MERCILESS

BOOK ONE: AGE OF CONQUEST

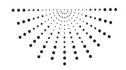

TAMARA LEIGH

WWW.TAMARALEIGH.COM

THE WULFRITHS. IT ALL BEGAN WITH A WOMAN.

A battle. A crown. The conqueror. The conquered. Medieval England—forever changed by the Battle of Hastings. And the rise of the formidable Wulfriths.

AN HONORABLE NORMAN

Chevalier Cyr D'Argent convinced himself he joined Duke William's invasion of England to reform its church and place its rightful king on the throne. But after a decisive Norman victory, the truth of his quest is revealed when his search for fallen kin leads to a Saxon grieving a boy slain by one of his own. Certain the defiant young woman will become the pick of the plunder, he forces her off the battlefield. Following a pilgrimage of penance, Cyr returns to England to seek his missing brother and claim the barony awarded by King William who stipulates he end the rebellion on his lands. He agrees, only to discover the woman he cannot forget is among those he must vanquish—and may even be their leader.

A REBELLIOUS SAXON

On a fateful autumn day in 1066, Aelfled of Wulfen's mistake leads to the death of her lady's son. Unforgivable—as is the silver-haired warrior who tempts her to put a blade in his back then does the unthinkable in protecting her from his fellow Normans. Now under the usurper's rule, faith crippled by her people's suffering, she finds her sanctuary threatened when she becomes a pawn of the rebel leader—and destroyed when betrayal delivers her into the hands of the man who haunts her dreams. As the fires of unrest scorch lives and lands, Aelfled struggles to shield her heart as well as her people. But perhaps love can unite Normans and Saxons. Perhaps she is meant to be here…with him…for such a time as this.

Thus begins the AGE OF CONQUEST series revealing the origins of the Wulfriths of the bestselling AGE OF FAITH series. Watch for FEARLESS: Book Two in Spring 2019.

For new releases and special promotions, subscribe to Tamara Leigh's mailing list: www.tamaraleigh.com

Cover Design: Ravven

eBook ISBN-13: 978-1-942326-33-5

Paperback ISBN-13: 978-1-942326-34-2

ALSO BY TAMARA LEIGH

CLEAN READ HISTORICAL ROMANCE

THE FEUD: A Medieval Romance Series
Baron Of Godsmere: Book One
Baron Of Emberly: Book Two
Baron of Blackwood: Book Three

LADY: A Medieval Romance Series
Lady At Arms: Book One
Lady Of Eve: Book Two

BEYOND TIME: A Medieval Time Travel Romance Series
Dreamspell: Book One
Lady Ever After: Book Two

STAND-ALONE Medieval Romance Novels
Lady Of Fire
Lady Of Conquest
Lady Undaunted
Lady Betrayed

INSPIRATIONAL HISTORICAL ROMANCE

AGE OF FAITH: A Medieval Romance Series

The Unveiling: Book One

The Yielding: Book Two

The Redeeming: Book Three

The Kindling: Book Four

The Longing: Book Five

The Vexing: Book Six

The Awakening: Book Seven

The Raveling: Book Eight

AGE OF CONQUEST: A Medieval Romance Series

Merciless: Book One

Fearless: Book Two (Spring 2019)

INSPIRATIONAL CONTEMPORARY ROMANCE

HEAD OVER HEELS: Stand-Alone Romance Collection

Stealing Adda

Perfecting Kate

Splitting Harriet

Faking Grace

SOUTHERN DISCOMFORT: A Contemporary Romance Series

Leaving Carolina: Book One

Nowhere, Carolina: Book Two

Restless in Carolina: Book Three

~

OUT-OF-PRINT GENERAL MARKET REWRITES

Warrior Bride 1994: Bantam Books (Lady At Arms)

*Virgin Bride 1994: Bantam Books (Lady Of Eve)

Pagan Bride 1995: Bantam Books (Lady Of Fire)

Saxon Bride 1995: Bantam Books (Lady Of Conquest)

Misbegotten 1996: HarperCollins (Lady Undaunted)

Unforgotten 1997: HarperCollins (Lady Ever After)

Blackheart 2001: Dorchester Leisure (Lady Betrayed)

*Virgin Bride is the sequel to *Warrior Bride; Pagan Pride* and *Saxon Bride* are stand-alone novels

For new releases and special promotions, subscribe to Tamara Leigh's mailing list: www.TamaraLeigh.com

THIS BOOK IS DEDICATED TO...THE WULFRITHS

Is it silly to dedicate a tale to the family of other tales culled from my imagination? So be it. Silly me dedicates MERCILESS, the first book in the Age of Conquest series, to the Wulfriths of the Age of Faith series who kept me company during long writing days for six lovely years. I hope the Wulfriths forged during the 1066 Norman Conquest of England are worthy of those who sprang from them, readers beautifully generous with their reading time, and above all, my savior who blessed me with the ability to weave God-honoring words into tales of men and women of ages long gone.

CHAPTER ONE

Sussex, England
15 October, 1066

*T*he battle was done. England was on its knees. And in the space between horrendous loss and brazen victory, a new day breathed light across the dark. But no beautiful thing was it, that splayed wide to the eyes more terrible than the moon had revealed and the ripening scent forewarned.

Bloodlust that had gripped thousands on the day past yet treading the veins of Cyr D'Argent, he felt it further displaced by revulsion and dread as he moved his gaze over the grey, mist-strewn battlefield.

Among the broken and torn bodies of numerous Saxons and numbered Normans, he glimpsed blue. But was it the shade that had eluded him throughout his night-long quest to recover the last of his kin?

Might his eldest brother and uncle yet breathe amid the slaughter? Might they be found the same as the third D'Argent brother whom Cyr had culled from gutted Saxons at middle night —though cruelly wounded, yet in possession of breath?

It did not seem possible a dozen hours after the death of England's king so decisively ended the battle few would argue the crown was destined for Duke William of Normandy. Still, Cyr would continue his search until he had done all in his power to account for the fate of those he held dear.

As he traversed blood-soaked ground so liberally cast with the fallen no straight path was possible, he questioned if his youngest brother and cousin remained among those searching for kin and friends. If not, it was because they succeeded where Cyr failed. Regardless, hopefully they would keep their swords close. Of greater concern than the daring Saxon women and elderly men retrieving their fallen were the profane of the Normans divesting the dead and dying of valuables.

"Lord, let us not search in vain," Cyr prayed. "Let my brother and uncle be hale and whole, merely seeking us as we seek them." Possible only if they had gone a different direction since Cyr looked near upon all who had crossed his moonlit path.

Another stride carrying him to a heap of bodies that boasted as many Normans as Saxons, he drew a deep breath and rolled aside two of the enemy to uncover the warrior garbed in blue. The face was too bloodied to make out the features, but the man's build was slight compared to a D'Argent. The only relief in the stranger's death was the possibility Cyr's kin yet lived.

He straightened, and as he turned from the sloping meadow toward the next visible blue, what sounded a curse rent the air and ended on a wail.

Farther up the slope, an aged Saxon woman whose white hair sprang all around face and shoulders wrenched on the arms of a warrior she dragged backward. Was it a dead man she sought to remove? Or did her loved one yet live?

Struck by the possibility his own sword was responsible for her struggle and heartache, Cyr was pierced by regret he did not wish to feel. It was the work of the Church he had done. Or was it?

Before the question could infect a conscience holding its breath, he thrust it aside and started to sidestep one of his own —a chevalier with whom he had crossed the channel. Younger than Cyr by several years, his eyes had lit over talk of the reward he would gain in fighting for William and the hope it was sizable enough to allow him to wed the woman awaiting his return home. She would wait forever, a Saxon battle-axe having severed links of his hauberk and breastbone to still the heart beneath.

Cyr swept his gaze over the bodies of long-haired, bearded enemies. Struggling against a resurgence of bloodlust that demanded justice for the young Norman, he reminded himself it was for kin he searched through night into dawn, not to wreak vengeance on the dead and dying.

Purpose recovered, he considered the bordering wood of Andredeswald where what remained of the Saxon army had fled on the afternoon past. Had his brother or uncle been amongst the ill-fated Normans who gave chase into the trees?

Only had they turned berserker, as sometimes happened to the most sensible and disciplined. That battle madness beyond courage had pried away Cyr's control when two chevaliers fell on either side of him. Surrounded by axe-wielding Saxons, he had yielded to the fury lest he join his fellow Normans in death.

Finding little comfort in recall of his superior skill and reflexes, he veered toward the wood where the ranks of dead began to thin. At the base of a hill to the right knelt a young Saxon woman.

The soft mournful strains of her song stirring the mist surrounding her, she bent over one whose head she cradled. Regardless of whether or not her kin yet lived, she bared her heart to loss. And her body to violation if the Normans picking over the fallen determined to plunder her as well. Until the duke granted the Saxons permission to retrieve their dead, they risked much in venturing onto the battlefield.

Concern for the woman distracting him from his purpose, he lengthened his stride to more quickly move past her.

To the left, a half dozen Saxons sprawled atop Normans, beyond them one of his own crushed beneath a bloodied and bloated warhorse. Ahead, impaled on a single arrow, enemy embraced enemy. But no recognizable blue.

As he neared the Saxon woman, more clearly he heard her song. Being ill-versed in the English language, her words held little meaning, but its lament made him ache such that were it not for what he glimpsed beyond her, he would have veered away.

The mist hung heavier there, the bodies deeper. Thus, he could not be certain it was the blue he sought amid the browns and russets of Saxons, but something told him there he would find kin.

Feeling blood course neck and wrists, hearing it throb between his ears, he moved toward the fallen with his sword going before him.

Of a sudden, the woman's song ceased.

Cyr rarely faltered, but he was jolted when she raised her head and her sparkling gaze fell on one responsible for the death of scores of her people. Like a candle beset by draft, emotions crossed her face, including alarm when her regard moved to the blade he had cleaned on his tunic's hem.

Once more regret dug into him, but it eased when he was past her and fairly certain his search yielded terrible fruit.

He sheathed his sword, and with strength he had thought nearly drained, cast aside Saxons who had met their end atop a Norman chevalier. The latter clothed in a blue tunic torn and blood-stained in a half dozen places, Hugh D'Argent's head with its close-cropped hair lolled upon the removal of the last enemy whose long hair his enormous hand gripped. There in the place between neck and shoulder was a cut that had severed the great vein, confirming the eyes staring east toward home would never again look upon France.

A shout sounding from Cyr, he dropped to his knees. He could not have expressed in words exactly what he felt for his uncle who had been coarse, hard, and demanding, but what moved through him dragged behind it pain that would go deeper only had the blue clothed his eldest sibling. He had cared much for the man who trained him and his brothers in the ways of the warrior. Now Hugh was lost to all, most tragically his son who would add another scar to the visible ones bestowed on the day past.

Eyes burning, Cyr gripped a hand over his face. An arm one of two younger brothers had lost to a battle-axe. A handsome face his cousin had lost to a sword. A life his uncle had lost to a dagger. And the eldest D'Argent brother who should not have been amongst Duke William's warriors? Whose fate would he share?

"Accursed Saxons!" Sweeping his blade from its scabbard, he thrust to his feet.

Bloodlust sweeping through him, his mind and body moved him to swing and slice and thrust, but somehow he wrenched back from a precipice of no benefit to any. Better he pursue those who had fled to the wood and yet had life to be let. However, as he stepped over a Saxon he had thrown off Hugh, he stilled over how slight the figure. And the face...

He looked from one who could be no more than a dozen years aged to the others he had tossed aside. Boys. All of them. Boys who had given their lives to bring down the mighty Norman. Boys determined to defend what was now no longer theirs to defend. Boys who would never grow into men. Boys soon to return to dust.

Another lay farther out. Smaller than the ones who had toppled Hugh, he sprawled on his belly, arms outstretched as if to crawl home and into his mother's arms. And the fifth boy was the one over whom the Saxon woman bent.

Her brother? Likely, for she was too young to have given life to one that age.

Guilt gaining a foothold, he reminded himself of the papal

blessing bestowed on Duke William for the invasion of England, as evidenced by the banner carried into battle. More than for the crown promised and denied William, more than for the land and riches to be awarded to his followers, the Normans had taken up arms against the heathen Saxons for the reformation of England's Church. Regardless of who had died on the day past, first and foremost they had done it for the greater good. Had they not?

Trying to calm this roiling that was no fit for a warrior, he breathed deep, filling mouth, nose, and throat with the scent and taste of death never before so potent. He expelled the loathsome air, but it was all there was to be had. Breath moving through him like a wind, chest rising and falling like a storm-beset ocean, he sent his gaze up his blade to its point.

Were we not justified? he silently questioned. *Was I not?*

Images of the day past rushed at him—the flight of arrows, slash and thrust of blades, shouts and cries from contorted mouths, blood and more blood. And laid over it all, the faces of ones who could barely be named young men.

Distantly separated from his uncle and eldest brother, Cyr's sword arm could not have taken any of the boys' lives, but considering how thoughtlessly he slew the enemy, ensuring those come against him did not rise again, it was possible had he been alongside his uncle, he would not have noticed their attackers were children. Like Hugh, he would have put them through.

"Boys," he rasped and dropped his head back. Neck popping and crackling, ache coursing shoulders and spine all the way down to his heels, he slammed his eyes closed. But more vividly memories played against the backs of his lids. And with ground teeth he gave over to them.

CHAPTER TWO

*A*elfled of the Saxons stared at the warrior in horrified anticipation of his desecration of the dead, and when it did not come wondered if here was God's answer to the prayer flung heavenward when the Norman pig drew his sword. Whatever stayed his hand, his survey of the savagery had landed on her and the boy before moving to a blade that had let much blood. The blood of her people.

Were she not pulled taut between the Lord whose comfort she sought and hatred over what had been done the Saxons, the barbarian might have made her tremble with fear. Instead, what spasmed through her was anger so reckless and unholy she dare not look long upon the warrior—just as she dare not allow him to see that from which she had turned back quaking fingers.

She tugged up her skirt's hem. Hoping she would not slice herself, she slid the beautiful instrument of death into the top of her hose, glanced at the warrior to ensure he had not seen, and returned her attention to the boy dragged away from the blue-clad Norman.

Lids flickering, chest rattling, he would not reach his eleventh winter. In her arms he would die rather than those of his mother who had lost her husband a fortnight past when he joined King Harold in defeating the Norwegian invaders at Stamford Bridge. Thus, it was for Aelfled to carry tidings to Lady Hawisa that another was stolen from her, this time by invaders from Normandy.

She looked around, wondered if any of those moving amongst the dead carpeting this portion of the battlefield was her lady. During the ride to Senlac on a horse shared by both women, time and again Isa—the name by which Aelfled best knew her lady— had risen above weeping and cursing to cry out to the Lord to keep her son safe. Were she not near, it was because she had moved her search farther out. Never would she leave until given proof of her son's presence or absence, be he alive or dead.

Soon dead, Aelfled once more pushed acceptance down her throat to her aching heart. Loathing herself for believing the word of one who, struggling to suppress tears over his sire's death, had spouted vengeance against any who sought to conquer England, she reeled in her searching gaze and paused on the boy's companions where they had landed when the Norman tossed them aside. Village boys, all of an age similar to the one she held, all christening themselves men by taking up arms against the invaders. To their mothers, Aelfled must also carry news of loss beyond husbands, fathers, and brothers.

"Merciful Lord," Aelfled whispered and caught back a sob as anger once more moved her head to toe. Merciful? Where was His mercy when Saxons sought to defend their homeland? Where was His mercy when boys abandoned childhood to wield arms? Where was His mercy in allowing Normans to cut down Saxons as if harvesting wheat? Where was His mercy—?

Appalled at the realization her faith was bending so far it might break its back, she gasped, "Pray, forgive me. 'Tis not for me to question You. But I do not understand, Lord."

"Aelf," breathed the one whose head her hand rested upon.

Blinking away tears, she bent closer, causing her throat to

spasm over the odor of spilled blood. During her search for her lady's son, the sight and scent of death had twice caused her to wretch, but though her belly was empty of foodstuffs, there was bile aplenty eager to make the climb.

"I was trying...to be a man, Aelf."

For that he brought sword and dagger to the battlefield, while the village boys carried any implement they could bring to hand. The sword and dagger of her lady's son were gone, but that had not stopped him. Though she could not be certain the weapon beneath her skirts belonged to the fallen Norman, it seemed likely, and as evidenced by its bloodied blade, it could have dealt the killing blow.

The boy whimpered. "Aelf?"

"Wulf?"

"I tried."

She attempted a smile of encouragement, but it was as if something learned was forgotten. "You more than tried," she choked. "You succeeded, and I am proud of your defense of England as I know your father would be and your mother shall be." Such lies, but perhaps they would ease the pain of his passing.

"Then you forgive me for...not keeping my word?"

They were both liars, but the damage done could not be undone. "Naught to forgive, Love."

His eyes widened, and the corners of his dry, cracked lips barely creased as if neither could he remember how to smile. "Love. Truly, Aelf?"

That she did not mean in the way he meant it, but what was one more lie? "Ever and ever, here on earth and in heaven, dearest."

"Love," he breathed, then passed from this world comforted by the belief the one he had vowed to wed when Aelfled entered his mother's service years past—she who was now ten and eight to his nearly eleven—loved him as a woman loved a man to whom she wished to be bound.

She touched her lips to his forehead, and as her tears fell on his slackening face, prayed, "Lord, receive this boy. Hold him close. Let him know Your peace and beauty. Give his mother—"

"Mon Dieu!"

She snapped up her chin, swept her gaze to the warrior who interrupted her audience with God as if he, arrayed in Saxon blood, were more entitled to call upon the Almighty.

Where he had dropped to a knee alongside his fellow Norman, he beseeched in a voice so accented it took her longer than usual to render Norman French into English, "Forgive me my sins."

Her breath caught. Never in her hearing had such humble words sounded so sacrilegious. With little consideration of what she did, she eased Wulf to the ground, staggered upright on cramped legs, and drew her meat knife from its sheath on her girdle.

The warrior gave no indication he heard her advance, and soon she was at a back made more vulnerable for being divested of chain mail. As she raised her knife high, she looked upon hair cropped short the same as most Normans. And stilled at the sight of so much silver amid dark. She had thought her enemy no more than twenty and five, yet he was silvered like men twice his age—though not as much as the one before whom he knelt.

She gave her head a shake, lowered her gaze to his back. But no nearer did she come to committing that heinous sin, her conscience forcing her to retreat a step and lower the blade.

"Pray, Lord," the Norman spoke again, "forgive me."

Dark emotions tempered by horror over what she had been moved to do, Aelfled said in his language, "Do you truly believe He gives ear to a savage, a murderer, a slayer of children?"

When he neither startled nor looked around, his still and silence made her question if this were real, but such sights and scents were not to be imagined. She was here. He was here. And her lady's son and thousands of others were dead.

He continued to ignore her as if confident she could not—or

would not—harm him. And so she waited, for what she did not know, and it was she who startled when he straightened. As he came around, revealing a face that confirmed he was below thirty years of age, she raised the knife to the level of her chest.

Though she had seen he was marked brow to toe by her slain people, she was unprepared to be so near evidence of his bloodlust and had to swallow to keep bile from her mouth—and breathe deep to match her gaze to his, the color of which could not be known absent the spill of light across the battlefield. Not that it mattered. To her, ever his eyes would be black.

They slid to her knife, the tip of which was a stride and thrust from his abdomen—were he of a mind to remain unmoving while she did to him what he had done to her people.

Returning his gaze to hers, he said with little emotion, "Offensive or defensive?"

Ashamed his words caused her lids to flutter, she bit, "Were I a man, offensive."

He inclined his head. "Were you, you would not have been allowed near my back—would be gasping your last."

That she could dispute only were her size and physique equal to his. Standing nearly a foot taller, shoulders as vast as any warrior, he had to be twice her weight.

"How do you know my language?" he asked.

The question surprised, though it should not. Few Saxons spoke Norman French, and even fewer among the lower class of freemen to which she belonged. But there was no cause to reveal she served in the household of one whose Norman husband's family had dwelt in England since the reign of Edward, the recently departed king who was fond of Normans owing to his exile amongst them previous to gaining the English throne—the same throne Harold had next ascended and from which Duke William had toppled him on the day past.

As Cyr waited on an answer not likely to be given, once more he considered the knife whose sole purpose the Saxon would have him believe was defense. Even if only for a moment, it had come close to being used offensively against one who had shed his hauberk to more quickly search among the dead.

He had sensed she came to put the blade between his ribs, but in the grip of prayer—more, something so foreign he could only guess it was that great slayer of souls known as apathy—he had done naught to prevent her from adding his death to his uncle's.

Returning his regard to her face, he realized he had fallen far short of one of the most important skills possessed by a man of the sword, that of being observant. Until this moment, he could not have well enough recalled her features to describe one whose pooled dark eyes, delicate nose, and full mouth were framed by blond tresses whose soft undulations evidenced they had recently lost their braids.

She might not be called beautiful, but she was comely enough to be among the pick of the plunder once less honorable Normans came looking for sport. Though her French might be nearly without fault, it would be of little use to one who numbered among the conquered, especially were she of the lower ranks as her simple gown suggested.

He started to warn her away, but in a husky voice almost sensual in its strains and likely beget of tears, she said, "You have not answered me."

Casting backward, he recalled words spoken while he beseeched the Lord's forgiveness. Did he truly believe the prayers of a savage, a murderer, a slayer of children would be heeded?

Offended as he had not been earlier, he fought down ire. There was much for which he required forgiveness, but he was none of what she named him. He was a soldier the same as her men with whom he had clashed. And she who had witnessed a humbling to which he had only subjected himself in his youth mocked him for it.

"My prayers are between God and me," he growled. "His forgiveness I seek, not yours, *Saxon*."

She set a hand on a thin psalter suspended from her girdle, its leather cover stained at its upper edge. "What of the forgiveness of a mother soon to learn one most precious to her is lost? What of she who shall mourn her slaughtered child unto death?" The woman jerked her chin at the boy whose blood had likely stained the psalter, then with more contempt than he had managed, added, *"Norman."*

Cyr was not steel against imaginings of such loss he knew must be greater than that felt for a brother gone too soon. Had the eldest D'Argent son not survived the battle, never would their mother recover.

The Saxon lowered her chin, slid the knife in its sheath, and stilled. It was the psalter that gave her pause, and as he watched her slowly draw her hand away, he knew she had been unaware of the blood upon it.

A sound of distress escaping her, she pivoted and started back toward the boy.

It was then Cyr became aware of gathering voices and looked down the hill across the meadow. The Normans who had slept off the day's battle were rousing.

"You should leave!" he called.

She halted alongside the boy and peered over her shoulder. *"I am not the one who trespasses."*

He shifted his jaw. "Those who have little care for who has the greater right to be here will care even less when the unfolding day allows them to look near upon their dead."

Her brow furrowed, and he knew she questioned his concern. Then she laughed, a sound that might have soothed a beast were it not so barbed.

"You are not safe here," he snapped.

She narrowed her eyes at him, swept them over the body-heaped meadow. "This I know, just as I know none of England is safe whilst beasts like you trample it."

"You are a woman alone."

Her hands curled into fists. "What care you?"

What *did* he care? She was no concern of his—unlike Hugh whom he ought to be delivering to his son. Still, he said, "Leave!"

"When I am finished." She lowered, whispered something to the boy who had surely heard his last, then slid her arms beneath him and drew him against her chest. What followed was so great a struggle she would not get far even if she managed to regain her feet. The boy was young but of a build befitting one destined to defend his people.

Cursing himself, Cyr strode forward and caught her around the waist. As he pulled her upright, the boy rolled out of her arms onto his side.

She swung around. "Loose me, *nithing!*"

He did not know the meaning of the word, but having heard it shouted by her people during battle, it was something to which one did not aspire. Staring into eyes the rose of dawn confirmed were so dark as to be nearly black, he demanded, "What do you?"

She strained to free herself, but she would go nowhere without his leave. Chest rising and falling against his, she said, "I would take him to the wood to ensure he returns to his mother as whole as he remains—that his body not suffer desecration."

That to which grief over Hugh had nearly moved Cyr. As if he had committed the ungodly act, the weight of guilt grew heavier. And urged him to atone. Though he longed to leave the woman to her fate, he set her back and scooped up the boy.

"Non!" She snatched the child's arm.

"I mean you no ill, Woman. I would but see you sooner gone that I may deliver my uncle from this carnage and resume the search for my brother. Now loose the boy and lead the way."

Lips parted as if to protest further, she searched his face for a lie she would find only were it imagined. Then her shoulders lowered. "I thank..." As though rejecting the expression of gratitude, she gave her head a shake and turned.

The wood was near, and though she did not venture far into

the deeply-shadowed place where what remained of the Saxon army had fled and some might yet lurk, he engaged all his senses lest he find himself set upon.

At an oak so ancient a dozen men could conceal themselves behind it, the young woman halted and turned her head in every direction.

"What is it?" he asked as he came alongside.

"Our horse. It is gone."

Cyr tensed further. "*Our* horse? You did not come alone?"

He more felt than saw the gaze she settled on him and the wariness there. "The boy's mother and I rode together."

"Then she has taken your mount and departed."

"Non, she would not leave without her son. Another took it." She looked past him toward the battlefield, and he guessed she intended to return there to search for one soon to grieve the death of a child.

Though Cyr wanted to command her to make haste to those of her own who would aid in delivering the boy home, it would be futile. If she heeded him at all, the moment he resumed his own search she would do as she wished.

So be it, little fool, he silently conceded, *it is not on me.* He would complete this act of atonement, give one further warning, then attend to his own kin.

"This seems a good place," he said.

She stepped around the backside of the tree, and he followed her several strides distant from the roots. As he settled the boy on the ground, she unfastened the girdle hung with psalter and knife and unsheathed the latter.

Immediately Cyr's hand itched for his dagger opposite the sword on his belt, but the intent of hers proved neither offensive nor defensive.

She dropped to her knees, planted the blade's tip in the ground, with great sweeps of the arms cleared the thin layer of leaves, then retrieved the knife and began assaulting the earth.

"Surely you do not think to bury him?" he barked.

A shudder moving her bowed shoulders, she turned her face up. "But a depression covered over with leaves to conceal him should your kind come to the wood." She swallowed loudly. "They will, will they not?"

Some would, whether to search out fellow Normans felled by Saxons during their retreat or plunder. "They will."

As she resumed digging, Cyr unsheathed his dagger and paused to consider the intricately fashioned pommel, hilt, cross guard, and blade. The rising sun scantily penetrating the canopy did not light the latter's silvered length, though only because he had not wiped it clean the same as his sword.

He stared at the stained steel and saw again those who had fallen to it when it had been necessary to wield two blades to preserve his life and the lives of other Normans. The shedding of blood was inherent in being a chevalier and certainly not unknown to him previous to the day past, and yet in that moment it seemed almost repugnant, and more so when he looked to the one at his feet.

For the first time he noted that, unlike the others pulled from atop Hugh, this boy was arrayed in finery not of the common. A chain was visible above the neck of his tunic, garments were fashioned of rich cloth, boots cut of good leather, belt buckle shone silver, and the empty scabbards at his hip were faced with polished horn.

"Who is he?" Cyr asked.

The woman stabbed the earth again but did not pry the knife free. Wisps of perspiration-darkened hair clinging to her brow, she looked up. "A child."

He gnashed his teeth. "Is he of noble blood?"

"He is—rather, was." She nodded as if to force the clarification on herself. "Just as he was of your blood."

It took Cyr no moment to understand, but he could not think how to respond.

The corners of her mouth rising in an expression too sorrowful to be a smile, she said, "Oui, on his sire's side."

Then he was born of a union between Norman and Saxon, the former likely drawn from one of the families who had long lived in England. If his father had sided with King Harold as seemed likely, he would forfeit all when Duke William ascended the throne—had he not already on the battlefield the same as his son.

"Who were you to him?" he asked.

"Were," she breathed, then in a huskier voice, said, "Maid to his lady mother and, on occasion, his keeper." A small sob escaped her. "As fell to me on the day past."

Did she think herself responsible for his death?

"If only we had not come south. Had we remained in Wulfenshire as my lady..." She squeezed her lids closed, shook her head.

"Wulfenshire?" he turned the name over. Though during the fortnight since the duke's army arrived on the shores of Sussex he had become familiar with the names of places within a day's ride of their encampments, here was one he had not heard. Wondering if it was near Yorkshire where England's usurping king had defeated Norwegian invaders days before the Norman landing and for safety's sake her lady had brought her son south, he asked, "How far north?"

The woman's eyes flew open, and there was alarm in their depths as of one surprised to find she was not alone. Then came resentment, and she dropped her chin and reached to her knife.

Cyr did not understand why he wished to know how the boy had come to be here, but what he did understand was it was not for him to question.

Huffing and grunting, the woman returned to driving her knife into the land to which she had been born. Again. And again.

He knew he ought to leave her, but he muttered, "God's mercy!" and pulled her upright. As she drew breath to protest, he said, "Do you stand aside, the sooner we shall both be done here."

"I do not need—"

"Stand aside!" He pushed her toward the boy, then it was her enemy on his knees. With one hand he plunged his blade into the ground, with the other scooped out displaced loam and rocks. Though reviled at making a tiller of soil one of two weapons that had elevated him above many a chevalier, there was satisfaction in the thrusts and twists that cleaned the blood from his blade as the wounded earth yielded up the depth he sought.

One foot, Cyr told himself, *then I shall leave her to whatever fate she chooses.*

So intent was he on a task unbecoming a man of the sword, once more he committed the deadly error of exposing his back to the enemy—not the woman but any number of her men lurking in the trees. However, not until he heard rustling leaves, skittering rocks, and labored breathing did he heed the voice urging him to attend to his surroundings.

Thrusting upright, he swept his dagger around. But as he closed a hand over his sword hilt, he recognized the one come unto him. The cause for the woman's great draws of breath was the boy she carried, he who had tried to crawl back to his mother, he who had aided four others in severing Hugh's life.

And whose young lives your uncle severed, his rarely examined conscience reminded. *Mere boys.*

Murderous boys, he silently countered, but with so little conviction it yet served, rousing anger better suited to the nephew of a dead man. "What do you?" he asked.

Near the boy Cyr had conveyed to the wood, she eased her burden to the ground, sat back on her heels, gripped her knees, and raised a face tracked with tears. "He also has a mother, as do the other three."

Darkness once more rising through him, Cyr looked to the depression in which he stood. Did she expect him to enlarge it to accommodate all who had spilled Hugh's life? Hugh who had yet to know such consideration? Hugh whose body might even now suffer plundering?

"It must be widened," she said.

He thrust his dagger into its scabbard, said, "Not by my hand."

She pushed upright. "Then by mine."

"So be it." If she had no regard for herself, why should he? As he started past her, she said, "It would be a lie for me to thank you."

He did not believe that. Not only had she drawn back from expressing appreciation earlier, but he sensed her declaration was an attempt to convince herself they were enemies. Still, it was good to be reminded they stood on opposite sides of the great fire set on the day past. Just as Normans would rebel against any who sought to yoke them, so would Saxons. Were the fire well enough fueled, it could rage for years across this island kingdom.

"Just as it would be a lie for me to welcome false gratitude," he said and, assuring himself he would think no more on her, strode toward the battlefield.

"Norman!"

He cursed, turned.

Hitching her skirts clear of her slippers, she hastened forward and held out the psalter.

Cyr spared it no glance, instead looked nearer on a face the rising sun confirmed was as lovely as thought—so much he was tempted to brush aside blond tresses to view all of it. And she must have seen the temptation, wariness softening the hard light in her eyes and causing her to retreat a step.

Still, she extended the psalter. "Take it."

He flicked his gaze over it, lingered over the blood. Was this spite? An attempt to bait him? Punish him? "For what?"

"Prayer and guidance, of which methinks you are in greater need than I."

The warrior wanted to reject that, but the man who felt

twisted and bent out of a shape so familiar as to be comfortable could not.

"It is in my language," she said.

He frowned. "As I know less of the written than the spoken, of what use?"

She tilted her head, causing a tress to shift and expose more of her slender neck. "Do you and yours not learn the language of the conquered, how will you govern your new subjects?" She raised her eyebrows. "Or is that not your duke's intent? Does he—do you —mean to kill us all?"

Baited, indeed. And yet he snapped at her hook. "It is not our intent!"

She thrust the psalter nearer. "I dare not ask for your word on that, but if you speak true, here is a good place to start—a means of enlightening your kind on how to rule those from whom you have stolen lives, hearts, even souls. And of course, let us not forget land."

He could not. Though he wished to believe he and his younger brothers had accepted the invitation to join Duke William's forces more for the Church than the possibility of becoming landed nobles the same as their father's heir, it was a lie.

Perhaps that was what made him yield though the woman greatly offended—and further offended when their fingers brushed as he accepted the psalter.

She snatched her arm to her side and, setting her chin high, said, "Methinks you will not mind the stain, *Norman.*"

As if he rejoiced in the blood of her dead. As if he had not shown her mercy and compassion. As if he had not sought to protect her.

Anger his only comfort and defense, he flung the psalter at her feet. "Take that and be gone."

She lowered her gaze, stared at her offering until raucous laughter sounded from the battlefield.

And so it began. "They come," Cyr warned.

She shifted wide eyes to his, and he was glad for the abundance of fear if it meant she would leave. "So they do," she said softly and turned away.

He stared after her as she moved toward the fallen youths. Though it was past time he left her, he longed for reassurance. "You will depart?" he called.

She stepped into the depression and began plying her knife. Were it only to accommodate the second boy, he would leave her to it, but if she intended to collect the other three...

As he strode forward, he glanced at the psalter fallen open to a page of precise text on one side and a simply-rendered cross on the other.

Halting before her, he demanded, "Will you take yourself from here after these two are covered over?"

"I will not."

He dropped to his haunches, but she continued to drive her blade into the ground. "For the love of God—if not yourself— leave the other boys!"

"Non."

Then it is on her, he told himself. But when she stabbed her blade into the ground again, he closed a hand over her fist gripping the hilt. "Unlike your lady's son, the others possess nothing worthy of plunder."

Her head whipped up. "Still they could suffer desecration, and if their bodies are moved they may not be found again." She swallowed loudly. "They must go home. They absolutely must. Now"—she jerked free—"collect your dead and leave me to mine."

As she resumed her assault on the earth, Cyr straightened. Assuring himself he had done all he could to save her and vowing he would forget her, he strode opposite.

CHAPTER THREE

*a*s Cyr exited the wood, the sunlight streaming across the battlefield revealed in more shocking detail all who had fallen. Perhaps worse, the carnage come to light seemed to have no effect on those plundering the dead, most appearing as oblivious to the bodies underfoot as were ants to the grains of dirt over which they clambered. And step by step, the scavengers drew nearer Andredeswald.

"Lord," Cyr rasped as he commanded his legs to carry him to his uncle, "I commend that woman into Your care. Let not spoils be made of her."

Blessedly, his uncle was as he had left him, yet in possession of the medallion around his neck, chain mail tunic, scabbard-hung belt, and boots. But though Hugh's sword was easily located, his dagger was not. Regrettable, it being a fine piece fashioned the same as those worn by all D'Argents, including Hugh's son who might one day have passed his sire's dagger to his own son.

Cyr hefted his uncle whose weight had grown more formidable these past years with the addition of fat that had surely lent to his downfall. Like the D'Argent heir, Hugh should have remained in Normandy. The painful irony of their accompaniment was they had not sought glory nor land but to fight side by side with younger kin to better ensure their survival. And now Hugh was dead and Cyr's older brother might be as well.

"Accursed Saxons," Cyr once more named the defeated, then shortened his stride to negotiate the massive number of bodies, the meadow's eastern flank comprised of twice as many Saxons as Normans.

Burdened by his uncle, fatigue, and the horrors he waded amidst, relief swept him when he sighted his younger brother.

As Theriot neared, the bit of lightness about him—surely born of hope their uncle lived—slid down his face and sorrow more deeply dug the few lines there.

"Guarin?" Cyr demanded though fairly certain of the answer. Had their older brother been found, alive or dead, it would have been unnecessary to ask.

Theriot halted. "Non," he said and offered no more as he settled his regard on their lifeless uncle. Relations between Hugh and him had been more strained than the older man's relations with the other brothers owing to Theriot's struggle with authority and penchant for revelry. But though he might not admit it, he had cared much for Hugh.

Keeping eyes lowered as if to conceal tears, he said, "I shall carry him."

As Cyr relinquished the big man, he asked, "How fares Dougray?" The third brother who had come seeking land.

Despite Theriot possessing a leaner build and standing four fingers shorter than Cyr, he did not strain beneath Hugh's weight. Settling the big man against his chest, he said, "The duke's physician concurs the arm must be removed and tells it is best done when next Dougray loses consciousness."

No shock, as mangled as it was, but Cyr had prayed it could be saved even if never again used to defend his brother's person. "Then he has awakened."

"Oui, and how he rages."

Doubtless against Cyr—as he had every right to do.

Though Cyr longed to go to Dougray, as well as his cousin who would soon learn of his sire's death, Guarin must be accounted for. "I shall continue my search for our brother."

Theriot started to turn away, paused. "Dougray is a man, as a man determines his own path, as a man chose to accompany us. Remember that no matter what he casts at your feet."

More likely upon my head, Cyr thought. "I thank you."

As the burdened Theriot began forging a path across the battlefield, Cyr returned his thoughts to Guarin. Having last seen him in the company of their uncle, both swinging swords and thrusting spears from atop their destriers, he would resume his search where Hugh had fallen after being unhorsed.

Once more seeking D'Argent blue, he spared only a glance for the three remaining boys responsible for his uncle's death—and determinedly withheld his thoughts from the woman intent on returning for their bodies.

But there was no ignoring his fellow warriors plundering Saxons and Normans alike. Whether or not Guarin yet lived, happily the scavengers would pick over the bounty offered by the D'Argent heir.

"Blue, Lord," Cyr rasped. "Reveal our blue, else never will I find him."

Over the next hour, as the sun warming the land furthered the stench and parted the shadows to cast light across the crimson of blood, silver of arms and armor, and brown of simple garments, Cyr searched. And prayed. For it, all he found was Hugh's downed destrier a good distance from where the warrior breathed his last. No evidence of Guarin nor his mount.

Further fatigued by the effort to move and shift bodies each time blue was glimpsed, mouth parched and belly groaning for sustenance it would surely struggle to keep down amid the dead, Cyr leaned forward and braced his hands on his thighs.

"Where are you, Guarin?" he grated. "I cannot return to France without word of what befell you." Though their mother would prefer to remain ignorant of her eldest son's fate that she cling to the hope he lived, if never Guarin was found it could prove more painful—and cruel. As for their father, he would be pained by the possibility of losing a son but anxious over his successor. Were Guarin lost, the heir would become Cyr who had joined Duke William to win lands of his own, not displace his brother.

A scream straightened his spine, and though he could not have said whence it issued, he sped his gaze to where he had found his uncle. Though he had ventured a good distance, he recognized the one who thrust an arm before her and saw light glint off the blade with which she threatened her enemy.

Guessing the two men meant to make plunder of her, Cyr snarled, "Fool woman," and drew his sword and ran.

As he neared, he heard her cry in Norman French, "Savages! Barbarians!"

The two laughed and dropped sacks whose bulging contents were looted from the dead.

As one moved toward her left flank, the other her right, she swept the blade side to side. Blond hair falling about face and shoulders, she spat, "Despoilers!"

"So we are, Wench." That one's guttural voice was familiar to Cyr, as were broad shoulders that were a poor match for narrow hips and thin legs.

The woman retreated a step, in her own language insulted them as first she had done Cyr. "Nithings!"

"Hear that?" called Campagnon's companion. "She names cowards those standing on the backs of men who cried out to their mothers as we watered the earth with their blood. A lesson in respect would do this Saxon good, do you not think?"

For answer, Campagnon lunged.

The woman's blade arced, and her attacker reeled back and clapped a hand over his face.

25

Naming her the foulest of those female, Campagnon's companion set himself at her.

She had no moment to recover—other than what Cyr provided.

Bellowing, he thrust his sword to the right of the man, snatched the back of his tunic, and flung him aside. Sparing the woman no glance, he swept around and saw Campagnon's companion land hard alongside a Norman archer whose empty quiver was aslant on his shoulders and bow just visible beneath his lifeless body.

Though aware the Saxon woman was once more at his back with a blade in hand and, confronted by three of her enemy, had more cause than earlier to wield it against him, it was his own against whom he must defend himself.

"You trespass, knave!" Campagnon shouted.

Cyr shifted his regard to him, from the amount of blood flowing from the gash across nose and cheek was certain he would scar, evidencing he had been bettered by a woman—and a Saxon at that.

"Campagnon," Cyr acknowledged as, out of the corner of his eye, he watched the miscreant's companion stumble upright.

Raymond Campagnon frowned, then his eyes widened and scorn curled his lips. "Cyr D'Argent. *Merciless* Cyr."

Though the byname was earned at contest and battle and Cyr wore it with quiet pride, it suddenly hung heavy and foul for what it revealed of him to the Saxon woman. Much of it true.

Campagnon looked to his companion. "You have heard of him. Eh, Merle?"

"I have, but surely one who thinks to show mercy to a woman —our enemy—cannot be the same."

Campagnon chuckled. "Perhaps he does not show mercy—but wishes her for himself."

"Leave," Cyr growled.

Campagnon dragged an arm across nose and cheek,

considered the blood trailing his sleeve, then set a hand on his sword hilt. *"After* I take the flesh owed me." His eyes flicked to her.

Silently, Cyr cursed the woman for not taking the opportunity to flee. "You shall not lay hands on her," he warned.

Campagnon blinked wide. "Else what? You will take up arms against your fellow warrior to defend a filthy little Saxon who insults her Norman betters? Now her masters?"

"You are not—will never be—my masters!" she cried. "You who tear at the dead like vultures, bathing your claws in their blood! You are heathens! Nithings!"

Almighty, did this begin with her? Cyr silently bemoaned. *Did she confront them over desecration of one of her own?*

Red rising up Campagnon's neck and face, hand on his hilt convulsing, he snarled, "Saxon whore!"

Watching for the moment he and Merle dared as they ought not, Cyr perfected his stance and angled his sword to once more judge lives on the edge of a blade. "Return to your scavenging, Campagnon."

The man glanced at Merle whose yellowed teeth crowded and overlapped such that it appeared he had twice as many as needed. He nodded, then both drew their swords.

"Back, Saxon!" Cyr shouted across his shoulder, then charged.

It was Merle with whom Cyr first crossed swords, that one reaching him first, but only in speed was he superior to Campagnon. A single meeting of blades sent his sword soaring and him scrambling backward lest Cyr's next swing slice open his unprotected belly.

Then came Campagnon.

Cyr's recovery was relatively sluggish and further delayed when he glanced across his shoulder to confirm the woman was in retreat. She was not, though she had distanced herself.

"Go!" he commanded and gave his attention to his opponent, sweeping his blade up and deflecting the blow coming at him from on high. With a roar, he broke the crossing of their swords and thrust, setting Campagnon back two steps.

The miscreant recovered his balance, bared his teeth.

Cyr bared his own, but in a smile. As mercenaries, the two had met during the private wars plaguing much of France—most often fighting on opposite sides—but for all Campagnon's skill and treachery, he had yet to best Cyr.

He raised his sword again, as did his companion who had recovered his own. "Non, Merle," Campagnon said. "D'Argent is mine."

"Truly?" Cyr raised his eyebrows. "We both know this ends as ever it ends. Save your strength for the defenseless from whom you can steal far more than ever you shall have of me."

Campagnon beckoned with his blade. "Come!"

Hardly had Cyr begun his advance than something drew his opponent's regard, causing him to lower his sword.

Cyr followed his gaze. In the distance, at the head of a dozen chevaliers and flanked by several more, Duke William moved in their direction.

Campagnon sheathed his sword, gestured to Merle. "Our reward awaits," he said, then to Cyr, "The Saxon wench—I give her to you."

As if she were his to give…

Cyr watched them depart and was not surprised they left their sacks. Though many were the plunderers and such was accepted in the aftermath of war, it would not garner the duke's kind regard. When the two returned for their plunder, by all that was holy, the Saxon woman would be long gone.

Cyr turned, strode to where she stood with the knife at her side. "For this, I warned you—"

"I am not his to give!"

In different circumstances, he would have liked that he first thought words she spoke, a sign they were of compatible minds. But these circumstances would never be other than what they were now—a great divide straddled by the conquerors, the conquered strewn across the jagged depths.

Peering down into a face bright with defiance, he demanded, "Did you invite their attentions?"

"I did not!"

"What did you do?"

"I came for another boy and found those two nearby. They knelt over a young man." She swallowed loudly. "I know not why, but it was more ghastly it was one of their own they…"

"What?"

"Bantered as if over a tankard of ale, one holding his hand while the other—Campagnon—cut off the finger to take a ring." She shook her head. "I knew I should run, but I commanded they cease and named them the foul things they are."

Eyes that had shone with defiance now smoldering with fear as if a gust of breath would move it to flame, she closed them. When she lifted her lids, she repeated, "I am not his to give."

He grunted. "But fool that you are and with one such as he, you were his to *take*."

Once more, defiance overwhelmed fear that she would do better to heed. "What of one such as you, *Merciless* Cyr?"

Did her question not so offend, he might have winced. "After all I did to prevent this from happening, though I have my own to account for, you ask this of me?"

Her lashes fluttered, shoulders sank, then with a note of pleading, she said, "How can you have slain so many on the day past and now aid those you slew—those who have more cause than ever to name you the enemy?"

"I am a soldier. A soldier slays that he not be slain. It was battle. And that battle is done."

"Done?" Her laugh was mirthless. "You think it ends here? Non. A great number we have lost to your duke's greed, but still we are many. If ever the fight to hold our country is lost, that loss will be long in coming."

He prayed not, that resistance would quickly wane so never again were so many lives sacrificed over the rule of England. "Regardless, the Duke of Normandy shall wear the crown."

Her eyes flashed. "Does he, never will it sit easy on the brow of William le Bâtard."

Cyr was not easily given to fear, that weakness trained out of him, but it sprang upon him—for her sake.

Though the duke and his party were yet distant and the growing din allowed none but the dead to attend to their exchange, he gripped her arm. Hearing her breath catch, feeling the rise of her knife-wielding hand, he put his face near hers. "Do not name him that. *Never* in his hearing or otherwise. Do you understand?"

"It is truth! All know his noble father did not wed his common mother, that he is duke only because there was no legitimate issue."

"What is your name, Woman?"

She seamed her lips.

He sighed. "It matters not. Just know many are the hands and feet lost by those who dared speak as you speak."

Her upper lip curled. "Barbarian."

"That he can be. And do not forget it." He glanced across his shoulder, saw Campagnon and Merle had joined the ranks of William's party. Though their advance was slow, they continued to move in this direction. "You must leave."

She shot her gaze to where the boys lay. "I have two more to take to the wood, then I must search for my lady."

He wearied of the argument. "Not in William's sight whilst he has yet to grant permission for your people to remove their dead. Thus, leave else suffer the indignity of being carried over my shoulder."

"But—"

"Decide!"

Her jaw shifted, and between her teeth she said, "I will go."

"And you are not to return until the duke grants permission, and only then in the company of others."

She jerked her chin, looked to where he held her.

He followed her gaze to smears and flecks of dried blood on the back of his hand. Though most belonged to Saxons, some had been flung by fellow Normans alongside whom he had fought.

Once more moved to guilt, he released her and looked to the duke. There was much on the battlefield to occupy the observant William, whether he happened on it himself or one vying for attention pointed out something of note. Thus, it was unlikely Cyr and the woman had come to his notice, but they would.

"What do you wait for?" he growled.

Her gaze wavered. "Who is Cyr D'Argent?"

He tensed further. He knew who he had been before and during the contest for England and wanted to believe he was as familiar with that warrior at battle's end, but never had he felt so raked and plowed—as if being prepared for seed never before strewn across his soul.

"Who?" she pressed.

Though he knew what his Uncle Hugh would say did he witness their exchange—words that would shame—he said, "Until all of England yields to Duke William, I am your enemy, little Saxon."

Was that hurt flickering amid rekindled anger?

"And I am sorry for it," he heard himself say as if new seed were already cast.

Had he wished her to express a similar regret, he would have been disappointed. "In the hope God yet gives ear to those He forsook on the day past," she said, "I shall pray for you."

It would serve until he forgot her, and he would as quickly as possible. He had a brother to find—God willing, alive, in which case Cyr would seek from William the reward promised for aiding in wrenching the crown from the usurping Harold.

"And perhaps one day it may be possible to forgive you,

Merciless Cyr," the woman added with a glance at hands evidencing those he had slain. Then she looked to the two remaining boys and started toward the wood.

Cyr turned from the one whose name he would never know, but had taken only a half dozen strides toward the approaching duke when compelled to look one last time at the woman.

He should not have, for she also looked around as if to gaze at him one last time. Despite compressed lips whose curve he would only ever imagine, he was drawn to this woman as he could not remember being drawn to another. Was it her strength and resolve, though he professed to prefer the fairer sex soft and easily swayed? Or was he merely too long outside the company of women?

The latter, he told himself and resumed his stride. Wishing it were possible to avoid his liege without offending him so he could resume the search for Guarin, he adjusted his sword belt.

As he drew level with the youths, he took in their pitifully slight bodies sprawled amid armored and helmeted men, some of whom were nearly twice their height and twice as broad. "Boys," he rasped, and though he set his gaze on William, his thoughts remained with the two he had forced the Saxon woman to abandon to trampled grass, bloodied mud, and feasting flies.

More than Hugh, more than Guarin, the boys should not have been here. More than Hugh, more than Guarin, they ought to have remained home with their families. More than Merciless Cyr, they deserved to walk away whole in body and mind.

He ground his teeth, growled, "It is done," and wrenched his thoughts off the path that sought to deliver him to the wood.

It was the path to William he must take, showing himself and giving account of services rendered to ensure when the new king determined who among his followers would be rewarded with English lands, Cyr D'Argent would be landless no longer. But though it was what he must do, what he wanted was to find his brother and take his kin back to Normandy.

Determinedly, he reminded himself he was a warrior, that by mastery of sword, spear, dagger, and destrier he excelled at feeding, clothing, housing, and entertaining himself. Still, the pride earned on the day past was so restrained he might almost think he had been but a bystander.

Fatigue only, he told himself. Were the Saxon woman's belief the crown would not sit easy on William's brow realized, in the days, weeks, and months ahead he would prove as formidable a warrior as ever.

England was Norman now, its people—perhaps even the world—forever changed.

CHAPTER FOUR

*S*he deserved worse than the back of a hand that would have sent her sprawling had it not stopped inches from her cheek. There it had remained, quaking so violently the air fanned Aelfled's face. Then a scream of grief. It dropped the lady over the neck of her horse where she convulsed and gripped and wrenched at the mane of the beast who suffered in silence as if in accord with the escort of six warriors that this was a mother's due.

Now, an hour after happening on her lady and delivering tidings more horrific than the recent loss of a husband, Aelfled led the way through Andredeswald toward three of the five boys who waited to be returned to their mothers' bosoms. Having dismounted minutes earlier, the small party went on foot, leading their horses to stealthily negotiate the wood.

Though thus far they had encountered only Saxons—soldiers fleeing Senlac with as much of their lives intact as possible and kin desperate to recover loved ones—they dare not risk announcing their presence lest any Normans who had followed their prey into the wood yet lurked.

"How much farther?" her lady demanded in a voice so raw it

was unrecognizable.

"Just over that rise near where we left our horse," Aelfled said and ventured a look across her shoulder at Isa who in that moment could be said to be beautiful—albeit darkly so—though only flatterers said she was beyond pretty.

Before wedding a Norman who, unlike Saxons, often adopted distinct surnames, Hawisa Fortier had been Hawisa Wulfrithdotter—daughter of Wulfrith. In keeping with her family's formidable reputation as warriors, as the last of their line she had not indulged in adornment of her person. Though it was told she had wed with her hair loosed as was custom, the tresses had been wildly disarrayed and in need of washing. And beneath a gown so simple she had looked more a slave than a noblewoman, she had worn chausses and boots.

Before this day, Aelfled could only imagine her lady in such a state. Now she could see how she might have appeared ten years past though, surely, her face had not been marked.

What had happened to her on the battlefield? she wondered again. How had she gained bruises on face and neck, a cut lip, scratches down her throat? Had a Norman laid hands on her? If so, she had to have prevailed. Being a woman, she had not been trained into a warrior, but better than many a man she was acquainted with that training and could defend her person.

Certain whatever had been done her during her search for her son had caused her to depart—and likely on foot since the horse the two women had ridden to Senlac was not amongst these— Aelfled nearly asked how she fared. But she bit back words that would not be welcome now that, once again, Wulf's mother was the last of her line.

"I am sorry, Isa," she spoke more words she ought not.

The woman's head snapped around. "Isa? That I was to you, but never again. Henceforth, you shall address me as Lady Hawisa —do you speak to me at all."

Aelfled did not need to be told that. She had known it ere

revealing the death of Wulf. It was the habit of years of friendship with one twenty and five years to her ten and eight that made her speak it.

She inclined her head, returned her gaze to the wood.

"Hold!" rasped the most formidable of their escort.

All stilled, waited for Vitalis to command them forward. When the stirring amid the trees proved a doe and her leggy fawn, the party resumed its trek. Shortly, Isa's escort set themselves around the perimeter of the ancient oak before which a fairly nondescript mound was covered over with leaves.

Standing alongside her lady, staring at it through tears and steeling herself for the possibility a hand would be raised to her again, Aelfled thought the shallow grave was larger than she had left it. Was it only imagining or...?

She caught her breath, did not realize she spoke his name until her lady gripped her arm. "What say you?"

"I..."

"D'Argent. You said D'Argent!"

Aelfled gulped. "I did."

"Why?"

She had not told of being aided by the enemy. There had been no opportunity amid her lady's response to her son's death, but had there been she did not know she would have revealed it for how much more it would pain and anger the grieving widow now mother.

Isa gave her a shake. "How did you learn that Norman name?"

Failing to swallow the lump in her throat, Aelfled said past it, "After I found Wulf, as I was holding him ere..." She gulped. "A chevalier came looking for kin and nearby found the man methinks slain by Wulf and the other boys." She nearly revealed she had the opportunity to put a blade in Cyr D'Argent's back, but that tale would be welcome only had she done the deed. "It was from amongst those atop his dead kin I pulled Wulf."

"He who slew mere boys ere drawing his last breath!" her lady cried. And shook—how she shook! Slamming her eyes closed, she drew shuddering breaths, and when the last went down, asked, "Did the chevalier desecrate my son's body?"

"Nay!" Aelfled was horrified over the suggestion, then recalled she had also feared the Norman's grief would cause him to take sword to Wulf's companions. But that need not be told. "Cyr D'Argent—"

"Cyr! You know his given name."

Determining how she had come by it also need not be told— nor that other terrible name by which he was called—she said, "He but gave aid, my lady, and I—"

"You paid his price?"

It took her a moment to decipher Isa's meaning, and it offended. Never would she offer sexual favors. Unable to keep anger from her own voice, she said, "He asked naught of me, and naught would I have given. He was..."

"What?"

She had nearly named him honorable, he whose sword arm had contributed to bathing the meadow in Saxon blood.

"Honorable," Isa revealed she knew her maid's mind.

Now she will do unto me as never has she though this day I give abundant cause, Aelfled once more prepared herself for a slap. Or worse.

But her lady laughed—if one could call a sound far from what Wulf had most easily roused from his mother. At the end of that false thing, she said, "I wonder how many silver-haired D'Argents fought for that thief."

Aelfled nearly stumbled where she stood. From the chevalier she had learned there were at least three of that family at Senlac, including his slain uncle and missing brother, but her lady's knowledge of silvered hair—no fit for a man perhaps aged twenty and five—told she had also encountered one. Cyr? The brother he sought? Another? Of greater import, had a D'Argent marked her face and neck?

"You knew the name ere I spoke it, my lady."

Isa released her. "I did. I do."

"How?"

A smile no more genuine than her laughter curved her lips, but she did not answer.

Thinking in this moment she was not even pretty, Aelfled asked, "What is it, my lady?"

Isa raised her eyebrows. "Private amusement born of a hating heart. And longing—so much longing to be worthy of my father and his father." She raised a hand, opened it to reveal a palm scored with crescents fingernails had pressed into her flesh. She stared at it, then once more curled her fingers inward—loosely, as if around a hilt.

"I am taken ill," Isa whispered.

"'Tis grief, my lady."

"Nay, revenge. It makes my head ache, throat burn, belly roil. Do I allow it, and I do not know why I would not, it will put me in the ground alongside my Wulf. But not until I feed it to bursting."

Such words from another lady would not have frightened. But this was Isa with the blood of warriors in her veins. And now vengeance.

She breathed deep, with what seemed effort moved her gaze to the mound. "So this is the Norman chivalry we are to esteem," she scorned. "Mere afterthought, but how very kind."

She delayed the inevitable—had been since before voicing her longing for revenge. But her next words told she believed herself ready to sweep aside the leaves. "Be gone."

Aelfled knew she ought to obey, but the friendship they had shared made her loath to leave her side—even if the only comfort she might provide was someone upon whom to beat out her anger.

"Hear me!" Isa snarled. "I am near the end of myself. And there will be no celebrating my arrival."

Aelfled inclined her head, whispered, "My lady," and withdrew a dozen paces.

When she turned back, Isa was on her knees beside the mound. She remained unmoving a long time, then said, "God give me strength," and began pushing aside the leaves.

In seeking to uncover her son, she also uncovered those on either side of him—four village boys though there ought to be two.

Aelfled sank to the ground and buried her face in her hands. Recalling when she had asked who Cyr D'Argent was, she saw him again and heard him tell he was her enemy until all of England yielded, then add he was sorry for it. She had longed to believe that last as she peered into eyes she had thought would ever be black to her. They were not. The eyes of the warrior who put England's defenders to the sword were green.

"I will forgive you, Cyr D'Argent," she whispered. "One day I shall."

A muffled wail brought her head up, and she saw her lady pull her son from the shallow grave. "Beloved Wulf!" Isa cried and, hunching over him, began rocking him as though he were an infant at her breast.

Hardly able to breathe for the guilt stuffing itself down her throat, Aelfled longed for the psalter gifted by her lady years past —the same now marked by Wulf's blood and rejected by Cyr D'Argent.

Thinking to retrieve it, she pushed upright and started toward the trees bordering the battlefield.

"Aelfled!"

Wrenched by the wrath with which her name was flung, she turned. "My lady?"

Bruised face flushed and moist, Isa peered across her shoulder. "Never shall I forgive you. Never!"

Aelfled caught back a sob. "As you ought not," she said and lowered her head and quietly wept for Wulf, Isa, her people, and an England she feared ever beyond recognition.

CHAPTER FIVE

Wulfenshire, England
Summer, 1068

*I*n the space of a fortnight, all had come together in a clash as of cymbals, the reverberations felt in every corner of Cyr's life. Hence, he had returned to England as he had known he must though he thought it would be many years before he ran short on excuses to stay out of the country he had helped conquer.

The first corner of his life to be jarred was that in which his brother, Dougray, slammed his bitter self time and again until commanded to leave their sire's demesne. The second corner was that in which Cyr's sister should have sat demurely, but having been far from reserved was now her brother's responsibility. In the third corner prowled Raymond Campagnon who had made Cyr regret the English lands chosen as his reward. And the fourth corner to be jarred—the only one he did not begrudge—was occupied by Guarin who might yet live if the one who professed to have seen him had seen right.

Did he live? Had Theriot found him? Was he at Stern Castle?

The possibility made Cyr long to defy the king's command he deal with Campagnon before presenting at the castle whose construction the youngest D'Argent had overseen in its lord's absence—could it be called absence since never had Cyr set eye or foot on the demesne upon which the fortress was raised. It was the name Wulfenshire, first heard spoken by the Saxon woman at Senlac, that caused him to choose one of several pieces of land carved out of that relatively small shire as his reward for being among William's worthiest followers.

Unfortunately, Campagnon had also been awarded a demesne here, though not of his choosing. According to Theriot, it was a relatively undesirable piece of land William tossed to one whose family name was likely responsible for him gaining favor. Fortunately, the tidings to be delivered Campagnon at Castle Balduc would eventually see him depart this shire, if not all of England.

"Mother Mary, Lord Jesus, Almighty Father, Heavens above, I am sore as sore can be," bemoaned the woman riding at his side. "We ought to have paused at that abbey."

Lillefarne whose imposing stone walls they had glimpsed in the distance a quarter hour gone where the abbey touched the borders of three baronies—Stern, Balduc, and Wulfen.

A heavy sigh. "How much farther, Cyr?"

Moving his gaze from the land he did not want, though it was where he would pass the remainder of his life if Guarin lived and was hale enough to reclaim the heir's mantle now worn by the second-born, Cyr looked to his sister.

Nicola the Reckless, the title teasingly bestowed by their eldest brother years past, raised her eyebrows.

As with each time he regarded her since his return to Normandy, he was struck by her physical transformation from girl to woman. If not for her scandalous behavior, a month hence she would have wed. As she had been pleased with the match made two years past, her intended being hale, hearty, and attractive despite the twenty years age difference, it had surprised she gave him cause to break the betrothal that left her with two choices—the convent or England where it was possible to pluck from among recently-landed Normans what their sire called an *unsuspecting* husband.

"As already told, at so leisurely a pace we ought to arrive at Balduc by early afternoon." He gauged the sun's position. "An hour and a half."

She groaned, dropped over her saddle's pommel, giggled, and snapped upright. "I am a D'Argent! I shall endure though much my delicate seat protests!"

"Nicola!" he rebuked as the regard of their escort too often upon her made itself more felt.

She rolled her eyes, tossed her head, and settling back in the saddle began humming.

Cyr narrowed his eyes at the soldiers, and when they returned to keeping watch over the road and bordering wood, once more assessed his surroundings. Those who followed their progress from the cover of trees were adept at stealth, remaining unseen and unheard, but he felt them.

Assured his party was in no immediate danger, Cyr considered Father Fulbert to his right—odd in appearance as well as pedigree. In looks, the only evidence of his godly profession was a tunic whose length was near that of a habit, skimming ankles rather than ground. Exceedingly tall and broad-shouldered, vast of countenance and deep of voice, so imposing a figure was he that children often named him Goliath. Of gentle soul and true to God, the man of near on two score years was no warrior—except in defense of innocent lives. As for his pedigree, he was a portent of things to come were William able to keep hold of his kingdom. Fathered by a Saxon, birthed by a Norman, he had been sent from England at a young age to receive training for priesthood in France. Most odd, indeed.

Surely sensing he was watched, he smiled but kept his gaze on the road. "You think it too quiet, Cyr?"

"I do, much like the day we met."

"I agree. And pray these do not dare as those dared."

Also Cyr's prayer. Having returned to Normandy months after the fight that saw thousands of Saxons and Normans bleed out their lives at a place now known as Battle and—more broadly—Hastings, he had delivered Dougray home. And brought with him tidings no different from those earlier sent by missive informing his parents that no body having been found, it was possible their eldest son was captured by Saxons during their retreat at battle's end and would be ransomed. After so long, it had been too slight a hope, and the shadows cloaking his parents had not shifted.

Weeks following Cyr's return, he had gone on pilgrimage hoping to gain some measure of forgiveness for those felled by his hand over more a matter of land than God. Absent his sword, having thought it sacrilegious to carry that which spilled so much blood, he had traveled alone until halfway through the journey when he joined a dozen others on pilgrimage. Days later, as dusk set in, brigands struck so brutally the pilgrims were quickly reduced to half. Side by side Fulbert and Cyr fought with daggers and fists—and prevailed, but not before losing another of their company, an elderly monk.

Awash in regret for having eschewed the sword that would have saved more of his fellow travelers, Cyr vowed never again to allow guilt—warranted or not—to render him defenseless in a world enamored of the defenseless. In the company of Fulbert, he had completed his pilgrimage, returned to his father's demesne, unbelted the bent and chipped sword taken from a slain brigand, and once more donned the weapon awarded him upon attainment of knighthood.

Now in the midst of what seemed a greater threat, he glanced at the hilt riding his hip. "With so large an armed escort, I do not think they will attack," he said. "They shall only have tale of our presence, strength, and destination to carry back to their leader."

Fulbert looked to the bordering wood and Cyr followed his gaze.

Still no movement, but they were there—rebel Saxons who refused to accept the rule of Normans. And he could not begrudge the natives their disaffection, especially those who suffered Campagnon.

Cyr recalled his last encounter with the miscreant. As ever, memories of the Saxon woman gave him pause, but he shook her off as was impossible to do when she trespassed on his dreams. Campagnon had been moved to violence over Cyr's interference, but it could not compare to how he might react once he learned of William's decree.

Upon Cyr's arrival in England, he had gone to the king as commanded and been upbraided for neglecting his English lands. Told it mattered not that Theriot administered them well, Cyr was forced to decide between taking control of the demesne or yielding it so it could be awarded to another of William's followers. Were it certain that follower was Theriot, Cyr would have made the decision then, even at the risk of finding himself landless should Guarin appear, but the king had played coy on the fate of Stern which his decree would render even more desirable.

Though Campagnon was aware of William's displeasure over his inability to control discontented villagers and capture the Saxon rebels who beset Wulfenshire lands with pillaging and, worse, the burning of crops, he could not know his burden would soon be lightened. The number of Normans giving proof of their mortality as they passed through Balduc having increased, the king's patience was at an end. Campagnon was no longer baron, his demesne to be absorbed into the one held by Cyr. However, he was not entirely set aside, William allowing him to remain as castellan of Balduc, answering to an overlord he detested.

It was either a game the king played, a test, punishment, or all.

William was no fool. He knew the enemy made of Campagnon would give his errant baron no peace. Cyr would have to watch his back—at least until he gained sufficient reason to remove Campagnon. When that day arrived, there would be a place for one of his brothers, be it Theriot or Dougray.

He glanced over his shoulder at where the latter rode behind Nicola. Though the mantle about his shoulders concealed the absence of the lower half of one arm, Dougray's dull eyes set in a gaunt face behind an unkempt beard evidenced the loss. However, since landing in England, an occasional light was seen in his eyes. If only it did not bode ill...

Had it been a mistake to bring him? Would it have been better to leave him in the hovel to which he had gone following banishment from his family's lands?

"It is well," Fulbert said low.

Though no longer greatly unsettled at being easily read by the priest, still it jolted Cyr. "You think so?"

"Time, patience, prayer, my friend." Fulbert smiled, revealing imposing teeth, then nodded to the wood. "Which they would also do well to heed, but how they are tempted! Their numbers must be great."

"Still, I believe they will stay the wood. Do they not, I am prepared." No idle talk. Though Cyr had vowed he would never again give any cause to name him *Merciless,* he would defend his family and people regardless of the cost in blood. Since it was only a matter of time before his vow was tested, he was grateful for the escort with which William surprised him—over a score of armed, battle-tested soldiers. Of greater surprise was the senior chevalier, in whose company Cyr had spent little time since his cousin's rejection of attempts to support him following the great battle.

Cyr shifted his regard to where Maël rode ahead and wondered as he had often these past days, what dwelt behind an easy smile that belied hard eyes set in a face counted the most striking of the D'Argents—before a blade put finish to it over a year and a half past and Maël buried his sire in English soil.

Though his prowess in battle had gained him a prominent position in the king's guard, Cyr had not expected he would long remain at William's side. After all, Maël's crossing of the channel to fight the Saxons had also been in the cause of gaining lands of his own. And lands he had not.

Once more, Cyr questioned why his cousin was overlooked, or if he had been. The battle had changed him as it had Cyr, but the manner in which he presented was a tight fit. A content-with-his-lot Maël was laughable. Regrettably, despite opportunities for the cousins to speak these past days, their only conversation of any depth was in regard to Maël's widowed mother.

Six months past, Cyr had honored his cousin's request to send her to England to aid Theriot in setting up Stern Castle's household. Though reluctant to leave Normandy, Lady Chanson had agreed in order to be nearer her son. But as told by Maël, he had seen her only once when he escorted her from London to Stern.

Silently vowing he would get enough drink into his cousin to loosen his lips, Cyr looked to the priest—and found he was now watched.

"I do not know that nut is ready to be cracked open," Fulbert said.

Wishing he could as easily travel another's thoughts, Cyr shrugged. "The breaching of some shells require greater effort."

"And a bigger hammer."

Cyr smiled.

"One I pray you will not have to use too forcefully in your dealings with the rebels," Fulbert returned Cyr to his immediate purpose.

"As do I. Once I have fixed a collar on Campagnon and settled my sister at Stern, I will begin ridding these lands of those who plague it."

"And the Lady of Wulfen Castle?"

His northeastern neighbor, the daughter of the departed Wulfrith so revered for training up England's defenders his reputation had years past pricked the ears of Duke William. Hence, that name had pricked the ears of Cyr's uncle who resented his duke's sly suggestion that Hugh D'Argent, esteemed for training up Normandy's warriors, would profit from a crossing of the channel.

When Cyr chose as his reward lands upon Wulfenshire, it had not occurred these could be the ones Hugh declined to visit, variations of the name *Wulf* fairly common in this island kingdom. But they were the same, the family of Wulfrith having controlled the largest portion of this shire until William began piecing it out.

Had the Norman husband of Wulfrith's daughter not been killed at Stamford Bridge weeks before the greater battle near Hastings, the land left to her might not have remained hers. But England's new king, having no proof his fellow countryman would have stood against him, allowed the Saxon widow to redeem a portion of her lands nearly equal to the pieces taken from her to award his followers.

Unlike many native landholders, she had possessed the required funds—or tribute as it was called—and William told he was mostly content with her submission. *Mostly* because he did not entirely trust her. *Mostly* because she denied him what he wanted perhaps more than coin—for Wulfen Castle to prove its reputation for training up warriors. For him.

That she could not do, she had sent word. Not only had the greatest of her family's trainers perished alongside her husband, but she and her young son were the last of their line. As she was but a woman relegated to the sharp point of a needle rather than a sword, she knew not the means by which her sire and grandsire and those come before trained up warriors.

Cyr had glimpsed William's ire over what she could not give

and was fairly certain were her son and heir not half-Norman, she would have lost all. Not for the first time, he wondered if she, a Saxon of Wulfenshire wed to a Norman noble, could be the same lady who had lost one of her sons at Senlac.

Likely, he once more concluded. Though the young woman aided following the battle had not spoken her lady's name, it seemed too much coincidence. However, Cyr had held close his knowledge of that noble youth. It was not from him William would learn one of the lady's sons might have fought against Normans and killed Hugh D'Argent. Enough lives had been lost to the conquering, whether by way of death or despair, and he would not add to those numbers.

Hopefully, the grieving widow and mother would give him no cause to regret withholding his suspicion from the one owed his greatest fealty.

Too long in answering his friend, Cyr said, "Forgive me, Fulbert. As instructed, I shall keep watch over the Lady of Wulfen to determine if she is truly loyal to our king."

The priest sighed. "Let us pray she does not abet the rebels. If she is the one you believe her to be, already she has lost much."

Cyr had shared enough of his encounter with the young Saxon woman that, following the king's discussion of Hawisa Fortier, Fulbert also concluded it was that lady's son conveyed to the wood ahead of four other boys.

"Hold!" Maël shouted at the same moment Cyr caught sight of two figures ahead.

Reining in with the others, hand on hilt, Cyr peered at two who came shoulder to shoulder on foot, moving with the awkward gait of those whose legs were bound together.

As their escort drew swords and closed around the ones whose safety they were entrusted with, Nicola said in near equal parts disquiet and curiosity, "Who comes, Cyr?"

"Soon we shall know. Fear not, you are safe."

"Sir Reynard! Sir Gilbert!" Maël called for chevaliers to accompany him forward.

"Remain here, Nicola." Cyr was tempted to command the same of Dougray, but he would do as he would. Moments later, Dougray followed his older brother who opened a path between two of their guard and put spurs to his destrier. Side by side, they reached Maël and his men as they reined in before the men who had staggered to a halt.

"Keep watch!" Maël ordered his chevaliers and sprang out of the saddle.

These unfortunates were known to him—and to a lesser degree, Cyr. Though their appearance was altered from this morn when they were sent ahead to deliver tidings to Campagnon that D'Argent, in the company of the king's men, would require lodging for the night, they were the same. Gagged, heads shaved, faces bruised, fine tunics exchanged for threadbare ones, feet bare, they were so disgraced it appeared the only good of their ordeal was that they lived.

More intensely aware of being watched by those in the wood, Cyr dismounted and drew his dagger to aid his cousin in loosing the men who grunted and babbled against dirty rags. As he sliced through the ropes binding one of the men's wrists at his back, Maël cut the gag.

The man tried to speak, but a coughing fit bent him forward. While he regained his breath, the cousins finished unbinding the two.

As Cyr came around, he noted the high color in Maël's face that rendered more stark the pale scar aslant it.

"Rebels?" Maël demanded of the second man who rubbed his jaw as he tested its range of movement.

It was as Cyr also wished to know, it being possible someone at court had alerted Campagnon of the king's decree.

A guilty flush dampening the messenger's seething, he nodded. "We were taken by rebels."

As if steeling himself for discipline, his companion touched his bald, scraped pate, stood taller. "It was she, Sire—Dotter."

Dotter, Cyr reflected on the word appended to a Saxon female's name to identify her by whose daughter she was in the absence of a surname. Thus, so impossibly common was the name that it eliminated only males as the leader of the rebels bedeviling this and surrounding shires. As Balduc was most often the target of their aggression, for this Campagnon forfeited his lands, William stating that if a battle-hewn warrior could not outwit the weaker sex, a lord he did not deserve to be.

"Did you put eyes on Dotter?" Maël asked.

"Non, Sire. A dozen rode us to ground, bound, and blindfolded us. Afterward, we but heard her voice and felt its breath on our faces. As others have reported, it sounded of an aged woman."

Gytha, the vengeful mother of the departed King Harold who had lost four sons in 1066? Cyr once more turned over the possibility toward which William leaned.

"Beyond your dignity," Maël said, "what did they gain?"

The soldier momentarily closed his eyes. "Lord D'Argent's missive. They know he comes to take possession of Stern and shall pass the night at Balduc."

Cyr filled his lungs with the gentle breeze upon which the rebels' scent might be carried from the wood. Had they not captured the messengers nor had spies at court, soon enough they would have learned whom the king provided an escort—that the lord of Stern had finally come. But did they know the reason he went the long way around Stern to stop first at Balduc?

"Their purpose in releasing you?" Maël pressed.

The one who had first spoken dragged up his tunic and from the waistband of ragged chausses drew forth an arrow. He held it out, though not to Maël. "She said to render this unto Cyr D'Argent—the merciless one."

Cyr reached, faltered as thoughts spun back to when Campagnon scornfully bestowed that well-earned name in the presence of the young Saxon woman. Was it possible she led the rebels, disguising her voice to conceal her identity?

"My lord?"

He accepted the arrow, slid his gaze from feathered shaft to keen tip, knew there was more. "And?"

"She said it was intended for you."

He tested a calloused thumb to the arrow's tip, acceded it was possible it would have found its mark from wood to road, but would it have penetrated his chain mail, embedding itself well enough to take his life? Likely not, but had the shot been most fortuitous, it could have found the flesh of his unprotected neck.

"And?" he asked again.

"Most curious, my lord, she said its absence from your heart wipes clean her debt."

Cyr stilled, returned to the present only when Maël turned a scarred, furrowed brow upon his cousin. "What debt?"

Ignoring his question, Cyr said, "I assume she conversed in Norman French."

"She did."

"Without fault?"

"Quite well, my lord, though I caught her Saxon accent."

One well-versed in the language of her enemies, a woman who owed him a debt...

He looked around, silently cursed the deep of the wood that denied him sight of one who could look upon him without being looked upon. Was she there? The one who told she would pray for him? Might so young a woman lead men in rebelling against their conquerors?

The thrill that went through him was short-lived. Had she sent the arrow—and who else could it have been?—her vengeance had wreaked terrible things on these lands, notwithstanding the letting of Norman blood. And neither did her own people go unscathed. Though the rebels mostly directed their efforts at Campagnon, the Saxon villagers were made to account for their

Norman lord's losses. Were a crop destroyed, an animal slaughtered, or a cart burned, the lord of Balduc confiscated the same and more from those who most needed it.

"Cousin?" Maël pressed.

Cyr met the gaze of William's man. Unwilling to relate his suspicions, though they had much meat on them, he said, "I seek the same answers."

Maël gave a grunt of disgust, returned his attention to his men. "At least a dozen set upon you, you say?"

"Oui, my lord, and took us well into the wood where there were more."

Survivors of the great battle as William believed? Cyr wondered. Common men whose common blood permitted them to flee to the wood unlike most Saxon nobles who believed it dishonorable to survive their king?

"Throughout you were blindfolded?" Maël asked.

"We were."

"Can you guess their numbers?"

"Four score, Sire? Five?"

Maël blew out a long breath. "The king will himself wish to hear your account."

The color drained from their faces. As evidenced by what had been done them, they had failed. And William had little patience for such.

"Sir Reynard, Sir Gilbert," Maël said, "take these men up behind you." As the two disgraced soldiers stepped forward, he turned full on Cyr. "I need not know what you know, would but remind you of what the king requires of your lordship."

"Be assured, Cousin, whoever she and her followers are, I shall end their rebellion." He slid the arrow into the scabbard housing his sword. "Now, we have a duty to discharge."

Beneath the eyes of those in the wood, the two returned to their destriers.

"It seems," Dougray said as Cyr settled in the saddle, "you have untold tales in your quiver." He glanced at the arrow. "If naught else, I shall be grateful for the entertainment they provide."

"You are not here for the purpose of entertainment, Dougray. Like it or not, you shall aid in ending the rebellion afflicting these lands."

Amid the beard, which was amongst the greatest of ironies, a smile appeared. For as much as Dougray hated the Saxons, he had adopted their unshaven, long-haired ways—albeit in no way groomed.

He showed more teeth. "Be assured, I shall like it well."

"*My* way," Cyr said. "Not the ungodly way of revenge."

Dougray shrugged the shoulder beneath which a portion of his arm was missing. "I do not think William will mind how it is done as long as it is done."

Cyr closed his mouth against argument, looked over his shoulder at the escort Maël commanded forward. As he moved his gaze between Nicola and Fulbert, he wished back the old Dougray. As difficult as his pre-conquest brother could be owing to the circumstances of his birth, *that* Dougray was far preferable to the one carried from the battlefield who had yet to cast blame on Cyr for his loss—at least by way of words. Hopefully, from beneath ire and bitterness, the pre-conquest Dougray would re-emerge.

CHAPTER SIX

Castle Balduc
England

*C*yr looked up from the missive to which the king had set hand and seal, noted the vein jagging Campagnon's brow up into his hairline, next the light scar across the knave's nose and cheek dealt by the woman it was best not to think on.

"Thus, your rights to this barony are forfeited," Cyr concluded. "They are transferred unto the Lord of Stern Castle to become one with my demesne. Do you wish, you may remain as castellan of Balduc."

Had the man's eyes fangs, the venom piercing his rival's would have killed. But though he must long to rage, he retained enough control Cyr had only to take hold of his sword by way of thought. Still, if Campagnon did not soon find something upon which to let his wrath, that vein might give.

Cyr turned the missive, extended it.

Fists white-knuckled atop the table behind which he stood, the former Baron of Balduc flicked his gaze over the parchment, shifted to Maël who had accompanied Cyr to the dais, then considered those beyond—Cyr's brother and sister, the priest, the king's men. He nodded as if in accord with dark imaginings, straightened, and gave a bow. "Baron D'Argent."

"Sir Raymond," Cyr afforded the only title left to him. "I assume you wish to accept the position of castellan."

With no tempering of sarcasm, he said, "I would be honored."

"Then until such time I deem it of mutual benefit we part ways, you shall administer Balduc and its lands as I direct."

A muscle at his jaw convulsing, Campagnon said, "Be assured I shall, *Baron.*"

Cyr looked to those on either side of the seat from which the former lord had arisen when Cyr and his escort interrupted their meal. Elevated above men-at-arms who occupied lower tables, eight chevaliers watched, among them Merle. And like Merle, they radiated resentment. To ensure few, if any, lasted longer than Campagnon, their ranks would be seeded with Stern chevaliers and men-at-arms.

"Before you and your escort continue on to Stern, you would be refreshed with drink and viands?" Campagnon asked.

Cyr rolled the missive and slid it beneath his belt. "We would. And as it grows late, we shall avail ourselves of lodgings."

The man's hands opened and closed as if seeking cold steel. "As you will." He stood taller. "Now it seems all that is left to me is to relinquish the lord's high seat and chamber."

"That will serve. For now."

He heard the whistling breath drawn through the man's nostrils, guessed it did little to calm him. Then Campagnon sidestepped, vacating the seat that remained his only in the absence of his overlord, and called for servants to erect more tables for their guests.

The Saxons who hastened forth were a nervous lot, and Cyr did not doubt they had good cause. Campagnon was surely the reason that of all the lands of Wulfenshire, those of Balduc were most afflicted with rebellion. Unfortunately, the king's greatest concern over the ills done those now Cyr's people was to prevent injustice from moving more Saxons from fear-driven acquiescence to deadly rebellion.

Campagnon displaced one of his men so he sat at the right hand of the rival who had become his liege, and several others to the left of the high seat to accommodate Cyr's companions, then called, "Wench!"

The young servant halted, bestowed a wary gaze that stunned though it was not directed at Cyr. "My beloved lord?" she said in a poor rendering of Norman French, but not so poor Cyr mistook the term of affection added to her obeisance. Just as certain was its insincerity.

"Prepare the lord's chamber for Baron D'Argent."

The Saxon dipped her chin, glanced at Cyr out of mismatched eyes—one brown, the other blue, in their depths fear and something else. Pleading?

Guessing her ill-used by Campagnon and possibly his men, that if she had virtue about her before the Normans' arrival in England it was long lost, Cyr offered her a smile he hoped would be interpreted as a sign her life would be different henceforth.

The corners of her mouth twitched, but had she thought to return the gesture, Campagnon's next words made her think opposite.

"Go, Wench!"

She swung away, ascended the dais behind which the chamber lay, and went behind its curtains.

Very different, Cyr silently vowed and turned to his cousin.

"There will be trouble here," Maël said low.

"So there will." Wondering how many tankards of ale it would take to unlock his cousin, Cyr raised his eyebrows. "You will join me at table?"

"I would, but I am sure King William would agree my place is with my men."

His place... Cyr inclined his head. "We will speak later."

"Perhaps." Maël turned on his heel.

Trouncing the impulse to follow and beat emotion into his cousin, Cyr gestured Nicola and Fulbert forward. As he took his sister's arm, a glance at Dougray confirmed he continued to lean against the wall to the right of the hall's entrance. Knowing it would be more a waste to invite him to sit on the dais than Maël, Cyr led Nicola and the priest to their places at high table and, as done never before, settled into the place of a lord.

The seat to which he had aspired when he wielded arms during the invasion was raised higher than others, expansive, and comfortably padded. And yet it was uncomfortable in that it made him feel almost a boy trying to walk in his sire's boots. He was a lord who knew how to lord only by his father's example, and the lives he would now control were those of an enemy unaccustomed and resistant to Norman rule. But here he would begin—and make the Saxons his people beyond the yokes worn since the great battle.

Much to Campagnon's discomfort where he seethed at Cyr's side, curtly answering questions regarding the state of Balduc and providing little insight, there was no quick end to the meal. Cyr let it drag from one hour into the next, using the time to become acquainted with faces, names, and the strength of each man's ill will, while allowing Campagnon's men to take measure of their new liege. For their sakes, he hoped they read him well enough not to challenge him. As a lord he would prove wanting for a time, but standing before this inexperienced lord was a warrior tested in the fires of the most brutal battle in England's recent memory.

"Wench!" Campagnon called.

The young woman who had exited the solar and resumed her duties in the hall lifted her pitcher from the rim of Maël's cup. As she hastened from the lower table, she cast those peculiar eyes upon Cyr.

"Eyes on me, Wench!" Campagnon snarled.

She shot them to the one reduced to a castellan and ascended the dais, but as she reached her pitcher forward, he snatched his goblet away. "Around this side, Wench."

Her lashes fluttered. "Oui, my beloved lord," she said and traversed the dais.

Cyr felt ache in his fist atop the table, only the certainty he would end such treatment of those who served at Balduc keeping him from driving his knuckles into Campagnon's face. And a glance toward his cousin told he was also so inclined. Not surprising. What surprised was Dougray.

A half hour past, he had taken a seat at the lower table occupied by Maël's men. He had presented his usual brooding self as he picked over the viands, but now his shoulders were unbowed, chin up, eyes moving between Campagnon and the woman. Interest, and not merely a spark—a light as if here was something worth dragging himself up out of the mire in which he had sunk following the loss of an arm. But though Cyr would like to believe his interest was of benefit to the woman rather than Campagnon, Dougray made no secret of his hatred of the Saxons.

Following his gaze to the servant, Cyr watched her draw alongside the one who summoned her. As once more she extended her pitcher toward his goblet, Campagnon slammed an arm around her waist.

"Loose her!" Cyr growled.

The knave dragged her closer, groped a hand up her side. "I may be yours to command in the keeping of Balduc, but you have no say over this woman."

A broken nose, Cyr decided on the first lesson that would lead to Campagnon's exit from Wulfenshire, but for the benefit of the knave's men, one more warning. "As I am the lord of these lands, the people of Balduc are under my protection, and I say what can and cannot be done with them."

"I do not dispute our king's decision to give Balduc unto you, D'Argent—er, Baron. What I dispute is my command over this woman." He looked up. "Tell him to whom you belong, Wench."

Cyr saw struggle on her face, whether it was to translate Campagnon's language into her own or summon the correct, loathsome response, he could not know.

She moistened her lips. "I belong to my beloved lord."

"See now!" Campagnon shot his regard to Cyr. "The witchy-eyed wench is mine. And do you doubt me, I have the papers to prove it."

Cyr frowned. "Papers?"

"She is not of Balduc. Good coin I paid for her at auction."

Nicola drew a sharp breath, on its exhale breathed, "Slavery. What heathen land is this?"

In this, heathen indeed. Unlike Normandy, England yet boasted that foulest of trades. Whether it was true the departed King Harold had engaged in the ungodly business ere claiming the English throne and his mother, Gytha, profited from the sale of girls shipped across the sea, the slaves made of men, women, and children accounted for between ten and twenty percent of the population. Until King William abolished slavery, there was nothing Cyr could do for the woman, nor could Dougray were he of a mind to aid rather than gloat over her circumstances.

Cyr glanced at him. His interest waned, hopefully because he also saw the futility of defending one whose life so completely belonged to another.

Or was it futile? Cyr considered the healthy purse on his belt, then guessing Campagnon would be more resistant to motivation driven by compassion than lust, ran his appreciative gaze up the woman. Her regard turned more wary, doubtless over the way he regarded her as he had not before.

"Your liege would like the woman for himself, Campagnon," Cyr said. "How much to buy her papers?"

He raised an eyebrow. "When I am done with her, we will speak of price. But fair warning, *my liege,* you may have a long wait. Much I like her in my bed."

Surely not as much Cyr's fist would like the crunch of the man's nose, but there was nothing for it. For now.

Feigning indifference, Cyr jerked a shoulder. "Providing she remains desirable, we may talk." A sideways warning that the less ill-used, the more coin she would bring.

"Much depends on her, eh Wench?" He drew her head down, kissed her hard, and thrust her away. "Be about your duties."

Nicola's nails sank into Cyr's arm. "Odious," she hissed.

Fulbert's verdict was the same, as told by his dark expression when Cyr looked past his sister.

"Remove your claws, Nicola," Cyr said low. "At this time, I can do naught."

She dropped her hand to her lap but leaned up and whispered, "You could kill him. Is that not what warriors do?"

"In this matter, dishonorable ones. Let us hope he gives me good reason in future."

She dropped down hard on her seat and sullenly spoke no more.

When Cyr called an end to the meal, Campagnon surged to his feet. "I shall ensure my wench put the solar in good order, *my lord.*"

Doubtless, to remove anything he did not wish his liege to happen upon. "You are all consideration, Campagnon," Cyr returned cordial artifice, "a much desired quality in a vassal."

The man's nostrils flared, but he suppressed the retort he would have given were he yet Cyr's equal. He smiled falsely, then strode to the curtains and snatched them aside. As they fell closed behind him, Cyr turned to his sister and the priest where they remained seated. Seeing their heads were together, certain they discussed England's slave trade, Cyr determined to leave them to it and further his acquaintance with Campagnon's men. But as he turned aside, he felt a presence at his back.

"Quite the undertaking," Dougray drawled.

Stealth even when stealth was uncalled for, but it was more his nature than learned. And once more it would serve him well did he leave off self-pitying and embrace what remained of the warrior—which was yet beyond that with which many a fighting man was endowed.

Dougray's shoulders shifted beneath the mantle. Though the garment concealed the loss darkening his soul, his bearded face did not. His smile its usual bitter self when it deigned to appear amid that which was shades darker than his flaxen hair, he said, "None of this will truly be yours until you rid these lands of its undesirables—and you know I speak not only of Campagnon and his mercenaries."

He knew, just as he knew that perhaps more than Balduc's deposed baron, Dougray wished England purged of what he named *Saxon dogs.* Until this day, Cyr had not questioned how deep that desire. If Dougray's interest in what had gone between Campagnon and the one known by the name *Wench* was born of concern for the latter, perhaps he was coming back to the man he had been ere the great battle. Albeit often with grudging, he had championed the oppressed—again, part of his nature, evident even before he learned the truth of his birth.

Cyr prayed Dougray would become that again, especially considering how dangerous he might turn if he did not forgive the injury gained from a battle-axe. Unfortunately, forgiveness came hard to one who had yet to reconcile himself to the fate dealt twenty-three years past when he was birthed as a result of their mother's relations outside of marriage. Because her infidelity was unwitting and her husband's faith of a strength to pardon her, the misbegotten child had been raised alongside his legitimate siblings. Now if only Dougray's faith were half as strong.

Though Cyr did not believe himself worthy to reacquaint his younger brother with God, he was determined to do so. If he failed, Dougray could be lost forever.

As determined before the crossing from Normandy to

England, they would start with the sword. Dougray would rage, but that anger would be put to good use.

"What?" the younger man mocked. "No words of wisdom to calm this beast?"

Cyr started to raise a hand to clasp his shoulder, but though such show of brotherly affection had not gone amiss prior to the loss of his lower arm, it would now. "The Saxons have become our people, Dougray. We will make peace and live and work alongside them."

There was no humor about the younger man's laughter. "*Never* my people. I would sooner see—"

"You will not, little brother. As you tried our father's patience, you will not try mine."

Ignoring Cyr's warning, Dougray said, "*Never* my father. And I wager I shall try your patience." He pivoted, tossed over his shoulder, "Truly, you ought to have left me to my hovel."

It would have been easier, Cyr concurred, but the voice belonging to the youth often trailed by his younger brother countered, *Easier in some ways, not all.*

Fulbert appeared at his side. Before the big man could say what too often he did regarding Dougray, Cyr said, "Time, patience, prayer. This I know!"

The priest wiggled his eyebrows. "So wise for one so young."

Cyr stared, and when Fulbert held his gaze without waver, grumbled, "I am not much younger than you."

"I suppose a dozen years is not terribly significant, but henceforth your responsibilities number greater than mine, Baron D'Argent. Though I may be held accountable for the souls of your people, I can tend them only if they come willingly whilst they yet have bodies in which to dwell."

Meaning give his thoughts and efforts to them now, Dougray later. Cyr inclined his head. "You are right, my friend. Let us begin."

~

FROM THE FAR ALCOVE HE watched, confident he could see but not be seen, hate but not be hated—at least, without good cause. But that would come.

The fire within so fierce he felt more a stranger to himself than usual, the former Baron of Balduc stared at the man ever taking from him—coin, victory, and reputation at contest, revenge on the woman who had scarred him at Senlac, and the demesne for which Raymond had risked his life to aid one who did not esteem so loyal a vassal.

Desperate to find something to cling to in a world so askew it threatened to let him slip through its cracks, he summoned imaginings of England's king put through with sword on that highest of seats...folding over the blade...dropping to his knees... falling on his face...

Not impossible, but of greater possibility was the demise of one who wished more than already he had taken. Fortunately, no matter D'Argent was now baron of these lands, he could not lay claim to the Saxon wench. She was Raymond's in full until he finished with her—or found himself in need of coin. But if first the latter, it would not be D'Argent to whom he sold her. Any but him. He would see her dead, purse woefully empty, ere allowing her to perch on the merciless one's lap.

Raymond looked to the thief who gathered around men who, henceforth, would answer to a D'Argent ahead of one reduced to a castellan. Doubtless, the knave sought to determine whose loyalty could be had. Likely a good number since mercenaries sought material reward above all else, but some would stay Raymond's side—providing he persuaded them their reward would be great once the rightful owner reclaimed all lost this day.

That he would do. Rather than pace away the days until even the keeping of Balduc was wrested from him, he would give D'Argent very good reason to hate him.

"Beginning now," he rumbled when he saw *his* slave answer the baron's summon to refill his tankard. She was quicker on her feet than when the one who had given coin for the witchy-eyed thing ordered her to his side. And was that a smile in answer to D'Argent's?

Raymond launched himself off the wall. "Wench!"

She swung around, causing a stream of amber liquid to streak the air and fall to the rushes.

"To me!" he snarled.

He saw her swallow, sensed she was tempted to appeal to D'Argent. But the Saxon-lover could do naught—nor his unkempt, one-armed brother who shot her owner a look of malice. Interesting. Considering what the heathen of England had stolen from the baseborn D'Argent, he ought to rejoice over the wench's fate. Raymond certainly did. And would have added to that fate the moment she came before him if not for a voice shrill between his ears insisting he await his *overlord's* departure.

The wench dipped her head. Then as was required of her, forcing her to dampen her loathing, she said, "My beloved lord?"

He raked his eyes down her, smiled the smile that, on occasion, could coax a visible shudder from her. This was one such occasion, and it eased his anger sufficiently to heed that shrill voice. The morrow was soon enough. Until then...

"Take you to the kitchen and remain there until I send for you."

"But your guests—"

He stepped nearer, lowered his voice. "Are you unwell, Wench?"

Her lashes fluttered. "My beloved lord?"

"You must be, for there is no other halfway acceptable excuse for questioning me."

She averted those mismatched eyes, and he was no fool to think it deference. She hated him, but though he told himself he did not care, he resented she did not appreciate how foul her life would be had he not outbid the one who wished to add her to the ranks of a half dozen joy women earning him good coin across Northern England.

"Am I right?" he rumbled.

"Most unwell, my beloved lord."

"Then all the more reason to hie to the kitchen."

Clasping the pitcher to her chest, she turned.

"And take the long way around my guests," he rasped.

She did as told, and he was pleased both D'Argents watched her retreat. *This* they could not control. Nor what was to come.

CHAPTER SEVEN

Lillefarne Abbey
England

*A*t last he came, as evidenced by the missive taken from messengers intercepted en route to Balduc. Of equal note was an increase in his holdings, though that was not written on this parchment but told by one who resided in Campagnon's household. Though forfeiture of Balduc to the Lord of Stern had to be of some benefit to the Saxons who suffered beneath the blade, fist, and heel of Campagnon, it could not bode well for the successor. Upon Senlac, there had been ill between the two men, and now...

Give that poltroon your back, and he will put a blade through it, oh merciless one, Aelfled silently warned the man who had likely forgotten her.

Releasing her breath, she lowered to the bench and stared at the name she had thought often since that bloody autumn morn when all the proof needed England had lost her soul was provided by the spill of sunlight across heaped, grotesquely splayed and bent men who would never again hold wives and children. Nor would they provide for or protect their families. Leading to more loss…more death…

Running the edge of a thumb across the name she had never seen written, she reflected on the number of times she had spoken it, then lowered her chin and let her tongue and lips form it. Strange it should affect her so deeply. But were she honest, and only with herself might she be, it was not the name that caused her heart to beat against the bars of her chest. It was remembrance of the warrior of short, silvered dark hair. He who had worn the blood of her people. He who had carried Wulf to the wood. He who had made himself a barrier between Campagnon and her. He who had delivered the last of the boys to the wood. He who had tossed the psalter back at her. And yet…

Was it he who took it? Though given little time to search for it whilst her lady wept and raged over her lost boy, Aelfled had required no more, clearly recalling where he had cast it. Had the man she thought never again to see retrieved it after ensuring none of the boys was lost to their mothers?

"It changes naught," spoke the one who had thrust the missive at Aelfled.

She looked up at the woman who worked vengeance on the Normans under cover of the name Dotter. Though she approached her twenty-seventh year, since the invasion she looked years older. And more so this day.

Because of an injury sustained in evading capture by King William's men who sought to end the rebellion on these lands following the murder of a Norman family? Likely, since the vigor with which the woman usually carried herself was absent, her movements slow as if planned in advance to ensure she did not undo whatever was done to piece her back together. However, there was enough light in her grey eyes to hint at blue and color in her cheeks, and Aelfled was certain it had all to do with Campagnon who was no longer baron due to this woman's well-trained rebels.

Aelfled rolled the missive, nodded at the length of bench beside her. When the woman did not join her, she asked, "What will you do now?"

"As ever we do."

Of course. As told, the long-awaited arrival of Cyr D'Argent and the transfer of Balduc to him changed naught. Dotter would continue that begun with Campagnon, and Aelfled would give aid with as little complaint as possible, even at the cost of her soul.

And very well it could cost her all, considering how often she was called upon to thieve and deceive. It was sin enough she broke God's commandments, but that she did so whilst residing here...

She looked to the wall that enclosed what had become her home the day of her return to Wulfenshire. Outside the abbey, her lady had further impressed on her former maid she had no hope her debt would ever be wiped clean—that there would be no end to the payments required of her. Then Isa had departed with her son whose death was to be kept secret as much as possible, though it had seemed not at all possible with his decay having become suffocatingly potent during the long, slow journey north.

Remembering his figure wrapped in linen atop a straw-stuffed pallet in the wagon she had walked alongside, Aelfled closed her eyes. Were there a God, He had not been with Wulf and those who followed him to Senlac. Were there a God, He had merely shrugged over the pleas of the Saxons. Were there a God—

She caught her breath at having once more acknowledged her battered faith was beyond battered. It continued to slip away— down through the places torn open by the conquering. Did she not catch hold of the threads trailing it, ever she might peer into the void. Utterly faithless.

Staring at her trembling hands gripping the missive against her knees, she whispered, "I believe You are here." Nearly a lie. "You have not abandoned us." Even nearer a lie. "You have to be here."

"Aelf?"

It was not the sharp tone that interrupted her attempt to catch hold of the blessed threads, it was the note of concern wrapped around the endearment. When was the last time any had called her *Aelf?*

When Wulf beseeched her forgiveness for deceiving her much as now she deceived others. The memory of his head in her lap transformed her trembling into a quake that ran head to toe.

A hand touched her shoulder. "What ill is this?"

Aelfled dropped her head back and looked into her beloved lady's face. "I fear have I not lost God, soon I shall. And if I do not have Him, who have I, Isa?"

The hand fell from her, grey eyes sharpened, mouth tightened, and once more it was Dotter before her.

Aelfled swallowed. "Naught ill, my lady, merely not enough time spent at prayer."

"Time better spent doing your duty to your people." Isa swept her gaze around the garden that provided for a good number beyond the abbey walls.

Aelfled tried to look at it through the other woman's eyes but saw it only through her own. Here sustenance for those who suffered most upon Wulfenshire—the people of Balduc from whom Campagnon took time and again, even when not in retaliation for what he lost to rebels.

"Duty well beyond this," her lady concluded.

Aelfled inclined her head. "When shall you require my aid again?"

"Come the full moon, we take the lord's hay upon Balduc."

She blinked. Though what was done at night was greatly aided by a lit sky, never had a full moon been attempted. "You risk being seen, my lady."

Isa flipped the hood of her mantle up over her hair. "A risk worth taking that Baron D'Argent and I become acquainted sooner."

Aelfled pushed to her feet. "You speak of more bloodletting?"

"As told time and again, 'tis rendered in defense of our persons. The slaughter of that Norman family was not of our doing."

Aelfled longed to believe her, but Isa knew her well—that no matter how much the one entrusted with her son abhorred the conquerors, and regardless how wrenching her guilt, she would not be a party to senseless slaughter.

"Aye, it is as you told," Aelfled said, then dared, "but did you tell true, my lady?"

The woman sucked breath between her teeth, thrust her face near to reveal glittering eyes that, like the barely breathable air between them, further evidenced anger.

Fighting down the impulse to cower with the reminder that even when she had caused her lady a greater grief than ever she had known, never had she landed a blow, Aelfled remained unmoving.

"The next full moon," Isa said, then pivoted and, with measured steps that bespoke discomfort, traversed the beaten path that would deliver her out of the garden.

Aelfled lowered her gaze to the missive surely gained at the expense of great humiliation to its bearers. She started to unroll it to look once more upon the name scrawled there, instead rebuked herself for wanting to gaze on what had been more intimately imprinted on her that day at Senlac.

Cyr D'Argent, the merciless one who had shown mercy to her and a handful of Saxon boys and their mothers.

Cyr D'Argent who, of all the lands he could have been awarded, gained those upon Wulfenshire.

Cyr D'Argent who, though she might not see him again, was now near enough to be felt.

"Why?" she whispered, but before she could guess the reason, she became aware of silence where there ought to be the scrape of feet. She looked up, saw her lady had turned at the center of the garden.

"When I returned the king's men, shaved and in rags," Isa said, "I had them deliver an arrow to D'Argent."

Aelfled frowned. "For what?"

"Rather than sight it on him, I sent it as a warning."

"W-with what message?"

"That its absence from his heart is payment in full for the debt owed him by she who intercepted his men."

Belly clenching, Aelfled gasped, "What have you done?" A valid question, for her lady's actions seemed impulsive—given too little thought by one who gave much to nearly all she did.

Isa's shrug was so slight it could have been imagined. "It shall be interesting to discover how he responds to my warning."

Suppressing the longing to scream, Aelfled said, "Surely you know that in giving him cause to seek me out, he may learn my name? Does he, I could lead him to you even though I speak no word against you."

Isa stared.

"He has only to enquire of others as to whom I served ere Senlac to discover you are the lady who lost a son at the battle. And how many Saxon lips can remained sealed against revealing you had only one heir, that the boy you present as—?

"Does he not already suspect the truth of my *son*, soon he will, for you gave him all he needed to piece me together when you revealed we were of Wulfenshire and the noble boy who died in your arms was half Norman." Chest rising and falling, Isa squeezed her eyes closed as if to slam shutters against imaginings of the life going out of Wulf—in arms not her own.

Finally, in a voice evidencing tight control, she said, "Upon this shire there is—was—only one other lady wed to a Norman, and her aged heart ceased beating when she lost her husband at Stamford Bridge the same as I."

Aelfled crammed nails into her palms. So frantic was she over the arrow that she had returned to an argument long ago lost—that against presenting another as Wulfen's heir. Even before the one who named himself King William took a portion of Isa's lands, Aelfled had thought it a great a risk, but a greater risk it had become when one of the men awarded those lands proved the only Norman aware of Wulf's death. However, the chevalier who delivered tidings of the new Lord of Stern after being introduced to Isa's son, had given her lady hope of holding close her secret.

Sir Maël, kin to Cyr D'Argent, had revealed his cousin had returned to France and if the eldest brother lost at Senlac was not found, the second-born would become heir to the family's Normandy lands. Hence, Cyr D'Argent would likely petition the king to allow him to pass Stern to the brother who administered it in his stead.

"It is on you," Isa returned her to the present.

Aelfled nodded. "I know it. But what will you do? Seek to slay the Lord of Stern as you did not when you could have put an arrow through him?"

Her lady raised her eyebrows. "I do not think that wasted opportunity. He was not fool enough to ride over Saxon lands absent armor and was too distant to ensure an arrow found exposed flesh. But I fear it will be necessary to—" She snapped her teeth. Did Aelfled not know her well, what was revealed by way of words caught back might have been lost to her.

For as much as Isa hated Normans, she was not eager to end the one who had aided Aelfled upon Senlac.

She raised her chin higher. "Though armed with a tale that will explain the boy who is now my heir should I be called to account, it is possible Cyr D'Argent will have to die."

Regardless of having glimpsed a heart Aelfled had begun to think not merely barricaded but buried, the words chilled.

"And now I have men in need of lessons." The lady turned.

"I am sorry," Aelfled called. "Ever I shall be."

That should have been the end of their audience, but Isa came back around. "It was reckless to send the arrow, more the words," she said. "Unworthy of my family's name and reputation. Vitalis has every right to be angered."

It did not surprise that the one upon whom Isa greatly depended to keep her rebels safe and effective disapproved of what his lady had done.

Isa pivoted, thrust her arms out to the sides to steady herself, then snatched them in. Weaving slightly, she went from sight and, minutes later, there came the sound of hooves as she and her escort departed the abbey.

Aelfled sank to the ground. Gripping the missive so tightly it would crease, she dropped her chin and addressed one it would be exaggeration to say she held to amid so much disbelief. "Dear Lord, how long ere D'Argent comes in the belief I sent the arrow? And how am I to cast suspicion off me—keep it from Isa?"

Despite the dismantling of her lands, the Lady of Wulfen played well King William's subject—so well it was told he believed King Harold's mother, Gytha, was responsible for the rebellions upon Wulfenshire the same as other shires across England. And it was possible the older woman was involved though such was not confided to Aelfled. Regardless, if Cyr D'Argent learned Isa had birthed only one son, he would know the lie of the full-blooded Saxon presented as born of her and her Norman husband.

"Pray not," Aelfled spoke into what she hoped was God's ear. She ached that there was no end to the warring between the two peoples across England, hated that even if her lady had not ordered the slaughter of defenseless Normans, likely her rebels were responsible. But of no benefit would it be to any were Isa stripped of what remained of her lands or made to wed another Norman to retain hold of her birthright by conceiving another heir.

"Twelve days ere the full moon," Aelfled informed the Lord of what He need not be told. "Too much light. And 'twill not be against Campagnon she acts now Balduc lands are D'Argent, but the merciless one who is not merciless."

She thrust upright. Ignoring the voice that warned her to enter the abbey by way of the fortified doors at the front, the same by which she accessed the garden outside its rear wall, she turned opposite the way her lady had gone. A dozen strides later, she slipped behind an overgrown hedge as she ought not during daylight hours.

Shrouded in shadow, she ran a hand over the rough stone wall that had been of wood before Hastings. Eight months later, it had become stone, the considerable cost funded by the Lady of Wulfen to ensure the safety of Saxon ladies who fled the conquerors to avoid being despoiled. But the wall had another purpose, one of which the Normans would approve even less.

When the stone beneath Aelfled's palm became smooth iron, she sought the catch. Releasing it, she opened the low, narrow door and ducked into darkness.

Once she secured the door behind her, cautiously she traversed the outer wall's hidden passage—alone, though come the full moon she would keep company with others. Those who previously sought refuge from the wrath of Campagnon would now flee the one known as Merciless Cyr.

CHAPTER EIGHT

Stern Castle
England

Stern Castle—absent both Guarin whom Cyr had prayed to find here and Theriot who had departed on the day past to once more scout the shire in the hope of verifying their brother's sighting.

Cyr swept his gaze around the stronghold. Despite how quickly it was raised to establish the presence of the demesne's Norman lord, it was formidable. Constructed of wood which would be replaced with stone in stages, the donjon was set high on a natural mound whose top had been flattened and sides sharply sloped down to a sizable bailey encircled by a palisade. Enclosing all was a ditch-turned-moat by way of water diverted from a nearby stream.

Formidable, and of greater import, exceedingly defensible. The youngest of the D'Argent brothers was to be commended.

Standing before the upper gatehouse, Cyr looked from the steps below cut into the side of the motte that linked donjon and bailey, to his aunt. Following a terse reunion with Maël who

75

assured his mother that once his men were settled they would speak further, she had offered to accompany her nephew during his survey of Stern. For nearly two hours, she had walked him through every room of the donjon and corner of the lowermost bailey with its barracks, workshops, stables, and chapel.

Now as if sensing his gaze, she looked up. "You are pleased, Cyr?"

"I am. Theriot has done well—better than his errant brother deserves."

Lady Chanson raised an eyebrow. "But?"

She saw, and he was ashamed his disappointment was read though it had nothing to do with the state of Stern. Before he could think how to answer, she said, "I could be blind, and still I would know you do not wish to be here. As neither do I. William may have been within his rights to claim the crown promised him, but how it was done and what it cost our people..." Her lashes fluttered as her thoughts surely turned to the man whose death had made her a widow. "And what it cost—and still costs—the Saxons... In that there can be little right. Can there, Cyr?"

He put an arm around her and drew her against his side as she had done him when it was he who stood a foot shorter. "It is done, Aunt, and if England is to prosper again, the rebellion must end."

"What of oppression? That which breeds rebellion?"

"I trust Theriot has been fair to those who work the land."

"Of course, but men like Campagnon—"

"He answers to me now."

She startled backward, and only after assuring her feet remained firm to the ground did he drop his arm from her.

"How is that possible, Cyr?"

"Much his oppression and the resulting rebellion displease the king. Thus, Balduc has been given to me."

He could not remember when last he had seen so genuine a smile move her mouth. "Then for that you passed the night there."

She wagged a finger. "I know not why you did not sooner deliver such glad tidings. Praise the Lord that devil is gone."

Cyr's own smile was apologetic. "He is not, Aunt."

Her eyes widened. "For what would you allow him to remain? Not only does he ill treat his people—now yours—but I am told he bought himself a woman. *Bought*, Cyr! A slave. Though he names the Saxons heathens, what is more heathen than one in the image of God owned by another—as though a piece of clothing or an ox for the plow?"

"Well I know what Campagnon is, Aunt Chanson—a man without conscience, a liar, a cheat, a ravager. However, the king has said he may remain as castellan, and so he shall until I have cause to remove him."

She gave a snort of disgust. "Ah, William. A wily one our Herleva birthed."

She would know. Her mother having befriended the common woman who gave the Duke of Normandy his illegitimate heir, Chanson had often been in the presence of the boy who had grown into a fearsome man as she grew into a woman.

"As methinks you have concluded the same as I," he said, "either I am tested, punished, or both. Regardless, Campagnon will depart Wulfenshire. Now I have a question. What know you of the Lady of Wulfen?"

She sighed. "Very little—that she is a Saxon who wed a Norman, one son she has of her husband who died at Stamford Bridge, and she is of such sickly disposition often she is abed."

She might think herself mostly uninformed, but what she knew of the woman could prove much. "Only one son? You speak of he who survived as others born of her did not?"

Her brow rumpled. "It is possible the boy had siblings, but I heard of only one child."

"His age?"

"That I know. Recently, Theriot saw him and told though he is twelve, it will be difficult to make a warrior of him does he not soon grow into his years."

Unlike the noble youth at Senlac who, had he lived, would wear well those years on the cusp between boyhood and manhood, Cyr mulled. Meaning Hawisa Fortier was not the lady of the Saxon woman to whom Cyr had given aid? That it was another lady upon this shire who had gone south only to lose a half-Norman son at the great battle?

Cyr resented disappointment which he should not feel that the young woman he had met at Senlac might be even further out of reach, especially as it had little to do with what seemed a good possibility she led the rebels.

"If you wish to know more about Lady Hawisa and her son," his aunt said, "it is possible Maël can enlighten you. It was he whom William sent to inform the lady a portion of her lands were to be awarded to you and Campagnon. He mentioned he had met the lad and told he was quiet and uneasy."

He would have been ten, had recently lost his father, and into his home came the conquerors to claim a sizable portion of his inheritance, Cyr reasoned away the boy's unease.

Deciding to turn the conversation to a matter of greater import, he said, "You say once more Theriot searches for Guarin. Did he give no idea of his return?"

"He did not. As with each time he goes looking for your brother, he returns at frustration's end, be it a day or a sennight."

"It is good he does not lose heart, that he yet believes the sighting is true."

Her smile returned, but it was sorrowful. "Methinks he has more hope than belief now."

"And you?"

She inclined her head. "As told, the man thought to be him was long-haired and bearded in the Saxon style."

"And liberally silvered for one of relatively few years."

"Oui, and therein the greatest possibility it was our Guarin. But as also told, he fled the Normans—indeed, did injury to one."

"But not grave injury as would be expected of a Saxon rebel."

"Because he did not wish it? Or was too eager to be away lest others set upon him?" She shrugged a shoulder. "Hold to hope, Cyr, but not so much it makes you neglect what is here and now." She nodded at the donjon behind. "Mercy, what was that sister of yours thinking? And what are we to do with her?"

He considered the young woman who stood outside the door watching them though she would have joined their tour had he not ordered her to remain inside. In that she defied him, but at least she was barely outside the donjon. "Father told I am to wed her away ere word of her dishonor crosses the channel. Know you of a Norman who would not incur the wrath of the D'Argents in taking her to wife?"

She laughed. "Pity the man who raises a finger against her. Did she not bite it off, her brothers would sever it."

Worse, Cyr silently amended.

"Non," she said, "other than Theriot's friend who recently returned to Normandy to gain his reward there, I have met none I would think capable of undertaking the mess of Nicola without making a greater mess of her."

"Theriot's friend?"

"The archer, who is even longer a friend to King William."

"De Morville," Cyr named the one who, were it not his arrow that put end to King Harold upon Senlac, was loosed by one under his command. "It is good he has found his reward," he said and rued it was too late to entice him to take a D'Argent bride. What might be hidden in England—at least for a time—could not be in France.

His aunt looped an arm through his. "Come and settle in, even if only until you are able to pass this demesne to one of your brothers so you may return to Normandy."

Entirely dependent on Guarin, she knew, and he hoped she

also knew that more than remaining his sire's heir, Cyr wished that mantle once more upon the eldest son's worthy shoulders.

As they crossed the small upper bailey, Nicola sprang down the donjon steps. "I do not know I like England," she said as she pivoted to ascend beside her brother and aunt that which she had just descended, "but more and more I am fascinated by the men's long hair and thick beards. And their fierce smiles amid all those whiskers—"

"Nicola!" Lady Chanson halted halfway up the steps, gripped her niece's arm. "Still thy tongue."

"But Aunt—"

"Still it!"

Nicola's half-opened mouth remaining thus, she looked to her brother. As if realizing she would find no ally in him, she snapped her teeth, puffed her cheeks, and blew out a long breath.

Cyr was grateful when his aunt loosed his arm and said, "As your time is better spent elsewhere, I shall deal with this silly creature. Go."

He needed no further prompting, and as he took the steps two at a time, he heard her say, "Such talk reflects thoughts you ought not have, Nicola—thoughts that led to the end of your betrothal and the beginning of your... Well, let us name it what it is—exile."

"Exile!" the young woman shrilled, and that was all, though surely not for Chanson on the other side of the door Cyr closed.

As he crossed toward the dais behind which the solar lay, he surveyed the hall and was pleased by the efficiency with which the servants prepared the great room for the meal to be shared at day's end. His aunt's doing, and unlike at Balduc, the Saxons seemed self-assured despite the occasional wary glance he received.

Chanson told they were well paid and mostly trusted, one having been discharged a fortnight past when caught listening in on Theriot and the steward as they discussed the demesne's finances.

Had the Saxon sought information to pass to the rebels? Cyr had asked.

Indeterminable, his aunt told and assured him his brother was keeping a watch on the man.

"Much intrigue," Cyr muttered and swept aside a curtain providing privacy between hall and solar. As the great swath of material fell closed behind him, he halted and once more surveyed the chamber Theriot ceded to the Baron of Stern—and Balduc.

A long table was positioned against the left wall, set around it four chairs. Against the right wall, a narrow table supported a pitcher and wash basin. Center of the room crouched the large bed, at its foot an iron-banded chest of such proportion it could easily hold both lord and lady's clothing. Had he a lady...

Cyr strode to the saddlebags he had earlier dropped atop the chest, tossed back the flap of one, and withdrew what he had kept close since Senlac.

He touched the stain that reminded him of the things he had done that he wished never to do again, as well as the woman who told she would pray for him though it was hardly believable, especially had she become the leader of the rebels upon these lands.

As ever regretting he had no name to fit to her face and voice, he set the psalter atop the saddlebag and submitted to the humbling Fulbert had modeled for him during pilgrimage. Going down on one knee, he pressed his forehead to his other raised knee and closed his eyes. He thanked the Lord for His mercy, guidance, and blessings, beseeched Him to heal England by making Saxons and Normans one people of one mind and heart, and pleaded with Him to return Guarin to his family, bring Dougray out of the darkness dragged around him, and scatter whatever shadows haunted Maël.

When he rose, the light slanting through the open window told day had significantly closed the gap between it and night. Though it was hours before Cyr would sleep, he was tempted by the bed which the Baron of Stern was long negligent in claiming.

Time aplenty later, he told himself, then stretched out on the mattress, clasped his hands behind his head, and set his gaze on the timbered ceiling.

The upper layer of the mattress being stuffed with feathers, it was softly supportive. Though on occasion Cyr had known such comfort as a warrior, far more he was accustomed to straw-stuffed pallets, forest floors, and the saddle. The lord's bed felt wonderful and yet...

He swung his feet to the floor, rose, and strode opposite that which was among the privileges of a landed noble—and which was nearly unbearable for how it made him feel a murderer and thief who had slit the owner's throat so he might steal into another's bed.

CHAPTER NINE

Village of Ravven upon Stern
England

*I*t was not her—too aged was she—but the face glimpsed amongst the villagers gathered to greet their new lord made Cyr look again. Too late. She had lowered her chin, and now she turned aside.

He might have shaken off suspicion, but the seemingly frantic manner in which she pushed her way past the others while fumbling with the hood down around her shoulders made him hold his gaze to her. By the time she slipped past those at the back of the crowd, her hood was draped over hair gone silver—or mostly, enough blond showing through a circlet of braids to further move his mind to the young woman at Senlac. Not that fair hair was uncommon among these people…

With such haste the woman departed the gathering that her shoulder struck the corner of the wattle-and-daub building whose alley between it and the church would provide shadow in which to conceal her. She stumbled, righted herself, and went from sight.

Something about him had alarmed her, and he intended to confirm or eliminate the possibility it had anything to do with the rebel leader.

He thrust his reins at Dougray who, the same as the first day of the Baron of Stern's tour of his demesne, had not wished to join the escort. However, given the choice of playing Nicola's keeper or riding village to village, he had submitted to the latter. Now if only he would submit to practice at swords as thrice he had refused since their arrival at Stern.

The hunch of his shoulders evidencing boredom as much as resentment, Dougray glanced at the reins. "You would have me do what with those?"

"Hold them." Cyr smacked the leather straps against the back of his brother's hand that rested on his saddle's pommel. "There is something I must attend to."

Dougray grunted, took the reins. "I think we would all like to relieve ourselves. Thus, the sooner we depart this miserable place, the sooner we can address our needs in yon wood."

Allowing him to believe as he would, Cyr swung out of the saddle. As he came around his destrier, he called in the Saxon language, "I am pleased to meet my people. Do you have any concerns or needs not being met, you are to come to me at Stern Castle."

They began murmuring, and he hoped he was understood, proving worthy of the effort expended by Fulbert to teach Cyr English during and following their return from pilgrimage.

"As well as I am able," he added, "I shall do right by you."

Exchanging glances with one another, they continued to speak low to their neighbors. Unsurprisingly, the hum of curiosity increased when he moved past them and between the two buildings. None followed, and he was fairly certain they, the same as Dougray, believed he sought privacy in which to empty his bladder.

Emerging on the backside of the buildings, he had only to

search for movement to once more set eyes on the aged woman. She moved slowly until, mid-step, her head turned as if to cast an eye across her shoulder. That she did not do, but she moved more quickly as if pursued. And she was.

Her destination was a pretty cottage with grass and flowers planted all around, and she slowed only when she was nearly at the door and Cyr a dozen strides behind.

Moments later, the tail of her skirt whipped up and barely cleared the space between the closing door and its frame.

Cyr halted on a barren threshold too well trod to allow grass to grow. He glanced behind, confirmed he had not been followed, and knocked. "Old woman, it is your lord. I would speak with you."

The door opened so quickly she must have waited on the other side as if certain she would be given no choice but to admit him.

He smiled. "I am—"

"How daft do you think me that I do not know whose presence in my village causes all to gather 'round?" she spoke from beneath her hood and in such a rush it took him some moments to make sense of her English. "I know who you are, Cyr D'Argent, just as I know who I am—and that is *not* an old woman. I am Bernia."

Feeling watched though he could not see her eyes, he said, "Pray, forgive me."

She drew a breath, and when she exhaled, the scent of mint rose between them. "Since I have no choice but to offer my Norman lord hospitality, enter."

Her words nearly made him withdraw, so pricked was he by guilt over the power wielded against these beaten people. But to do so would cost him time. If he did not scratch his curiosity and give answer to suspicion, he would have to return another day. "I thank you, Bernia."

She turned, and he entered the single-room dwelling and closed the door. The shutters of four windows having been turned back, every corner was revealed. Assured no other was inside, he eased his hand from the hilt he had settled it on before raising the other to knock.

"I can offer no wine, no ale," she said as she crossed to a table with a stool set on either side. "But I have goat's milk." She pointed at the clay pitcher on the table, settled on a stool, and nodded at the fire pit at the center of the room over which a small pot hung. "There is porridge from this morn, thick though it has gone."

He lowered onto the stool opposite her, grimaced as its frame groaned beneath weight that had to be twice her own. "I thank you, but I am well sated."

"And unaccustomed to common fare," she said and swept the hood back off her head.

Cyr was shocked by what the light filling the cottage revealed that he had been given no opportunity to note when first he looked upon her. Were she not entirely sightless, she was nearly so, the clouds across her eyes obscuring their color.

Had this affliction only made it appear he had set her to flight, rousing hope she might lead him to one much younger than she? Certainly it had caused her to miscalculate the space occupied by the building against which she had struck a shoulder. But what mattered was whether or not she was kin to that young woman.

He let his eyes rove features that, on close inspection, were more familiar. In her younger years, she would have been lovely, so much that she remained a handsome woman in her older years.

Had her colorless eyes been as dark as those of the one he sought? Her nose was nearly as fine, mouth as wide though lips thinner, and the skin of her throat was loose and sloped as, surely, once it had not been.

Wishing she would smile so he might also compare teeth, he nearly startled when her eyebrows sprang high. "Have you looked your fill, my lord?"

Discomfited at having believed her sightlessness made it

possible to delve her face without her knowledge, he said with forced nonchalance, "Enough."

"And your conclusion?"

"I am thinking you are her grandmother."

She frowned. "I am to know who *her* is?"

If she did know, one word should suffice. "Senlac."

Bernia went still, momentarily lowered her lids. "I know what went there, just as I know my granddaughter did not give her name and would not wish it given now."

"Regardless, I would hear it." And if she refused, she must know he could learn from others in the village the name of the child of her child.

"Methinks that is not all you would hear, my lord. You would gain more than her name, hmm?"

"Have you more that you are willing to give."

Despite the lines cornering her mouth and small gaps between upper teeth, her smile was pretty, and it was easy to imagine that bowing of lips on her granddaughter had the young woman something over which to smile.

"Willing," she mused. "Only if Cyr D'Argent, Baron of Stern and now Balduc, is truly a man apart from Campagnon."

He tensed. "If you know of my meeting with your granddaughter at Senlac, you must know he and I are nothing alike."

"It is as I wish to believe, and that you will not put out my eyes as I have heard your king does when denied something." She snorted. "Aye, too late to steal my sight, but the pain... Torturous, I imagine."

Again, the delay in translating her words, but when he understood enough to make sense of them, he could offer no defense. He wished what was told of William was not true—more, that his liege had not done far worse, including cutting off the hands and feet of enemies who, during a siege some fifteen years past, mocked him for his bastardy and mother's humble birth.

"Whether or not you tell what I wish to know," Cyr said, "I vow to do you no harm."

She mulled that, said, "A bargain I will strike with you."

"Bargain?"

"You have looked upon me, now I would look upon you so I might know you better. Do you agree, I will speak my granddaughter's name—and more for which she will not thank me though I believe it will aid in keeping her safe providing you are honorable as she told."

That she had thought him honorable, stained as he had been by the blood of her people, made his chest constrict. "I agree. How is she called?"

"Aelfled."

He let the name wind through him, then cross his tongue. "Aelfled," he murmured. Though he did not know its meaning, it fit. "I thank you, Bernia. Now where can I find her?"

"Ah nay, my lord. You must fulfill your end of the bargain—allow me to look upon you."

Suppressing impatience, he said, "What would you have me tell?"

"D'Argent—meaning of the silver," she translated his name into English. "Is it true so young a man is as silvered as I?"

"Not yet, though do I follow the path forged by my sire and his sire, in a score of years what is now more black shall be more silver."

"It is the same with all your brothers, is it not?"

He hesitated. "All but the third-born."

"What color his hair?"

"Flaxen."

"Unmarked by silver?"

"That is so."

"And the sister you brought to England?"

She was well informed. "Nicola's hair is dark but sparsely

silvered, though given a few more years it may present the same as mine."

Bernia nodded, and keeping those clouded eyes on his, put her head to the side. "Does your sire know he was cuckolded?"

Having ignored the voice warning it was in this direction they moved, Cyr was nearly as angered with himself as her. Dougray was not part of their bargain, but as he summoned words to rebuke her in Anglo-Saxon, she held up a hand.

"Forgive me, Baron. 'Tis you I wish to look upon, not family secrets you wish kept buried."

He drew a deep breath. "I am done being looked upon. Now I would know where I can find your granddaughter."

"'Tis no small thing you ask, my Norman lord. To ensure I not harm one I love well, I must look nearer yet."

He ground his teeth, said, "Look."

She surprised by rising, and further when she moved around the table. If she but intended to put more questions to him, for what did she draw so near? He took inventory of her, and confirming the only thing of consequence on her person was the meat knife on her belt, remained seated. However, lest she possessed concealed weapons, he set his mind on his own blades and angled his body toward her.

She halted alongside. "As your breath barely stirred my hair when first we spoke, I know you to be tall. And as much as my stool protested when you sat on it, I know you are of good weight. What I do not know are your features." She raised a hand, ran a thumb across her fingertips. "These are my eyes. Will you allow me to touch your face?"

Cyr tensed further, and she laughed, a sound that jolted only because it was a poor fit for eerily sightless eyes in which light could no longer dance in time with that joyous sound. "Would you have me remove my knife, my Norman lord? Mayhap search me for other weapons?"

The warrior feeling a coward, he took her hand and set it on his jaw. "Look as near as you like."

She stepped close and slowly began mapping his features. But she did not stop at his face. After lingering over the size and shape of brow, eyes, nose, mouth, and chin, she moved her fingers over his hair and ears and down his neck. "I think you must be handsome, Cyr of the silver. That she did not tell—though I hoped it was so."

"Hoped?"

Her eyebrows flitted upward and the bit of a smile became more, but rather than give account of that hope, she slid her fingers from the base of his neck out to the bounds of his shoulders. Then she dropped her hands, lowered to her heels, and said, "Merciless."

He jerked. "*That* your fingertips tell?"

"Nay, that is as Campagnon named you when you defended my granddaughter. I believe you can be—and certainly have been —merciless, but not that day nor this. Nor do I believe it of your brother, Theriot. But Dougray…"

Of course she knew the name of the one who kept Stern for him, but that she also knew the name—and vengeful nature—of the third son told she was well versed in matters of the D'Argents. There were informers afoot, doubtless within his own household.

Further she disquieted him when she said, "You are not wed, are you, my lord?"

"I am not, but I shall take a wife to get an heir." Though that he would not do until he could determine as best as possible whether he was heir to his sire's lands or these awarded by William. Did he lord Normandy lands, a lady of France he would take to wife, one whose dowry would either expand his demesne or fill his coffers. Did he lord English lands, a Saxon lady he would aspire to wed to better secure his hold on this demesne.

Bernia settled a hip against the table's edge. "A lord must have an heir." She appeared to consider his face. "And all the more acceptable your son shall be to your new people does he boast Saxon blood."

Then she understood the way of things, as he supposed she ought to since other Normans awarded English lands had taken Saxon wives, regardless of whether the ladies were willing. But as it seemed a game she played, rather than benefit her, he determined to move his own playing piece onto a parallel path of benefit to him.

"I think you must be right, but tell, for what did your granddaughter's lady wed a Norman a dozen years past whilst these lands were Saxon?" He was pleased by a shift in the air that bespoke now she was moved to discomfort, and when she did not answer, added, "I speak of the Lady of Wulfen." The air shifted further. "She whom Aelfled served as a maid ere the great battle, the same who lost a son upon Senlac."

A fluttering of lashes.

Needing no further confirmation that, as thought, Hawisa Fortier was that same lady, he said, "Most blessed she had another son, do you not think?"

He nearly missed the bob of her throat.

Then perhaps she did not have another son... "Though it benefits her now to have wed a Norman since her heir has half that blood, she could not have known what would come to pass."

The breath Bernia drew raised shoulders she turned into a shrug. "As with many a noble marriage, 'twas arranged. And King Edward—God rest his groaning soul—was pleased by the match made with one of his Norman favorites."

Groaning soul... Because he had fathered no children, the absence of which gave Harold and William cause to spill the blood of thousands to decide who had the better claim to the throne.

"But enough about that noble Saxon lady," she said. "Speak to me of the brother who went missing at Senlac. Has he a wife in Normandy?"

Now it was he who caused the air to shift, so swiftly standing and placing himself over her she stepped back. "What know you of Guarin?"

She tilted her face up, and the slight curve to her lips evidenced she was pleased once more he was the one moved to discomfort. "Only that he is believed to have been sighted near or upon Wulfenshire, and for that Sir Theriot's search for his eldest brother finds no end."

Hating that once more his playing piece was on her side of the board, he said, "I find it curious that of all the English lands upon which he might be sighted, it is these distant from Hastings, the same given to me."

"That is curious, my Norman lord. Now the question is which is the imposter? Be it truth? Be it coincidence?"

He clamped his fingers into fists, not to use against her but to hold back hurtful words bred by the desperate longing to learn his brother's fate. "What else do you know of Guarin?"

"Naught, my lord."

"Then guess. Did he survive the great battle? Was he the one seen on these lands?"

"A guess in your favor would give hope I have no right to bestow. All I can offer is assurance that as our people have more heart than your own, a greater chance you have of recovering your brother than were you Saxon."

So bold, as if either she did not feel his anger or fear it.

But there was another possibility—that she tested it as a means of looking nearer upon him before revealing what more than ever he longed to know. This test he would pass.

Wondering when last he had so often filled his lungs to their full depth and breadth, he drew back a step.

Immediately, she turned aside and crossed to the fire pit. When her searching hand found the ladle's handle and she began stirring the porridge, she said, "There is another coincidence that ought to be addressed. How is it that of all the lands you could have been awarded, you were given ones upon Wulfenshire where resides the woman you aided at Senlac?"

Not coincidence, he silently conceded.

"Too much coincidence," she said, "and yet only now you come to relieve your brother of his lordship."

Determining to end the game, he strode to her. "I have more than held up my end of the bargain. Now I would know where I can find your granddaughter."

She turned her face down as if to consider the pot's contents.

"Surely you know you bear a resemblance to Aelfled," he prompted.

"So all say."

"Thus, I believe it possible it was by design you led me here."

She looked up. Rather than a face wreathed in denial, it was garlanded with a smile. "And look how you followed, Norman. That told much of my new lord, though not as much as I know now."

Feeling ashamedly bared and vulnerable, he snapped, "What it tells is that I wish to end the rebellion which more afflicts your people than mine."

Her smile dropped, and as if to herself she said, "So it does. And I fear there is no going back to the way we were, that we will become but a whisper amid the howl of ages do we not mix with your people..." She ceased stirring. "...do we not make children with our Norman conquerors."

That he could not argue. Knowing he was too long gone and were his men not searching for him, soon they would, he demanded, "Where is Aelfled?"

She swung around and crossed the room.

He followed—and slammed a hand to the door when she began to open it.

Those sightless eyes lifted to his. "I cannot tell where to look for the rebel leader, Cyr D'Argent, only that it was not my granddaughter who sent the arrow and, thus, she remains indebted for what you did for her and the mothers of those boys."

Anger once more expressed by his hands, Cyr said, "With or without your aid, I will find Aelfled."

"I pray you do—and soon."

Despite her attempt to persuade him her granddaughter was not the rebel leader, was this a warning from one who professed the belief Normans and Saxons must mix were the latter to survive? "What does she plan, Bernia?"

She shook her head sorrowfully. "Not what you fear, though neither do I approve of what she is moved to do."

"Tell!"

She sighed. "It is difficult—often impossible—to undo vows given the Church."

"What say you?" he demanded.

"My Aelfled wearies of the collar 'round her neck, the leash dragging her where she wishes not to go. So chafed is she I fear she will don the habit of a Bride of Christ ere long."

That alarmed, though he told himself it was only because her motive for becoming a nun was surely for the cover and protection afforded by the Church that would allow her to more easily coordinate her rebels.

Bernia's mouth curved slightly. "You have what you came for. Now leave this Saxon to her pale porridge."

Cyr understood. Without speaking the name of her granddaughter's sanctuary, she revealed it. "I thank you," he said and removed his hand from the door.

She started to open it, paused. "My granddaughter is all I have, my son slain by brigands and his wife taken by pox whilst Aelfled was too young to deeply feel the loss of her parents. Thus, I shall entrust you with her safekeeping."

Uncertain how to respond to the responsibility, he inclined his head.

She opened the door, and as he stepped outside, added, "At peril of failing yourself, do not fail me, Cyr of the silver."

The squeak of hinges sounded again, and as he looked over his shoulder, he glimpsed her crown of braids before there was only the door before him.

"I will not fail you and certainly not myself," he muttered, "providing you know Aelfled better than the rebels know her."

"My lord!"

He looked around. As expected, his men were searching for him. As not expected, this day the abbey that stood on the borders of Stern, Balduc, and Wulfen would receive Baron D'Argent.

CHAPTER TEN

Lillefarne Abbey
England

*W*ere she here, for what would you wish to speak to her?"

Concluding it was futile to attempt to identify Aelfled amongst the white-robed and veiled women moving through the cloister below, especially as her grandmother believed she had yet to make her profession, Cyr turned from the window and settled his gaze on Abbess Mary Sarah—a Saxon who, though upon their introduction proved proficient in Norman French, had reverted to her own language. Veiled aggression, but aggression all the same.

"I would speak with her of the great battle—specifically, the circumstances under which we met upon Senlac."

A shadow flitted across her face and off. Rising with such grace from her padded bench it appeared she floated to her feet, she said, "We do have amongst us a Sister Aelfled, but that cannot be the one you seek."

Then Bernia's granddaughter *had* made her profession, would nevermore be of the world of men—providing she was not the rebel leader. Feeling as if something had fallen out of him, refusing to look upon what it was, he said, "Regardless, I must speak with her."

Eyes bright in a well-boned face of so few years she had surely obtained her esteemed position by way of high nobility and favors owed, she stepped before him.

Not much more than twenty and five years, Cyr concluded. And prettier than at a distance when he had focused more on a brow upon which hair peaked lower than most, a defined jaw, and gently cleft chin. Center of that were large eyes, a somewhat snub nose, and a generous mouth.

"That is not possible, Baron." She clasped elegant hands at her waist. "Sister Aelfled is in the infirmary, so ill that does the Lord not heal her broken places, within a sennight she will find her reward in heaven."

What had fallen out of him now felt trod upon.

"Most tragic," she murmured, and in that moment he saw more clearly her dislike and was certain much of the light in her eyes was satisfaction over emotions he had not hidden. "Fortunate for you, Baron, I hold it is another you seek—one of far fewer years."

He nearly jerked over the revelation the woman in the infirmary was old. Satisfaction, indeed.

She nodded. "Does the one you met upon Senlac reside within these walls, it would be Aelfled Sorendotter."

Daughter of Soren, Cyr silently translated the closest the Saxons came to surnames. But was she also Dotter who led the rebels? Chest tight with a surfeit of breath, he said, "Also professed?"

"Not yet and may never be, though when she came to Lillefarne near on two years past, it was as she desired."

"You are saying she declined to speak vows."

"Nay, I declined."

"For what?"

"She was not ready."

"And still is not?"

She raised her eyebrows, called, "Sister Rixende!"

The door opened, and the nun who had escorted Cyr into the apartment looked first to the right at the far end of the room where a large desk sat with a chair behind it and two before it, then to the left at the sitting area where her mistress had received her Norman visitor.

The abbess stepped around Cyr, crossed to the young woman, and leaned in. They conversed in their language and too low to know what passed between them, then the nun withdrew.

Abbess Mary Sarah crossed to the chair behind her desk, lowered, and gestured to the chairs opposite. "Sit, Baron. It may be some time ere Aelfled appears."

Then she was summoned, would soon stand before him.

That which had been ground into the dirt having picked itself up and shaken itself out, Cyr started forward. And halted at the realization his back would be to Aelfled when she entered, giving him no time to look upon her before she looked upon him.

"I shall remain here." He turned back to the window overlooking the cloister.

"As you will." The rustle of parchment sounded, and when he looked around, he saw her dip a quill in ink to resume the work he had interrupted.

A quarter hour later, no nearer the one he sought, Cyr wondered if rather than summon Aelfled Sorendotter, the abbess had warned her away. "She does not come at your command?" he asked.

The woman looked up. "She does when she can be found."

"The abbey is hardly of a size in which one can long remain hidden."

"You know not all our nooks and crannies, Sire. Forsooth, we have many. But you are correct, Lillefarne is not large. It is the wood beyond whose frame makes a picture of our Lord's house that is large."

His gut tightened. "Aelfled is outside these walls?"

"Likely. Oft she goes to the trees, whether to walk, pray, or gather nuts, berries, and mushrooms for our table."

Was she so naive to believe Aelfled's exploits beyond the abbey were innocent? Or did this Norman hater know full well what went in the wood and ignore it in the hope the rebels would restore England to the Saxons?

He started for the door.

"Baron!"

He looked across his shoulder.

"Aelfled will come." She pointed her quill's feathered tip at the ceiling. "Do you not hear the bells?"

He did, and not for the first time. But it was of little note since bells marked all hours of prayer and other matters within a house of God.

"It tolls for her," she said and returned to her correspondence.

Knowing this moment Aelfled might more greatly distance herself, Cyr struggled over whether to believe the abbess.

"I vow you are not deceived," she said, keeping her head down.

"A bell that tolls for *her*." He made no attempt to soften his suspicion. "For one who is but a resident of the convent?"

Her eyes rolled up and met his across the distance. "It tolls not only for Aelfled but any who depart the safety of Lillefarne whom we must call back at the approach of danger. Such was not necessary ere the Normans stole our lands. A wooden palisade was all that was needed to keep out those we did not wish within. Now a stout wall of stone is required."

He had noted—and wondered at—that.

"As for the bells, in this instance they are rung to accommodate *you*, Baron, rather than protect my charges from men like Campagnon and his followers. And I do it for you only because your brother and his men have yet to give me cause to fear them. Thus far, they honor the name D'Argent as much as possible for one come across the narrow sea." She raised her chin. "Tell me that will not change beneath your lordship."

"It will not."

"Is that a promise?"

"It is."

"One I shall hold you to though not as fiercely as shall the Lord."

Feeling the need to offer further assurance, he said, "You know I am also now Baron of Balduc."

"All know. Now the question is—how long ere your castellan is removed?"

"As soon as I can satisfy King William I have cause for relieving him of his position, he shall be gone."

"Certes, the nithing shall provide cause aplenty, though it could prove your death do you not watch him closely."

Feeling as if schooled, and by one who never had and never would wield a blade, Cyr said, "I am well aware, Abbess."

She jutted her chin at the window he had abandoned. "It should not be much longer."

Grudgingly, he passed another quarter hour watching those who came and went in the cloister below, while behind him, the abbess scratched at her parchment.

As the last of his patience dripped from him, a knock sounded. Though the one beyond did not await permission to enter, the door opened with what seemed caution. And inside slipped a woman he did not recognize for all the dirt scuffing her veil to chin to hem.

The same as the nun sent to summon her, she looked first to the desk. Finding it occupied, she did not glance at where he stood, evidencing she was uninformed of the reason for her summons.

Hastening toward the one who retired her quill to its ink pot and sat back, she brushed at her bodice and aproned skirt and said in a sweetly raspy voice that caused hairs to rise on Cyr's arms, "Pardon, Abbess. I would not have kept you waiting were it not of import what I—"

"Silence, Child!" the woman said with authority that made her sound thrice the age of the one she rebuked though she looked little more than half a dozen years older.

"But I must tell you—"

"Aelfled!" The abbess raised a staying hand, then swept it toward Cyr and said in Norman French, "Our visitor shall think it rude do you continue to speak in a language with which he is not as familiar as are we with his."

CHAPTER ELEVEN

*a*elfled, once of Wulfen now of Lillefarne, daughter of Soren, so abruptly halted she nearly tipped forward. Forgetting the explanation rehearsed as she ran from the wood in answer to the bell well beyond its first sounding, forgetting her frustration over losing half a basket of mushrooms, she stared at Abbess Mary Sarah.

Dear Lord, he has come, she sent heavenward. *He is here. How could I not have felt him as much I feel him now? And how did he find me as he had no name as he has now? Is this Isa's doing?*

The abbess's slight nod confirming what she knew, Aelfled swallowed hard. And turned.

He stood before the window in the sitting area, as tall and broad as remembered, arrayed in fine, spotless garments as not remembered. And his eyes...

It seemed more they looked into her than at her. Did he search for confirmation of what had brought him to Lillefarne—the belief she had sent the arrow?

"Merciless Cyr," she whispered and did not realize she had done so until she felt breath across her lower lip. And saw his lids narrow. Had he caught her words or did he but question what she spoke?

She startled when a hand touched her arm, looked to the woman who had come around her desk.

"You remember Cyr D'Argent," the abbess said without question.

The woman knew the tale of Senlac, Aelfled having shared it in the vain hope of unburdening herself of that horrific night and day. And Wulf's death.

Returning her gaze to the warrior whose eyes she knew to be green though the color could not be seen at this distance and with light at his back, she said in his language, "It has been a long time." And wished it far longer so this ache might have gone dull. Were it possible...

"The baron would speak to you, Aelfled."

She sank fingers into the material of her apron, clawed up a handful. "Of what?"

"A good question, Child." The abbess stepped in front of her charge, blocking her from D'Argent's view. "As I have matters to attend to, I shall leave you to discuss whatever business brings him to us."

Aelfled opened her mouth to protest, but when the woman's wide-thrown eyes told there would be no argument, pressed her lips.

Abbess Mary Sarah turned aside. "Sister Rixende shall be outside the door do you require anything," she said, surely more a warning to the man within than a courtesy to those left behind.

Aelfled glanced at him, noted how tight-lipped the smile he gave the woman before inclining his head as if in gratitude for the consideration.

Moments later, the door closed, leaving Aelfled staring at it. And alone with one she had thought never to see again the last time he had gone from her in the wood. But as she had not feared the

Norman then, she feared him now, though not because her virtue was at risk. She had been alone with him in the aftermath of the great battle, and he had proven honorable—unlike the vile Campagnon—and more honorable in delivering the rest of the boys to the wood.

Awareness of him growing palpable, the feel of his eyes causing her skin to prickle and flush, she pressed her shoulders back and yielded her gaze.

The corners of his mouth convulsed as if he might smile, but only that. "Do you still pray for me, Aelfled of Senlac?"

Were her tongue not rooted, she might have choked on it. How painfully fitting that she, only ever known as being of Soren, Wulfen, and Lillefarne should be named that. Doubtless, her embittered lady would also think it fitting.

She splayed her fingers, immediately wished the bunched material back in her hand to give her something to hold to in this emotion-tossed sea.

"Do you?"

"Non, Cyr D'Argent, I do not pray for you." It was nearly the truth. So rarely did she allow her enemy-turned-savior to intrude on her time with the Lord that only when he shouldered his way in did she keep her word.

"Did you ever?"

She clasped her hands at her waist.

He stared long into her face, then moved his gaze down her.

She would have been ashamed at being arrayed in dirt inherent in digging for mushrooms did she not remind herself she had looked no better at Senlac. Worse, for on that field she had also worn blood. But not as much as he.

His eyes traveled back up. "Neither have you forgiven me?"

That she had not promised, had only expressed the possibility one day she might. "If you recall, you told you were not in need of forgiveness." Hoping to end their audience, she added, "Why are you here?"

He strode forward, and it took all her will not to retreat

around the desk. When he halted, near enough she could smell the scent of his hard ride but not so much she had to strain her neck to hold his gaze, she was not as staggered by his effect on her as she might have been had she not already spent many a night with Cyr D'Argent.

Too often, remembrance of the warrior kept her awake until she forced her thoughts elsewhere—of necessity, having learned only then might he remain outside dreams that were not always of Senlac and blood. Even so, at times he awakened her, his presence in her small dark cell so strong she clasped her hands close lest she reach to him. And find him there.

Silly, she named herself, but it never stopped her from feeling him.

"There is something I wish to return to you," he coaxed her back to daylight and his indisputable presence.

It took her some moments to arrive and more to translate his words. Dare she hope he wished to return the psalter he had rejected and she had been unable to find? "What would that be?" she prompted.

He reached to the left side of his belt, but there was only a scabbard there. And it was not the sword he drew from its throat but another thing of good length hidden on the other side of the hilt.

Isa, she silently bemoaned, *you did deliver him unto me.*

Praying she revealed no recognition of that which she had only been told, she fit puzzlement on her brow. "I am unaware of having lost an arrow." Did she sound as breathless as she felt? She raised her gaze from the black-feathered shaft to green eyes. "Indeed, I did not know I possessed one."

His lids narrowed. "The day of my arrival upon Wulfenshire, two of the escort the king provided were captured by rebels, abused and humiliated. The unseen leader known as *Dotter* had them deliver this with the message its absence from my heart wipes clean a debt."

"You think I am that woman?"

"If I am owed anything, in all of England there are only a handful who might feel indebted—the young woman I aided upon Senlac and the mothers of the boys whose bodies were recovered. It could be any, but most likely it is you...else the mother of the noble boy whose death in your arms has left her with but one son to pass her lands to."

Once more, Aelfled rebuked Isa. Fiercely, her lady strove to protect what remained of her family's holdings—and to keep safe those who did her bidding. However, the thoughtless act of sending an arrow to her Norman neighbor could undo all to which she aspired, leading to the loss of what remained of her lands and more blood-tainted streams and blood-soaked ground fed by Saxon lives.

"I should take your lack of denial as admission?" Cyr D'Argent said.

She blinked, wondered how it was possible not to see him for however long she had allowed Isa to put hands around her throat. Were this man capable of becoming one with his surroundings, it ought to require much more effort.

"You should not." She sent up a prayer for forgiveness. "Beyond what you tell, I know nothing."

A muscle in his jaw jerked. "I believe you do." He extended the arrow.

She ignored it. "I believe I do not."

Catching up her left hand, he slapped the shaft across her palm, then released her. Though his touch was momentary, it stole her breath.

"Admit it, deny it, it makes no difference," he said. "Even were you not at the end of that arrow when it was given unto the king's men, I am fair certain you know who was, what they do, and when they do it. And this I tell, Aelfled of Senlac—"

"Not of Senlac!" As if this time being named so horrendous a thing had the weight of a fist behind it, she dropped the arrow and stumbled back against the desk. And once more knew his touch when he gripped her arms...chest brushed hers...breath moved the hair across her eyes...

Supported more by the warrior than the desk, she looked up. And when she found herself further touched by dark green eyes, trembled.

Desperate to distract him from what had moved from beneath her skin onto its surface, she said again, "I am not of Senlac." And hated it was with so little conviction it sounded as if she pleaded for agreement.

Breath flaring his nostrils, he released her and stepped back. "Until the raiding, burning, and killing across Wulfenshire ends, else you prove you have no hand in such, that you are to me."

She longed to curl her fingers over the desk's edge behind to ensure her softening knees did not betray her, but she resisted lest she reveal exactly how much he affected her.

"I will end the rebellion, Aelfled of Senlac. Whilst I lord Stern and Balduc, there will be peace amongst its Saxons and Normans."

"Peace!" That word and further offense over being named of that ungodly place, firmed her knees and raised her chin. "My people lived well enough in peace before your William set to murdering us and stealing our lands to award them to his fellow bloodletters, *Merciless* Cyr."

That last was retaliation for what he named her. But though there was little satisfaction in causing his eyes to darken, she told herself she did not care what she wrought since it was blood-soaked truth she spoke.

"They will live in peace again," he growled.

Ignoring the voice warning it was reckless to further aggress— that she acted the same as her lady who sent the arrow—she stepped into the space from which he had retreated. "Even do you give my people cause to forgive you for what happened at..."

She detested the name, and all the more now he sought to identify her by way of that meadow. Determining to call the place of her people's defeat that by which most referred to it now, she said, "After what happened at Hastings and what has happened since, I do not know it possible to live in peace with your kind."

He lowered his face nearer hers. She caught her breath, not because now he aggressed on her, but for how softly—as if to soothe a wounded animal—he said, "England can never be as it was. And if you are honest enough to open your eyes to the country lost, you will see your people did not live in peace. Oui, there is much suffering now, but there was suffering then, Aelfled."

Only Aelfled, not of *that* place. And how different her name sounded come off his lips than off any other's. It was more than the deep of his voice...more than his accent...

Upon her shoulder he set a hand so large and warm her knees loosened once more. "When the rebels who darken these lands become reconciled to Hastings—"

"W-what of Campagnon who darkens these lands more than those who but give answer to what he does to their people?" she retorted. "He may no longer be baron, but he shall continue to plague us."

"You know I have no care for him. As told your abbess, as soon as I have cause to send him from this shire, I shall."

"Cause being beatings, even deaths, of more Saxons? Is that what it will take?"

He sighed heavily. "I am bound by the wishes of our king. And those wishes—rather, orders—include ending the rebellion."

Of which he believed her a part. And rightly so, though not as thought. She looked down, and seeing the arrow she had dropped, sidestepped and bent. "I do not raid, burn, or kill, nor lead those who do." She straightened and offered the arrow. "This is not mine."

He studied her face, looked to that which she reached to him, then cupped his hand around hers on the shaft. "What do you when you go to the wood, Aelfled? Certes, this day you dug in the dirt, but for what other purpose were you there?"

His touch again, of greater alarm than what he asked of her—until she followed his gaze and saw what he saw. And remembered when last she was with him and her hands had been as fouled. As had his, perhaps more so.

"Not to hide the bodies of slain children," she whispered and felt his hand tighten. "To dig for mushrooms...gather nuts...pick berries." It was true. He need not know she had also left a message beseeching Isa to rethink the full moon, nor that Aelfled would go to the wood on the morrow to leave another message, this one alerting her lady Cyr D'Argent had come.

"I am not the one you seek," she said.

"As Bernia would also have me believe."

Aelfled snatched her hand free. "You have met my grandmother?"

"This day in the village of Ravven. When she came to my notice, so much she resembled you I guessed she must be kin and determined I would speak with her."

She swallowed loudly. "Surely she did not reveal I reside here?" Her nearly sightless grandmother would not knowingly endanger her. But if she had trusted him...

As I may have given her cause to, Aelfled recalled all she had told of their encounter and how Bernia had praised the Lord for placing in her path the only godly Norman amongst the thousands.

"She did not tell I would find you at Lillefarne," he said. "A guess brought me here when she bemoaned that as you weary of being led where you do not wish to go, you aspire to don a habit."

Wily Bernia, Aelfled silently rebuked, *more than Isa you led him to me.*

He put his head to the side. "Is her fear founded? If so, for what would you spend your life within these walls?"

To escape what Isa requires of me, she could not say. *Were I a Bride of Christ, only then might my lady absolve me of a debt I can never repay.*

Though Isa was angry with God for not keeping her son safe and surely tested His patience over her involvement with the rebels, Aelfled was fairly certain she yet believed. And perhaps more so than Aelfled whose faith was so frayed, the abbess did not believe her charge was ready to make her profession.

"Mayhap you but seek the protection and cover afforded by the Church, Aelfled of Senlac," D'Argent submitted.

Setting her teeth against further protest over what he once more named her, she accepted that on the protection side of it he was right—she wished relief from the debt owed Isa—but not the other side that alluded to gaining cover to coordinate the rebels.

She cleared her throat. "What Bernia told is true. I am not the one you seek."

"I pray it is so," he said with what sounded sincerity.

Here a means of turning the conversation. "Do you really pray, Cyr D'Argent?"

"More than ever, as advised when you gave me your psalter—for prayer and guidance you said, of which you believed I was in great need."

"But you cast my gift aside."

"Wrongly so."

"Then after you brought the other boys to the wood, did you...?"

His sorrowful smile made her ache. "I did, and I have carried it since and every day looked upon its stained cover and read and prayed its words and wondered if you miss them. Do you?"

She did, though the Lord gave her little reason to feel so bereft.

"I think you must," he said, "that now you are in greater need than I."

Because he did not believe what she and her grandmother told?

"Thus, when next we meet, I shall return it to you."

"Next?"

"And the arrow…" He glanced at where she clasped it against her abdomen, its feathered shaft angling up from her hip, its point center of her chest. "It shall remain absent not only from my heart but those of my men. Are we of an understanding?"

The thought of it piercing him nearly made her shudder. "As told, it is not for me to understand." She thrust the arrow forward. "As also told, this is not mine."

He took it. "Then I shall have to increase my efforts to discover its owner."

Heart convulsing, she held his gaze.

He turned and tossed over his shoulder, "I give warning. You will fare well to stay out of the wood, little Saxon."

As would he and his men, especially come the night of the full moon when the rebels moved again, making no allowances for Normans they happened upon, overwhelming those who sought to turn them from their purpose. And this time it could be the warrior who had been her savior upon Senlac.

"As you would fare well to gather in that which can easily be taken from you, Baron of Balduc," she heard what seemed another's warning. But it was she who voiced it before she could think better of it.

Slowly, he came around. "I thank you for the warning." He bowed low, straightened. "I shall heed it, as I pray you heed mine."

He opened the door, wished Rixende a good day, and went from sight.

"Lord," Aelfled breathed, "what have I done?"

It is but hay, she told herself, *not that which keeps my people from starving.* But she fooled herself. Hay was of great import, providing winter fodder for animals who supplied fresh meat, breeding stock and, occasionally, surplus to be sold.

But now it will be different, she countered. *Just as Theriot D'Argent did not take from the Saxons of Stern any more than they could give when his crops were lost, neither will his brother. And no more will Campagnon be allowed to take from the people of Balduc.*

But what of Dotter? It was not just hay and wheat to her. It was vengeance. And that she was not done with.

"He is gone, Aelfled."

She looked to the woman in the doorway. "I thank you, Rixende."

"Are you well?"

"I am but tired. I think I shall seek my rest."

Minutes later, Aelfled knelt in her small cell and reached beneath the cot upon which she spent many a Senlac-haunted night. She drew forth the bundle, unfolded the wool cloth, and looked from the intercepted missive informing Campagnon of Cyr D'Argent's arrival, to the hilt from which she had turned back Wulf's fingers.

So deadly a dagger with so horrendous a history did not belong at the abbey. Nor had the arrow she returned to Cyr D'Argent.

She folded the cloth back over missive and dagger, slid the bundle far beneath the cot, then went to the kitchen and wielded an entirely different sort of blade against what remained of the mushrooms.

～

"I HAVE HER."

Fulbert inclined his head. "As thought. Is she the one who sent the arrow?"

Cyr settled in the saddle, retrieved the reins once more passed to Dougray who had shown no interest in the reason for the detour to Lillefarne. "I pray not."

"Pray or think?" the priest called him to account.

"Does it matter?" Dougray growled. "They are all of them devils."

Feigned disinterest, Cyr silently corrected the depth of his brother's presence in the conversation. "If it was not she who sent it, Fulbert, then likely one of the mothers of the boys who died at Senlac by my uncle's hand." He glanced at Maël who sat with his men beyond the abbey's outer wall, was glad he not hear again the shameful manner in which his sire was felled. "Had I to guess, I would say it was the Lady of Wulfen since she is of a line of esteemed warriors and, better than any, would know how to breed and lead rebels. And all the more did she under the direction of King Harold's mother, Gytha."

Or Edwin Harwolfson, he reflected on another rebel leader plaguing William from the depths of Andredeswald where the Saxons had fled when their king fell. Believed to be the only one of Harold's bodyguard to survive the great battle, it was said Harwolfson was dragged nearly lifeless from the field by a hag who enlisted the devil to return him to the living. Not for the first time, Cyr wondered if the cursing, wailing white-haired woman he had seen struggling to remove a warrior's body from Senlac was the one named Dora.

"If the Lady of Wulfen sent it, then she cannot be bedridden." Dougray again, voice so bitter it would be unrecognizable had Cyr not become accustomed to it since his brother's return to consciousness and discovery the lower half of his arm had been removed.

"That I had hoped to determine this week," Cyr said. "Unfortunately, my audience with her must wait."

Dougray narrowed his eyes. "For what?"

"We must harvest the lord's hay."

Fulbert made a sound of dissent. "Did not your aunt say it would be done twelve days hence providing two more days of good rainfall? That it is then the villagers next owe service to their lord?"

"She did, but Aelfled of..." He paused, told himself she gave him no cause to regret attaching her to that place where he had met her. But he did regret it, as when she had recoiled. Had he not aspired to provoke her to reveal what she held close, he would not have further pained her.

"Continue," Fulbert prompted.

"Though Aelfled of Lillefarne revealed very little, upon our parting she advised the Baron of *Balduc* to bring in what can easily be taken from him. I think it must be the lord's hay upon that barony, a warning if it is not harvested before its time it will be burned the same as last year."

"Witch!" Dougray growled.

Letting that pass, Cyr recalled the missive Theriot had sent last June to report the loss of the lord's hay and assure his brother he had not retaliated against the rebels by taking the villagers' crops as done by Campagnon upon Balduc. Instead, he had ordered what remained of the hay be harvested lest it was also lost to flame and stored it at the castle to apportion it between lord and villagers throughout the winter. When the hay ran low before frost's end, more had been purchased from a southern shire.

Surely of frustration to the rebels, the torching of the lord's hay had proven of benefit to the D'Argent demesne. It prompted Theriot to place a guard on grain crops until they were harvested two months after the hay. Thus, nearly all crops that would keep the people of Stern from starving were saved, unlike those of Balduc to which the rebels had turned most of their efforts. Doubtless, when Cyr toured those lands added to Stern he would discover much misery among the Saxon folk. And death.

The rebels—and Campagnon—had much to answer for.

"Reconcile yourselves to a long day," he said. "The tour of Stern shall be completed ere night's fall so we may acquaint ourselves with Balduc on the morrow."

"What of Stern's hay?" Fulbert said.

"We shall begin with Balduc's. Since that is where the rebels concentrate their efforts, I believe they will strike there first, and all the more likely while Stern hosts a great number of the king's men." Cyr looked to his brother. "Once more I give you a choice, on the morrow ride with me to Balduc or stay Nicola's side."

Light leapt in the younger man's eyes but was too quickly extinguished to determine its source. "That is no choice," Dougray muttered and put heels to his mount.

"Time, patience, prayer," the priest reminded.

"Already much is expended," Cyr grumbled. "Hopefully, soon we shall see the fruits of our efforts, even if it is against Dougray's will he returns to life."

Fulbert shifted his regard to the third son, and when Dougray passed between the doors propped open to admit visitors and halted alongside Maël, said, "I am thinking Balduc is not merely the lesser of two evils for your brother."

What had he seen in those eyes that Cyr had not? Had the fleeting light anything to do with the one Campagnon called *Wench?* That possibility made him question the wisdom of Dougray's accompaniment. Until his brother submitted to training a body much changed from Hastings, the defense of his person was doubtful. It might be better to leave him behind.

CHAPTER TWELVE

Castle Balduc
England

*S*o soon returned!" The castellan of Balduc halted before Cyr at the center of the hall, gave a stunted bow.

"My visit is two-fold." Cyr drew forward the woman who had persuaded her nephew she would be of better use at Balduc than Stern whose household and books were in impeccable order. "My aunt, Lady Chanson, assures me if the accounting of my new demesne is not comprehensible, she can make it so the same as Stern's."

The man's upper lip quivered, evidencing he struggled against baring teeth the same as a dog ere attack. But as if to compose his face, he bowed his head in a show of deference. "Dear lady," he addressed the floor, "I am honored to have my home graced by the widow of a much-esteemed warrior so...*tragically* lost at Hastings."

Chanson tensed—and doubtless Maël behind—but in a fairly level voice she said, "As I am honored to be welcomed at Balduc, Sir Raymond. And I do not doubt I shall be impressed by how well you keep this castle and its books for my beloved nephew, your Baron."

When Campagnon lifted his face he wore as near a smile as possible for one who seethed. "I believe you will find naught of consequence out of order, my lady." He offered his arm. "Allow me to escort you to the high table where you may be refreshed with drink and viands whilst my steward collects the books."

She glanced at Cyr, arched an eyebrow, then took her host's arm and allowed him to lead her forward.

"As told," Cyr called, "my visit is two-fold, Campagnon."

The man halted, peered over his shoulder. "The second fold, Baron?"

"A tour of Balduc to become acquainted with my people and survey the villages and crops." The knave did not need to be informed of the early harvesting. Yet.

Campagnon's smile was strained. "Better you than me. Most grateful I am our king has relieved me of such tedious tasks. I wish you Godspeed." He continued toward the dais.

Were he to remain castellan, he would be severely schooled in those tedious tasks. Blessedly, that was not to be.

As Cyr started to turn toward Maël and his men, a handful of whom would remain at the castle, Campagnon called, "Come hither, Wench!"

Cyr saw the young woman hasten from the corridor that gave unto the kitchen, wondered again when William would ban slavery in England, and hoped it would not be too late for her. Then he felt an otherworldly nudge that Fulbert told was of the Lord and corrected himself. He would find a way to aid her.

He pivoted, strode past the king's men, and was not surprised Dougray was positioned to the right of the doors, a vantage he liked much in enclosed spaces. It afforded a good view and an easy exit when he could stomach no more boasting, cheer, and laughter that had become as foreign and distasteful to him as Saxons.

Drawing near, Cyr said, "We ride."

Only Dougray's eyes moved, shifting from the high table to his older brother. "Maël accompanies you, oui?"

Cyr halted before him. "He has said he shall."

Dougray nodded. "I think it best I stay and keep watch over our aunt."

"The king's men will ensure her well-being."

"Still, I would remain." He returned his gaze to the high table.

Cyr looked around, noted how flushed and stiff his aunt as she stared at Campagnon who ordered his slave to provide refreshments for his guest. "Very well, watch, Brother. And that is all."

"All?"

"I do not like him any better than you, and he will test your patience as he tests mine, but you are not to engage."

Dougray narrowed his lids. "You think me incapable?"

"What I *know* is you are long without practice, albeit that is easily remedied. When it is, *then* you may engage if so moved."

Jaw clenching, Dougray raised his arms beneath his mantle. And faltered over the stance that, before Hastings, had been so habitual a show of defiance his brothers teased him. But unlike other times since his loss, he did not jerk his arms back to his sides. He angled his chin higher and clasped one arm and a half over his chest. "Does Campagnon give me no cause to engage, I will not."

Cyr wanted more assurance than that, but it would not be gained without argument that would reveal D'Argent vulnerability to Campagnon—and delay the tour of Balduc. He inclined his head and strode through the doorway followed by his cousin and the men he commanded.

"You may regret not binding your brother and tossing him over the back of his horse," Maël said as they descended the steps.

Cyr glanced at him. "I pray the men you leave behind are capable of preventing him from getting into deep trouble."

"They are, but exactly how deep depends on how great the fight within Dougray wants out. Though I do not doubt he would prefer to loose it upon Saxons, for now he might make do with a certain Norman."

Perhaps over a certain Saxon slave, Cyr silently concurred and swung into the saddle and set his mind on Balduc's people and the crops soon to fall to the scythe.

~

EACH VILLAGE upon Balduc was much the same—far more women and children than men, all poorly garbed, few responding beyond nods and curt greetings, wattle-and-daub huts in varying states of disrepair, scarce farming implements, and few animals worthy of plowing or providing meat. Unlike the people of Stern, those long under the heel of Campagnon suffered much. And yet...

Cyr considered those working a nearby field who had not joined others from their village in welcoming their new lord. They continued to toil, which he could not begrudge them considering how great the need to feed their families. Even now they did not pause to watch the entourage depart.

Cyr looked behind at the dispersing villagers, many of whom had set their feet on the dusty road to return to laboring over life-sustaining crops that, unlike hay, required more tending before being harvested at summer's end.

"Once more, your brow rumples like that of an old man," Fulbert said.

Cyr looked to the priest who rode alongside. "Do you not find something peculiar despite all the poverty witnessed this day?"

"That the Saxons have not all stolen away." It was said with no small measure of sarcasm.

Cyr smiled tautly. "For what would they flee Balduc?"

Fulbert's eyes bulged. "Their garments are little more than rags, the greatest comfort of their homes is they yet have roofs, and the crops they scratch out of the dirt are so pitiful the people may barely survive starvation this winter—and only then if their grains are not seized as done last year."

"Exactly, and yet most of the Saxons have stayed the land though fear of reprisal from Campagnon cannot be worse than death from lack of sustenance. Look at them. Though we are just come out of spring, none appear to be recovering from near starvation."

Fulbert snorted. "What is starving to you? A man laid prone? A child so weak he cannot even crawl?"

"Certes that," Cyr said, then jutted his chin at a woman ahead who walked the side of the road, hand held by a girl of six or seven skipping to keep up. "But not that." Though both wore garments so worn it seemed a miracle their seams held, one had only to look beyond the clothing to see neither wanted for food. Indeed, the girl carried excess weight, her face ruddy with good health.

"That is peculiar," Fulbert acceded, then peered over his shoulder at those returning to the fields. "It is the same with those who greeted us in the village." He shook his head wonderingly, returned his regard to his friend. "You are most observant."

"Not soon enough," Cyr muttered, ashamed what had been buzzing about him like a fly only now settled long enough to be looked near upon. "Regardless, they are being provided for. And well, as if to ensure they remain upon lands once of—"

"—Wulfen," Fulbert spoke over him.

Cyr nodded.

"You believe that lady supplies them with what is taken when rebels set the lord's crops afire?"

"I can think of no other willing or able to do so for the people of Balduc. And yet how is it possible to provide for so many extra mouths, especially as some of her own grains are lost to the rebels in retaliation for her bending the knee to King William? Could her crops be vast enough to weather those losses and still have enough to give to those no longer in her care?"

"And secretively," Fulbert mused, "a great undertaking to prevent Campagnon from confiscating what she supplies."

Cyr nodded. "I must meet Hawisa Fortier and look near upon her lands. But first we bring in the hay." He considered the distant field where stalks swayed in sunlight.

You would fare well to gather in that which can easily be taken from you, Norman, Aelfled had said in her husky little voice. He was certain she spoke of his hay, and for the dozenth time wondered why she had given warning. Had it been unintentional? Had she—?

He gripped the reins tighter, told himself it did not matter. Though the hay was not as tall and mature as it ought to be, there was nothing for it. Regardless how much the villagers protested giving service to their lord earlier than due, they would answer summons delivered before dawn on the morrow and the harvesting of the lord's crop would commence at sunrise. But for now...

From the sun's position, there was time to visit the last village before the press of dark forced them to return to Balduc Castle where they would pass the night. The prospect of once more sleeping beneath the same roof as Campagnon was unwelcome, but necessary. Balduc lands being more vulnerable than Stern's, Cyr and the king's men would oversee the harvesting of the field earlier noted as being in close proximity to Lillefarne Abbey.

Convenient, he once more named its location. And as before did not answer the question of to whom it was convenient— himself or the woman who, if she did not lead the rebels, surely aided them.

THE DRAWING of blood was of Norman on Norman. And yet it was very possible a Saxon woman bore the blame—at least in part.

As taught by his uncle, Cyr had begun his assessment of the scene he and the others burst in upon the moment he crossed the kitchen's ember-lit threshold.

Center, toppled stools around a skewed table.

Right, the back of one whose figure cast a broad, elongated shadow on the far wall.

At his feet, a man whose shaggy hair and beard told all as he began to rise.

Left, the slave who pressed herself in the narrow space between rear door and wall.

"What is this?" Cyr thundered as the former Baron of Balduc swung around.

Despite the dim, there was no mistaking Campagnon's high color and bared teeth—nor the hatred in eyes moving from Cyr's face to the sword advancing ahead of the one made his overlord.

"What is this?" the knave mocked and turned to the side to reveal he had no weapon to hand other than the fist he opened to jab a finger at the man he had bettered. "It is your wee lame brother trespassing where he has no right to go regardless of whom I answer to."

Protective instincts were a force to be reckoned with, Cyr acknowledged as he struggled against acting on them the same as Maël surely did where he came behind. If not that Dougray was quick to regain his feet and his fierce expression revealed he was more wrathful than injured, Cyr might have yielded to putting Campagnon through.

"Leave off, Cyr—Maël!" Dougray barked. "I will finish the miscreant."

That miscreant dropped his head back and sent laughter around the room.

Cyr and Maël did not leave off, but it was not Campagnon at whom they set themselves after casting aside their swords. One-armed though Dougray was, wrestling him back from his opponent was like throwing off a boar who but appeared injured enough to approach.

Campagnon's laughter sounded louder, making it more difficult to subdue Dougray who would have drawn blood from his own kin had he a blade in the fist he swung.

Finally, Cyr and Maël took him to ground, and the latter commanded his men who had followed him inside, "Remove Campagnon!"

"Not without my property!" the knave shouted as he was dragged toward the door. "Get here, Wench!"

"She stays," Cyr ordered.

"She is my prop—"

"Silence him!" Maël yelled across his shoulder and landed a knee to Dougray's chest to prevent him from bucking free.

The sound of flesh-covered bone being struck was not an unpleasant one, and more pleasant it was when no further protest passed Campagnon's lips.

Not so Dougray. He cursed and shouted until Cyr said, "Eventually you will forgive me," and landed a blow to the jaw as effective as the one dealt Campagnon.

Dougray dropped his head back and was further dumbed by his skull striking the stone floor.

Maël blew out breath. "That did it," he muttered. Still, he was watchful of his senseless cousin as he lifted his knee off his chest. As well he should be. Dougray was not the strongest of the D'Argents nor the most skilled in weaponry—that honor belonged to Guarin—but in addition to having once swung a blade with the left hand as well as the right, he had an amazing capacity to endure pain and quickly recover from blows.

Cyr straightened and crossed to the door. "Return to your beds," he instructed those anxiously peering inside, and as he began to close the door glimpsed the retreating figure of Campagnon's man, Merle, beyond the priest and his aunt.

"But Dougray is—"

"Humiliated, Aunt." He looked between her and Fulbert, noted she gripped the priest's forearm, not for the first time wondered if it was attraction he sensed between them. "For it, he will not thank you for bearing greater witness to what was done him."

She sighed. "You are right."

"Fulbert, ensure my aunt is returned to her rest," Cyr said and closed the door. He nearly retrieved his sword from where he had cast it aside, but as his destination was the Saxon woman, he let it lie that she not feel more threatened—and slowed and shortened his stride when she sidled away.

"I mean you no harm," he said in her language. "I but wish to know what transpired here."

She tensed as if for flight, then sagged when a glance past him confirmed she could not escape.

He halted five feet distant. "By what name are you called?" he asked.

During earlier encounters he had seen wariness in those mismatched eyes, but though there was less light here, he thought the sparkle there was of defiance. And was certain when she said, "I am called *Wench*."

He raised his eyebrows. "As I have been called *Merciless*, but that is not my name. I am Cyr. You are?"

She stared until Dougray's groan flew her gaze to him.

Though Cyr hated he should know her only by the object to which Campagnon reduced her, he said, "For what did they meet over fists?"

She raised a hand toward her throat, in the next instant snatched her arm to her side. Too late. Having drawn attention to what he might not otherwise notice, he considered the smudges on her collarbone and up the sides of her neck. Bruises? Or merely marked by dirty hands?

"Was it you they fought over?" he asked tautly. And hoped it was—evidence Dougray *was* coming back to himself.

A huff of laughter parted her seamed lips. "Certes not. Your brother hates Saxons, cares not what Campagnon does to me. He came to the kitchen to ease an aching belly, interrupted my *beloved lord* whom I am prone to displeasing, and the two traded insults that led to blows. That is all."

Stepping nearer, causing her to press herself more firmly to the wall, Cyr verified the manner in which she had been marked. She believed Dougray unconcerned with her plight, and that was possible, but far less possible if he had seen her bruises.

He dropped back a step, said, "I intend to free you from Campagnon. I know not how, but I will have no slaves on my lands. And given time, I am certain King William will abolish the heinous trade from all of England..." Here was the place to speak her name, such familiarity assuring her he saw her as a person. Instead, all he could say was, "...whatever your name is."

She raised her eyebrows, and the glow from the embers clearly showed the brown eye opposite the blue. "Slavery has its place. It is not all bad."

He could not keep surprise from his voice. "Of course it is."

"Nay, it saved the lives of what remains of my family. Now if you will permit me to pass, I shall seek my rest. Most assuredly, the morrow will be long."

Would she suffer Campagnon's anger in lieu of those upon whom he could not let it? Cyr wanted to ask, but it would be wasted breath whether she refused to tell as seemed likely or that he could do little about it. Yet.

He stepped aside, and she walked wide around him.

Upon reaching the door, she turned. Her gaze lingered over Dougray whose long, low groan told he was recovering his wits, shifted to Maël who readied to once more pin his cousin, settled on Cyr. "To you who are not merciless, I am Em. But never name me that in his hearing. Pray, never." She dipped her head, opened the door only wide enough to slip into the corridor, and was gone.

"Em," Maël said when Cyr returned to his side. "Of the name Emma, you think?"

Before Cyr could respond, Dougray groaned loudly and narrowly opened his eyes.

Cyr dropped to his haunches, gripped his brother's upper arm. "What I think," he said loud to ensure Dougray heard, "is I must return this wayward D'Argent to Stern first thing on the morrow."

Maël's smile was all sympathy. "I concur."

CHAPTER THIRTEEN

The villagers were not pleased, having had the harvesting sprung on them as was necessary to protect the lord's hay should Aelfled seek to undo what she had done in giving warning.

Balduc's castle guard were not pleased, two-thirds ordered to work the fields alongside the villagers to sooner bring in the crop.

The king's men were not pleased, set to watch over the labors beneath an unclouded sun.

And perhaps most displeased was Campagnon, ordered to arrange a feast for all come the end of the haying. "Woman's work," he had growled, no longer smug as when he watched the brooding Dougray depart before dawn.

Then there was Aunt Chanson who declined to accompany Dougray though she had made quick work of Balduc's accounting on the day past—consisting of only two books, she reported, and so poorly kept the pages listing income and expenditures numbered fewer than a dozen. The steward, whom she pronounced derelict, was now schooled in what would be expected of him. *If* he retained his position.

Now where she sat astride a palfrey alongside her nephew, she appeared neither displeased nor pleased by this day's events. But when next she spoke, it was obvious she was disposed toward the former. "A bold, unseemly thing to set men of the sword to harvesting, Cyr. Regardless of the threat, I do not think your uncle would approve."

He inclined his head. "He would not. Too great a regard had he for hands calloused by the hilt to see them calloused by the scythe, even were the latter all that stood between a man and starvation."

"You are certain the threat is real," she asked, "that it is necessary to bring in hay that would grow to greater quantity given a sennight longer?"

"I believe the warning to be true, that this will be lost do we wait."

"You will also gather in Stern's lord's hay before its time?"

He hesitated. "I thought to once the greater threat to Balduc's was eliminated, but I shall allow Stern's to grow a while longer." What need not be told now was it could prove a neat trap in which to catch rebels who, plans for Balduc thwarted, would have to move quickly and less cautiously to take Stern's hay.

"What of the villagers' crops?" Chanson asked.

"Safe, I believe. It is the lord's to which the rebels set fire."

"And for which Campagnon retaliates by claiming the people's," she reminded.

"True, but he shall do so no more."

After a long moment, she said, "When the rebels are denied, what do you think they will do?"

"Search out another vein to slice open. My hope is before that happens, they will be persuaded things are different now Balduc is given unto me."

"That will take time. Beneath Campagnon, the Saxons have been mistreated, starved, even murdered."

"Not starved, Aunt."

She frowned. "I may have spent these six months upon Stern

where its people are treated more fairly, but I am not deaf to the groanings of those upon Balduc."

"They have not starved as they would have us believe—and Campagnon surely does."

She shifted in the saddle to look nearer upon him. "I do not understand."

"And I am just beginning to."

She set her head to the side, causing the fat braid made of her waist-length hair to slide off her shoulder. "What of the Saxon men who have died—not in the great battle but in denying themselves nourishment so their children and wives may eat?"

"I think it mostly a deception, that many of those said to have died live."

"You have proof?"

"What I have seen with my own eyes. Though Campagnon confiscated the villagers' crops, those who stay the land are far from starving and likely never were. I believe absent fathers, husbands, and brothers watch over their families from amid the rebel ranks, keeping them well supplied with food."

"Where would they come by such and how would they deliver it without alerting Campagnon?"

"I have my suspicions, though I expect to have more before long. Now..." Cyr glanced at the sun climbing the sky, its position marking the passing of two hours since dawn. "...there is a scythe that needs wielding."

She slid her gaze down his figure clothed in the most worn of the tunics, chausses, and boots he possessed. "Even more, my Hugh would not approve of a D'Argent working the land."

Neither did it appeal to Cyr who would prefer practicing at arms. However, not only was he now responsible for the well-being of the people on his lands, but they answered to him only because they were forced to do so. He must earn their trust and respect, and this seemed a place to begin.

"In that you are right, Aunt, but it must be done, meaning it is time to pass you into the care of your son." He nodded over his shoulder at where his cousin sat the saddle amid a half dozen men who kept watch over this side of the field.

"As you will, Cyr, though I would be of better use aiding Campagnon in preparing the feast."

"Even did I not require all the king's men to keep watch over the harvest, after what transpired between that knave and Dougray last eve, I would not leave you at Balduc—nor would Maël."

She looked to her son, in a sorrowful voice said, "What has become of him, Cyr? How long before my boy comes back to me? Back to himself?"

Cyr set a hand on her shoulder. "Whether the losses were dealt our own bodies, minds, and souls or those of ones we held dear, we were all changed by the great battle—some for the better, many for the worse."

"The worse," she breathed. "As it was for you when you returned to Normandy. But the pilgrimage and Father Fulbert set you aright."

He looked to the left of the king's men where the priest sat atop his mount with his head back to take sun upon his face. "As much as possible."

"If only he could do the same for your cousin."

"Maël would have to be receptive."

She nodded, sighed. "And then there is Dougray."

"So there is," Cyr said with finality that he not be further drawn into discussion over what was to be done about the third-born son.

It being past time the Lord of Balduc and Stern dismounted, he turned his destrier toward his cousin who remained much in need of a good quantity of drink to loosen his tongue. Could it be loosened...

Soon, he vowed. *Soon you shall speak what you do not, Maël.*

~

WIELDING a scythe was far different from wielding a sword.

Cyr had not expected a similar heft or swing but been confident his training at arms compatible enough with taking a blade to hay that he would soon master the stroke of a farming implement against barely resistant stalks.

Were Balduc's villagers not wary of their new lord and his men-at-arms who struggled to keep pace with those of the soil, Cyr was certain the smug amusement about their mouths would have been voiced as loudly as the laughter with which Campagnon had taunted Dougray on the night past.

"My lord?"

He looked up from applying a whetstone to the long, curved blade that had dulled again. "Aye, Waring?" he acknowledged the grizzled man limping toward him who supervised those younger and fitter of body in bringing in the crop.

"With your permission, the workers will go to the wood to gain the shade, quench their thirst, and satisfy their hunger."

Cyr glanced overhead, from the sun's position guessed six hours had passed since the scything began.

"But an hour's rest, my lord, and they may recover sufficiently to bring in all the hay ere nightfall," the man said as if to counter refusal.

Regretting he thought his lord unconcerned over their well-being, Cyr said, "Whatever you determine the workers require, be it an hour, be it two."

Surprised widened the man's eyes and parted his lips amid a thick beard. "I thank you, my lord."

"You need not seek my permission should the workers require further rest. I trust you will do right by them. And me."

Waring hesitated. "I shall," he said, and as Cyr returned to working the whetstone, added, "It is good you keep your blade sharp, my lord, but elsewise you and your men make more work for yourselves than required."

Cyr raised his eyebrows.

"I have watched you."

As Cyr knew, just as he was aware of being watched by other Saxons here—*most* aware lest any think to wield a scythe against flesh rather than hay.

"In swinging the scythe, you must keep your arms straight, blade closer to the ground, steps smaller. Do you, the cut will be more consistent as will the row of mown hay."

Cyr looked behind, compared his work to that on either side cut by Saxons who had long ago passed him. His row was crooked, its stubble jagged. "I thank you, Waring."

The man inclined his head. "And rest. You need it as well, though…"

"Aye?"

"The workers will be more at ease do you leave them to our own whilst they break." He held up a hand. "No insult, my lord. They are unaccustomed to laboring alongside a nobleman."

"I understand."

As Waring shouted for the workers to break, Cyr resumed sharpening the scythe's blade. A quarter hour later, he strode toward where his horse nuzzled grass in a copse opposite the bordering wood where the villagers gathered. There, Chanson and the half dozen men Maël left to watch over his mother had dismounted to satisfy their own hunger and thirst. Though Cyr intended to join them, he paused over a sound so distant it took a moment to identify it as pealing bells.

Of the abbey that lay two leagues distant? It had to be, tolling the hour of sext as it had surely done the earlier hours whilst those working the field were oblivious to all but the sounds of their labor.

Aelfled would be there. Or would she? Perhaps she was with her rebels despite his warning to stay out of the wood.

"Pray, join me, Cyr."

Resuming his stride, he looked to his aunt who waved him to the blanket spread for her, considered what he ought not—a quarter hour to Lillefarne, a quarter hour back. Time aplenty before he resumed haying.

"I thank you, Aunt, but there is something I must do."

"What you must do is rest, dear nephew, though first I suggest soap and water. Look at you!"

He did not need to, from his scent and clinging clothes well aware he was far from presentable.

"Never have I seen you so foul, not even when you were a boy."

And yet he had been fouler—upon Senlac when the color with which he was splattered was red rather than brown. He halted alongside his destrier and reclaimed the belt earlier fastened to the saddle.

"Cyr!" Chanson protested as he girded his sword.

"I shall return soon." He thrust a foot in the stirrup, swung into the saddle, and tapped heels to the animal's flanks.

Though tempted to go by way of the wood that would save time despite a reduction in speed, he dared not underestimate the rebels' ability to stay apprised of their enemy's movements. Were they worthy adversaries as believed, already they had learned of the harvesting and set men to keep watch who would not hesitate to act against a Norman caught out alone.

But soon it would be safe for Normans and Saxons alike to travel the wood and roads of Wulfenshire, he silently vowed. For that, he did this.

Only when he neared Lillefarne did he enter the wood to observe without being observed. Listening for a break in the chatter of birds and small animals that would warn he was no longer alone, he considered the yet distant abbey against a soft blue sky. In height and width, the stone wall enclosing the community of nuns was formidable. As the cost would have been great, and all the more considering the speed with which the wall was raised, Lillefarne must be well endowed.

By whom? The departed King Edward? The slain King Harold? The vengeful Gytha? The Lady of Wulfen? Certes, not King William whilst a staunch Saxon served as abbess.

All still at the front, the abbey's great doors closed and, doubtless, barred, Cyr dismounted. Keeping to the trees, he moved to the western side. It was quiet there as well. But not so the rear.

In the midst of a sizable garden knelt a woman, hair fashioned into a braid that shifted across her back as she worked the patch of vegetables before her.

Was it Aelfled, also of blond hair he had imagined would shine as bright in sunlight? Likely, since the abbess had admitted to allowing her unprofessed charge to leave the safety of the walls.

She rose, and with her a large basket in each hand that made her stagger. As she regained her balance, Cyr confirmed it was not a habit she wore but an aproned gown like that upon Aelfled two days past. Though there was too much distance between them to be certain, she appeared the right height, and when she lifted her skirt and stepped to a patch of low-lying plants, her carriage was familiar. As she returned to her knees and began adding more bounty to her basket, he determined it was the one he sought.

And allotted more time to this foray for the chance to learn something that could be of benefit in defeating the rebels.

CHAPTER FOURTEEN

Lillefarne Abbey
England

*W*as this happiness?

She had never liked working the earth no matter the blessings yielded up, but as there was peace in toiling beneath the sun amid silence upon which only the sounds of nature trespassed, this could be counted happiness, could it not?

Aelfled pondered it a moment longer, then dropped the last bunch of slender carrots atop onions barely of a size to unearth, sat back on her heels, and swiped perspiration-dampened hair off her brow.

Until the people of Balduc were assured their new lord would allow none to take the bounty of their own gardens, there was satisfaction, if not happiness, in providing them with food from what she had planted among fruit trees following Campagnon's arrival on these lands.

She had not expected her vegetables to thrive, but they had last year and again this year. Though wary of delving dirt in which beastly insects and slippery worms made their homes, she was pleased with all she had achieved. And might have succumbed to pride were she yet the self-assured young woman who could be entrusted with her lady's son.

Drawing a deep breath, she felt a presence and looked left and right, but it appeared she was alone—unless the Lord deigned to walk with *her* in a garden.

She almost laughed, but someone *was* here. She stood, turned all the way around, and confirmed no one was visible between the garden and wood nor atop Lillefarne's stone wall. Was it possible it *was* the Lord here? If so...

She hesitated, then lowered her chin and silently addressed Him who might or might not be present, pleaded with Him who might or might not listen, pried at Him who might or might not forgive her for wandering so far from His flock as to have left it— the same as He appeared to have left her people.

"Pray, Lord, show me You have not abandoned us," she concluded her prayer and opened her eyes on laced fingers so fouled they were less recognizable than when she had stood before Cyr D'Argent two days past. She raised them, turned them front to back.

She had not aspired to become a lady, that possibility so rare for a commoner it was nearly all dream, but as Isa's maid she had taken great care with her appearance—and more refined it had been by her lady's gift of good cloth that, several times, had caused her to be mistaken for one of the nobility. But no more...

What she would do for five minutes in her lady's cooled bath water! Clouded by soap and scented with herbs, it had been wondrous. Several times, Isa had washed Aelfled's hair in that water, giving back as she was given unto. And once when her husband blundered in, red-faced blundered out, and called through the door it was unseemly for a noblewoman to serve a commoner, she and Aelfled had laughed. Such friends they had been...

Eyes wet, nose stinging, she decided she would have a bath,

albeit cold and clear and unscented. She bent and hefted baskets that were overfilled so only one crossing to the wood was required.

Straining beneath the weight, she carried her burden from the garden toward the wood, weaving as she moved shade to shade provided by fruit trees born of venturesome seeds that had long ago rooted distant from the abbey.

The wood was considerably cooler, its canopy full and extensive. Though welcome in that moment, less so it would be when she submerged herself in the chill stream as she did two and three times a month during the summer.

She lowered the baskets before a berry-ladened bush, one at a time lifted them over its top and down into the cleared center that would conceal them until they were collected under cover of night. Then she raised her skirt's hem and turned in the direction she took to leave and receive messages.

She did not remain on that path long, veering away when she caught the shush and gurgle of water and glimpsed the sparkle of sunlight across its surface. Though it was possible a message awaited her in response to the one informing her lady Cyr D'Argent had found her at the abbey, she would check after she bathed the better to enjoy the shedding of dirt and easing of muscles.

Shortly, she emerged from the trees onto the bank of the widest and deepest part of the stream coursing this portion of the wood. She jerked frayed ties out of their loops, cast off the apron, and began plucking at her gown's side laces.

"You disregard my warning to stay out of the wood." The deep, heavily-accented voice speaking her language spun her around.

He stood between two sturdy oaks, Cyr D'Argent and yet not, this one very different from the one who had come to her two days past. No longer did he look the lord, not even a common soldier. If not for his short hair, she could be forgiven for believing him a common Saxon.

That which must have once been a fine brown tunic evidenced hard labor, from dirt flecking and streaking the cloth to perspiration molding it to his muscular frame. Hose encasing long calves was snagged and torn, and short filthy boots would not long keep their soles.

Was it *his* presence felt in the garden, so strong he had but watched from the wood?

"What do you here?" he asked before she could demand the same of the one who might have seen her leave food for Balduc's needy—blessedly, of far less detriment than had she provided proof she colluded with the rebels in checking for a message.

"Do you not answer because you have something to hide?" he baited.

More than *something.*

"Aelfled?"

She almost wished he would not speak her name. It made her center go askew, but it was naught compared to how she would have felt had he revealed his presence after she unclothed.

Nervous laughter escaped her, and therein was opportunity to throw him off whatever scent he followed. "Certes, I have something to hide." She scooped up her apron, dangled it. "It can be no more obvious I am here to bathe than that you are in greater need of scrubbing than I."

His lips curved. "We have both been hard at our labors—you tending your garden, I harvesting hay."

She tensed over verification he had seen her in the garden, meaning he had seen her conceal the baskets. And were he working the land, difficult though it was to believe of a noble, it was surely because she had warned him to attend to what could be taken from him. In the first instance, she acted against Normans, specifically Campagnon. In the second, she did injury to her own by denying the rebels the lord's hay.

When D'Argent strode forward, she retreated a step, her slippers sinking into moist soil a reminder the stream was at her back. Though she considered drawing her meat knife and running opposite, neither would aid in escaping this warrior. But she was not without hope—that of being fairly certain that just as he had done her no harm the first time they were alone in a wood, he would do her none now.

He halted, and though several feet separated them, the scent of his labor was so strong she felt as if clasped close. Or was this but an attempt to explain away her breathlessness?

"Though you did not heed my warning to stay out of the wood," he said, "I found merit in *your* warning."

And her language. How had he become so versed in it when it was told the one awarded Stern had returned to Normandy after his duke was crowned?

"Thus," he continued, "since dawn, Balduc's villagers, my men-at-arms, and I have gathered in the lord's hay."

She moistened her lips. "Men of the sword working the land. Unimaginable."

"And more difficult and strenuous than expected. But worth the effort, and for that I am grateful to you."

Had the rebels learned what he did upon Balduc? If not, they would soon. Would they guess it was she who had betrayed them? Would they turn their efforts elsewhere?

She swallowed loudly. "Also you bring in the lord's hay upon Stern?"

"Later—unless you know it to be at immediate risk as well."

"I know naught. What you think a warning was but a response prompted by anger and a good guess after what befell the lord's hay a year past—and for which Campagnon retaliated against those beneath his yoke."

"As well you are aware, they are no longer beneath his yoke."

She raised her chin higher. "As well *you* are aware, still he rules people who cannot know life will be different beneath a new lord."

"I do not think my brother, Theriot, could have made it more clear the D'Argents are different, and for that, far less your rebels—"

"Not my rebels!"

He shrugged his mouth. "Far less the rebels harry Stern than Balduc."

"You fool yourself in thinking they have more liking for a D'Argent than Campagnon."

"If they are not your rebels, how know you that?"

"It is no secret that vile Norman is to be feared only for being a brute, that he is so deficient in strategy and leading men he makes a better target than a D'Argent—and a more desirable one for how much suffering he causes."

"Then the rebels do have a greater liking for my family."

Realizing she was working herself into a hole, and more quickly for how flustered she was at being so near him, she sidestepped to put more distance between them. "If by *liking* you mean respect, perhaps."

He stared so long it took all her will not to look away. Finally, he said, "I need your aid, Aelfled."

She narrowed her lids. "Mine?"

"To end the rebellion. To return men to their wives and children. To see Stern and Balduc prosper in an England struggling to rise from its knees. To make Wulfenshire among the first to stand and serve as an example for how Normans and Saxons can live and work alongside one another."

She tried to seal her lips but the words pushed past. "Alongside?" The distance between them closed, and only when she halted so abruptly she swayed did she realize she was the one who had moved. "There is naught *alongside* about what your people do to ours. Your king sets Saxons *behind* Normans, yoking us so if we do not follow we are dragged, and if we resist we are choked to death."

As she replenished her breath, she noted the creasing of his brow and wondered if it was over what she said or because she spoke so rapidly he struggled to make sense of her language. "You came for land and took it," she continued, "and with it life as we knew it and would have it be again. The Saxons who rebel do so because there is no *alongside* with Normans who regard even our nobles as inferior. Aye, many of your men seek marriage with our ladies, but only to strengthen their hold on stolen lands. They—"

Moisture on her inner lip tasting of salt, she snapped her teeth. Now she felt the burn of tears and the wet on her cheeks, heard the quick breaths moving her shoulders.

"Aelfled." Calloused fingers pressed the soft underside of her jaw and raised her chin. Though already her eyes were on his, she had been looking through him as she loosed accusations and emotions against a Norman who gave her less cause than any other. Now as she more deeply smelled his unwashed body and wondered why it did not offend as much as it should, she saw herself in his eyes.

He bent his head, but though she feared he meant to kiss her, he said, "I am Norman, the lord of lands taken from a Saxon and given me by one who is now king—he who, do I not serve well, will award them to another the same as he gave Campagnon's lands to me. But unlike whichever Norman would eagerly take my place and could prove the same as Campagnon, you know me."

"I do not. I have kept company with you for...three hours in all?"

A frown gathered his eyebrows, and she wondered if it also seemed more to him. "Aye," he said, "but I believe a life could be made of so few hours—who I was to you at Senlac, who I became between Senlac and Wulfenshire, who I am to you now I am upon Wulfenshire. Though I have much to answer for and may never be acquitted of what I did on that battlefield, I aspire to be worthy of the words inscribed in your psalter."

When last he was at Lillefarne, he had told he had read and prayed those words, but that profession had not moved her then as it did now that he inserted her in all the months between their first meeting and this.

A chill went through her—of wonder that a warrior and enemy should speak thus, of hope he was as genuine as he sounded, of greater hope that just as it seemed his faith had been elevated, hers might be restored.

"The prayer book is so beautiful, I am loath to lose it," he continued, a reminder he had said he would return it when next they met. But that was not this day, it being nowhere visible on his person.

"By way of prayer and guidance found there and aid of a priest met on pilgrimage, I repented for the animal I was before and upon Senlac—that which previously made me proud of being named *Merciless,* that which made me join William more for the promise of land than Church reform. And of great benefit to many of those wronged, your psalter showed me how to govern your people."

As she had challenged him, albeit derisively.

"And that I shall do. If I stay."

She blinked, said in a rush, "Then it was not to take your place here that at long last you crossed the narrow sea?"

This time she glimpsed teeth in his smile. "At long last? The wait for my arrival seemed a very long time?"

She told herself to retreat, but light though his touch, she could not move. "Your absence from lands awarded you is fact," she snapped, "not of any yearning for the return of a Norman."

"Not just any Norman. One you know, Aelfled."

"I do not know you."

He moved his gaze from hers, sent it around her face, settled it on her lips. "You do." He angled his head as if…

Once again, he did not, and she shocked herself by asking, "Do you mean to kiss me?"

His lids flickered, and when his eyes returned to hers, she

noted as she had not before how long his lashes. "Would you allow me, Aelfled of Lillefarne?"

Lillefarne, not Senlac. That acknowledgement weakened her, tempting her to catch hold of his foul tunic to remain upright. Resisting the pull of him, she pressed nails into her palms. "Would you?"

Tell him nay, demanded a voice within. *Tell him never would you allow a Norman such intimacy.* But the voice was so small she thought it possible she misunderstood and said as she ought not, "I would not know what to do."

"Have you never been kissed?"

She had not, though there had been occasions she wished it. "Were my heart right, a virtuous Bride of Christ I would make."

"Then selfishly"—he leaned in—"I am glad your heart is not right, my little Saxon."

My?

She would have tugged on that to determine how strong its threads, but he brushed his lower lip over hers and the contact was so dizzying she did not know if it was the fabric of her gown suddenly filling her hands or his tunic.

"You were not meant to be a nun, Aelfled." His breath fanned her lower face. "You were meant to be here with me. Like this."

She opened eyes she had not meant to close, looked into his, breathed his scent and told herself it was unpleasant. But she did not wrench away—not that it would be necessary. From the feel of the fine, tight weave that ought to be coarse and loose, it was she who held to him.

"Why?" It was all she could think to say. But though uncertain what she asked, she knew she should not have when that one word brought her lips into contact with his.

He slid his hands up her back and neck, pushed fingers into her hair, and pressed his mouth to hers.

Still she did not know what to do, but he did, the deepening of his kiss making her feel as if she fell down something very high and steep. Or did she fall up? Was that possible? And when he coaxed open her lips, inwardly she reached for something to slow her. But descent or ascent, there was naught to hold to—until he ended the kiss and pressed her head beneath his chin, her face to his collarbone.

"*That* is why," he rasped, breath warming her scalp, chest heaving, heart pounding.

Her body was guilty of the same, and though she commanded herself to push him away, she felt weaker than before.

They might have stood there a minute, looking the lovers they were not, it might have been ten, but it seemed seconds for how much she longed to remain thus.

"Release me," she said with so little outrage she could hardly have been offended had he laughed.

His arms eased, then his hands traveled the same path taken when he had drawn her near—sliding out of her hair, down her neck and back, lowering to his sides. But he did not retreat, and that had all to do with her.

She looked to fingers filled with damp, begrimed fabric, against her knuckles felt the stone of muscles and movement of his heart. Did her own beat as fiercely?

She released him that she might set a hand to her chest. Blessedly, she realized how much more the fool it would make her appear and snatched her arms to her sides. "I should not have allowed that." She raised her gaze from rumpled material that evidenced how fast she had held to him and seeing he watched her, whispered, "Why did you do it? For what did you kiss me, Cyr?"

CHAPTER FIFTEEN

*N*ow the watched was the watcher.

Feeling exposed beneath Aelfled's beautifully dark gaze, especially for how moved he was to hear her speak his name without *Merciless* or D'Argent attached to it, Cyr wanted to refuse her an answer. But though he could tell himself all day every day he had kissed her only to seduce her into aiding him, all day every day it would be a lie—and contrary to all to which he aspired since the great battle.

"Why, Aelfled? Not because I could for the yoke you believe around your neck. I kissed you because I wished to."

"But why would you wish it?" she said in that husky voice that sounded of long winter nights beneath a feather-stuffed coverlet amid the flickering light of an exhausted fire. "Why me?"

Discomfited, he fought down the urge to walk away by reminding himself of what had nothing to do with that wondrous meeting of mouths—that he did want her aid, and all the more if sooner it solved the mystery of Guarin and returned the eldest son to his family.

Despite the ache of slicing open the warrior and letting his pride spill out, he determined his best chance of gaining her cooperation was to be honest about all the days and nights since that first meeting when, more than ever before, he could not think quite right around a woman. And finally understood his uncle's warning not to allow one so near he neglected his reason for being.

However, before he could begin softening Aelfled, she said, "You think to use me. You say I am meant to be here with you as if we have a future, but we do not—certes, not an honorable one. As I am but a commoner who keeps a garden, I cannot aid you in securing your lands."

"You do far more than keep a garden, Aelfled. I saw the food you brought to the wood. For the rebels, hmm?"

"Not the rebels!" she said so vehemently he was inclined to believe her.

"Then?"

She looked down.

"Aelfled, I have only to detain you—to prevent you from warning away those who come for the food—to verify for whom you leave it."

She sighed. "It is for the people of Balduc. Thrice a week I replace some of what Campagnon steals from them."

There was sense in that, especially as the villagers were not as ill fed as they ought to be for all that was taken from them. And yet, two baskets three times a week could not supplement many. There had to be others who provided. "Who collects the baskets?"

"Villagers."

"I want names."

"Why?"

"If what you tell is true, they have naught to fear from me. I would but assure them that should they require sustenance beyond what their crops yield, it need not be collected in secret now I am lord. Meaning no more must you venture beyond the safety of Lillefarne's walls—unless 'tis but an excuse to conceal another reason you come to the wood."

"As you yourself bore witness, I came to bathe. Concealed, aye, but you must agree it is not something a woman alone—and a Saxon at that—wishes known."

"Still, I think you play with me."

"And I think you would use me for your own ends, that you kissed me to gain aid you believe I can give."

He stepped nearer. "As told, I kissed you because I wanted to. Why? Because you have been with me since Senlac and only now is it possible."

She caught her breath. "I do not understand."

"Then *I* have not been with you since Senlac?"

Her gaze wavered.

"I believe I have, Aelfled. And quite possibly, just as often you visited me at night whilst there was a sea between us, I visited you."

Silence.

"You know it was no coincidence these lands were given me. I chose them."

She nodded. "And yet only now you come. And you say you may not stay."

"I may not, and had not much conspired against me, it is possible never again would I have set foot on English soil." A breeze moving through the wood stirring up the scent of his body, he grimaced and turned to the stream, lowered to his haunches, and splashed cold water over head and shoulders.

Aelfled stepped alongside, so near her skirt brushed his arm. "Conspired?"

He straightened. "What returned me to your shores was, foremost, what may have been a sighting of the brother for whom I searched on the battlefield."

Though he watched closely for her reaction to talk of Guarin, he saw only what seemed genuine regret.

"I am sorry he remains lost to your family, just as I am sorry for all the Saxons who, having no bodies to bury, also hold dear the hope their loved ones live."

"You know my brother, Theriot, searches for Guarin?"

"I have heard."

"If he is alive, he will be found. And those who took him from Senlac shall answer for all the ill done him."

She thought on that, said, "You tell foremost it was for your brother you returned to England. What else?"

Did discomfort cause her to change the topic, or was there nothing more to be said?

Yielding, he said, "The king nears the end of his patience over my absence from Stern and threatens to award the demesne to another. If my brother is dead and I am our sire's heir, I choose to live in Normandy. However, as I do not wish to lose these lands, more greatly I aspire to end the rebellion in the hope William is more easily persuaded to allow me to pass them to one or both of my younger brothers."

"You hate England, then."

"I do not. What I hate is what was done here, and that in part I am responsible for the deaths of five boys. And that is but the greatest of my regrets, though it should not be yours."

Pain flashed across her face.

"Their lost lives are not upon you, Aelfled."

She did not gainsay him, but sensing his words landed against a sturdy wall, he continued, "I am not alone in my regrets. Many are the Normans who fought at Senlac and afterward wanted naught more to do with William's conquest. You have heard of the Bloodlust Warrior of Hastings?"

Did she startle over tales that, were they true, made the chevalier more worthy of being named that than ever Cyr had been of *merciless?*

"Maxen Pendery," she said softly. "Long his Norman family has resided in England."

"You know him?"

"I am acquainted with the Penderys. It was to them at Trionne my lady's husband sent her and their son to ensure their safety."

Son, Cyr snatched hold of that. *Only one.* Unless for some barely conceivable reason a second son was left behind, the one Lady Hawisa now presented as her heir was deception.

"Pendery lost a brother upon Senlac," Cyr said.

"The same as you."

"I pray not the same—that mine lives. Regardless, after all Pendery did that day which saw him well rewarded, he committed his life to the Church and William permitted him to pass his English land to a younger brother as I hope he will allow me to do if I am, indeed, my sire's heir."

After a long silence, she said, "If great your regret for what you did, why did you not enter the Church?"

"Methinks, like you, my heart is not right. Nor am I desirous of living out my days in a monastery. As, I wager, neither are you."

She averted her gaze.

The shifting of sunlight alerting him he was too long gone from the harvest, he returned to that which they had danced away from. "Still I can right some of my wrongs, Aelfled. And for that, I would have your aid."

Her eyes flew back to his. "Believe me or nay, I do not lead the rebels."

"In that I think you speak true, but I am not convinced you do not aid them. Hence, I would have you deliver a message—"

"I have no contact with them."

"Deliver them this message," he repeated. "Do they disband and return to their homes, they will not be questioned nor made to account for treasonous acts. I will be fair in our dealings and, as soon as possible, remove Campagnon from Balduc."

She blinked. "You are saying all will be granted pardon no matter their offenses against William, even their leader?"

Here what could ruin the chance of a peaceful resolution, but he would not lie. "Nearly all. The king requires those who slaughtered the Norman family be given over to him."

"Then he assumes the rebels on Wulfenshire are to blame. What if they are not?"

"I think it more than assumption, Aelfled. Regardless, do they wish absolution, it is for them to discover the murderers, whether they are amongst their own or beyond them. And quickly. If they do not disband and yield the ones who slew that family by summer's end, King William will send an army to harry this shire."

"Dear Lord," she whispered.

He touched her shoulder. "Is the Lady of Wulfen their leader? The one called Dotter?"

She staggered back a step. "She is not!"

Once more the watcher, noting her protest was less genuine than in denying the food was for the rebels, Cyr said, "If you do not know who leads them, how can you be certain?"

"Because such is beyond my lady who has not the heart nor health for it."

"I know the reputation of her family, Aelfled, that she is the daughter of Wulfrith Wulfrithson, in years gone was esteemed by King Edward for being the greatest trainer of England's defenders."

"That is so, but she is a woman."

"As was Aethelflaed, the renowned leader of men and daughter of King Alfred, and Boudica before her."

She drew her teeth over her lower lip. "Is that as your king believes?"

"He entertains it, but as the Lady of Wulfen plays his subject fairly well, he is more disposed to it being Gytha, mother of King Harold. Still, he suspects your Saxon lady is not entirely ignorant. Just as I suspect the same of you."

"You are both wrong."

"As I wish it. But if we are right, I would have you deliver my message."

"Would that I could the sooner to see an end to the suffering, but I have naught to do with the rebels, thus no means of communicating with them."

He wanted to believe her but dared not. "I must return to the field. Ere I depart, will you give me the names of those who collect the food?"

She hesitated. "I shall, though only because I trust you more than other Normans, believe you will do them no harm, and it will prove the food is not destined for rebels. Near always it is Waring and his son."

Cyr laughed. "Unless there is more than one Waring, it is the same who supervises this day's harvest."

She nodded. "There are two—old Waring and his son."

"I will speak with him, and if I am satisfied, he can come for the baskets, though after this day he is to present himself at the abbey."

"As you will. Now I would like to bathe—"

"Non, Aelfled. You will return to your sanctuary and leave its walls only to tend your garden."

"But—"

"Until I end the rebellion you claim to have no part in, there is no place for you beyond Lillefarne."

Anger leapt in her eyes. "I am not yours to command."

Considering their kiss to which, for all her inexperience, she had responded with such enthusiasm it had become dangerous, he could dispute that. But he said, "True, but you are mine to watch. And that is all the warning I give. Do I catch you in the wood again, I will assume you communicate with the rebels." He gestured in the direction of the abbey. "Go."

A huff of anger escaping her, she pivoted, swept up the apron she must have dropped whilst they kissed, and ran.

151

"Heed me," he muttered as she grew distant. "I would have you lead me to the rebels but not at the cost of ill befalling you, my little Saxon. Do not return here."

CHAPTER SIXTEEN

*A*nother lie she must count among the many. But no matter she believed Cyr D'Argent could be trusted, it was not for her to do where Isa was concerned. Wulf was dead, and she might herself die were she responsible for harm done his lady mother.

Thus, she must defy the man who had done more than kiss her, who had made her welcome his mouth upon hers. It was a risk, but if he had set a watch on the wood to verify it was Waring come for the food, surely by now his men were gone. When next the bells tolled, it would be two hours since the baskets were collected.

A small risk, she assured herself, but worthy of caution. She lowered to her knees alongside her cot and withdrew the bundle. When she raised the dagger to candlelight, as ever she marveled at how beautiful something so deadly could be. And hated that last it had fit the hand of Wulf who had likely used it to slay its owner, Cyr D'Argent's uncle.

She rose, removed her relatively dull meat knife from its scabbard, and replaced it with one whose purpose was to shed the blood of men as she hoped she would not have to do should she happen on one other than Cyr D'Argent. The blade barely fit, being wider, thicker, and longer, but well enough she could more easily bring it to hand than were it hidden beneath her skirt.

Her cell was so small she had only to turn to reach the table at which she had composed the message she would leave in the wood. Wincing over the splotch of ink on the parchment's upper left corner, quickly she read the words there.

He came again, this time to the wood, did not show himself until after food was left for those of Balduc. Though he knows not this place where I leave the message, it is no longer safe. There is more to tell but best done in person.

No signature. None needed.

If Isa did not come to the abbey herself, she would send another, and to that trusted person Aelfled would pass D'Argent's message, as well as King William's threat of what would happen at summer's end if resistance continued.

Aelfled folded the parchment into a small square, slipped it down her bodice, and snatched up her slippers. In stockinged feet, she left her cell and moved past those in which others of the convent slept with less troubled hearts—and fear.

Outside the dormitory, she pushed her feet into the slippers and continued to the place where a concealed door accessed the stone wall's inner passage. Once inside, she traversed darkness with the aid of a hand running the outer wall and, shortly, slipped into the garden.

Though there was much moon this night, a great amount of cloud cover aided in concealing her as she made the crossing from abbey to wood. Upon entering the trees, she moved more cautiously, knowing if any lurked, the dim could be of greater benefit to them.

All was as quiet as possible for a place given to the chirp, buzz, click, and scrabbling of night creatures, and yet fine hairs on her neck prickled as she veered toward the berry-ladened bushes. Was she watched again as when Cyr D'Argent had watched her? Was he or his men here?

The possibility tempted her to return to the abbey, but it was imperative she leave the message, and so she persuaded herself what she felt was only fear of being watched. Still, she turned her thoughts heavenward.

If You are here, be with me, Lord. I know I am a liar, but how else am I to protect those You forsake?

Immediately, she regretted seeking His aid since more likely her prayer offended than pleased. But it was done.

After verifying the food had been collected and the baskets left behind, which she would retrieve upon her return to the abbey, she continued on the path taken earlier though not as far as the stream. When she glimpsed the silhouette of great slabs of rock ahead, she paused and looked around. No sight or sound that did not belong here.

Assuring herself she was alone and would soon be curled on her cot, whispering childhood songs to keep thoughts from straying to Cyr D'Argent as he would have her believe oft his strayed to her, she continued forward.

As she neared rocks that rose to more than twice her height, moonlight slid through a break in the clouds and down through the spaces and cracks in the leaved canopy—enough by which to read the response to her tidings that the Norman baron had found her at the abbey. Had one been left for her.

She halted at the eastern tip of the rocks where one great slab thrust up from the earth to the reach of her waist and two others appeared to have been dropped atop to hold it down. It was mostly seamed all around, but here was space enough that if one slid a hand flat between the two lowermost slabs they might find something in that darkness.

As ever, she held her breath lest her fingers happen not on parchment but something living.

Blessedly, it was the former. She drew it out and stepped back.

As she unfolded the parchment, the clouds moved across the moon again, but she had just enough time to read the message—though only for how short it was.

Be still, her lady had written.

"That is all?" Aelfled rasped. *"Be still?"*

The crackling of leaves snapped her chin around, the heavy tread of boots made her release the parchment and bring the dagger to hand. But as she swung the blade in the direction of him who had awaited her on the other side of the rocks, he swept his hood back to reveal hair to his shoulders that looked brown in the night but she knew was near red in the day.

"Vitalis," she gasped.

Her lady's man reached down, retrieved Isa's message, thrust it at her. "Had D'Argent not been warned the lord's hay upon Balduc was to be taken, *be still* would have sufficed until the full moon."

As she had known, the rebels had learned of the early harvesting and guessed she was the betrayer. And God help her, she was.

∾

IT WAS no easy thing to be a warrior and merely watch as instincts that felt as if bred into him shouted for him to draw his sword and set himself at the man who seemed his equal in stealth.

Until the sword-girded Saxon had shown himself, Cyr had thought it only Aelfled and him here—and Maël who had returned an hour past after furtively following Waring and his son to the hand cart into which they loaded the food and conveyed it to their village.

Feeling his cousin's gaze, knowing he also longed to act against the rebel, Cyr glanced at him where he stood behind a tree fifteen feet distant, shook his head.

The one named Vitalis, short-bearded, hair gathered back off his brow and skimming his shoulders, stepped nearer Aelfled.

Hold, Cyr commanded himself. Though obvious the man was angered she had given warning of what the rebels intended, he did not move to take the dagger from her. Likely did not see it as a threat.

"How came you by so fierce a weapon, Aelfled—more, one of such worth?" he asked. "Had I not my own upon my belt, I might think you had stolen it."

She lowered it. As she did so, moonlight once more slipped in and out of the wood, and what it momentarily revealed moved Cyr's hand from his sword to his own dagger. It was not only that what she held was no simple blade for cutting meat at table, it was the flash of color beneath the hilt.

Where had she come by so fine a weapon, indeed? Though it was no rarity for the wealthy to indulge in elaborate hilts, pommels, and cross guards, that hers was set with a sapphire to which the D'Argents were partial seemed too much coincidence.

Might it be his uncle's lost at Senlac? Before Cyr located Hugh's body, Aelfled had pulled her lady's son from that grisly scene of boys who felled a great warrior.

Cyr looked to Maël, was certain his gaze was also on her dagger. Were it not Hugh's, it could belong to Guarin who had been sighted in the vicinity of Wulfenshire. Regardless, the possibility it was of a D'Argent was overwhelming—more even than how divisive the woman who possessed it.

Returning his regard to the big Saxon, Cyr sought proof of the dagger he alluded to also being of great worth, but though his mantle was off the shoulder of the side upon which his sword was belted, it draped the other.

"Tell, Aelfled," Vitalis prompted.

"I found it."

"Where?"

When she did not answer, he said with more accusation than question, "It was you who betrayed your own."

"I will explain myself," she said. "To *her.*"

157

Dotter, Cyr silently named the rebel leader and, feeling his sense of betrayal deepen, knew for this his heart pounded. Though logic told he was a fool to be so affected by Aelfled's lies— that he had no right to expect better of her—he felt as if it were kin who broke faith with him.

Disgusted, he told himself he was no youth in the first blush of infatuation, that she was not the first woman with whom he was intimate nor the first he wanted beyond kisses. However, there was no denying she was the first to whom he gave enough power over him to risk being thoroughly compromised. How had she done this to one who, beneath the warrior, had been foremost a son, brother, cousin, and friend? Certes, it had begun at Senlac with what passed between them there—what he had done for her when he ought to have been doing for his uncle and brothers. Then there was the score of months during which he had felt her presence outside her presence. And now their kiss.

Of a sudden, Vitalis stepped nearer Aelfled, and despite how much Cyr did not wish to care for her, he readied mind and body to defend her.

"You know in this moment I could carry out the sentence due a traitor," the Saxon said, "and few, if any, would think ill of me for saving her the trouble."

Head tipped back to hold his gaze, Aelfled said, "I know it, just as I know she prefers to deal with me herself."

"Methinks you are wrong, Aelfled, that she wearies of you."

Her shoulders rose with breath as if steeling herself. "Regardless, she will wish to speak with me." She took a small step back, worked the dagger into a scabbard too small for its size, then reached down the front of her gown and removed a piece of folded parchment. "Give this to her and tell her I await an audience."

The big man was a long time reading it, whether because he lacked proficiency with the written word or there was too little light. When he looked up, it was not at her but around the wood.

Whatever she had written made him more wary. And tempted Cyr to prove his fear founded.

Hold, once more he commanded himself. *Herein may be the means by which you end the rebellion. Remain the absent enemy they believe you to be.*

"You came alone?" Vitalis said low.

"Of course I did."

He snorted. "There is no *of course* about it."

"My word I give."

She spoke true, Cyr mused, though only because she did not know what transpired following the harvest which had seen the lord's hay carted to Castle Balduc. After that which barely passed for a feast was provided for the workers, Cyr had returned to the abbey with Maël to verify who collected the food. He had not expected Aelfled to come again—certainly not so soon—but while Maël ensured the food was truly destined for villagers, Cyr had lingered. Had Aelfled defied him a quarter hour later, he would not have known.

Vitalis held out her missive. "Deliver this yourself."

"What say you?"

"I will take you to her."

Her disquiet rippled across the air, but even as Cyr's hand convulsed on his hilt, he was stirred by anticipation. Were that truly the man's intent, soon the rebel leader would be within reach.

"You know I am not to leave Lillefarne," Aelfled said.

"And yet you do." He grunted. "You think it is not known you visit your grandmother once, sometimes twice a month?" The Saxon lifted her hand, thrust the missive into it. "Follow me." He turned, and when only his feet rustled the leaves and scraped the dirt, he swung around. "Had I determined to carry out your sentence, I would do it here. Now do you truly wish to explain yourself to her or nay?"

"I will come with you." She followed, as she rounded the rock he had earlier come around, glanced behind as though to ensure they were alone.

Cyr and Maël let a half minute pass before making prey of them.

It was a challenge to do so without alerting them, but they were aided by Aelfled being less proficient in stealth. The greater challenge would come if Vitalis had left a horse nearby as surely he had done were Dotter not close. Thus, until Cyr and Maël retrieved their own mounts, they would have to continue on foot, putting to good use Hugh's intense training. But they would have several things in their favor—no weighty chain mail, the cover of a mostly clouded night, the pound of hooves to mask the sound of their own progress, and the rebel's horse slowed by the weight of a second rider.

Of a sudden, Vitalis changed direction—opposite where Cyr and Maël had left their own mounts. Several minutes later, it was revealed a horse awaited his return. More daunting, Vitalis had brought a second. It was no decision of the moment to deliver Aelfled to Dotter. He had come to take her from Lillefarne.

"Non!" Maël wrenched back his cousin and slammed him against a tree, rasped, "Let her go."

"He came for her," Cyr growled as he peered at where Vitalis aided Aelfled in mounting the horse.

"Oui, he came for the one who possesses a D'Argent dagger, be it my sire's or your brother's." Maël thrust Cyr harder against the tree as if to knock sense into him. "Dare not let her mean more to you than that."

Dare not? He more than dared. He *did,* and that angered him as Maël would have it do. And rightfully so.

Cyr shifted his regard to his cousin who had required an explanation for riding to the abbey this eve, as ever regretted what a Saxon blade had done to a face one should not name beautiful for being borne by a man. But it had been.

"You are right, Maël. Now loose me."

He complied, said low, "We shall pursue them as far as we can that we come as near as possible to the den of rebels, oui?"

Were it daylight, the pursuers would soon be left behind, but the lack of visibility would slow the pace of the pursued, ensuring the safety of riders and horses. "Oui, Cousin."

Maël gripped Cyr's shoulder, flashed a dark smile. "Think of it as competition—which of us can outrun the other?"

As chevaliers in training, they had been equally matched. Or nearly so. When angered, Maël won, even if only by a stride.

"And the prize might be finding Guarin," he added and turned to watch Vitalis settle in the saddle. When he and Aelfled of *Senlac* put heels to their mounts, the cousins ran as they had not in years.

"WULFEN!" Where Maël bent over, hands on knees, he laughed. "Of course they are upon Wulfen. Where else would they be but where we cannot go?" He peered over his shoulder at his cousin, straightened. "Rather, where they *think* we cannot go?"

Cyr eyed the horses growing so distant he identified them only because he knew where to look, then heavily seated himself on the ground. He pushed a hand back through wet hair, was grateful he did not number among the Normans beginning to adopt the long hair and beards of the conquered.

How long had they run? An hour? More? Regardless, they had been on Wulfen lands for quite some time. "It seems..." He breathed deep. "...it is time I met...the Lady of Wulfen. What say you, Maël?"

Once more, his cousin laughed without genuine humor. "I say..." He dropped to the ground, slowly rolled his head on his neck. "...I am eager to meet that lady again. And of course her son and heir...see if I can get the lad to talk this time and learn how proficient he is with Norman French...as well he should be since that is the language of the one said to have sired him."

Cyr had done much talking during the feast, revealing to Maël nearly all he had learned and his suspicions. The next time, it would be Maël doing the talking. But how to get enough drink into one who, before the great battle, had often imbibed to excess, and since the battle could make a single tankard of ale last two and three hours?

Cyr blew breath up his face, asked, "How distant is Wulfen Castle from here?"

"A good league. Were we not nearly tasting blood, this eve you would have seen its rare beauty, of credit to that woman's Norman husband. But on the morrow, oui?"

"The morrow." Cyr sank back on his elbows and looked to the break in the clouds to the east and the pricks of starlight. He tried to think on how lovely it was so he would not think on the woman gone from him. But Aelfled was not truly gone. Just as when he had been on the other side of the narrow sea, she stayed with him.

Dear Lord, he silently prayed, *do not let ill befall her in my absence. Let not Vitalis or Dotter lay hand to her.*

"You disturb my rest," Maël growled. "Think on other things— other women more worthy of thought."

Cyr saw his cousin had lain back and propped his head in his hands, resented him for knowing him so well.

"A Norman lady," Maël continued. "Of noble blood, sweet virtue, kind heart, and tame unlike these…Saxon women."

"A Norman lady like my sister, Nicola?" Cyr retorted.

Maël groaned. "She is spoiled and young. Regardless, a better wife she will make a newly-landed Norman than one born to these heathen lands."

Seeing a door into Maël crack open, Cyr asked, "Were she not your cousin, would you take her to wife?"

"Perhaps, but I am without lands and have no interest in gaining any, so I am without appeal."

"You came for lands."

"A fool mistake that was." Maël rolled to his hands and knees, staggered upright. "Our horses and whatever sleep remains of the night await us," he slammed closed the door Cyr had hoped to throw wide. "Shall I once again prove I am more fit than you, Cousin?"

Cyr rose, straightened his damp tunic. "One loss is one too many. Let us see how long you keep me in sight."

CHAPTER SEVENTEEN

Wulfen Castle
England

*A*re you..." Aelfled swallowed, and knowing it must be asked more gently, said, "Pray tell we are not losing you, my lady."

Isa had not looked well at the abbey. Now in the light of middle morn cast through the windows, she appeared worse— painfully thin, pale, and a rattle in the long breath she drew.

"The physician assures me if I heed him henceforth, I shall recover."

From what? Aelfled longed to ask. The injury she was said to have sustained or something else?

"So either I remain abed and leave my people to fend for themselves a fortnight, else I do what needs doing and, quite possibly, leave them to fend for themselves the remainder of their lives." She sank into the pillows stacked against the headboard. "What think you I should do, Aelf?"

Aelf again. She closed her eyes and savored the endearment surely spoken without thought, especially since she had owned to betrayal that could prove the end of her. When next she looked to Isa, she was watched—not with accusation but what seemed sorrow.

Aelfled stepped around the foot of the bed where Vitalis had left her following hours awaiting this summons. "You must not leave us, Isa." She lowered to the mattress edge, caught up her lady's hand. "Heed the physician and allow me to once more make my bed alongside yours so I may tend you night and day until you are restored."

"We are not who we were, Aelfled," Isa said dully. "Those women are gone, the same as my Wulf." She pulled her hand free, gestured at the missive she had cast on the coverlet after commanding Aelfled to elaborate. "Do you think it true—Le Bâtard will send an army at summer's end?"

"I do, my lady, just as I believe Cyr D'Argent..." She trailed off, wished she had thought through her answer.

"What?" Isa said sharply. "You think he will make a better lord to those taken from me than whoever replaces him does he not end the rebellion?"

"I do."

Her lids narrowed. "You have not told all. What else happened in the wood?"

Wishing she had not drawn so near, Aelfled lowered her gaze, but her lady caught up her chin. "Methinks the last time you were so flushed was when that young thane mistook you for a lady and left the wet of his lips all over your soft hands. What else did D'Argent seduce out of you besides the warning to bring in Balduc's hay?"

Aelfled shook her head. "I have told all of which we spoke."

"But not of what you did." Isa's lips curved slightly. "You kissed. And what else, Aelfled?"

She longed to deny it, but it would be another lie—and futile. "Only a kiss. I do not know why I allowed it, but it will not happen again."

"Such an opportunity would require I trust you enough to provide another occasion for that vile Norman to lay hands on you." She loosed Aelfled's chin, set her hand on her own chest, and grimaced as if pained. For a long while, she did not speak, and when she did, her voice had lost volume. "What am I to do with you?"

Aelfled drew a deep breath. "Methinks Vitalis wishes me dead."

"What he wishes and his willingness to act against my orders are two different things. And he knows to which he must defer."

Aelfled hesitated, said, "He loves you still."

"'Tis wasted emotion to feel much for one beyond one's reach." She angled her head. "You know that outside of sinful intimacy, never can you be with Cyr D'Argent?"

Defensively, she said, "You imagine I wish him within reach."

"No such imagining, Aelfled. Your sorrow is nowhere near my own, but it has been your most faithful companion near on two years. Methinks what keeps it from turning so bitter it becomes you, is you did not lose all hope at Senlac. Why? Because your *honorable* enemy left you with just enough that no matter how cracked your soul, you possess nearly all its pieces."

"As do you, my lady."

She laughed curtly. "If 'tis so, not for much longer. She who was once your friend and now a childless widow is barely here."

Aelfled took her hand again. "You are young, my lady. Do you disband the rebels, turn your efforts to discovering who slew that family, you could start again...wed again..."

Isa pulled free. "Another husband?" Her voice was stronger, grey eyes brighter, and color bloomed in her cheeks. "One of that loathsome race responsible for my boy's death?"

"My lady—"

"What think you of a D'Argent? As there are five to choose from—likely more in Normandy—there must be one I can control, possibly even this Cyr."

Aelfled felt slapped. Though she knew Isa was all mockery, if there was any Norman she could be persuaded to wed, it would be the one who held the lands taken from her. And there was something else that bothered nearly as much—the number of D'Argents cited.

Beyond the uncle slain upon Senlac and the brother whose fate might be the same, only Cyr, Theriot, Dougray, and their cousin, Maël, were known to be in England. The number of which Isa spoke was one too many unless she believed the eldest brother lived—knew it was Guarin sighted upon these lands.

Though Aelfled hated reliving that day at Senlac, she returned to it and swept past Wulf, Cyr, Campagnon, and Cyr again to her lady, remembered how Isa had reacted to the D'Argent name. What had she said?

I wonder how many silver-haired D'Argents fought for that thief.

When Aelfled had pressed, she had admitted she knew the name but not told how.

"What is it?" her lady asked.

Aelfled returned her to focus. "You say there are five D'Argents to choose from, but I thought there only four in England."

Something flickered in her eyes. "Did I say five? I misspoke."

"Then you do not think the eldest brother lives?"

She shifted against the pillows as if to find a more comfortable position. "I heard one resembling Guarin D'Argent was seen upon our shire, but as he had long hair and a beard, 'tis more likely one of our own."

"But were he kept captive since Senlac, his hair would be—"

"Aelfled, I am sick unto death of talk of the D'Argents. Let us finish with what I am to do with you so I can gain my rest."

Aelfled did not doubt she needed sleep but was familiar enough with her lady, even in her state of ceaseless grieving, to know she hid something. Was that something *someone*?

"So what do you suggest?" Isa prompted.

No choice but to leave be the matter of Cyr's brother, Aelfled said, "Allow me to remain here and serve you as before."

"You have so little care for me you would have me even more reminded of my greatest loss?"

For which Aelfled was responsible no matter that Cyr said otherwise.

Aelfled stood from the bed, clasped her hands at her waist. "I do not wish to pain you, and as you have good cause to distrust me, there is no longer a place for me upon Wulfenshire."

Isa considered her, said, "You shall return to the abbey."

"You wish me to make my profession—become a Bride of Christ?"

"Nay, to serve me as before."

Aelfled knew she heard right, but it was all wrong. Might Isa no longer be of sound mind? "My lady, I warned D'Argent about the lord's hay."

"I do not forget. But I believe you regret acting against your own people and you did it with little thought and much longing to end the unrest and injustice. Providing you remember and embrace who you are—a Saxon strong of mind, body, and spirit— you can yet aid in ousting the Normans. Will you remember it? Embrace it?"

She did not want to. It would mean more lies and, likely, further encounters with the man it would be best she never again set eyes upon. But though her debt to Isa could never be erased, the least owed her was payments. "I will, my lady."

"And you must be of the mind you owe naught to our oppressors, be they of Campagnon's ilk or Cyr D'Argent's allure."

"Aye, my lady. But what of William's threat?"

"For now 'tis only that. Two months we have before summer's end. Two months to send the Normans from our lands."

"Truly, you believe it possible?"

Isa rubbed her brow, drew her hand down her face. "There is much at work here of which you know naught. Now give your word that for love of Wulf and penance due him, you will act the woman and not the fanciful girl who allowed our enemy to seduce her."

"My word I give."

Isa closed her eyes. "Vitalis will escort you to the abbey."

Aelfled stared, was tempted to offer to braid the tangled mess of hair cast across pillow, shoulders, and coverlet that ought to be darkly golden not ash-brown. It needed washing, fragrant oils, and hundreds of gentle strokes. Was there any more capable than Aelfled of returning it to the glory over which Isa's husband had been enthralled?

Certain she would hurt all the more when her lady rejected the offer, she turned toward thick, heavily-pleated curtains that provided visual privacy to those in the lord's bedchamber. However, in the absence of din in the great hall beyond, it was possible what was spoken here could be heard. For that, Isa had ordered the hall cleared before granting the betrayer an audience. But as Aelfled crossed the room, she heard the great doors open and boots across the stone floor.

She halted, gasped when the curtain was swept aside and Vitalis entered.

"What goes?" Isa demanded.

"It is who *comes!*" he snarled. "Cyr and Maël D'Argent with a dozen escort—chevaliers all."

Aelfled swung around.

Her lady had pushed off her pillows. Shoulders bowed, she peered at her man from beneath her lashes. "Did they see you?"

"Nay, they remain outside the walls awaiting permission to enter, but do you grant it and show yourself, it may ease suspicions over your involvement with the resistance."

Isa grunted. "They could not have chosen a better time to call on me. Aid me, Vitalis. I shall greet them in the hall." She pushed the covers off, slowly lowered her feet to the floor.

A moment later, he was at her side. As he scooped her into his arms, Aelfled saw on his belt a scabbard, in it a weapon of beauty to which the night past had done no justice. But of greater note was how familiar the cross guard and hilt. For this he had marveled over the blade she had drawn on him.

Aelfled would wager much that here was another D'Argent dagger—and it belonged to Guarin. If he yet lived, he must be near.

"Follow, Aelfled," Isa said as she was carried past. "Once the D'Argents are inside, Vitalis will escort you to Lillefarne."

Aelfled snatched the coverlet from the bed, her lady's robe from its hook, and hastened onto the dais outside the lord's chamber.

Vitalis ordered the housecarle Ordric, a bodyguard equivalent to a Norman chevalier, to carry the lord's high seat from the dais to the hearth, doubtless to provide Isa's visitors a better view of her. After he settled her in the chair, Aelfled helped her lady don the robe, but when she tried to put order to her hair, Isa commanded her to leave it be.

As Aelfled arranged the coverlet around her lower body, tucking it in and hurting over muffled sounds of discomfort, Vitalis directed the housecarles, servants, and Wulfrith who was not Wulfrith where to stand to best protect and represent their lady. Then he kissed Isa's hand, murmured something, and ushered Aelfled through the kitchen and out into the garden.

A quarter hour later, the signal was given the D'Argents were inside the donjon, and the two departed Wulfen Castle.

CHAPTER EIGHTEEN

I am pleased to once more be welcomed into your home and presence, Lady Hawisa," Maël said in Norman French and bowed.

Certain the woman's smile, slight though it was, required effort, Cyr shifted his regard to the one who appeared barely a young man where he stood erect to the right of the woman who claimed him for a son.

Maël straightened. "Allow me to present my cousin and your neighbor, the long-awaited Baron of Stern, Cyr D'Argent."

"Neighbor," the lady drawled in the conqueror's language. "In another life, my *vassal* and *keeper* of Stern."

Cyr returned his gaze to one he sensed, despite her appearance, was not to be underestimated. Wondering if it a good thing she did not hide her bitterness, he stepped forward. "I am honored to meet you, Lady Hawisa Wulfrith*dotter* Fortier."

There—a gleam in her pale eyes over his emphasis on *dotter*, a name that hardly fit were she the rebel leader—at least not this day and, perhaps, not any day in recent memory. Hers was no feigned illness. He would not be surprised had it been necessary to carry her from bed to hearth.

Belatedly, he bowed, straightened.

"It would be false to say *I* am honored, but..." She was a long time replenishing her breath, and it seemed to cause discomfort. "...I am grateful for the aid you gave my maid upon Senlac."

Then she knew it was useless to deny she was Aelfled's lady. One less game he must play. "I am sorry for your loss, Lady Hawisa, and that of the other mothers whose boys died. A great tragedy."

"For you as well—more, your cousin." She shifted her gaze to the right, nodded. "Oui, Sir Maël, when first we met and you gave your surname, I knew it was your sire slain by mere children, but I was fairly certain you were unaware my son was one of those boys. I was correct?"

Cyr could not be more grateful for having revealed this to his cousin during the feast. Still, Maël would not welcome discussion of it with her nor in the presence of his men.

"Quite so," he said more lightly than expected. "And now I am curious, my lady."

She raised eyebrows beneath hair so wildly tangled Cyr was reminded of the Saxon hag who sought to drag a warrior from Senlac. But this woman was of no great age and her hair far from white. "Well I know how uncomfortable—near painful—curiosity's itch," she said, "so how might I salve yours, Sir Maël?"

"All those boys died, including the noble amongst them, and as it is told you had one son with your Norman husband, who is this boy at your side?"

Cyr expected that one who had heretofore stood unresponsive, albeit alert, to evidence confusion since Maël believed him deficient in Norman French, but his eyes sharpened, chest puffed, and he took a step forward. Clearly, he well enough understood what was spoken, whether Maël was mistaken or much the boy had learned since last the king's envoy visited.

"Non, Wulfrith," Lady Hawisa caught his arm. "It is for me to correct what this Norman insinuates."

"But my lady mother—"

"For me!" she snapped, then sucked breath between her teeth and bent forward slightly.

The housecarle over her left shoulder came forward, but she raised a staying hand and shook her head.

"My lady," Cyr said, "perhaps you ought to rest." He glanced at the curtain behind the dais, not for the first time wondered if Aelfled and Vitalis were on the other side. Even if Hawisa was not Dotter, increasingly he was convinced she kept company with the rebels. "If you would provide our party with drink and viands, we will wait until you are better able to discuss those things which brought us to Wulfen."

She eased back, looked up at the one she named Wulfrith, and whatever passed between them it was sufficient for her to release his arm.

As he stepped back, she drew a shuddering breath. "Let us finish this now. I have not the stomach nor heart to prolong it."

Further evidence she did not want them inside her walls.

"May I ask what ails you?" Cyr said and, from the glitter in her eyes, was certain she would not answer.

Thus, she surprised. "The physician knows not, so perhaps it is grief—for my eldest son, my husband, my country. Will it kill me?" A one-shouldered shrug. "Time will reveal what only the Lord knows."

Eldest son. Therein the answer—lie or not—to the question Maël put to her. She had more than one son with her Norman husband.

"This is Wulfrith"—she nodded at the boy—"he who, until his brother's passing, was named Alfrith. As is custom in many a Saxon noble family, the eldest son is given the name of his sire from whom he gains his inheritance. As these lands belonged to my family rather than my Norman husband, our son was named for my sire. As is also custom with my family, should the heir die or prove unworthy, his name is passed to the next in line who sheds the one given him at birth. So it was with my sons."

Exuding disbelief, Maël said, "Inquiries were made, my lady, and though most are unwilling to speak of your family, a few told you gave your husband but one child. So who lies?"

"None."

"Then?"

"It is the superstition of the—" She coughed, pressed fingers to her lips, reached toward the housecarle who retrieved a goblet from a table before the hearth and passed it to her. Hand shaking, she carried the vessel to her lips and closed her eyes.

Feeling Maël's impatience more than his own as she wet her mouth with numerous sips, Cyr used the time to observe the second Wulfrith who was of a lesser build than the one the Lady of Wulfen would have them believe he had replaced. He had not the height nor breadth of the boy with whom Cyr had aided Aelfled over a year and a half past, and though Cyr's aunt had told he was aged twelve, she had to be misinformed. Unless this boy was a runt, he could not be more than ten.

"As told, none lie." Lady Hawisa lowered the goblet and cradled it against her abdomen. "Superstition of the ignorant is the reason many believe I birthed only one son. Tell, Sir Maël, is your king so intolerant—even fearful—of those things rare that the educated might name him uneducated?"

"Certes, he is not, Lady Hawisa. No heathen *your* king."

"Then I need not fear for my Wulfrith whom I birthed minutes after his brother." She inclined her head. "He is a twin."

Were that true, definitely a runt, Cyr reflected, and though the boy may have shared a womb with the one who died upon Senlac, he was not of the class of twins whose face and body mirrored the other's. But there was some resemblance.

"Naught to say, Sir Maël? Or, unlike your *educated* king, do you believe twins are of the devil?"

"I do not."

"I am relieved, though still there is that other belief twins are proof of a woman's adultery—two children, different fathers. Would you accuse me of such, deny half my Wulfrith's blood was drawn from your own little Norman stream?"

Not to be underestimated, Cyr silently reaffirmed. As ill as she was, she had all her wits. And they were keen.

"I would not," Maël said, "but there remains the question of how none knew you bore two sons."

As if grown weary of him, she looked to Cyr. "Is it really so different in Normandy, Baron D'Argent?"

He arched an eyebrow.

Though her lids were only half raised, he saw the roll of her eyes that evidenced disgust. "Only those trusted knew I bore two sons—including my husband who cared enough for his reputation and mine to ensure neither of us was besmirched by the superstitious. Thus, Alfrith was raised by a trusted Saxon family and reclaimed when my eldest son—yet a mere boy though now he would be a young man—was murdered by your cowardly uncle."

"Maël!" Cyr gripped his cousin's arm. Now it was he preventing the other from acting as he ought not in the presence of Saxon warriors who not only numbered more than Vitalis on the night past but stirred as they readied to defend their lady.

That lady reached behind, and when the second Wulfrith placed his hand in hers, drew it onto her shoulder. "Now," she said, "what other business have I with my *neighbor*?"

"Loose me," Maël growled.

Cyr glanced at him and, hoping he had settled sufficiently, complied and narrowed his eyes at the Lady of Wulfen. "It is more the king's business than my own, though I am to oversee it."

"Speak."

He moved his hand to his sword scabbard, slowed when the housecarles stirred again. As he drew the arrow from alongside the blade, he watched the lady, but if she understood his intention, she hid that knowledge behind a brow lined with confusion.

"An arrow, Baron?"

"Would you do me the kindness of looking near upon it?"

"For what?"

"To determine if you recognize it. A great service you would do your king to whom you have given your allegiance by aiding in returning this to the rebel who sent it to me."

She snorted, coughed, and continuing to hold to the boy's hand on her shoulder took another sip of wine. When her nose showed above the goblet's rim, she said, "How would I know one arrow from another? I am no archer. I am a lady."

"You are also Wulfrithdotter. If all that is told of your family is true, I cannot believe you ignorant of weapons. My own sister, young though she is, has enjoyed the benefit of many brothers trained at arms."

She handed the goblet to her housecarle and motioned Cyr forward.

Two strides and he stood before her, potently aware her guards would be upon him should he present more of a threat. Thus, he left it to her to draw nearer to take the arrow.

As she examined it tip to feathered shaft, he said, "The message delivered with it was that it was intended for me and its absence from my heart wiped clean a debt owed. Thus, I thought your Aelfled sent it, but no longer."

She looked up. "Your belief that little mouse could be responsible tempts me to question how fit you are to hold and defend Stern, Baron."

Little mouse? Did the woman not realize how false that rang to one who had met Aelfled on a bloody battlefield? That he had only aided in retrieving the boys to ensure the determined woman was not ravaged? He might think of her as his *little* Saxon, but there was no equating a Saxon with a mouse. The Normans had defeated these people, but no easy victory had it been. Had any other single, decisive battle lasted so long?

"Non." The lady extended the arrow. "It is far more believable I had this delivered to you since I am hardly pleased my son's inheritance was greatly reduced to reward Normans."

"Then you are the rebel leader known as Dotter?"

As if slipping into a deep, hot bath, she released a long breath, smiled softly. "Oh, that I were. Such would have made my sire proud. However, as much as I dislike your William, for the sake of my son and people, I am now his subject the same as I was King Harold's and King Edward's before him. Thus, you may be assured an enemy does not dwell within these walls." She thrust the arrow nearer, but still he ignored it.

"Regardless, my lady, the rebellion upon these lands must cease. Do they not, at summer's end King William will send an army to root out the rebels and no mercy will he show."

In her widening eyes he glimpsed alarm as expected of one in receipt of terrible tidings heretofore unheard. Then Aelfled had not delivered his message? Or was this an act?

Continuing to watch her closely, he said, "It is decreed that should the rebels disband and hand up those responsible for the murder of the Norman family, without fear of reprisal they may return to their homes and resume their lives."

"Resume," she said with sorrow as if recalling life before the Normans. Then she lowered the arrow to her lap. "A generous offer. I pray it reaches those desperate men so they may act upon it. Too much and too long the people of Wulfenshire have suffered."

She was believable, but Cyr did not believe her.

"Are we finished, Baron? I am exhausted."

"One more thing. Have you word of my brother, Guarin? It is believed he was sighted on these lands a month past."

"I know only that your youngest brother is so certain it was this…Guarin, he neglects Stern to search for him. But chances are that just as I lost a son upon Senlac, you lost a brother." She shook her head. "A difficult thing to accept in the absence of a body." Her eyes moistened, and she blinked. "As told, I am grateful for the aid you gave Aelfled in ensuring I knew my son's fate. I wish you good day."

Cyr inclined his head. "We shall meet again, Lady Hawisa."

"Your arrow." She offered it again.

Still he ignored it. "I believe it is where it belongs, my lady. Good day."

Having been refused hospitality, with parched mouths and grumbling bellies Cyr, Maël, and the chevaliers rode from Wulfen Castle.

At the center of the meadow skirting its walls, Cyr reined around and once more took measure of the fortress. Until William's conquering, castles were exceedingly rare in England, especially those constructed of stone. Doubtless, it was under the guidance of Hawisa's Norman husband that a relatively defenseless wooden home had been replaced with this formidable structure. It would take years, perhaps a dozen to transition Stern to stone, but it would be done. Just as in Normandy, the castles rising across England were here to stay.

"She is a liar," Maël said as he drew his mount alongside.

Cyr inclined his head. "I believe so, but if she is Dotter, she may not be that for much longer."

"I think you are right. When first I met her, she was quite lovely despite the pallor of grief she had me believe worn only for her husband, but now she is so gone I hardly recognized her. I wonder—" He grunted. "It matters not what afflicts her. So to Stern?"

"To Stern." For the time being they were done with Balduc— the lord's hay brought in, the books in good order, a dozen of Cyr's men-at-arms and four chevaliers seeded amongst Campagnon's men, and his aunt escorted to Stern this morn before Maël and he rode on Wulfen. And found no evidence Aelfled was or had been there.

"Let us go by way of Lillefarne," Cyr said.

Maël muttered something, said, "I ought not be surprised. But what will you do if she has not returned?"

"For now, I can but verify her presence or absence." *And pray,* he silently added.

"Poor Cyr, my sire was right. Though ever you have been discerning with the fairer sex, one most unsuitable shall prove your downfall."

Though discomfited, Cyr laughed. "He said that of you, Maël, not me."

"Did he? Then perhaps he said it of all of us. Mayhap we shall each in our turn fall to a treacherous Saxon woman like Hawisa Wulfrithdotter."

Or Aelfled Sorendotter, Cyr silently acknowledged the one who fit his hands well but not his future. Though he wished to see Guarin restored as their sire's heir, he yet longed to return to Normandy—and all the more to distance himself from Aelfled.

But for now, he must again draw near his little Saxon who was no Dotter but certainly no mouse.

CHAPTER NINETEEN

Lillefarne Abbey
England

She was not here. That conclusion, which seemed the only one to be had a half hour into their wait, twisted Cyr's insides.

Where was she? If Wulfen Castle had been Aelfled's destination on the night past, there she might have hidden whilst Cyr was within its walls. Or Vitalis could have taken her to the rebel camp that, were it not upon Wulfen, was surely nearby. But far more disturbing was the third possibility—the sentence due a traitor carried out, whether by Vitalis or the one who cast the shadow of Dotter.

God's eyes, Aelfled, he silently called to wherever she was, *I told you to stay out of the wood!*

"I think you must accept it, Cousin. We are not entering and she is not coming out."

Cyr looked to Maël, saw he perspired heavily beneath the nooning sun, his dark silvered hair glistening, tunic adhering to shoulders and torso. "So I must," he acceded, though far more of a mind to pound on the abbey door again and demand to speak with the abbess who should have presented herself in the absence of Aelfled. But then, if the holy woman wished to conceal that one of her convent residents had gone missing, she would have to lie. Far better she avoid the opportunity to do so.

Deciding to check the garden again as he had done upon their arrival, Cyr said, "Tell your men to make ready. I shall return anon."

Maël gave a sour look and spurred his destrier to where he had left the chevaliers at the edge of the wood to provide a good vantage and present less of a threat to those of the abbey.

Cyr fit his hands into leather gloves removed earlier, but as he urged his mount to the left to reach the garden at the rear, he heard the groan of hinges and reined in.

Slipping out the short, narrow door set in one of two larger doors through which horses and carts could pass came Aelfled.

Such a peculiar rush of emotions went through him he could only stare. He was angered she had kept him waiting so long he had imagined the worst. He was relieved he had not made an unforgivable, irreparable mistake in letting her go with Vitalis— one, he realized, he would have regretted to his end days.

"Baron D'Argent?" she said as she crossed dry, balding grass— stiffly, he noted, hopefully the result of being long in a saddle to which she was unaccustomed. "You wish to speak with me?"

Calm, he counseled as her seemingly guileless question raked nerves so raw anger once more spurted through him. She had to know how long she had kept him waiting and how he might interpret that in light of his warning not to leave the abbey. But what she did not know was he had proof of her defiance—worse, her collusion with rebels.

She halted alongside his destrier's neck, raised a hand to shield her eyes from the sun beating on Cyr's head. "I did not expect to see you again so soon—if at all."

Stalling for time in which to compose his countenance and

thoughts, he picked off his gloves and hooked them beneath his belt, angled his body toward her, and set a forearm on the saddle's pommel.

Though her face was shaded, he confirmed it and her neck showed no signs of abuse. One less thing the rebel Vitalis must answer for.

He lowered his gaze down her, noted the meat knife was returned to the scabbard on her girdle and was disappointed as he should not be. D'Argent dagger or not, a fool she would be to wear it in his presence.

"I came as bid," she prompted. "For what?"

He returned his gaze to hers and determined to do what William would not approve of. Though with her unwitting aid he might sooner bring the rebels to heel, did he provide proof she was watched—that whatever service she performed for the rebels was compromised—surely other plans would be made. And hopefully, in no capacity would they include her.

"I wished to tell it was verified you spoke true that Waring and his son come for the food."

A corner of her mouth convulsed. "Then you set someone in the wood last eve. Or was it you?"

It was one thing to give her good cause to stay out of the wood, another to reveal what he had confirmed of her allegiance on the night past, and quite another to lose the chance of catching Vitalis near the abbey again. "A man-at-arms followed the men to the nearest village. After confirming the food was given to its people, he reported to me at Balduc. I am glad it was not for the rebels, Aelfled."

"I spoke true."

"And you have obeyed me and not gone to the wood since last we spoke?"

She stiffened. Because his choice of words once more asserted she was his to command? Or did she fear he had made good his claim she was his to watch, and it was not only Waring and his son seen in the wood?

"I have left these walls only to tend my garden," the little liar lied. "And now to answer your summons."

More anger he suppressed by telling himself she could be excused for the untruth. She was under threat of being sentenced as a traitor, and unless he could offer his protection—and she accepted it, which he did not believe she would do—it was in her best interest to stay the side of the Saxons. Thus, she must lie, as would his sister were Norman lands taken by Saxons.

But though Aelfled was of the conquered, he of the conquerors —enemies despite whatever made this rope between them draw them nearer though each strained opposite—her warning to bring in the hay was surely the result of a struggle between loyalty to her own, faltering hope the Saxons would prevail, and the possibility of peace restored beneath Norman rule.

"I am glad we are of an understanding," he said. "I would not see ill befall you."

Her smile was tight. "It is kind of you to have a care but unnecessary. No more shall I venture beyond the bounds of my garden."

"And the baskets will be collected from the abbey," he reminded, which was also a reminder to himself to inform Waring of the means by which he would henceforth gain the food grown in her garden. One more stop along the road to Stern.

"I am glad for that," she said. "The more I think on it, the more I am persuaded the wood is no longer safe."

An insult to the Normans, though Cyr did not doubt it due ones like Campagnon.

"Especially for a woman alone," she added.

In that moment, she sounded so meek he was tempted to laugh at she who had gone to the wood again, done so in the dark of night, brandished a deadly dagger, and rather than attempt to flee the man who threatened to deliver the sentence of a traitor, agreed to accompany him to answer to one very likely known as Dotter.

Struck by impulse, he commanded himself not to touch her again—then caught up the hand shielding her eyes, drew her near, and peered into her startled face. "I care not what your lady would have me believe. You are no mouse, Aelfled of..."

He looked to the small hand in his. She had lovely, slender fingers though the dirt of her garden was beneath her nails. And he might have kissed it if not for a sudden awareness of being watched. Though Aelfled stood between the abbey wall and his destrier, Maël and his men could see enough to guess that what Cyr did with this woman was no mere exchange of words. But it was done, and as she had yet to recover from the surprise of his trespass, he held on.

"Aelfled of what?" he said. "Not Senlac, you say. And now that you are of the abbey, not Wulfen. But neither Lillefarne, I say. So Aelfled of what?"

He caught the tearing of her eyes before she lowered them. And rather than tug free, she curled her fingers over his and whispered, "Of no place. All that is left of me is Aelfled of the Saxons, and so unrecognizable has she become I do not know I like her, though..."

"Though?"

"It matters not what I feel for her."

Certain what she alluded to had much to do with what had awaited her last eve when she delivered her missive—and his message—to the rebels, Cyr longed to demand she explain herself. But Aelfled of the Saxons who hardly knew herself would not tell. That she lived and had returned to the abbey despite the inability of the rebels to destroy the lord's hay upon Balduc told somehow she had redeemed herself sufficiently to be trusted with whatever was asked of her.

So what had redemption looked like beyond threats to her person? Had her grandmother also been threatened?

Cyr released her hand and straightened in the saddle.

"I must return to my work," she said.

"Then you would not ask after my meeting with your lady? For what she named you a mouse?"

She looked up, once more shaded her eyes. "When did you meet with her?"

Was it truly a question to which she lacked an answer? As she had not earlier risen to the bait left for the mouse Hawisa named her, he would have guessed she did not need to ask it.

"This morn we rode on Wulfen Castle. We came here directly afterward."

"How fares Lady Hawisa? I understand she has yet to recover from an illness with which she is long afflicted."

"She appears quite ill. So much, one wonders if she is dying."

She caught her breath. "I pray not."

"Then there are some you do pray for," he reminded her she had told she did not pray for him though at Senlac she had said she would.

She shrugged. "I do not think He listens to me—nor any Saxons—but much I love my lady and so I try to gain His ear."

Then perhaps she had not wandered as far from God as she led him to believe.

"I met her son," he said.

She caught her lower lip between her teeth, nodded.

"Though he resembles the first Wulfrith, he is small for his age."

Another nod.

"Were you one of those who knew the truth of his birth?"

Her hesitation was palpable, and when she neither confirmed nor denied it, he knew she had closed up and would not be pried open. Because she had not been entrusted with what might be a lie and feared any response would reveal it for that?

She tilted her head. "For what did Lady Hawisa name me a mouse?"

Certain she was so uncomfortable with talk of the second Wulfrith she sought to speak elsewhere, he said, "When I presented her with the arrow first I presented to you and asked if she recognized it, I said I had wrongly believed you sent it. She assured me you were too much a mouse to do so, though I disagree. And neither do I believe she thinks it, that she but... Well, I am not certain. Does she seek to protect you or to throw me off your scent? Both?"

"Scent?" she exclaimed. "Had I one, no longer do I now you know I supply the villagers of Balduc with food."

He smiled. "Certes, you have a scent, Aelfled. More than one. Do you so soon forget how near we stood on the day past? I do not. Cannot. Your scent was of earth and—"

"Good day, Sir Cyr." She pivoted and began retracing her steps.

"Stay out of the wood, little Saxon," he gave one last warning and watched her until she went from sight.

Once the door was secured, Cyr turned his destrier. As he guided it to where Maël and his men waited, he hoped she would heed him. And give the man he would set in the wood no cause to report anything of consequence—where *she* was concerned.

HE HAD WARNED HER, but she had hoped he had not acted on that warning. So how closely had his man watched for her? Certes, enough to see Waring come for the food. Might he have witnessed her meeting with Vitalis?

Not likely. Wulfen-raised since the age of six when sent to the renowned family to ensure the most promising son worthy to take his place as a thane of England, Vitalis was not only a master at arms but stealth. Surely, he would have been aware of the presence of another warrior in the wood long before that Norman became aware of him. And Vitalis would have made a quick end of Cyr D'Argent's man.

"We were not seen," Aelfled said aloud and believed it a little more as she stared at the altar distant from the bench she perched on. Still, it was good Vitalis had agreed to move the place where messages were exchanged to one opposite the direction of where she could no longer leave baskets of food. But that was all he conceded.

Though she had revealed Cyr's warning she not venture to the wood and his threat to watch her, Vitalis had asserted the taking of hay at the full moon would stand. And before departing Lillefarne, he had said Aelfled could be forgiven only once for betraying her people and because Isa believed it unintentional, that he was less certain of her innocence, and her vow to be true to her lady meant being true to the rebels. Lastly, he told if plans changed he would leave a message.

Less than a quarter hour after his departure, word brought Cyr D'Argent was outside the abbey and would speak with her. Lest whatever he wished to discuss proved of short duration, she had made him wait to give Vitalis more time to distance himself from the Normans. Then heart halfway up her throat, she had gone to Cyr and learned much of what had passed between Isa and him though naught of how her lady had explained a second son.

It was obvious Cyr was not convinced of the tale told him, but neither had he outright rejected it. Rather, he had sought Aelfled's aid in determining which way to believe, and for that she had seamed her lips.

"I will not fail, my lady," she whispered, then brought the cross on the altar to focus and raised her voice. "Lord, let me not fail her again. Lord, heal her. Lord, move her to do what best serves her people rather than revenge." She closed her eyes. "Lord, return to my people ere we are lost to the ages."

She tried to feel His presence. Waited for something— anything—and feeling nearly as empty as when she had entered the chapel, pushed to her feet.

She had a message to write, though of few words it would be and there was no hurry since Vitalis or another would not check for two days. But it would be waiting, revealing *he* had come again, and as feared, watched her closely—so closely it was imperative they alter the plan.

CHAPTER TWENTY

Stern Castle
England

*E*mpty-handed, but at last Theriot came.

Wishing he had not spent so much hope on the eldest brother returning with the youngest, Cyr tossed aside the weighty, heavily nicked training sword. "No Guarin," he called to Maël, "but now we are four again."

His cousin straightened from where he bent to retrieve the pike he had nearly proven was superior to a sword for its longer reach and his exceptional skill, followed his cousin's gaze beyond the fenced yard outside Stern's walls.

Staring at the dozen guiding their mounts toward the castle, he said, "Guarin may not be out there, Cyr. He may have fallen upon Senlac the same as my sire. Methinks your time and Theriot's—and Dougray's if you can move him out of self-pity— would be better spent putting an end to the rebels. And making better use of my men and me ere the king recalls us. Whoever rules Stern must be present at all times to ensure it remains in

Norman hands. Thus, you must decide soon—these lands or your sire's? As William told, you cannot have both."

Once more, Cyr considered leaving England. It was what he wanted. But not all he wanted.

Refusing to look nearer on what was here for him in this island kingdom, he said, "Oui, I must decide soon, though I shall delay as long as possible so we might first learn my brother's fate." He strode forward and swung over the fence.

Shortly, Theriot reined in, ordered his men to continue to the stables, and turned his destrier sideways. Smiling wearily, he extended a hand. "Welcome to Stern, Cyr. Forgive me for not being here to pass the keeping of these lands to you."

There was still something boyish about the youngest brother, though the soft was mostly gone from his face and he sported an abundance of whiskers many a night beyond the scrape of a keen blade.

Cyr gripped Theriot's hand, released. "Of far greater import is finding our brother."

The younger man sighed. "Indeed."

Maël halted alongside Cyr. "You bring tidings of Guarin?"

Theriot raised an eyebrow. "And good day to you, Cousin. I trust you have found your lady mother in good health and spirit?"

With a note of chagrin, Maël said, "I believe she is happy here. I thank you for being the son I have not been."

"Much she misses you." Theriot shifted his regard to Cyr. "Let us speak inside."

Upon their entrance into the great hall that had come alive with the return of the dozen warriors who were being poured drink at the high table, Chanson and Nicola hastened forward to embrace Theriot.

"You have grown, Sister!" He pulled back. "Not only in height but daring, I am told."

She blushed prettily, hooked an arm through his, and turned him toward the hearth.

"Dougray?" he asked of her as he had done Cyr at the stables and been warned the third-born was still far from the brother remembered. Theriot had assured Cyr that, as he had always been the closest with their half-sibling, he would set Dougray aright.

"Aunt Chanson has sent for him," Nicola said. "Beware, he is more surly than usual."

Because of what had transpired at Balduc that had seen him returned to Stern ahead of the others, Cyr had no doubt.

"But I am sure he will come," she added.

"Where is Father Fulbert?" Cyr asked.

"The priest is not yet returned from the village he walked to this morn."

His introduction to Theriot would have to wait. And it was probably for the best as eager as Cyr was to learn Theriot's tidings.

When the D'Argents were seated before the hearth and served drink, Theriot sat forward. "I am certain Guarin is somewhere near. Laugh at me if you will, but I feel him."

Years ago, all thought it exaggeration he possessed that sense in greater portion than other D'Argents, but time and again he proved he was gifted with something well outside the realm of close observation—that which Hugh had likened to a child born of a perfect marriage between all five of the natural senses.

"What of your inquiries?" Cyr asked. "Is anyone speaking?"

"The Saxons are mostly close-mouthed, but if you happen on children out from behind their mother's skirts and father's scowls, there are things to be learned."

"Such as?" Maël said.

Cyr glanced at him where he sat beside Theriot, past his shoulder saw movement so slight as to be nearly imagined. Dougray stood in shadow alongside the stairs.

"Just over the Wulfenshire border in Lincolnshire," Theriot said, "my men and I paused at a stream to water our horses and came upon two boys fishing. Blessedly, they were more hungry than wary and accepted my invitation to break fast with us. One kept stealing looks at me, and so I teased I took no offense and told he could look on me as long as he wished since surely he had never seen a young man with so much silver in his hair. The boy blurted he had seen another, and that one had more silver, then said perhaps it only looked more since his hair was long and he had silver in his beard as well."

Theriot glanced between Cyr and their cousin. "I think you both hold your breath."

They exhaled in unison, and Maël demanded, "Continue."

"It is the same description given by a soldier William sent to investigate the murder of the Norman family. But this boy saw something else. After assuring me he but traversed the wood that day to sooner reach home, that he was not hunting deer, he said the silver-haired man shared a horse with another. This was also told by the Norman soldier, but as not told, the boy said it was a woman." He let that settle in a moment. "One side of her tunic was darker than the other, and he thought it blood."

"What color her hair?" Maël asked.

"Golden."

"Then the arrow thought not to have found its mark in one believed to be a man did land," Cyr concluded.

His brother nodded. "Now I wonder if it is no mere sickness from which the Lady of Wulfen has suffered since around the time of Guarin's sighting."

As Cyr also wondered. "Maël and I met with her on the day past."

Theriot's head jerked. "Did you?"

"Oui, and it is no false thing she is unwell." Cyr shifted his gaze to his cousin. "Tell me her hair is golden beneath all that unwashed mess."

"Quite." His smile was so genuine not even the ugly scar above it could detract from perfection over which many a maiden's heart had fluttered before Hastings. "She has him. It has to be her."

"It is the nearest we have come to confirming Guarin lives," Theriot said, "but still we may reach too far."

Cyr did not want to hear that. He wanted to ride on Wulfen. But above the hum of excitement rang the clear bell of reason. Wulfen Castle was a fortress like no other seen in England and would require much planning, effort, and time to breach. And it could prove for naught if that lady held his brother there and was given time and opportunity to move him. Or she kept him elsewhere—worse, destroyed evidence of having imprisoned one of William's followers. Had she not already slain Guarin...

Theriot cleared his throat. "Here the difficulty. It makes no sense Guarin, in possession of his injured captor, rode not toward Normans who could aid him but away as if *they* were the enemy."

There was that, Cyr silently conceded. And a possible explanation. "I understand it is rare, but I have heard tale of captive men and women whose minds and bodies are so broken they begin to sympathize with their abusers."

"Non." Theriot said. "Of any other I might believe that, not Guarin."

A gasp sounded from Nicola. "But if he has been terribly abused, perhaps he *is* lost inside himself."

Wishing he had thought to send her away before offering an explanation for Guarin's behavior, her unusual silence having made him forget her, Cyr said, "It is only something we must consider, Nicola."

"But likely true," Dougray said, striding forth. Ignoring Theriot who surged to his feet and swung around to greet the one he had not seen since Senlac, he held his gaze to Nicola. "These Saxons are heathens, would think naught of torturing—"

"Enough!" Cyr was distantly aware of lunging out of his seat, but when Dougray opened his mouth to spout more bitterness, he was intimately aware of the hand with which he gripped the neck of that foul tunic, his aunt's cry of protest, and the fist swinging toward his face.

He caught bunched fingers in his other hand, grunted over the force of knuckles seeking to crack bones, and propelled Dougray to the side and backward, stopping only when they came up against the wall to the right of the hearth.

"Clear the hall!" Theriot shouted.

As chairs scraped across the dais and boots pounded over the floor, Cyr stared into the face nearly level with his. Bloodshot eyes glared, nostrils dilated and pinched, upper lip convulsed above teeth no longer well-cared for.

When the great doors slammed closed, Cyr barked, "Until once more you prove worthy of the name you trample—and dare not disavow it again!—you will not gainsay me nor challenge any beyond your ability to land a blow and do it well."

"Cyr!" his aunt beseeched.

He shoved Dougray harder against the wall. "All I would hear from you is you understand and shall comply."

Dougray kept him waiting, finally said, "I understand. But comply?"

"Then leave!"

"Pray, Cyr…" Their aunt gripped his arm.

"I am done walking wide around him," Cyr snarled. "Done having our name sullied by one who could have bested Campagnon were he half the man he was before Senlac."

A bark of laughter sounded from Dougray. "I am half—"

Another shove bounced his head against the wall, knocking back the sarcastic rejoinder.

"Non!" Cyr's saliva sprayed his brother's face. "You will not own to that. You are not half a man. All here know it a self-pitying lie. You but act the part, and not well. So cease and come back to who you are, Dougray D'Argent!"

His brother's mouth opened, closed, then he snarled, "Release me."

"Non."

"Non?" Dougray growled.

"Stand away, Aunt," Cyr commanded, and when she hastened to the side, said, "Find your own release, Dougray—even if you must imagine me your enemy."

"You think that hard to do? You whom I followed to England to gain lands only to lose an arm to a Saxon pig?"

There. Words he had not heretofore spoken though long they dwelt behind his teeth. Words more true than Cyr had wanted to believe even when, upon bloodied Senlac, he began to accept what he had done was more for personal gain than bringing ungodly men to God.

He nodded. "It is good you do not find it hard, providing it gives me what I want—a man capable of besting me, not the boy who could only boast one day he would do so."

In Dougray's eyes was the longing to prove he could triumph over his older brother, but there also was the longing to refuse Cyr what he sought.

Hoping moments from now he would find himself on the floor being pummeled, Cyr waited. At last Dougray wrenched his fist free and drove it into his brother's nose and mouth.

Cyr should not have kept his feet beneath him, ripe as he was to be taken to ground, but Dougray did not strike again. His shoulder slammed into Cyr's as he shoved past.

Theriot sprang into his path. "Pray, let us speak, Dougray."

The fist again, this time to the jaw, and as Theriot stumbled back, his attacker continued to the doors.

"Dougray!" Cyr shouted. "A sennight I give you to decide. Aid in retrieving Guarin and set your mind and body to serving and protecting Stern or ever be less than you are—a wayfarer...an outcast...whatever feeds that bitter soul."

Dougray threw open the door and strode outside.

Moments later, Maël thrust aside the descending silence with, "That is a beginning. And not a bad one. But can you truly turn your back on him, Cyr?"

"He leaves me no choice." Tasting the blood running from his nose, Cyr drew a hand across it, then fingered his aching front teeth. As he confirmed they had not cracked or loosened, a great sob sounded from behind.

"Merciful Lord!" His aunt hurried to Nicola, patted her niece's shuddering back, stroked her bobbing head. "Come now, Dear. It is just men being men, little different from boys being boys."

In that she was wrong, but Cyr ground his teeth and looked from Theriot who rubbed his jaw to Maël who appeared satisfied. Whether or not Dougray would admit it, progress had been made, and it had cost their cousin no blood or bruise. Had it, Dougray might not have walked away. He might have crawled.

Though Maël had a great care for his cousins, it was not quite the same as being their brother. He would have followed Dougray and given back what was done him.

"Oui, a good beginning," Maël said. "But what comes next? And what part would you have me play, not only in restoring Dougray to the D'Argent name but finding Guarin?"

As near a brother as was possible, Cyr silently acknowledged. "Though I long to ride on Wulfen, I think we must move cautiously lest we incite Guarin's captors to dispose of him have they not already. As for Dougray... What think you, Theriot?"

"I cannot think now. I am weary, near starving, and my aching head has begun to pound." He nodded. "But Dougray and I shall speak. And soon."

CHAPTER TWENTY-ONE

*T*heriot's *soon* came sooner than expected. And Aelfled was to blame.

Well before dawn, the young man-at-arms set to watch the abbey returned to Stern Castle with proof Cyr's little Saxon remained defiant.

Garbed in undertunic and chausses he dragged on, Cyr received him amid torchlight brought into the solar.

After apologizing for awakening his lord, the man drew from his purse a piece of parchment many times folded to fit the palm. "She left this, my lord, though not at the stacked rocks."

Then she and her rebels thought that place no longer viable. "Where?" Cyr asked as he unfolded the message.

"So opposite a direction she would have gone unseen had you not told me to watch for movement in the garden at the rear. As suspected, a door must be there. When she entered the wood, I followed at a good distance and saw her leave the message in the rotted center of an ancient oak, then as directed followed her back to ensure no harm befell her. Unfortunately, I was too distant and the garden too deep in shadow to determine the secret door's location."

If need be, Cyr would find it. He turned the creased parchment toward light and read, *He came again. Certes, he watches closely. Pray, reconsider your course. More, what you would have me do. I fear I am so compromised as to be dangerous. I beseech you leave answer soon.*

"Would you have me return it to the oak, my lord?"

It was the same Cyr asked himself. Return it so she might warn away the rebels as intended? Or keep it and let the plans of disaffected Saxons proceed?

He lowered into a chair and read her words again. The answer was there. As she revealed naught of the rebels' *course* and the part she played, it was of little benefit to withhold her warning. But were he honest with himself, the greatest argument for returning the parchment was for her sake. If she was heeded, surely the danger to her would be snuffed. Except to toil in her garden, she would stay inside her walls. Or so he prayed.

He stood, folded the parchment, and crossed to his man. "Place it where you found it."

"You would have me resume my watch?"

As Cyr looked into eager blue eyes, he thought how young the man was, guessed it was likely as a squire he had served at the great battle. "Oui, but ere you return to Lillefarne, quench your thirst and hunger and resupply yourself with enough food and drink to pass several days in the wood. I would not have you distracted or caught out hunting."

The man pivoted and pushed through the curtains to make his way past those his arrival had awakened who now strove to return to their rest.

"Sir Theriot," Cyr heard him acknowledge the one to whom he had answered before the Baron of Stern's arrival.

Hating his fatigued brother had refused to avail himself of the lord's solar and made his bed on a pallet in the hall among the restless, snoring masses—and been further disturbed by the delivery of Aelfled's missive—Cyr strode to the curtains and out onto the dais.

By the dim light of torches, he saw the man-at-arms move in the direction of the kitchen whilst Theriot crossed toward the great doors.

To relieve himself, Cyr guessed and would have turned back if not for the purpose in his brother's stride. Had Theriot determined now was the time to speak with Dougray? Was his destination the stables where, during supper, the master of horses reported seeing the one who had yet to return to the donjon?

As Theriot quietly closed the door behind him, Cyr saw his cousin rise from a pallet.

Moments later, wearing only chausses, Maël ascended the dais. "I say we follow," he said. "I am not certain he can handle *this* Dougray alone."

Cyr nodded. "He will not be pleased, but I think you are right. Don your tunic."

Shortly, amid torchlight sufficient to move unopposed by guards who recognized their lord and his cousin, the two entered the outer bailey and caught sight of Theriot.

As expected, his destination was the stables, but within fifty feet of the building, he came around.

Cyr did not begrudge him that keen sense, having no desire to steal upon him. But beyond marveling over it, ever it unsettled.

"I thank you for your concern," he said low as brother and cousin halted before him, "but I am capable of defending myself should Dougray receive me no better than earlier. Or worse."

The latter was a good possibility, Cyr considered, especially if the third brother had overly imbibed without benefit of viands. "I do not question your abilities, Theriot. More than many a warrior, you proved yourself during the great battle, but this is different. This is no enemy to be thoughtlessly slain all the sooner to engage the next who seeks your life. Though what earlier transpired prepares you for a much-changed Dougray, you may not be sufficiently armed, especially as what was once a good friendship renders you more vulnerable than Maël or me."

Theriot's bruised jaw hardened. "You are not my nursemaid, Cyr. Like it or not, I go in alone."

"No need, little brother," Dougray's voice presented itself ahead of his figure parting from alongside the stable doors. "I am here."

Stealth. Of benefit against many a man but usually less so Theriot with that unnatural sense of his. Doubtless, Dougray had escaped notice only because the youngest brother had first trained that sense on Cyr and Maël.

Theriot turned, rebuked, "Sooner you ought to have revealed yourself."

Walking a straight line, Dougray moved into torchlight. Blessedly, just as his body evidenced no great quantity of drink, neither did his face.

"Had I, I would have missed hearing myself compared to the enemy." Something almost a smile appearing amid his tangled beard, Dougray settled his gaze on Cyr. "It was due me," he surprised, and again when he said, "I do not require a sennight. I shall give answer now."

Hoping his calm was born of honorable resolve, Cyr waited.

"Much anger I have wasted on those less deserving though once more my enemy surround me—hives of them. And the nearest hive holds captive our brother. Thus, I shall aid in retrieving Guarin. Do I not give my life to do so, by the sword I shall serve these lands so ever they remain Norman."

Cyr did not know how to respond. He wanted his brother back as well as the warrior capable of protecting family, people, and home, but there was no doubt Dougray's decision was fueled by vengeance. Once he took up arms again, could he be controlled? If not, surely better a fist-wielding than sword-wielding Dougray.

Feeling Theriot and Maël's disquiet, Cyr glanced at them.

"Does your offer stand?" Dougray prompted.

Wishing Fulbert were here rather than the chapel where he

made his bed, Cyr recalled the holy man's oft-repeated words —*time, patience, prayer.* An abundance of the first and second had been expended, but were the offer not rescinded, much more of the third would be required.

So be it, he accepted what could prove the only course to pull Dougray back from the edge of the dead. "My offer stands, providing in serving me you act within the bounds of my orders."

Dougray inclined his head. "Whilst I serve you, Baron D'Argent."

And afterward? Cyr nearly asked. *Prayer,* he reminded himself. "You do know that means protecting these lands and its people, most of whom are Saxons?" At Dougray's hesitation, he decided here was an opportunity to delve what had happened between his brother and Campagnon. "Those who cannot defend themselves," Cyr added, "like Em."

Dougray's brow furrowed. "Em?"

As thought, he did not know her name. "Campagnon's slave."

Cyr was rewarded with a glimmer of interest and a softening about the face that evidenced his brother yet possessed compassion enough to feel for the oppressed—even one of Saxon blood. But as if remembering she was of that people responsible for his loss, his face returned to its familiar hard lines.

"Were I moved to aid her, which I am not," he said, "it would be impossible. As she is a possession, she is neither yours nor mine to protect. She is Campagnon's to do with as he pleases."

"True, and most unfortunate that." Determining enough was said on the matter—for now—Cyr said, "Thus, to the training field we go."

His brother started to turn away. "I shall meet you at dawn."

"Non. We go there now, Brother."

"Now, Cyr?" Theriot exclaimed. "It is three or more hours ere dawn."

"Which we will put to good use without the sun beating down on us. You will join Dougray and me?"

A hesitation, then, "Of course."

"Maël?"

"I am for sleep. But be assured, Dougray, when we meet at swords again, I shall demand more of you than, I suspect, your brothers shall—the same my sire required of you."

Dougray grunted. "You flatter yourself. There was only one Hugh, and if any can come near to replacing him, it is Guarin."

Cyr felt the incoming tide of his cousin's anger, then the outgoing tide, and it did not come again to that shore. "Hence, all the more reason we must find your brother," Maël said. "And for you to make good on the surname gifted you." He turned on his heel.

"Gifted me," Dougray muttered as he watched his cousin depart. "So it was." He looked to Cyr and Theriot, then pulled the brooch from his mantle and heaved his shoulders back. The covering dropped to the ground, revealing the lower portion of his tunic's left sleeve was empty of limb from elbow to hand. "I shall require a sword." His having been lost upon Senlac and, doubtless, now a passenger in a scavenger's scabbard.

Pushing past the pain of seeing his brother bare his loss, Cyr said, "I shall secure a worthy one. Until then, a training sword will suffice."

Dougray shrugged.

"And your dagger. From this day forth, you shall wear it on your belt, even if only to remind you of what was required to earn it and will be required to once more wear it with pride."

"I would think it better to wait until—"

"You will unpack it. You will don it. You will practice with it when you are not at swords. And you will cut your hair and beard."

"Non, I will not cut them."

"You look the Saxon you profess to hate, Brother."

"More than profess. But as I come right of mind, I find there could be an excellent use for so long neglecting my appearance—

that of providing cover." He looked between his brothers. "Not only do I lack the identifying D'Argent silver amid dark hair, but over the face of a Norman I wear that of a Saxon which will allow me to move unseen among the heathens. And for that, I must become better acquainted with their language."

Further proof he had done more than brood all day. Albeit greased by vengeance, the cogs of his mind were turning in a direction worthy of a warrior—more, a brother.

"I withdraw that last requirement," Cyr said. "Now let us resurrect your sword song."

"You play me foul!" Dougray snarled as he carefully turned his head to peer behind at the one who had set a dull blade against his neck.

"Foul?" Cyr raised his eyebrows. "Far less than your enemy shall, Saxon or otherwise."

The breath of his seething causing the morning mist to puff and swirl before his face, Dougray remained unmoving while beyond him Theriot regained his feet and slapped at his rear to scatter the dirt gained in being bested—only for the third time in all the hours since Dougray's trials had begun amid torchlight.

Cyr had not intended to intervene, but this time when Dougray felled Theriot, there had been anger about him rather than triumph as if he guessed his brother showed mercy to encourage him—and bring an end to this training session which Dougray had refused to do a half hour past, though all were weary, dry of tongue, wet of body, and filthy.

"So what will you do now your enemy has stolen upon you whilst you allowed anger to distract you, Dougray? Yield? Or fight Theriot *and* me?"

"Two against a one-armed man?" he scoffed.

"Many a time you faced and bested several opponents, even

whilst wielding a single blade. And it is not as if now you are without a sword arm since, unlike most, you possessed two to begin with."

Still he seethed, though the mist moved less enthusiastically before his face.

Cyr looked to Theriot. Seeing he had retrieved his sword, he removed his own from Dougray's neck and came around. "If any warrior can recover his skill at arms, it is you who was not only as adept at wielding weapons with the left hand as the right but better than most able to endure and quickly recover from blows."

Dougray glowered, but amid that dark was a gleam Cyr thought might be the old Dougray. Hoping to coax him farther into the light, he said, "Perhaps the Lord, seeing this day, made you thus."

Dougray set his sword's tip to the ground, and with rivulets tracking his dirty face, said, "You spend too much time with that half-Saxon priest. I liked you better when you were merciless and more ungodly than godly."

"Then even more I am glad you are not me," Cyr attempted to lighten the confrontation.

"Of course you are glad. You would not wish to trade places with this lowly brother—even did I yet possess both arms."

Wondering how best to respond and finding no good answer, Cyr was grateful when Theriot said, "Attend! A rider approaches."

Hearing the sound and feeling vibration beneath his feet, Cyr turned and studied the thick mist. Just left of center, it billowed as the moist air behind was displaced by horse and rider pushing through. Readying his sword, he glanced around to ensure the men on the wall were also alert to the one come unto the castle.

The half dozen there who had watched the brothers practice before the castle showed they were well aware of whoever rode with the urgency of one bearing tidings of import.

From King William? Cyr wondered and hoped it was not recall of Maël and his men.

Shortly, the rider emerged from the thick of the mist and Cyr saw it was the young man-at-arms who had hours earlier departed to continue his watch over Lillefarne.

"We are done here," Cyr said and, as he strode forward, put over his shoulder, "Refresh and rest yourselves. The next session will demand more of all of us."

"My lord!" the rider called as Cyr exited the yard. "I bear tidings from Lillefarne."

Cyr halted, and when the man dismounted, said, "Deliver them."

"I was too late in returning the missive to its hiding place. When I sought to do so, I found another message there." He reached inside his tunic and withdrew two folded parchments. "The smallest is that which I was to return. I thought it best not to do so until you looked upon the new message."

"You thought right." Cyr unfolded the larger one and had to strain to read it by torchlight. In a bold, untidy script likely inked by a man—perhaps Vitalis who had taken Aelfled to meet Dotter —was written, *No longer the full moon, now the night before, we take from Stern what he denied us upon Balduc. Be prepared to render services esteemed by one owed your loyalty.*

Cyr drew breath between his teeth. Ill-timing rendered moot his attempt to remove Aelfled from danger by allowing her to give warning he had hoped would be heeded. But there was gain to be had in the change of plans less cryptically told than expected. Now armed with a good chance of ending the rebellion and freeing Guarin, Cyr would not risk losing it.

When two nights hence the rebels attacked the lord's hay upon Stern, a sizable host would await them rather than the handful of men who had watched over it these past days. The rebels would be brought to heel, and surely among their numbers were some who could lead the way to their nest—or hive, as Dougray preferred.

So what to do with this new missive? If he did not return it,

Aelfled would not be prepared to give aid a day sooner, and that would be interpreted as evidence she betrayed her people. If he returned it, she would assist the rebels in whatever was required of her, proving her loyalty and—for a time—keeping her safe from the sentence of a traitor.

It was no choice. It must be the latter. Hopefully, the lack of response to her warning would not raise her suspicions. She would assume her fear and protest were ignored.

He folded the missive, handed it to the man. "This one you will return to the tree. If what it tells proves true, in two nights she will steal from the abbey, and I would not have her slip free."

The man inclined his head.

"Tarry an hour that we may speak more on this," Cyr said and, as he motioned him to follow, tightly folded his fingers over Aelfled's intercepted message and assured himself this was the only worthy course. And of added benefit, he would learn the role she played in the rebellion—hopefully, one outside of Guarin's imprisonment.

~

Lillefarne Abbey
England

THIS HER ANSWER? One night ere the full moon rather than the night of? Complete disregard for her warning?

Teeth so tight they ached, Aelfled stared at the words inscribed by Vitalis. Had Isa spoken them? Had her man merely set them on parchment? Or was this all him, Isa too ill to provide direction?

She read it again. It had to be all Vitalis. Her lady was too wise to reveal so much—not only time but place. Blessedly, the message was received by the one for whom it was intended.

Still, Cyr D'Argent was no fool. By way of her warning he ought to have harvested the lord's hay on Stern immediately after

Balduc's. Regardless of the reason for the delay, he had to have set watch over the field the same as he had done her and might yet do. And if the rebels...

With jerks amid the sound of snagging cloth, Aelfled slid her back down the rough bark and sank to her haunches. "Dear Lord," she breathed as she swept her eyes over this part of the wood she was fairly certain was unknown to Cyr D'Argent, unlike where she had left food. "Work me a miracle. Speak into Cyr. Tell him to bring in the lord's hay upon Stern this day or come the morrow. And if You will not do that for me or Your forsaken people, let him be done keeping watch over me. Two nights hence, I must keep my word to aid my lady's men. I cannot fail them as I did Wulf."

Of a sudden lightheaded and nauseated, she clamped her eyes closed and dropped her chin to her chest. She counted each shuddering breath required to settle head and stomach. Five... ten...fifteen...

She lifted her chin. "You are Saxon, strong of mind, body, and spirit," she whispered Isa's words. "Remember. Embrace. No more will lose their lives because of you. You will preserve them, Aelfled Sorendotter of..."

She was tempted to name herself of the Lord, but her faith was so scarce it would be sacrilegious—merely an attempt to flatter God who could not be fooled.

It was a struggle to rise, though less due to weakness than the tree's bark being even more grasping as she straightened against it.

She stepped away, pulling her snagged mantle free, then folded Vitalis's message and tucked it into her bodice. Upon her return to her cell, she would put it to flame, then retreat to her garden and fill a basket for Waring.

CHAPTER TWENTY-TWO

Barony of Stern
England

They came.

Even before Cyr had shared with his brothers and cousin the intercepted message, he had considered the same as they that it could be intended more for his eyes than Aelfled's. Thus, though the bulk of his men and Maël's were set over the lord's hay upon Stern, small contingents patrolled other parts of the barony under orders they not engage if they encountered anything suspicious—providing no innocents were in danger. They were to put heels to their mounts and report to Cyr. But as revealed by the message, it *was* the lord's hay upon Stern they meant to burn.

On foot, surely having left their mounts at a distance to steal upon the field they had to know was guarded, eight cloaked and hooded men hunched low and crept forward amid moonlight muted by thinly-scattered clouds. As they did not carry fire, they were surely armed with flints and, once they made use of them, would quickly retreat.

"How much nearer will you allow them to draw?" Dougray rasped from the other side of Theriot.

Cyr had not wanted him among those chosen to bring down the rebels, but Dougray had been determined and Theriot sided with him, citing were any needed to act with great stealth, none was better than Dougray.

Hoping he would not regret yielding, Cyr said, "No nearer," then gave the signal.

The thunder of hooves and whinnying of horses too long kept in check sounded all around as he and his men surged forward and fanned wide to ensure closure of the noose drawn around the rebels.

Desperately wishful, Cyr silently named the rebel's hope of escape. They were had, and no matter how skilled with the weapons they drew, many would fall and enough would be captured it was possible some could be made to talk—rather, betray.

One did escape the noose, but before Cyr could set after the rebel capable of more speed than most, Dougray swerved aside.

"Do not kill him!" Cyr shouted and knew if his brother defied him without good cause, it could be blamed on his inability to hear the command. Believable, but like the others, he had been instructed to draw as little blood as possible to ensure a greater number of loose tongues and more rebel lives to offer up for the return of Guarin.

Seven of eight rebels wielding swords and daggers turned all around in search of escape from the small Norman army surrounding them.

"Throw down your weapons and live," Cyr commanded in their language as, out of the corner of his eye, he saw Dougray launch out of the saddle onto the back of the one he pursued.

Let him not overreach, Cyr silently prayed, then continued, "Hold to your weapons and die."

One of the men whose hoods had fallen to his shoulders

swung around, and before Cyr could voice recognition of the man, Maël snarled, "That is no Saxon!"

"I have Campagnon's man, Merle!" Dougray bellowed.

Cyr looked to where his brother had an arm around the man's neck, pinning him against the length of his own body, then more closely considered the other two whose faces were revealed. He knew few of the names of Campagnon's men, but moonlight shone bright enough to place them at Balduc Castle.

It made no sense. The message told the rebels would...

"Dear Lord, I have been had," Cyr muttered.

"It would seem the message left for that woman *was* intended for you," Maël also concluded. "Doubtless, the rebels work ill elsewhere whilst we are distracted by your vassal's plans passed to them by someone in his household."

Had Aelfled known? Cyr wondered and berated himself for *his* wishful thinking she not be a party to this deception. Time was better spent discovering how the rebels worked this obscenity to what could prove their great advantage.

"Lay down your weapons or die for Campagnon!" Cyr shouted.

Most were mercenaries. Though hardened men, it was not in their nature nor best interest to remain loyal to one who had set them a task for which they would have to answer to the King of England. Their only defense was they followed the orders of their direct superior of whom they dared not ask questions. But providing William was in a forgiving mood and he could make use of men indebted to him for his mercy, it could prove a reasonable defense.

With reluctance, the men cast off their weapons, and all that were visible were on the ground by the time Dougray marched Merle into their midst.

Cyr guided his horse nearer, stared into the man's florid face that shone with defiance despite the arm hooked beneath it whose hand grasped a keen blade that Dougray had but to draw sharply downward to sever the great vein in the neck. "Do you survive this attack against the king's man, Merle, you shall have to find another lord to serve. Doubtless, Campagnon will hold you responsible for exposing his treachery."

The man shifted his head clamped against his captor's shoulder, between his teeth said, "You think that poor excuse for a lord who cannot keep hold of lands *I* should have been awarded has the mind and might to act against a pack of D'Argents?"

Yet another surprise this night delivered—could he be believed. Cyr narrowed his gaze on the one who sounded sincere in his disregard for the man to whom he had seemed a companion. Was this an act to protect Campagnon and his position at Balduc? Or had Merle acted on his own?

"Oui, *I* dared where never would he," he continued, "as all those who believed in me ahead of Campagnon shall attest. What say you, warriors mine?"

There was a murmur of agreement that seemed of relief. Because Merle provided a good tale? Or because the self-confessed leader would bear the brunt of punishment?

Hating the web of intrigue and lies, Cyr's anger rose to such height he was tempted to order Dougray to make good use of his dagger. But that gained under Fulbert's direction and beneath the Lord's gaze would be lost and Cyr would be merciless once more...

He breathed deep. "A pity these *warriors* believed in one such as you," he forced humor into his voice. "Doubtless, they regret it now. And shall more so later."

"Riders!" Theriot called, once more the first aware of their approach.

As Cyr ordered his men to secure the prisoners and Maël commanded his to prepare for battle, the youngest D'Argent added, "Two. No more than three."

Moments later, two appeared against the dark of night from the direction Merle and his men had come. Were they the enemy, they would be witless to advance on so great a gathering of warriors. Thus, Cyr guessed here came those set to watch over another area of the demesne.

It was so, as told by their announcement, "Balduc Castle has been attacked."

The sticky web seeking to encase him, Cyr clenched his hands. For the diversion that held the greater force of his men here, had the rebels revealed the lord's hay upon Stern would be burned? Or was the attack on the fortress also of Merle? Perhaps he sought Campagnon's death, not only for revenge if he truly despised him but to gain whatever wealth the former Baron of Balduc had accumulated in oppressing the Saxons.

Cyr looked to where Dougray had moved his captive back and to the left. "Is this your doing, Merle?" At the man's hesitation, he snarled, "You would not also like to claim responsibility for the attack on Balduc?"

It was not he who answered but the one who delivered the tidings. "Non, my lord."

Cyr swept his regard back to the soldier.

Confusion center of his face, the man said, "I know not what Campagnon's man does here, but half a dozen Saxon rebels burned a section of the outer wall and a quarter of the harvested hay ere your men scattered them."

"Were any taken prisoner?"

"One, my lord," the second soldier said with what seemed regret. "Backed into a corner with only a dagger to fight her way past two armed with swords, she turned the blade on herself."

Cyr stiffened, and it seemed as if that inside his chest ceased beating. "She?" he said in a choked voice. "You are certain it was a woman?"

"Oui, my lord, I saw her myself."

"Young? Old?"

"Young."

Non, dear God, he cast heavenward.

"Rather, what I consider young, being near on fifty myself," the man said. "Had I to guess, I would say she was aged thirty."

Had Cyr's heart truly ceased beating, it determined to make up for those lost beats. Not Aelfled. That was not the part she played in the rebels' plans. Another thought struck, though it hardly seemed possible after that to which he himself had borne witness. "What color the Saxon's hair?"

"Black, my lord, cut to the shoulders."

Neither Hawisa Wulfrithdotter Fortier, she who was said to have long, golden-hair beneath the filth and was surely too ill to attempt such. "Have you anything more to tell?"

"Only that it was your men at Stern who quickly routed the rebels, my lord."

To whom Cyr must compose a missive informing them of Merle's betrayal and ordering them to keep close watch on its castellan. He started to turn his horse aside, looked back. "Did you see Campagnon?"

"I did, my lord."

"His reaction to the attack?"

"Anger, though his mood lightened when he saw the Saxon woman was dead."

"What did he say?"

"That of course it was a woman, all the more dumb-witted for being a Saxon. And likely all had been of her sex, so poorly executed was the attack and of few numbers. Then he spat on her and returned to the donjon."

More than expected and worthy of pondering, Cyr mused as he urged his mount toward Maël who had drawn near enough to listen to the exchange with the soldier. Though it was not Aelfled who had taken her life, it was possible she had been among the five who fled, having slipped past her guard in the wood. It was unfortunate not a single rebel was captured alive. But of greater import than learning if Aelfled was among their ranks was discovering where Guarin was held. Failing that, had a good number been captured, they might have been used to bargain for his release.

Though frustrated by the night's events, Cyr forced himself to look on the good of it. The loss of Stern's hay was averted, and the rebels' plan to use Merle's betrayal as a diversion to wreak damage on Balduc had mostly failed.

Or had it? Only six had attacked the castle. Though Merle had reduced the castle's defenders by eight, still there remained dozens only a fool would set so few against. Might there have been more rebels in hiding who awaited a signal never given? If not, might the fires set at Balduc Castle been a second diversion?

"What are you thinking?" Maël asked as Cyr drew alongside.

"That this night my lordship might be the victim of not one but two diversions to allow the rebels to work greater ill elsewhere."

Maël frowned. "So how are we to stop them—if it is not too late?"

"Aelfled of Lillefarne. Were she among the rebels who fled Balduc, likely she returns to the abbey. Were she not, she has a part to play." He nodded. "I shall give charge of Merle and his mercenaries to Theriot and, if God is with us, this night we will remove these hooks from our mouths and use them to catch our enemies."

CHAPTER TWENTY-THREE

Lillefarne Abbey
England

*P*ast middle night. Were they coming or not? And if they came, were there any Normans in the wood to alert Cyr?

Where Aelfled crouched against the wall, clouds overheard spotting her with cool drops, she pressed fingertips hard to her temples, then thrust fingers back through her hair.

Cradling her head, she closed her eyes. "Lord, keep them from the blades of Normans. They but seek to take back their lives and country. Pray, aid me in keeping them safe from whatever foul winds blow this night."

A hoot sounded, and she so forcefully snapped up her head it clipped the wall behind. Was it of owl or man? Glimpsing no movement amid the scattered fruit trees between her garden and the wood, she waited.

Now two hoots. Silence. Three hoots.

She pushed upright, and as she moved along the wall toward the hidden door, saw movement.

They trickled in, advancing tree to tree, perhaps as many as a score. As she had never sheltered so great a number, it portended much ill had been worked on Cyr D'Argent. Until the danger of him was past, she must keep Isa's rebels here. If he came to her with questions and accusations, she would lie as she must for her lady, though had God in His heavens not entirely turned from her, she gave Him more cause.

In that moment, she longed to clasp her lost psalter between her palms, press its spine to her lips, and seek comfort in repeating the prayers within—until she recalled the blood staining it.

"Attend to the now," she whispered. "Serve your lady well."

It surprised Vitalis was the first to appear. On nights she sheltered his men—and the occasional woman—rarely did Isa's most trusted man present himself. Instead, he and others led their pursuers astray, and the next day or the day after Aelfled would begin receiving instructions as to which men should return to the encampment—two at once, at times as many as half a dozen.

"What do you here?" she asked as Vitalis motioned forward those who followed him.

"Too many D'Argents," he rasped. "Though we struck hard and well, we are to exercise greater caution." Then almost to himself, he muttered, "A risky venture this. Accursed Jaxon."

Then it was Isa's first in command who chose to ignore Aelfled's warning she was too closely watched to ensure the rebels' safety. She was not surprised, nor that Vitalis was angered. Unlike Jaxon, he thought first of those under his command, whereas the former thought first of vengeance. Were Isa not so ill, surely she would put an end to Jaxon's disregard for the lives of those fighting to regain that stolen from them.

"The one whom Baron D'Argent set to watch over the abbey met an unfortunate end," Vitalis returned her to the present with tidings that stole Aelfled's breath. "Though Sigward was under my orders to—"

"Sigward?" she gasped the name of one she had no liking for, he who was not directly under Vitalis's command.

"Aye, as my scout took ill, Jaxon sent him."

Then Sigward had been in the wood hours ahead of the rebels' arrivals to ensure they remained clear of the enemy.

"I do not believe it was necessary to slay D'Argent's man to quiet him, but the result is in our favor—no warning can he deliver his lord."

Ache lancing her breast, more certain than not the vicious Sigward had killed without cause, Aelfled whispered, "His death will reveal rebels were here."

"Sigward hid his body well. Thus, it will appear the man has gone missing. Who can say it occurred here or upon his return to Stern?"

Cyr D'Argent, Aelfled silently answered.

As the rain fell with slightly more enthusiasm, Vitalis motioned two of his men to enter the secret passage, then said, "Let us pray the silence of a dead man and the Normans having much to occupy them after what we wrought this eve keeps them from the abbey long enough for us to rest ourselves. God willing, we depart on the morrow."

Would God be willing? Aelfled wondered, then forced her thoughts from the murder of Cyr's man to that which made little sense. Since even when she sheltered only five or ten their departures were spaced at least a day apart, she said, "Surely not all will depart on the morrow?"

"If possible. Much depends on the reports of the scouts I send out."

She shook her head, and as two more men hurried past toward the passageway, said, "You underestimate Cyr D'Argent. I think he will come soon, perhaps this night, and he will think me a party to this."

"He might wish to come, but when he receives word of what happened in the north, as he shall shortly has he not already—"

"North?" This time Aelfled interrupted. "You speak of Balduc? Was it not the lord's hay upon Stern referenced in your message?"

"It was, and that was set upon as well." She caught the shadow of his smile. "Though not by us."

"I do not understand."

"If ever there is a time and place for you to understand, it is not now and here." He considered the sky. "The Lord is gracious to only now send rain."

It being too late to reveal the trickery worked on the conquerors, she reflected. By now, the fires had consumed all evidence.

Vitalis looked behind, called low, "Make haste." The men did so, and when they were past, Vitalis returned his attention to her. "The only things with which you must concern yourself are doing your duty and preparing to depart Lillefarne." At her startle, he said, "Your time here is at an end."

Was she to join the rebels? Of course she was. There was no other place for her upon Wulfenshire. Then what would be asked of her?

What I cannot do, she silently answered and sent her thoughts in the direction of Lincolnshire and Nottinghamshire where it was possible she could begin again—providing her grandmother could be persuaded to accompany her. She could not leave Bernia behind. But what of the word given her lady?

"You are to return to Wulfen Castle," Vitalis said. "Once more you shall serve Lady Hawisa."

She gasped. Was she forgiven sufficiently to be restored to her position? Might she once more be fast at her lady's side? Caring for her? Returning her to health?

As much as she longed to believe it, it seemed impossible, especially considering her most recent meeting with her lady. Her reception had been so chill she had not expected her betrayal easily forgiven or excused—if at all.

Perhaps it is not, fear whispered. *Perhaps you were lulled into proving yourself loyal only that you give aid this night. Perhaps the same as Cyr's man in the wood, you shall go missing. Perhaps the silence of a dead woman will be your fate as well.*

"Aelfled?"

Through tears, she saw Vitalis frown.

"Are you not pleased?" he asked. "She believed you would be, as did I."

She swallowed. "Of course I wish to serve my lady as before, but..."

He beckoned forward two more rebels, and when they went behind the hedge, prompted, "What?"

She nearly shrugged off the question, but she wanted an answer of which, hopefully, she might discern the truth. "Is that truly my destination, Vitalis? Or am I no longer of use to my lady?"

His brow grew weightier. "Have you betrayed us again?"

"I have not."

"Then as told, Wulfen Castle is your destination."

She did not believe herself gifted with reading well another's face and body, and it was all the harder to do by the light of the moon forcing its way through the clouds, but had she to decide one way or the other, she would name him sincere.

"Let us get the rest of these men inside and settled," he said.

She nodded, asked what she should have earlier, "Are there injuries?"

"Blessedly, we met little resistance, and those who sought to interfere with our work were quickly subdued."

Then not dead like Sigward's victim. Bound and easily found come morn, albeit arrayed in humiliation.

"Beyond a few minor hurts and strains," Vitalis said, "we have only to deal with a self-inflicted injury."

"Self-inflicted?"

"As ever, Gerald ignored my warning to retreat as soon as the flint yielded flame and this time paid the price for his love of fire.

I do not think his burns serious, but to his end days he shall carry on his person proof of this night we inflicted much damage on our enemies."

Much? It sounded more than the lord's hay upon Stern, but there was no time to discuss it. "There are bandages and salve aplenty to ease his pain," she said.

He inclined his head, and over the next few minutes beckoned forward the remainder of his men. As the last one crept across her garden—nay two, a rebel with a limp bringing up the rear—Vitalis preceded them into the passage.

Hoping the last man's injury was no more than a twisted ankle, Aelfled followed him inside. Though the latch engaged when the door settled in its frame, as ever she lowered the bar into place lest the abbey's hidden entrance was discovered.

Amid darkness that allowed no telltale light to shine from the passage outside or inside the walls, she instructed, "Stand to the left." Though most knew from past experience what was required to negotiate the narrow space, among their ranks could be one or more for whom this was their first time joining those who worked havoc in the night. Too, sometimes the rebels who had shared this passage before were too fatigued or injured to think clearly.

Despite her warning, her shoulder bumped that of the last man who entered and she stepped on his foot.

As he quickly drew back, she whispered, "Forgive me," then set a hand on the right-side wall to guide her forward. "Follow me," she said once she was past all.

Their boots scraping the packed, earthen floor, she led them toward the far end and around the corner into a passage twice as wide where she had amassed all required to sustain them until they could safely return to their encampment—medicinals and bandages, drink, food, blankets, and candles they would light with the same flints used to make fire this night.

Fire that had destroyed another crop. Or so Cyr D'Argent would be made to believe.

HASTILY LAID PLANS make for hastily severed limbs and lives, Hugh's warning returned to Cyr as he and ten of his men surged out of the wood toward the abbey's eastern wall. Unfortunately, there had been no time to lay better plans when, what was on the cusp of being deemed a fruitless wait bore fruit upon the discovery they were no longer alone in the wood. And were nearly outnumbered.

Cyr and Maël's men had held until the rebels determined it was safe to approach Aelfled's garden. Then Cyr and his cousin's plan was set in motion, though not that toward which both first leaned—attack before the rebels entered the abbey's hidden passage.

Lest they scatter amid the wood, yielding up fewer of their numbers whether by escape or death at the hands of their pursuers, it was determined that, even at the risk they claimed sanctuary within Lillefarne, it was better all were trapped inside walls they must leave eventually. But if everything went to plan, they would come out this night.

Praying Dougray's hatred of the Saxons did not unveil one whose appearance made him the best choice to slip unnoticed among the rebels as they moved from wood to garden, Cyr bent low and came out of the wood's shadow into moonlight diluted by clouds that loosed gentle rain.

Praying the long-haired, bearded D'Argent could open the door surely barred from the inside, providing access to Maël and his men who even now surrounded the garden, Cyr glanced left and right at his own men negotiating the open ground.

Praying he could prevent Aelfled from admitting the rebels into the abbey so they could be taken ere claiming sanctuary, once more Cyr searched the walls for a watch that would be required were this a fortress. No movement. No watch.

Praying the missing young man set to observe Aelfled's movements outside the abbey was but remiss in his duty, Cyr slowed as he and his men neared the wall and was grateful they made little sound, all having divested themselves of chain mail. Still no movement above.

God willing, soon the rebels would be had and good use made of them. And Aelfled...

He thrust her from his thoughts. When he was done here, he would make time aplenty to decide what to do with his little rebel.

There being only the barest of shadow in which to conceal themselves at the base of the abbey wall, all moved into it save the one who had assured Cyr he could send the hook-ladened rope over the wall and secure it. Having padded the hook before departing the wood, he stood twenty feet back from the wall, twirled the rope with increasing speed, then sent it soaring high. And over the wall.

Hoping the thud was as barely perceptible to those inside the walls as outside, Cyr watched the man reel in the rope until it tautened and a light scrape sounded.

With a low chuckle of satisfaction, the man strode forward. "It is secure, my lord."

Cyr took the end of the rope. As he tested it, he beseeched the Lord to forgive him for breaching the walls of this holy place, of which even King William might not approve. Thus, another problem with hastily laid plans, but he could conceive of no better time or opportunity to deal a blow capable of bringing the rebels to heel. And if by some small miracle he was able to take them without disturbing the abbey's inhabitants, surely he would be more easily forgiven.

Looking to those on either side of him, Cyr said, "One at a time. Once you are in position on the walls, remain out of sight until you hear my signal." He nearly smiled. "As there are owls about this eve... One hoot, you go back down the rope. Two, you give my cousin the signal to proceed. Three, you descend to the courtyard and aid me."

Receiving nods, Cyr released the rope and positioned himself before it facing the wall. He jumped high and grabbed a length one hand over the other. Engaging the muscles of his arms, he raised his body, drew up his knees, and hooked a foot around the rope. Having fashioned a rung beneath his boot, he pushed upright and gripped the rope higher. So it went until he reached the top where he paused to confirm none were on the wall. Then he swung over and, crouching low, searched for movement amid the buildings below whose layout he knew from his reunion with Aelfled.

All was still.

Those of the abbey slept the sleep of the innocent—all but Aelfled who made much of the night by harboring rebels amid the godly. As there appeared no others present to aid her, that which he hoped for might prove possible. The abbess and her charges unaware of what went in the night, likely Aelfled would confine the rebels to the passage. When it was believed danger was past, they would slip out by way of the garden.

How many times had she performed this service following the destruction they wrought, making it appear they vanished like the smoke of fires they set and for which their own suffered? Often. The abbey being nearly at the center of Stern, Balduc, and Wulfen, the majority of rebels had only to reach the walls of this place whilst their pursuers were led astray by others. For this, Aelfled dwelt here.

"Not much longer," Cyr rasped, then hearing the soft grunts of the man climbing the rope after him, went in search of her.

As it seemed the best way to locate the passage's inner door was from atop the wall, he bent low and, rain flecking him, moved in the direction of the garden. At the joint between eastern and rear wall, just past steps that accessed all below, he stopped and searched beyond the roofs of buildings and bare stretches of wall. All remained still.

In the space between Cyr leaving the wood and ascending the wall, had Aelfled exited the passage this side of the wall? Worse, had the rebels? Of such great numbers were the latter, it did not seem possible.

Show yourself, he silently prodded the infuriating woman. *Show me where to find the door.*

As if she heard and was of a mind to obey, a gowned figure emerged from a small shed built against the eastern wall almost directly below him. She eased the door closed, and he smiled at the realization rebels were beneath his feet in this section of wall twice as wide as the rest to accommodate steps built into it and of greater length than necessary other than to disguise its hidden purpose.

If it fell to him to set Stern in stone—as seemed more possible the nearer he drew to recovering Guarin—he would see the same incorporated into his castle.

He straightened enough to be visible to his men on the walls, raised a staying hand, then from his vantage watched Aelfled's progress toward what he guessed was the convent. Once certain she was distant enough she would not hear his descent nor see him if she looked behind, he moved down the steps.

Shortly, he entered the shed. Leaving the door open to allow moonlight to turn the black gray, he considered barrels stacked two high on both sides of a narrow aisle. Knowing what he would find behind them, he took two strides to the stone wall. The barrels touched it on the right. As solid and immovable as they were, their purpose was not purely concealment.

Not so those on the left where there was space enough for one the size of Aelfled to slip through sideways. Too, the barrels were easily shifted to accommodate Cyr's greater bulk, allowing him to enter a relatively wide, empty space. It being nearly pitch black here, he had to feel for the door and found it in the far corner—low, fashioned of iron, a bar laid across it.

Though much Aelfled risked in harboring rebels, of which Cyr could not believe Abbess Mary Sarah would approve no matter her loyalty to Saxons, she was not remiss in protecting those of the abbey. Providing Dougray had been able to unbar the other door, the rebels could be taken without overly disturbing the residents and, quite possibly, none the wiser their inner walls were breached.

Cyr exited the shed and quietly closed the door. Though he meant to ascend the steps to give the signal and join his men and Maël's in bringing out the rebels, there was movement where there should not be. Aelfled had returned.

CHAPTER TWENTY-FOUR

a man where there should be none. And no mere mortal this. A warrior.

It mattered not whether it was the one she knew, though in this moment she feared him more than any. On no night was it permissible for a man to be inside Lillefarne. And what it portended this eve…

The ice pouring into Aelfled that so abruptly halted her advance her hood fell to her shoulders, melted. As the surprised warrior also came to life and lunged at her, she whirled away.

Her skirts were her undoing, flaring out behind her and into the grasp of her pursuer. He yanked so hard she would have landed on hands and knees if not for the arm that slammed around her waist and wrenched her back against a chest so firm she lost her breath. She drew another, but before she could cry out, a hand clapped over her mouth.

Then words warmed her ear. "Swallow your scream, Aelfled."

With so many lives depending on her, there was no relief in knowing it was Cyr who had her. Better one who sought to ravish a Saxon woman.

"Swallow!"

There being little she could do against one far stronger, she released the breath through her nose, jerked her chin.

"I know you to be a liar," he said, "but if you agree in the sight of God you will not scream—more for their sake than yours—I shall chance removing my hand."

Their sake? How she hoped it was those of the abbey to whom he referred, not the rebels—that he was unaware they were near.

"You have but to nod again."

She did so and gasped when he spun her to face him, lifted her off her feet, and pinned her against the shed's wall with the length of his body.

"Once more, you and I meet in the dark of earliest morn," he forced upon her memories of Senlac as she peered into what could be seen of his face in the shed's shadow. "And once more, I search for one of my own."

His uncle who had died at the hands of Wulf and his friends, his eldest brother who might also have spilled his life upon that meadow. And now...

"Where is my man, Aelfled?"

She felt the rip in her heart begun by Vitalis's revelation lengthen.

"Tell what happened to the one I gave watch over you!"

She longed to feign ignorance, but it would be useless and prove her more a liar. She lowered her chin.

He lifted it. "If he is dead..."

No more did he make of his threat. No more was needed.

"What do you here?" she whispered, "How did you get in?"

She felt his impatience amid anger, heard it in his voice when he said, "Not the way of your rebels."

She had thought herself prepared, it surely too much to hope he had not seen those who stole into Lillefarne, but tears stung her eyes. She had failed. Again. More than having the happiness of once more serving her lady stolen from her, that rendered impossible even were she able to reach Isa, she was pained by the fate of those she had not kept safe.

Cyr had not come alone. Doubtless, his men were in her garden and would this moment be in the passage slaughtering the rebels had she not barred the outer door. And that he was here, outside the shed, meant he had seen her exit that place concealing the inner door.

Had he gone inside? Discovered it?

"Why did you so soon return?" he asked, and when she gave no answer, said, "The barrels. You forgot to push them back against the wall."

Straining throat muscles to keep from sobbing, she held his glittering gaze.

"This night, your rebels belong to me, Aelfled. I thank you for securing the door so they cannot enter here and claim sanctuary."

Surely there was hope for them, she told herself. Unless he meant to further violate God's house by bringing soldiers inside, unbarring the door, and attacking those in the passage, the rebels could be let into the abbey later. For a time they would be trapped here, but eventually the watch would ease sufficiently to allow some if not all to escape. Of course, much was dependent on how well the garden's barred iron door held against the Normans' efforts to breach it. And they would try, but if it resisted long enough to get her people inside...

She startled when Cyr turned his head over his shoulder and hooted the same as the rebels had done to send a message to their own—twice.

What did it mean? "Cyr?" she whispered and winced at the fear in her voice.

"Rebel though you are," he murmured, "I like that you call me Cyr."

Had she?

"Baron D'Argent—"

"What is said is said, little Saxon. Now listen."

She stopped breathing, and as she strained to hear some thing in the night she was to fear whilst he savored it, she became more aware of his muscular body against her soft curves. And remembered his kiss.

"Pray, release me," she beseeched.

"So you may seek to unbar the door and deny me my due? Non, I am most comfortable. And very interested in your reaction to the message now being sent by my men upon these walls to the king's men in the garden.

Lord in Your heavens, she silently prayed, *let the door hold. Have mercy on the Saxons. This night, turn Your face back to those You forsook.*

What seemed minutes passed, and only when sounds muffled by stone reached her did she realize she had closed her eyes and dropped her head forward. She raised her chin, and feeling the loss of warmth against her brow, was ashamed she was so weak she had set it against the base of Cyr's throat.

"There," he said. "My cousin and his men are inside, and those who do not resist will live to answer for their crimes."

"So soon?" she breathed. "How?"

"The last *Saxon* who entered the passage ahead of you, feigning a limp so you not question why he lagged, was my brother. And it seems Dougray had no difficulty unbarring the outer door."

The man she had bumped into in the dark, who had not responded to an apology not due him. Either unlike Cyr he did not know the language of the Saxons, or he had feared his accent would reveal him.

If not for the sound of pounding on the iron door in the shed, she might have cried. Vitalis and his men were desperate to escape the trap laid them, and there being nothing she could do caused anger to sweep aside sorrow.

"Norman pig!" She began struggling in the hope of freeing herself and unbarring the door to let the rebels in.

"Cease!" Cyr barked when she tried to bring a knee up between his legs. "It will be over soon."

She did not heed him, and surely only because he was averse to hurting her was she able to loosen an arm and rake nails down his jaw and neck.

"I said cease!" He caught up her wrists and pinned them to the shed wall alongside her head.

Panting in his face near hers, hoping her breath foul, she felt her stomach wrench, then bile blaze up her throat.

She did not know how Cyr knew she was about to empty her stomach, but he sprang back and yanked her down to rain-dampened ground. Then he was alongside her where she hunched over hands and knees, sweeping back her hair as she retched.

When her stomach would give no more, she hung her head between her arms. "Why did they not heed my warning to stay away? This would not have happened. You…" She turned her whimper into a sound of disgust, shifted to the side and pushed back onto her heels. As Cyr released her hair and it tumbled around her face, she said, "There is my reaction. Does it please you? Make you feel superior? More the conqueror?"

He did not respond, and she forced herself to attend to sounds beyond the patter of rain.

The pounding on the inner door having ceased, from the other side of the wall where her garden lay, she heard chain mail, voices raised in anger and defiance, whilst others issued commands. Had what transpired not already roused Lillefarne's residents, it would now.

She raised her gaze to where Cyr was on his haunches before her, now out of the shed's shadow saw the lines she had scored into his flesh and wondered who had bruised one side of his nose down to his lip. Telling herself she did not care, she returned her thoughts to those for whom she did care.

"I failed them," she said more to herself than he who did not need to be told. "Now they shall think I betrayed. Again."

After a long moment, he turned his head and gave a single hoot.

This time she did not wonder at its meaning. He had won mightily, whether one rebel yet breathed or a score.

"I am done here, Aelfled," he said, "as are you."

It was true. There was nothing left for her here, just as there was nothing for her at Wulfen Castle.

He stood, reached to her. "Come."

She frowned. "Where?"

"I know not what I am to do with you, but for aiding the rebels you are as much my captive as they."

There seemed no benefit in resisting him beyond the satisfaction of doing so. But she recalled Isa's words.

Remember and embrace who you are. A Saxon strong of mind, body, and spirit.

She did not dance to Cyr D'Argent's song, would not go meekly. If he truly wanted her, he would have to expend more effort than commanding her to follow.

Neck aching over how far she tilted back her head to hold his gaze, she said, "You have no hold over me whilst I am within these walls and have the right to claim sanctuary."

She caught the flare of his nostrils, heard his deep breath. "As you say, they will blame you for this night, Aelfled. You are not safe here."

She laughed. "Safer here than with Normans I count as my enemy and who count me as theirs. Safer here than where you shall decide the fate of those whom I do not count as my enemy though you have made them count me as theirs. Non, I remain."

He took a step toward her, but just as she accepted she would have to fight him to resist being taken over the wall, he stilled. "As you will, but be it the morrow or a month hence, I shall bring you out so you can aid my enemies no longer."

"I assure you, I shall not be trusted to aid them again. Leave me and think no more on this Saxon rendered harmless."

"Not possible. My word I give, I will come for you."

Even if she claimed sanctuary he would breach the walls again, force her out?

As he started to move toward steps that would deliver him to the wall walk, she tossed at his back, "You will discover I have donned the habit of a Bride of Christ." They were mostly words since she doubted the abbess would allow her to make her profession. And Mary Sarah would be right not to do so, but if the threat kept Cyr from coming again…

It did not portend well that he returned to her though he had been set to leave. And as seemed ever her burden, she wished she had thought through her words.

He dropped down, and despite how little light there was, she could see every line of anger in his moisture-flecked face. And the swelling red lines she had scratched into it. "Truly, you have so little regard for the Lord you would make mockery of vows so you not be made to answer for working ill on your Norman lord *and* your people?"

Once more, she was bereft of breath.

"Non, Aelfled of Senlac. No matter how godless you have become, *that* I will not believe of you."

"You do not know me!" she spewed again and wished him away so she could recover enough of her wits to bind her tongue.

"I know not all of you, but as told, I am certain you were not meant to be a nun."

Do not say it, she silently begged, then said it. "As also told, I was meant to be here with you? Like this? On my knees, emptying my belly whilst those I was to protect begin numbering their days rather than years?"

"Not here, not like this." He thrust to his feet and once more offered a hand. "Do not prolong this, Aelfled. Come with me."

"Non."

He lowered his arm. "Then I shall collect you in a manner you will like even less." He turned and strode to the steps.

"What manner?" she called.

He ascended the steps two at a time and did not look back, nor down upon her as he traversed the wall walk overhead.

When he went from sight, doubtless to lower himself over the wall he had scaled, she would have bent over herself again did she not become aware of women's voices and, moments later, that of the abbess.

Aelfled would have to answer for this night, and even had there been the narrowest possibility she would be allowed to take holy vows, her use of the abbey to aid the rebels would put finish to it.

Determining she would slip from the abbey and persuade her grandmother to leave the village of Ravven, she whispered, "Lincolnshire or Nottinghamshire." And pushed upright.

"Aelfled?"

She swung around.

The abbess halted, from beneath her hood searched her charge's moonlit face, then looked around. She paused over the shed, the steps, the wall walk, then heaved a sigh. "It seems you have been caught out, Aelfled. And of greater, more serious consequence, our rebels as well."

CHAPTER TWENTY-FIVE

Barony of Balduc
England

*T*wo diversions as feared. But since the damage was done, the fire likely extinguished more by rain than the villagers' efforts, and the perpetrators apprehended at Lillefarne, Cyr had not immediately set out following his return to Stern where he learned the villagers' hay in the northernmost village of Balduc had been burned.

Those tidings delivered by the guard set to watch over that village, three of whom had been bound and humiliated in the same manner done those who delivered the arrow to the baron come unto his lands, Cyr had cursed rebels so bent on revenge they cared not if their own suffered—and been tempted to once more prove merciless.

Lest he yield, just as he had given charge of Merle and his mercenaries to Theriot, he had given charge of the score of rebels marched to Stern in the rain. Then at Fulbert's insistence, Cyr and the priest had gone to the chapel and talked and prayed.

Afterward, he had slept little, mind fevered with what had been done on the night past and must be done on the day to come. He would do penance for trespassing on the abbey, though King William would approve of the result, but mostly he was troubled by his encounter with Aelfled.

He knew how to bring her out. Having conceived the idea before leaving her, this morn he had sent Maël and his men to do his bidding. However, more than to ensure she not further aid the rebels, he feared what was perceived as betrayal would see her as dead as the one set to watch her whose body had yet to be found. Too, Cyr could not put from him that he had taunted her over what Maël and his men did in her garden.

Fear had shone from her, as much if not more than at Senlac, and for a moment he thought she lost consciousness when she dropped her brow to his throat. Determining he would not further taunt her, he had only interpreted for her the muffled sounds coming from the inner passage as being capture of her rebels. And been nearly unmanned for it.

How he had known when that mix of anger and fear made her belly turn on her, he could not say. It had been a feeling one surely ought to have only for another known long and well. Such a cur he had felt for causing so violent a response—worse that all he could do was hold back hair whose silken strands his fingers remembered even now whilst grasping reins.

Knowing he deserved her anger, he should not have risen to it again, but when she refused to leave the abbey and threatened to take the veil, sentencing herself to remain ever separate from the world of men—his world—he had given back.

"Fool that I am," he muttered. Once more pushing Aelfled from his thoughts, he returned to the humid air rushing past as he and his men neared the fields over which a mist not of morn but of dampened smoke eddied. The destruction was as vast as told— crop after crop of hay lost to those who needed it to feed animals that would provide meat and milk to sustain men, women, and children through winter.

As he slowed, Dougray came alongside, and Cyr glimpsed in his brother's eyes a glimmer not born of resentment... anger...vengeance...

Having dealt the rebels a terrible blow last eve in gaining so many captives and without loss of life on either side—a surprise with Dougray in their midst and considering how easy one rebel had made it for him to assume his place—something had been wrought in the third-born who played no small role in the victory. The warrior was showing through the layers in which he had wrapped himself nigh on two years past.

Dougray frowned. "For what do you smile?"

Cyr drew rein, and when his brother and the men behind followed suit, said, "I am thinking how glad I am you refused to cut your hair and beard. And wondering how next to use my Norman in Saxon's disguise to protect this demesne."

Dougray grunted. "I am sure you will think of something. Until then, it is on the training field I ought to be, not inspecting the crops of heathens destroyed by fellow heathens."

Cyr would have left him at Stern if not for his brother's almost deadly altercation in Aelfled's garden with Vitalis, whom Cyr was certain had led the rebels to Lillefarne.

The Saxons had resisted when the Normans entered the passage and been so ferocious that, if not for the hopelessness of being trapped like mice and Vitalis commanding all to stand down, there would have been dire casualties on both sides. Men of the soil the rebels may have been before the conquest, but exceptional training had transformed them into men of the blade. Though divested of their arms, every precaution had been taken to ensure they did not stir to life outside the passage. But Vitalis had stirred—and mightily—when something was spoken between Dougray and him and the two men had to be pulled off each other.

Whilst preparing to depart the castle this morn, Cyr had happened on his brother and seen animosity in his gaze as it prowled amongst the rebels. Upon noticing Cyr, Dougray had cleared his eyes and face and advised Stern's outer and inner walls be fit with cells in which to imprison those who acted against D'Argent rule. A better means of separating foes and sheltering prisoners from foul weather such as that which had turned dirt to mud in the earliest hours of morn, he had said, then grumbled England seemed more susceptible to the wet and chill than Normandy.

Cyr was not fooled. Knowing Theriot and the men-at-arms had enough to deal with between the two paddocks in the outer bailey—the western one holding Saxons, the eastern Merle and his men, he had commanded his brother into the saddle.

Now as Cyr dismounted, he said, "I agree you require much time on the training field, but you shall have hours in which to practice this afternoon. Dismount."

"Surely you do not intend to draw nearer?"

"I do."

"The crops are gone. What else must be told?"

Likely, he was right, but once more Cyr was disturbed by the reaction of bedraggled villagers, in this instance those whose faces were marked with the soot of fighting fire. Since the loss of hay could mean the difference between surviving the winter and not were the new Lord of Balduc the same as its former lord, Cyr had assured them their animals would not go hungry. He spoke in truth, though it meant he would be unable to sell his own excess hay to increase his revenues and would have to purchase more beyond that.

The expressions of some had reflected surprise and disbelief, but most prevalent was disregard where there should have been despair at worst, relief at best. Regardless of his promise, the loss of crops should not lack for lament—and anger.

Where was disillusionment with rebels who worked ill on

their own? It was as though the fire was of little consequence, and Cyr did not think faith in the Lord cast away their concern. It was something less, and he intended to discover the answer. And be as satisfied with it as with the sense made of that other ponderable—that the villages on Balduc and, less so, on Stern boasted few men of good age, whereas young women were plentiful and many had babes on hips or in slings.

Cyr suspected some of the children were fathered by Normans, Campagnon and his men having seduced the conquered women or forced their attentions on them, but he guessed most were sired by rebels who occasionally stole home to their women.

Returning Dougray to focus, he said, "Join me."

His brother sighed and dismounted.

The two strode across muddied ground to the nearest field. "Here the rebels were last eve whilst our attention was diverted by Merle's failed attack on Stern and the rebels' half-hearted attack on Balduc." Cyr peered across the hazy field. "Do you see anything I do not?"

"Only if you do not see a burned field. But what I do see that I worry you do not is how dangerous these Saxons are—so much that never can you give them your back."

Reminding himself of time recently spent with Fulbert, Cyr narrowed eyes stung by smoke. "Though it might seem safer to believe that true of all Saxons, I believe it will prove more dangerous in the end, preventing us from finding a place of peace in which our two peoples can exist together."

Dougray gave a huff of disgust. "Thanks to that priest, you wear the blinders of your god."

Cyr's jaw tightened. "He is also your God."

"Is he?"

The question returned Aelfled to mind, she who seemed nearly as bereft of faith. And therein a response for his brother. "I am surprised you do not feel a kinship with the Saxons who must feel as abandoned by God as do you."

Dougray's eyes and face brightened, but though Cyr steeled for an eruption, his brother shifted his regard to the field. Perhaps his interest began as pretense, but his brow became weighted, then he turned aside and began traversing the burned field's border.

Cyr followed to its end where Dougray considered the field again and said, "Do you not think it peculiar the perimeter is more heavily laid with ash?"

Cyr looked nearer on the blackened field. And saw what his brother saw. "I am thinking I ought to climb a tree."

Shortly, perched thirty feet above the ground, he surveyed what was put to flame well before the rain. With the exception of a ten-foot expanse at the rear of each field, the perimeter was darker and thicker with ash than all within.

"You see it?" Dougray called.

"Oui, and a passage at the rear of each field and the remnants of tracks as of ladened carts." Cyr descended and jumped the last feet to the ground. "Though the rain washed away much evidence, for certain the tracks lead from field to wood."

Dougray grinned.

Cyr slapped his brother on the back. "It appears the rebels are not as destructive nor uncaring toward their own as believed. Only after harvesting and carting away the bulk of crops under cover of hedges do they set the fields afire. And I wager, it is the same they have done since the beginning."

"Then the villagers are not in terrible straits as they would have their Norman lord believe."

"They are not. And here further proof the mortality of their men is not as high as it appears. Doubtless, most joined the rebels who bring in the crops that feed them and the families they leave behind."

"Plaguing the Normans without harming their own," Dougray

mused. "When Campagnon's crops were supposedly burned and he retaliated by taking those of the villagers, it substantiated the death of men who sacrificed themselves to ensure their families ate. And all the while, the Saxons were ensured a continuous supply of food."

Cyr nodded. "For this, the villagers show less concern for losses than warranted over a matter of life and death. Whether or not it is the lord's crops taken or their own, they are provided for."

"Clever, but how is it possible to store and disperse so much hay and grain without being caught?"

"I have an idea, but first we follow the tracks. Though likely most have been washed away, that is the place to start."

Dougray showed teeth in so nearly a genuine smile Cyr was struck by how handsome his brother was despite how little care he took with his appearance. "Dougray."

The younger man raised his eyebrows.

"If not for your sake, then the sake of the woman you one day wed, do something about your teeth ere they rot out of your head."

They disappeared behind his lips, though not from shame, Cyr guessed, but over mention of marriage. He had nearly caught back those words, but no matter how they offended, he had determined that just as Dougray must learn again proficiency with weapons, he must learn how to control his emotions.

"And wash your body," Cyr added. "It is most foul and not due to this day's mud."

"Like my hair and beard," Dougray finally spoke, "it serves well this Norman in Saxon's disguise."

"You err. Not even the foulest of those I worked alongside in bringing in the hay boasted the strength of your scent. Scrub your teeth and body ere you take up arms again else I shall enlist Maël and Theriot to do it for you." Cyr turned and strode toward their mounts and his men.

Following three hours that, time and again, ended in wide streams and marshy ground, only two things were known for certain. The carts had gone separate ways and all moved in the direction of Lincolnshire or Nottinghamshire. What was not known but seemed the best explanation was the bounty was sold on other baronies, coin being easier for rebels to transport and disperse to villagers who could then buy hay and grain as needed.

Clever, indeed.

CHAPTER TWENTY-SIX

Lillefarne Abbey
England

*B*lood.

Unable to gaze long upon her trampled garden where Vitalis and his men had been fettered as rain fell harder, only now with chin lowered did she notice streaks on bodice, skirt, and rimming the hem.

She had expected to find blood in the passage. Though not as much as feared, it had been on the stone walls and darkened the floor. For hours she had cleaned away evidence of the night past, unaware she would wear those near-frenzied efforts—and her failing—upon her person.

Following the pounding on the door to which she had been unable to respond, many were injured. Had any died? She had to believe not as no bodies were left behind, but that did not mean none had died since.

Pressing her back more firmly against the wall she had crouched against on the night past while awaiting the rebels, Aelfled closed her eyes, breathed deep, then lifted her head and forced herself to look upon her garden for the last time. It was mostly destroyed, but once she was gone others could set it aright.

"Lincolnshire or Nottinghamshire?" she repeated as done often while cleaning the passage.

Though it mattered not to her, she guessed her grandmother would choose Lincolnshire where dwelt her youngest daughter, rather than Nottinghamshire where Bernia's brother lived. All that mattered was they leave Wulfenshire—and all the sooner for what she found concealed beneath the blankets in the passage.

She had not been certain until she looked at in daylight, but now she was convinced of its kinship with the one beneath her cot. She lifted it from her side, tilted it to coax the sun's rays into the gem set in it. It was not identical to the dagger taken from Wulf's convulsing fingers, but nearly so. And just as the letters H D A were scratched into the steel of the one that had likely slain its owner, here was inscribed G D A.

It was surely Vitalis who had removed the dagger from his belt and hidden it before he could be made a prisoner of the brother to whom this belonged. The question was whether Guarin D'Argent yet lived. And was he upon Wulfenshire?

She longed for the answer, unable to content herself with the answer made of this dagger's presence and her lady's recognition of the name D'Argent at Senlac. The same as Aelfled, Isa had encountered one of that family whilst searching for Wulf.

Had the eldest brother been less honorable than Cyr? Had he harmed—perhaps violated—one of the few Saxon women who dared search for her dead before being granted permission? Was he dead for it, his dagger given to Vitalis who had known the danger of it being found in his possession?

The sound of footsteps made Aelfled tense for flight, but though she had space aplenty to return to the passage and bar the door if any entered the garden, the one moving toward her did so from inside the passage.

It was the abbess who stepped out from behind the hedge. "I

thought to find you here." Her eyes fell upon the dagger, and she lost what little smile she had. "What is this?"

Wishing she had lowered it out of sight, Aelfled stammered, "I f-found it in the passage."

The unusually attractive woman halted before her, extended a hand into which Aelfled set the hilt. She pointed its tip heavenward, turned the blade side to side, drew it close to her face. "G D A." She looked past the dagger. "You think it of a D'Argent—the missing one? What is his name?"

"Guarin. And I do think it, Abbess."

She inclined her head. "Much it resembles the one I saw on Cyr D'Argent's belt when he sought an audience with you. How do you think it came to be in the passage?"

Unwilling to name Vitalis, Aelfled said, "It had to have been in the possession of a rebel."

She raised her eyebrows. "So is it proof Guarin D'Argent lives or is dead? Or proof of naught?"

"Who can say? But as its blade was clean, methinks whoever left it behind did so knowing they would fair ill were it found upon them."

The woman returned her gaze to the dagger. "It is of some worth beyond its value in giving greater hope to the D'Argents their lost brother lives."

"What shall we do with it?"

"I will lock it away so the family does not increase its efforts to find him since it would bode ill for those of Wulfenshire."

Aelfled nearly protested, but it was true. Were the D'Argents provided further proof beyond the sighting, their search for Guarin could turn aggressive.

"I saw you cleaned the passage," the abbess said. "I thank you. It was unsightly."

Aelfled had not known she had gone into it after Cyr and his men departed with their prisoners, but of course she would wish to confirm the defenses were once more secure.

244

"You are done here," the woman said. "Join me in my apartment for the nooning meal."

She wished to speak with her in private? Of what? Leaving Lillefarne as Aelfled had already determined to do? Likely, since she had greatly endangered the residents. That reminded Aelfled of what she had wished to ask when found outside the shed.

"Abbess, last eve you called the rebels *ours* as if—"

"As if they are my people? Rebels or nay, they are, Aelfled. I may be wed to the Church, but I am a Saxon the same as you and want the Normans gone from our lands. Though I cannot approve of all the rebels do, I understand their reasons. And pray they succeed."

Aelfled nodded. "Of course, but did you know…?"

"What?"

"I have harbored them?"

A soft laugh. "I know not why the Lord gifted me with keen intelligence and an education rarely provided women even of the noble class, but those who stand against me would fare well not to mistake me for being of the ignorant class."

It was not a direct answer, but answer enough. "I hope you do not think I stood against you, Abbess. I but fulfilled a duty given to atone for…"

"Wulf," she said.

Then she knew Isa was no stranger to the rebel cause? Though Aelfled wanted to ask, she kept her tongue. But if the abbess thought to press *her* for more information, that dread was replaced by the dread of approaching riders.

"Visitors," Mary Sarah said. "Normans, I guess. Come." She slid the dagger beneath her girdle, slipped behind the hedge, and it was she who barred the door before leading Aelfled through the passage.

The abbey was more astir than it would be if not for the night past, Aelfled noted as she exited the shed and started toward the dormitory.

"Nay, follow me," the abbess said, lifting her skirts and ascending the steps to the wall walk.

My due, Aelfled told herself. Were it Normans come unto these walls, likely it was a result of her failure to keep the rebels safe.

At the front of the abbey, above the great doors, the abbess motioned Aelfled to stand back, then crossed to the wall and peered down.

"Abbess!" a man called in heavily-accented English.

Not Cyr. Were he of the D'Argents, whom had he sent in his stead?

The abbess caught her breath, took a step backward.

Someone known to her, Aelfled guessed. And, it seemed, someone feared. Not for the first time, she pondered the same as many at Lillefarne how the relatively young woman had come into so esteemed a position when the old abbess passed shortly after the Norman invasion.

"Abbess!" he bellowed again.

Returned to what was of greater import, Aelfled wondered if the one who came was sent by the usurper to punish the abbey for hiding rebels. Possible only were he near.

"Is it William?" Aelfled whispered.

The abbess looked around. "Nay, one of his men who—"

"Abbess!"

She sucked breath, pressed her shoulders back, and stepped forward. Though her eyes were surely on the man below, her chin remained level as if to intentionally look down her nose at him.

"It is the abbess you address," she called. "For what do you come to God's house?"

"I am to bring out Aelfled, daughter of Soren."

Aelfled clenched her hands.

"By whose authority?"

"Baron D'Argent's."

"Ah, he who trespassed on holy ground last eve."

"That he might take what was due him without shedding blood inside your walls, Abbess."

Her head tilted. "Were you to tell me it was on the authority of a bishop—even a Norman one—I might tremble a little. But see, I tremble not. Only by my say shall Baron D'Argent enter these walls to take from them."

"Unless the one he wishes comes willingly," the man responded.

"I believe I can speak for Aelfled Sorendotter in saying she will not."

"And I believe she will after she is delivered this missive."

"Its tidings?"

"It is for her eyes, not yours nor mine."

After a long moment, she said, "Approach and pass it through the door's grate. I will see it delivered. If she chooses to respond, you shall have her answer forthwith."

"I know her answer. Were she with you upon the wall, the missive would not be necessary."

Aelfled's heart beat faster. Of what did he speak?

"Pass it through," the abbess repeated, then turned and stepped past Aelfled. "Open the grate," she called down.

It was done, and soon a young nun ascended the steps. Out of sight of those beyond the walls, she passed the missive to the abbess.

As Aelfled accepted the missive from the latter, she noted Mary Sarah did tremble and looked up. "Of what are you afeared, Abbess? That they will—"

"Naught," she said sharply. "Read it."

She untied the string, unrolled the parchment.

Aelfled Sorendotter, it said, *I have been merciful. For naught. Thus, if you wish to see your grandmother again, come to me. ~ Cyr D'Argent, Baron of Wulfen and Balduc*

Now it was she trembling so much the parchment rattled.

"It could be a lie," Abbess Mary Sarah said after reading it.

"Nay. He knows who she is and where she is. And this is surely what he warned of last eve when I refused to leave with him. He has her." But would he turn merciless again? She could not believe he would harm an innocent old woman, but...

He also had Aelfled who would not leave Wulfenshire without Bernia.

"Aelfled Sorendotter!" the man called. "Do you require proof, show yourself."

Stiffly, she stepped forward and wished there were comfort in being accompanied by the abbess.

The warrior on his great destrier below with a half dozen soldiers at his back, smiled. "I thought you there."

Though the turn of his lips was mocking, it was a handsome smile in what had surely been an exceedingly attractive face before a blade disfigured one side of it. As she moved her gaze over what was visible beyond the mail coif covering his head, she wondered if it had happened at Senlac, then said, "Your proof?"

He looked over his shoulder, raised an arm, returned his gaze to her. "The day is too hot for one of aged bones. Watch the wood."

Two riders came out of the trees, seated before one a slight figure with a head crowned by silver hair. It was too distant to see her features, but it was Bernia.

"Proof enough?" he asked.

She jerked her chin.

"Good. Collect your belongings quickly so we may reach Stern Castle well before the supper hour—all your belongings. You will not return here." His eyes shifted to the abbess. "As told, she is willing."

Feeling the woman's anger, Aelfled looked to her. Nose no longer set on high, Mary Sarah glared at the man.

"Have we met, Abbess?" he asked.

She swung aside, traversed the walk, and led the way to the

dormitory. At the steps, she turned to Aelfled. "I am sorry I cannot aid you."

"Cyr D'Argent has my grandmother, and though I do not believe he will harm her, I must go to her."

"I shall send word to Lady Hawisa of what has transpired."

Would she believe Aelfled innocent of further betrayal? Did it matter? "I thank you."

As Aelfled stepped past her, the abbess said, "Speak not of the dagger found in the passage."

Aelfled inclined her head and, ignoring the curious looks cast upon her by nuns and those of the convent, entered the dormitory.

It did not take long to gather her possessions, so few were they. The delay was in determining what to do with what she had long hidden beneath her cot—another D'Argent dagger and Cyr's missive to Campagnon intercepted by Isa.

She shifted the brazier coals, pushed the missive to the bottom, and covered it over. The next time the brazier was lit to warm the cell, all evidence of Isa's visit to Lillefarne would be destroyed.

Aelfled bundled the dagger and placed it at the bottom of her pack. Cyr knew she had harbored rebels, so he could hardly think worse of her that she possessed what had belonged to his uncle. Since Hugh D'Argent's wife was at Stern, Aelfled would give it to her as soon as she found an opportunity to do so in the absence of her son. Though she thought it possible the lady would find solace in its return, she did not believe a warrior as sentimental. More likely, it would anger him.

Only when Aelfled donned her mantle did she realize she yet wore her blood-stained gown. She yearned to change into her second gown, but she had kept Cyr's man waiting long enough.

She departed the dormitory and saw the abbess awaited her alongside the smaller door set in a larger one. The woman surprised Aelfled with a quick embrace and whispered in her ear, "You are Saxon. Never forget it. Ever embrace it."

As Aelfled recovered breath over words strikingly similar to Isa's, the abbess drew back and unbarred the door. "God be with you, Child."

Aelfled ducked beneath the low lintel and stepped out onto moist ground. As she lifted her eyes to the man who awaited her, the door closed and bar dropped.

"I began to think you had no care for your grandmother," he said, then to the chevalier beside him, "Take her up before you."

The man dismounted and motioned her forward, but when he set hands on Aelfled's waist to lift her atop his destrier, the one who commanded him said, "Inspect her pack."

The dagger. Would he think it a weapon she meant to turn on one of his own? Panic rising, she reminded herself he acted for Cyr. He would not like what he found, but he would do no more than take it from her.

The chevalier loosed her, stepped back, and in his language said, "Give it to me, Lady."

He thought her a lady. She would not correct him, certain soon Cyr would do so. Until then, perhaps he would treat her with some respect.

As she passed the pack to him, she caught the deceptively pretty ring of a great number of chain mail links. Ignoring it, she let her mind travel down the road she had not fully ventured upon.

She was as much a prisoner as those taken on the night past. Would she be held with the rebels, some of whom—if not all— would believe she had betrayed again?

Nay, no matter the anger of the man now given proof she aided his enemies, no matter he believed he had been merciful for naught, she did not think he would do that. As for her grandmother, neither would he harm her even had Aelfled refused to leave the abbey. And he had known she would not refuse, that he had only to take Bernia from Ravven to bend her to his will.

The chevalier gave a grunt of satisfaction, stepped to his commander, and handed up the bundle from which the dagger's hilt projected. "She is armed. And well."

Seeing the hand reaching for it falter, Aelfled looked higher. And shuddered.

The one sent by Cyr had lowered his coif. Though his short hair was surely all the more dark for the perspiration shaping it to his head, amid the black were silver strands that had no right to sprout in such abundance from the head of one so young.

Another D'Argent. And the eyes he slammed to hers revealed which one.

CHAPTER TWENTY-SEVEN

Stern Castle
England

I have her," Cyr murmured, and knew it was not the first time he boasted of that to the man at his side, the first instance after the old woman who this day served as bait revealed where he would find her granddaughter.

With what sounded a smile, Fulbert said, "Else she has you."

Cyr looked from the riders approaching the drawbridge to the priest.

The man shrugged. "You sound more pleased this time. And I thought you rather pleased then."

"She aided the rebels—is the reason time and again they slipped free of Theriot and Campagnon. This ensures she can be of no further use to their cause."

Fulbert chuckled. "Non, last eve ensured that. As well you know, this is protection."

He did know, having first discussed it with Fulbert. Turning defensive only made him sound a youth.

"And methinks it something else more bothersome," Fulbert added.

Cyr returned his gaze to Aelfled whose hood would soon cover her head. Even at a distance she was lovely beyond the blond tresses his fingers refused to forget. "Oui," he admitted, having asked for prayer to aid in overcoming what he named lust though Fulbert submitted it was more serious—albeit more pure.

Cyr turned from the land before the castle to the wooden railing overlooking the outer bailey and considered the paddock holding Merle and his men and the one opposite. The hands of the rebels were bound behind their backs where they sat against the wall, excepting those of four who hunkered over bowls and cups. Once hunger and thirst were satisfied, they would be bound again and another four loosed, among them Vitalis to whom Cyr intended to grant an audience.

"You have determined how best to make use of them?" Fulbert asked.

"If my cousin does not soon return to William's service, I shall have my own men deliver Merle and his fellow mercenaries to the king to decide their fate. As for the rebels, regardless of whether they can be made to reveal their own to sooner end the rebellion, my greatest use of them is recovering Guarin, alive or dead. And lest William does not agree with me, it must be done quickly."

"Then in addition to praying for an easing of lust, we must pray the king is in a forgiving mood should he not agree."

Cyr smiled wryly and returned to the wall.

He frowned. Maël and his party were near enough for him to act on the instructions given him. Why had he not? Surely he had not forgotten?

As his cousin neared the drawbridge, Cyr noted how dark his face, hard his jaw, unmoving his gaze. Such depth of anger he had last seen on Maël's face the day before the great battle. Just as Cyr had never learned its cause, he did not know it now.

"D'Argent!" he bellowed.

Even had the coif now made a collar covered Maël's head, he would have heard, but he did not respond.

Cyr moved his gaze over the men just behind and on either side of his cousin. Their eyes were on him—as were those of the women who shared their saddles. Though one stared sightlessly at Cyr upon the wall, the younger woman saw him well as evidenced by a defiant expression surely masking fear.

But if Maël did not do as told, that mask would slip. And in this instance, Cyr wished it firmly in place.

Having no desire to display her or her grandmother before the rebels, he called, "Cover their heads!" and silently cursed that those in the bailey might hear and guess what he sought to hide from them.

What Maël would not order for whatever godforsaken reason, his chevaliers did as they guided their mounts over the drawbridge, drawing the hoods up over the heads of their charges.

"Something has gone afoul," Fulbert said.

Had the body of Cyr's man-at-arms been found in the wood? The murder of a Norman would anger Maël, but this seemed too much like the day ere the great battle, seemed too... Personal?

When Maël passed beneath the portcullis into the bailey, Cyr strode to the steps. As he began his descent, he looked to those entering and knew the moment Aelfled saw the rebels in the western paddock. Head turned that direction, she startled, and he hoped her hood cast enough shadow to conceal her face. But had it, she rendered it useless in sweeping it back as her mount drew level with the paddock.

A murmur rose from the Saxons, and Cyr was a half dozen steps up from the bailey when he saw one of those unbound rise from the wall and draw back an arm.

"Get her away!" Cyr shouted at the same moment another shout sounded from the paddock.

But the stone flew, and no sound did Aelfled make as it

knocked her head to the side and slumped her over the arm fastened around her waist.

Bloodlust. It poured into Cyr as he jumped the last steps to the ground and drew his sword.

Bloodlust. It thrummed through his veins as he lunged toward the paddock whose bound prisoners gained their feet.

Bloodlust. It carried him over the fence and set him at the one toward whom the other rebels moved as if to defend him.

Bloodlust. It blinded him to the one who called his name and wrenched hold of his sword arm—the same who took an elbow to the jaw but did not let go, not even when others arrived and aided in dragging their lord to the fence and holding him to it.

"Cyr!" Theriot shouted as his other men surged toward the amassed rebels with swords and daggers drawn.

Though beyond his brother Cyr saw the biggest of the rebels—Vitalis—taken down first, the warrior continued to struggle and curse those depriving him of vengeance.

"Cyr!" It was Fulbert's voice at his back, his hand gripping his friend's shoulder.

More than the efforts of Theriot and his men-at-arms, that was the beginning of the end of Cyr's struggle. Bloodlust ebbing, knots in mind and body easing, he began to return to a semblance of the man beaten into a different shape between Senlac and his return to England.

He knew the transformation showed when Theriot released him, stepped back, and commanded the others to do the same.

As the men cautiously complied, Theriot shifted his jaw that had first been bruised by Dougray and would be further bruised by Cyr. "I understand your anger," he said, "but not your actions. Though I do not doubt many a rebel life would have been lost beneath your blade, their greater numbers would have seen you severely injured if not slain ere we could beat them back."

Cyr straightened from the fence and felt Fulbert's hand on his shoulder lift. "The enemy did not slay me upon Senlac. And those who came nearest to doing so were not bound nor weaponless."

"That is as true as it is that you wore mail and helmet and had others at your sides and back." Theriot raised his eyebrows. "More, you fought for William, fellow countrymen, land, and your life—*not* over the casting of a stone at one of the rebels' own."

"A woman!" Cyr said, then seeing again the moment Aelfled was struck by the stone, looked across his shoulder at where Maël and his men had drawn rein before the inner gate.

Several had dismounted and were yielding their horses to stable lads, though not the one who held Aelfled, his back to Cyr shielding her from view.

To the right, Bernia stood small alongside the man with whom she had shared a saddle, her hand gripping his arm. Though anxiety pitched her voice high, the only sense Cyr could make of her words was her granddaughter's name.

Movement returned his regard to the chevalier given charge of Aelfled, and he saw the man dismount. She was conscious, as evidenced by her partially upright posture, and when the man reached to her, she pushed his hand away.

Cyr looked to Theriot. "You saw the one who cast the stone?"

"Oui."

"He requires special treatment."

His brother inclined his head.

Cyr shoved into the scabbard the sword he had kept hold of, climbed the fence, nodded at Fulbert, and strode forward.

Behind, above the gruff, angry voices of men-at-arms separating the rebels and issuing commands, rose the sound of clapping. Cyr did not look around, not even when Merle called, "Might the baron be a lover of Saxon women?"

Catching Maël's eye as he neared, Cyr saw much of his cousin's anger had abated, though not such that he looked remorseful. Likely, Aelfled would have lowered her hood even had the king's man been the one to order the women covered. But he had explaining to do.

"Out of the way!" Cyr thrust aside the chevalier whose tone told he sought to coax Aelfled down, stepped into his place, and peered up at her where she held to the pommel with one hand, the horse's mane with the other. Though she remained upright, her chin was down, head turned opposite, blond hair curtaining her face streaked red.

Subduing the impulse to drag her down, he set a hand on her knee. "It is Cyr. Come down."

She quaked. "I need a moment."

"Aelfled!" her grandmother called from the other side of the destrier. "What has happened?"

"I...my stomach is unsettled. That is all."

"I have ears, Child. Where were you struck?"

"'Tis a small cut. I am nearly ready to...dismount."

"Cyr of the silver hair," the woman said imperiously, "I entrusted you with the safety of my granddaughter."

So she had told that day in Ravven. And so he had sought to do since—though not necessarily for her.

"Do not fail me further. Aid her."

Though she offended, especially in the presence of men who would question their lord taking orders from a Saxon woman, Cyr moved his hand to her granddaughter's arm beneath her mantle that hung askew. "Turn to me, Aelfled. I shall lift you down."

She drew her arm tight to her side. "I need not be carried."

"I will set you on your feet."

She remained tense.

"My word I give. I would but aid you in gaining the ground."

He heard her swallow, then she shifted around. When he saw what was revealed, he clenched his fingers into a ball of ache to keep bloodlust from resurfacing.

The stone had struck hard, its edge surely jagged. Past the fall of her hair and too much blood, a gash ran from the corner of her left eye and angled to the center of her temple. Hopefully, the worst she would suffer was a scar since such a blow could permanently damage one's mind. And some killed.

Cyr slid his hands inside her mantle, gently gripped her waist, and when she released pommel and mane, pulled her down.

She sought to keep her head up, but it fell onto his shoulder as her trembling body sank against his.

"You have her?" the old woman demanded.

"I have her, Bernia."

"Do not set her down."

"I will not, Bernia."

Aelfled lifted her head, and her dark eyes flickered. "You…gave your word."

"I lied." He settled one arm across her upper back, slid the other beneath her knees, and raised her against his chest.

All the ill felt toward her on the night past slipping away, he peered into her face. And nearly cursed when he saw the true extent of her injury. Stitches would be required. "I did not want this, Aelfled. You should have stayed under your hood."

Her lowering lids lifted. "I am one of them. Will not hide as though…I betrayed last eve." She frowned, lifted a hand toward his jaw she had scratched, in the next instant gripped the neck of his tunic and gasped, "Do not drop me!"

"Of course I will not."

"Be still." She squeezed her eyes closed. "Pray, s-stop turning."

Not caring if she spewed on him as narrowly avoided last eve, he clasped her close and strode past the others up the walk, acknowledging tight-mouthed Maël with a nod and one word. "Soon."

A quarter hour later, his aunt ushered him out of the small chamber abovestairs in which she and Nicola slept and upon whose bed he had laid the barely conscious Aelfled and seen her grandmother settled in a chair beside her.

Though Chanson was accomplished in stitching flesh as done for the boys and young men injured while training under her husband and the chevaliers who battled alongside him, Cyr turned as the door started to close behind him.

"As little scarring as possible, Aunt. The fewer reminders of this day, the better."

She frowned, then seated the door.

Now to find Maël.

"I TOLD you I would not have them displayed like spoils of war, that when you brought them into Stern their heads were to be covered."

Maël, having cleared the great hall in anticipation of answering for his breach of trust, remained unmoving where he stood with a shoulder to the doorframe looking out across the land. Fertile land. Once Saxon land. Now Norman land.

"What were you thinking?" Cyr demanded as he closed the distance between them.

The warrior who had yet to remove mail tunic and coif drew a breath that broadened his shoulders and turned the scarred side of his face toward Cyr. "I was not thinking. I was feeling. And not of things I would wish upon you. Though if you have a great care for that Saxon wench as you make it appear, I might wish it."

Cyr knew his cousin was not fond of the conquered, having spent months after months stamping out their rebellions, but something had moved him toward that which was more the face of Dougray. And when he halted alongside him, Maël offered an explanation by way of the dagger he raised from his side.

"This was among the possessions she brought out of Lillefarne."

The first thing Cyr noted as he accepted it was the quality evidencing only a noble could pay for its forging. The next, of greatest importance, was it was of the D'Argents. He need not look upon the letters scratched into steel to know to whom it had belonged.

"Mayhap she dealt the killing blow," Maël ventured where Cyr would not.

"Non," he said. "I told you of that morn when I discovered your sire. She was there to find her charge and had dragged free the boy to deliver him to his mother. Whether she found the dagger on the ground, took it from Hugh's hand, drew it from the body of Lady Hawisa's son or his hand that put it through your sire, I do not know. But I am certain she could not—would not—kill."

His cousin turned his face fully to Cyr, and sunlight slanting across it was cruel to the scarred side. But more cruel was the emotion seeking to become Dougray's mirror. "All can kill, Cyr, including that priest of yours—even if only in self defense, out of neglect, or by way of words or actions that move another to yield up his own life as he would not otherwise do."

That Cyr could not argue, but none of those applied to Aelfled upon Senlac. Though she had come to his back to put her dull meat knife in him rather than a keen dagger that would have ensured her success, she had turned from vengeance and taken no other opportunity provided.

"It was not by her hand your father breathed his last, Maël. Even did she confess it, I would not believe it. I was there. I saw the mournful woman come too late to save her lady's son."

Maël expelled breath above his head. "All this time she had the dagger. How could a D'Argent captive be so fool to believe her enemy would not search her to ensure she did not slip it between his ribs? How could she believe it would not be recognized and taken from her ere she could do harm?"

"Where did you find it?"

"In her pack."

Of little or no use there, Cyr reflected. But had she hidden it beneath her skirt...

It was possible she would have drawn it, but surely only to defend herself, he was certain—and knew Hugh would have been disappointed in him for not being exceedingly mindful of guarding his back.

His uncle had been many things good and a few things bad, but one thing he had not hidden well even from the godly-when-it-served-him William, was how nearly godless he could be.

Think the worst, act on it, he had once rebuked Cyr. *If you are proven wrong—even do you do another grave ill, ever a priest can be found to give ear to your repentance and absolution for a coin or two.*

Cyr's sire had overheard that, and so great an argument had ensued between the brothers all had known of it. Hugh had departed, and when he returned months later, his son's and nephews' training had intensified. But for a time he had been more discreet in imparting wisdom his brother named godless and over which his wife and sister-in-law wrung their hands.

"I should have been there, fighting at his side," Maël returned Cyr to the present, a time in which the dagger's owner no longer existed outside of memory.

Seeing his cousin's head was back, eyes upon the sky, Cyr asked, "What would you have done, Maël?"

"Protected my sire as was my duty."

"Even if it meant killing boys?"

Maël turned his gaze on his cousin. "Boys. That is not how a warrior ought to die. Such humiliation..."

Cyr set a hand on his shoulder. "We may never learn what happened there, but all knew Hugh for a mighty warrior, including William. Any who believe boys—only one of whom had training at arms—were the death of him, are either foolish or of jealous bent. Hugh had to have first been seriously wounded by Harold's warriors for boys to bring him down."

Maël turned his face forward, thrust a hand back through his hair. "Had I been there, I could have saved him."

Cyr did not know if now was the time to ask the question he had never found the right moment to ask. It was indelicate, but Maël had opened a door heretofore locked, and if ever he was vulnerable enough to answer, now seemed the time.

"Why were you not at his side, Maël?"

His cousin closed his eyes.

"I saw you across the battlefield, and fierce you were as your sire trained you to be. But you did not fight with the D'Argents. Why?"

He opened his mouth, hesitated, closed it.

"Whatever your reason, Maël, is it why you are landless though esteemed by William? Is it why you would not return to Normandy to yourself deliver your mother news of Hugh's death? Is it why there is no joy about you where once there was?"

Maël turned to him. "I failed my sire, my mother, Dougray, Guarin, and myself. That failure made a corpse of Hugh D'Argent and a widow of my mother, led to the loss of Dougray's arm, and capture—if not death—of Guarin, and left me fatherless. That is all there is to say." He lowered his eyes to the dagger Cyr held. "I had thought to give that to my mother, but better you. Now I must speak with my men." He bowed curtly and descended the steps.

CHAPTER TWENTY-EIGHT

*S*he knew what had happened to her, remembrance having sought to fit itself into a dream of wee Aelfled picking berries with her grandmother—a fit so poor it awakened her.

What she did not know was why the bed upon which she lay on her side was soft and warm. The last time she was so wonderfully cradled was the night before Isa's husband sent wife and son south to safety that had proven the death of the latter. But it was not possible Aelfled was on her feather-stuffed pallet at the foot of her lady's bed.

Though she could lift her lids and discover where she was and if it was night or shutters blocked daylight, she wanted to return to sleep to lighten what felt a weight on her head. But memories of all that had happened since Cyr D'Argent's return to England flashed behind her eyes.

She shifted her head on the pillow, whimpered as the dull throb at her temple sharpened. Was her injury as serious as the amount of blood made it appear?

Lifting an arm from beneath the blanket drawn over her, she

reached to her head. But another's hand turned around hers and drew it away.

"It is stitched and bandaged," spoke one who should not be here with her—wherever *here* was.

She opened her eyes on a candle-lit room and focused on the man seated in a chair beside the bed. Spread knees bracing him forward, one elbow on his thigh and closed hand before his face indicating the hand holding hers had been clasped with the other, he stared at her.

Feeling as if unclothed though she felt the soft of a well-worn chemise against her skin, Aelfled shifted her gaze over walls and the bit of ceiling that did not require her to move her head. No prison this. Though the chamber was not the size of Lady Hawisa's nor as lavish, such would be given one of import—not a Saxon commoner who aided rebels.

The only explanation was the injury done her, and that was not explanation enough. Returning her gaze to Cyr, she noted the scratches she had dealt him, once more wondered at the bruising of his nose down to his lip. "Where am I?"

"My aunt and sister yielded their chamber to—"

"Grandmother!" she gasped, ashamed only now she remembered the one who had been allowed to no more than assure Aelfled she was well before they departed Lillefarne.

"Bernia sleeps on your other side," Cyr said.

She started to look behind, but the slight movement made her groan.

"Do you listen, Aelfled, you will hear her."

She attended to the sounds, and beyond the sputter of candles caught her grandmother's breathing. "What of your aunt and sister?" she asked.

"They pass the night in my solar."

"And you here. Why?" The moment she asked, she became aware of the caress of his thumb across the back of her hand.

She looked to it and knew he followed her gaze when he

released her, returned his elbow to his thigh, and clasped the fist made of that hand beneath the other.

"I wished to speak to you when you awakened," he said.

Though she knew it best to accept there was naught more to his presence, she remembered their kiss, and now his caress of her hand despite proof she aided the rebels and her refusal to accompany him from Lillefarne.

"You would not have harmed my grandmother," she said, aware she did so with little thought but too discomfited by her injury to think more on it. "I came to you because I could not leave without her."

Cyr tried to blame his reaction on fatigue, but though he had no night of good sleep in recent memory, that one word—more than her threat to take holy vows—made him speak back, "Leave?"

A slight nod and wince. "We cannot remain upon Wulfenshire. As you have seen, in the eyes of my own, now I…" Her lashes fluttered as if she struggled for words, then she sighed. "Now I appear more conqueror than conquered. More Norman than Saxon."

Cyr's mind moved in a direction it should not go—the same as when she had spoken of becoming a Bride of Christ. Though he told himself it was for her protection he forced her out of the abbey, there went Fulbert who believed it something more. And knew Cyr well.

"Thus, if you will accept my word my grandmother and I will leave Wulfenshire and no more come upon it," she said, "on the morrow we will go where we are not known and begin anew."

As Cyr forced himself to consider her remedy for the danger in which she had placed her and her grandmother, the sense that was his in smaller measure than Theriot's made him attend to the woman on the other side of Aelfled. Bernia's breathing had changed, and though it might yet be of sleep, he thought it more likely she listened. Was she as versed in Norman French as her granddaughter?

"Pray, think on it," Aelfled alerted him to how long he made her await an answer.

Though unintentional, it served one who had no answer to give, but he *would* think on it.

"What have you done with the one who threw the stone, Cyr?"

Determining this time not to comment on how well he liked the informality of her speaking only his Christian name, he said, "He is called Sigward. You know him?"

The widening of her eyes and paling of her face was all the answer needed. But she gave more in a rush as if desperate to explain herself. "Sigward was of my village of Ravven, a few years older than I. Does he live?"

"Oui, though a terrible beating he took."

The rest of the color fled her face. "Was it the fist of Merciless Cyr?"

"It would have been had not my brother and men prevented me from casting myself in the midst of captives who believe they risk little in openly killing a lone Norman."

She searched his face as if questioning actions that revealed more of him than he ought to permit, said, "Then one of your brothers beat him."

Dougray would have liked to no matter Aelfled was the victim, but it had been another. And one not entirely unexpected. "Non, it was a fellow rebel."

The same, Cyr guessed, who had shouted as he himself had done when he saw Sigward draw back his arm. The same who, during the rebels' march to Stern, had questioned how his scout came to be replaced by a Norman. Sigward had told he was knocked unconscious before he could follow the others to the abbey. And was overheard by Dougray who drew nearer and said it was no difficult thing since the coward fled opposite. Sigward denied it, but as evidenced by what was done him this day, he was not believed.

"It was Vitalis who took him to ground." As disbelief rose on

Aelfled's face, Cyr continued, "Sigward is the Saxon my brother replaced, rendering him unconscious when, rather than follow his own into the abbey, he ran. This your Vitalis learned, and he and the other rebels took the opportunity of his attack on you to render justice unto a traitor."

"He betrayed," Aelfled breathed.

She knew something, Cyr realized and probed, "Fear can make a traitor of many a man."

"Not fear. I think he knew that you…"

She closed her mouth, but he understood. Was there dissent among the rebels? Had Sigward led his own into a trap made of Normans to rid their ranks of Vitalis and his men?

"Is Vitalis well?" she asked.

Her question moved Cyr to another matter. "Regardless of whether he believes you also a betrayer, the one who has a care for you fares better than Sigward."

She frowned. "A care? Vitalis feels nothing better than disgust for me."

Was that a lie in her voice and on her face? And what of Cyr's own? Might she hear and see his jealousy?

He recalled the man whom Theriot escorted to the hall. The one who had met Aelfled at the great rocks and taken her to Wulfen had been cut and bruised during the struggle to drag him off Sigward, but that could not disguise he was in possession of good looks, nor that his tall, muscular frame and proud bearing were forged of great discipline. Likely, the warrior was of the esteemed class of housecarles who served Saxon landholders before the conquest.

Cyr had questioned him about the attack, but Vitalis had refused to answer. Only when he was led away did he speak, and then to pose a question of his own.

Watching Aelfled closely, Cyr said, "Certes, he attacked Sigward for fleeing, but I think it also for the injury done you. And that you seek to hide what he feels for you and you for him."

"I do not."

He leaned nearer. "I had him brought to me, and no word did he speak, not even in his defense, until I ordered him returned to the paddock. You wish to know what he asked? How you fare, naught else but the fate of one who does not share the discomfort of his imprisonment."

She lowered her gaze to the mattress.

Cyr told himself it mattered not what Vitalis and she felt for each other. Until he made good use of them, the only thing left for them to feel was captivity.

He nearly left her to her rest and healing, but Theriot and Dougray had reminded him of that which he assured them he need not be reminded—if Guarin lived, every day that prolonged his captivity drew him nearer death.

He sat back. "I am aware Vitalis is the one with whom you rode to Wulfen the night of the day I found you in the wood."

Her eyes flew to his.

"Oui, I was near the great rocks with my cousin. We followed on foot as far as we could—well onto Lady Hawisa's demesne. You met with her that night, did you not?"

"Non," she whispered, and he heard fear in that word surely born of a lie.

"Hawisa Fortier Wulfrithdotter," he mused. "If not for appearing so ill when she received me in her hall the next day, I might think her the rebel leader known as Dotter."

Aelfled's gaze wavered, and he saw from the shuddering of the blanket her breathing had quickened. She knew something of her lady she did not wish to reveal, but did she know anything of Guarin?

"Were you still at Wulfen Castle when I arrived?" he asked. "Did you listen in on my audience with your lady?"

Her tongue clicked off her palate. "I know naught of what you speak."

"I think you do." He sat forward again. "Whether or not Lady

Hawisa is or ever was Dotter, all I require from you is what you know of my brother—if he lives, where he is held, if he does not, where he is buried."

"I know naught of him, my word I give."

"And easily you do so. But not believably, Aelfled."

Her eyes brightened, and more forcefully she said, "I do not know if he lives or is dead. I know not if he is or ever was upon Wulfenshire. No lie."

"Only in this?" He looked nearer upon her. "I am wondering, if I agreed to escort you and your grandmother to the shire of your choice, might you then know something of my brother?"

"I would not." It was said with little hesitation and what sounded genuine regret.

"If you did know, would you tell?"

Much hesitation.

"Aelfled, you said your own people regard you more as the conqueror and the Norman. As you are now outside them, what have you to lose in aiding me in recovering a beloved brother? Little, I say, and much to gain."

Once more, she looked to the mattress.

He waited until, reaching the end of his patience, he rose and started toward the door.

"Cyr!"

His name on her lips, rustle of bedclothes, and low moan of pain turned him before he reached the foot of the bed.

Having rolled onto her back, she pressed a hand to her bandaged temple and peered at him through narrowed lids. "As I am of no use to you, send my grandmother and me from Wulfenshire."

"Non." He glanced at the old woman facing opposite her granddaughter. Had she not listened in before, she did so now, so still was she as if too deep a breath would make it difficult to hear.

Hoping there was benefit in her attending to the exchange— that she would persuade Aelfled to tell what she knew, Cyr said,

"Did you aid me in ending rebellion on these lands, at least in part I could justify to William the release of one whose efforts permitted the rebels to flourish. But you give me nothing."

"I have nothing."

"Nothing you are willing to give. Though you have proven useful, all I have gained from you had to be taken by deception and force."

Her mouth trembled, reminding him of a kiss taken neither by deception nor force.

As if she also remembered, she drew her lower lip between her teeth and looked sidelong at her grandmother's back. Then in a lower voice, she said, "How did you know I was to hide the rebels last eve?"

He owed her no explanation, but the impatience that had ejected him from the chair waned amid memories of her at the stream. Did she know the power she had over him that no woman before had possessed? A power Hugh warned his son and nephews to resist for how easily they made a man vulnerable?

The youths they had been had scoffed at the possibility any woman could turn a true warrior from his purpose. But proof of such had first been given by Dougray—and now Cyr who had sent away his aunt to himself keep watch over Aelfled. Until she awakened, how long had he watched her sleep though he also needed rest? An hour? Two?

Regardless, it was not only concern that bid him observe her as her mind traveled other worlds. Though previous to this night he had no desire to watch a woman in that unguarded state, he had been intrigued.

She bewitches me, he silently admitted.

"How did you know?" she asked.

Recalling where their conversation had left off, he stepped nearer. "By way of the message you left in the tree warning you were too closely watched and urging the rebels to reconsider their plans."

She startled.

"They did not ignore it, Aelfled. It was delivered to me by my man in the wood who remains missing and is likely dead at the hands of your rebels. I ordered him to return it. You would know why?"

"I would."

"In the hope they heeded you, protecting you from whatever danger you place yourself in to give aid—even though the absence of warning might have sooner delivered the rebels into my hands." He breathed deep. "But it was too late. When my man gained the tree, the rebels had left a message of their own ordering you to prepare to receive them the night ere the full moon when they would take from Stern what I denied them at Balduc. Thus, I determined to capture the rebels. And you with them."

If she knew of what he spoke, it did not show. Where alarm had been was wary interest. It was possible she was unaware of what the rebels who sought to evade capture had wrought. "Whoever leads them has a keen wit," he continued. "It was not Vitalis and his men who came to burn Stern's hay. Somehow the rebels learned Campagnon's man, Merle, intended to set it afire and used that knowledge to distract me from their true purpose."

Aelfled's frown deepened. "But to distract you, you would have to know—"

"Oui, the contents of the message my man intercepted and returned so you could make preparations to shelter the rebels. Methinks that message was meant as much for me as you—at the very least written in such a way as to mislead me if it fell into my hands. As said, their leader is intelligent, and all the more for that second diversion."

In near equal parts, her confusion and interest deepened, and unlike her earlier denials and evasions, he glimpsed no lie. "Tell," she prompted.

"Hardly had we captured Merle and his men than I received word the rebels had attacked and fled Balduc Castle. Believing it the true target and thinking my greatest chance of capturing the rebels was to seek the one who aided them, we rode on the abbey. And long we waited, but just as we prepared to withdraw, a far greater number of rebels than those who attacked Balduc Castle came seeking shelter until their pursuers abandoned the hunt. Two diversions, you see."

"For what?"

"To allow them to take the villagers' hay in the northernmost village of Balduc."

As if she well chose her next words, it was some moments before she said, "Did the rebels burn it all?"

"That is as they wish me to believe, but not all, Aelfled. Only enough to make it appear so."

She slid her regard to her hands gripping the blanket to her chest. She knew of their trickery and likely justified the part she played with the knowledge the destruction was only enough to mislead the conquerors—that her own would be provided for.

"Clever, do you not think?" he submitted.

Feeling her struggle to return her gaze to his, he said, "I now know as you have known that the rebels' crimes are not as extensive as believed. Though I cannot condone their actions, they are not unforgivable. Hence, had I not a good use for those captured last eve, after gaining their submission, most I would return to their families to work the land."

Her eyes fell upon him. "Good use?"

"Very good use."

He expected her to press further, but as if realizing it would be a waste of breath, she said, "Were any Saxon or Norman lives lost last eve?"

Cyr's thoughts moved to the man set to watch her movements, but she spoke of those gone into the passage and those who brought them out. "Non, it was mostly token resistance as of rats trapped in a corner. And for that be glad you were given no opportunity to unbar the door."

She hesitated, said, "There was so much blood in the passage, I feared—"

"You returned there?"

"Oui. I am responsible for the mess made there, so it was for me to clean."

"The dried blood on your bodice and skirts." Cyr was glad for an explanation of what had disturbed him when he settled her on the bed and aided Chanson in the removal of her mantle. It was Nicola who assisted his aunt in removing the gown so it could be laundered.

"I should have changed," she said, "but already I had kept your men waiting long. I did not realize your cousin was the one come for me, though I would have had he not worn his coif when first I looked upon him."

The telltale D'Argent silver hair.

"When I came out and he ordered my pack searched, I regretted what I had brought with me."

"His sire's dagger."

"The same I took from Wulf's hand at Senlac."

Cyr tensed over knowing more of his uncle's final moments.

"When I learned you were his nephew, I dared not return it to you. It was fearful enough you guessed Wulf and his friends were the death of him, but to give proof…"

"Why did you take it to Lillefarne?"

She shook her head, grimaced as if pained. "I should not have."

"For what was it among your possessions, Aelfled? Offensive or defensive?" Hardly had the words exited his mouth than once more he was returned to Senlac where he saw the meat dagger drawn on him and asked that of her there.

So sorrowful and knowing was the turn of her lips he knew she had joined him on that bloody meadow. "The same as that day, not offensive," she said, "but neither defensive. I wished to return the dagger to your aunt that it might be of comfort. But certes, it was of no comfort to her son. I do not know why your cousin did not strike me."

"That is not the way of D'Argents," Cyr made no effort to temper the offense taken.

"Perhaps not, but this day methinks it was nearly the way of Maël D'Argent—as, I understand, it is the way of your king."

That tale, Cyr recalled William of Normandy's reaction to the refusal of Matilda of Flanders to wed him for being baseborn and far beneath the station of the King of France's niece. It was said the duke had beaten her, leaving her bruised and weeping. Yet how true could it be, that lady having later agreed to wed him— and no evidence since that theirs was anything other than a satisfactory marriage? Unlike many a lord with coin aplenty to keep women besides a wife, William appeared to be devoted and faithful to his Matilda and she to him.

Returning the conversation to Maël, Cyr said, "My cousin *was* angered, the dagger a reminder of a father lost and the humiliation dealt by those who say Hugh was felled by mere boys when, surely, your charge and his friends but put finish to what Saxon warriors began."

"You think that true?"

"Few warriors are as mighty as was my uncle."

What seemed relief eased her brow.

"Maël asked me to give the dagger to his mother, and I did, but I do not think she found comfort in it any more than her son."

"I am sorry. I should have left it at Lillefarne the same as…"

Cyr raised his eyebrows. "What did you leave at the abbey?"

Once more, she averted her gaze.

Too many secrets. Too much distance between Saxons and Normans. Still, he was determined to close that distance though it might prove impossible with her. "Ere I leave you to sleep, is there anything you require?"

She looked to the bedside table where a cup of watered wine sat, but said, "Non. Good eve, Baron."

"I am not above serving you, Aelfled." He retrieved the cup, lowered to the mattress, and gently raised her. "Drink." He placed the rim against her lips.

As she sipped, he noted how short and thick her lashes that darkly contrasted with her fair hair. For this, he guessed, her eyes seemed otherworldly dark and beautifully large. And wished them once more upon his.

As if to grant his wish, she swept up her lashes.

"Enough?" he said tightly.

She nodded, and he eased her back. And missed the feel of her.

Far too much power over me, he silently cursed his weakness. *Dear Lord, is this what made Dougray do what he did not wish to do? Is what I feel a portion of what he felt? Was it this more than anything that caused him to bend to my persuasion?*

Cyr had known a woman was at least partially responsible for turning Dougray's mind to gaining land in England, but perhaps that woman deserved even more credit.

He set the half empty cup on the table and, as he stood from the bed, said, "We will speak more when you are better recovered."

"You will think on sending my grandmother and me from Wulfenshire?" she asked as he crossed to the door.

He peered across his shoulder. "I will, but expect no more than that. Rest well, Aelfled." He moved his gaze to the still figure beside her. "And you, Bernia."

CHAPTER TWENTY-NINE

She had not rested well though, blessedly, her grandmother had continued to feign sleep following Cyr's departure.

Now as the two women picked at viands the bright-eyed Nicola D'Argent had delivered, Aelfled shifted where she sat propped on pillows and asked, "How much of what Baron D'Argent and I discussed last eve did you understand?"

The fingers lightly patting the platter between cold slices of venison and chunked cheese stilled, then Bernia raised unseeing eyes toward those of her child's child. "Enough to advise, Aelfled."

"On what?"

"That which cannot be changed as Cyr of the silver hair knows and the rebels ought to accept the sooner to end the bloodletting and begin making babies."

Aelfled was not unaware of the direction her grandmother had set her feet not long after the conquering, but since it was opposite Isa, it was best not to speak there. "No longer am I welcome upon Wulfenshire. As my kin, neither are you, Grandmother. Thus, I must persuade the baron to permit us to leave."

"It is not merely a matter of being unwelcome." Bernia pinched a piece of cheese. "That you were knocked near senseless is evidence of that." She popped the morsel in her mouth, and as she set to chewing, Aelfled touched her bandaged temple whose ache had eased considerably.

"As you yourself told," Bernia continued, "to our own people you are as much the enemy as those who stole our lands. Now tell, who made you that?"

"Grandmother—"

"Aye, Hawisa Wulfrithdotter. A good, honorable woman she was. For that, I sent you to Wulfen when she called for girls of a good age to present themselves for consideration to enter her service. And a good woman I still believe her to be beneath vengeance that has not allowed her to grieve properly and rise above her loss."

Aelfled sighed. "As discussed well enough to be long settled, I pledged myself to her, and that pledge stands all the stronger for my failure to protect her son—"

"He is more at fault for his death than you, Aelfled."

Something else previously discussed and on which neither would be moved.

"You must tell Hawisa what he did."

"It will not change that he is dead and will more greatly pain her," Aelfled said too sharply, then murmured, "Forgive me," and moved the discussion back to where it had begun. "Could I yet be of use to my lady, still I would do as she bids no matter my conscience or desires. But all that is left to me is to distance myself—and you—that I do her no further harm."

Bernia narrowed lids over clouded eyes. "What of the harm done you, that which will be all the greater do you abandon your home?"

"It is no longer my home nor yours. It belongs to a Norman."

"Aye, and one I rather like who likes my granddaughter."

Bernia smiled. Though her teeth were slightly gapped, the bowing of her lips made her appear younger.

Aelfled wanted to deny Cyr felt anything of consequence for her, but there was some truth to it and she was too tired to argue it.

"And you like him," Bernia added.

Again, the temptation to argue. Again, resistance. But Aelfled acceded, "Albeit Norman, he is many things a woman could wrap her arms around knowing even if her hands were pried from him, his would not be pried from her. But I am Saxon, common, and proven as much a rebel as those now in his power. He might like me well enough to take me to mistress, but I do not want that nor do you. Now let us speak no more of the impossible."

It could not be known whether Bernia would have complied, for a knock sounded and the door opened.

The lovely woman who entered ahead of Nicola D'Argent was the same who had aided Cyr in removing Aelfled's mantle on the day past. There had been no introductions, but before Aelfled lost all sense, she had heard Cyr call her *Aunt* and now knew she was the one delivered the D'Argent dagger.

The lady halted alongside the bed, clasped her hands at her waist.

Seeing her eyes were mapped red and lids slightly swollen, once more Aelfled wished she had left her husband's dagger with Mary Sarah the same as done that of the lady's missing nephew.

As the widow considered the young and old woman, Aelfled wondered at her age. Though her son appeared between twenty and thirty years, it would surprise were she more than two score. As it was not unheard of for those between girlhood and womanhood—as young as twelve and thirteen—to wed, and some survived birthing from a body not yet of good size and maturity, Aelfled guessed the lady at the far side of her thirties or the near side of her forties.

"I am Chanson D'Argent," she said. "You may call me Lady Chanson."

Aelfled inclined her head. "I am Aelfled. This is my grandmother, Bernia."

"This I know. Now if you will lie down, I will examine your stitches, clean your injury, and replace the bandage."

"I thank you and your niece for the care given us." Aelfled glanced at the younger woman who stood at the foot of the bed. "We—"

"Do you prefer to remain seated?" the lady spoke over her.

No comfort the dagger, Aelfled reminded herself of what Cyr had told, then eased down the pillow.

"Nicola." Lady Chanson motioned her forward, and the young woman came around the bed, set a bag atop the coverlet, and opened it.

Shortly, Lady Chanson pronounced her stitches strong and well worked and predicted the scar would heal well enough it need not be hidden behind hair. After securing a clean bandage over it, she said, "We are done."

Aelfled sat up quickly, grimaced over the discomfort. "Lady Chanson?"

"Oui?"

"I am sorry for the loss of your husband and any pain caused by the return of his dagger."

Her mouth tightened, and Aelfled was certain she would be rebuked, but then the lady's pale pink lips eased. "I loved him more than I should have and miss him more than I ought to," she said. "I know you meant well, and I am grateful you sought to ease my loss. Now I must attend to one of my nephew's men whom I do all I can to ensure he does not lose a leg."

"A leg?" Aelfled exclaimed. "I understood injuries gained at Lillefarne were minor on both sides."

"Those were, but not the one dealt this day by rebels when my nephew's men were en route to Stern to return the body of a man-at-arms found in the wood near the abbey."

Aelfled caught her breath.

The lady inclined her head. "His death comes as no surprise, but my nephew is..." She sighed. "It is good he knows not which of his prisoners is responsible. Although if he determines to punish all..."

Sigward, Aelfled silently named the one Cyr told had taken a terrible beating from Vitalis whom he believed had feelings for her. Though years ago Aelfled had been unable to hide from Isa her infatuation with Vitalis, and her lady had teased that if another maid as dear and adept could be found she would arrange a marriage, never had the warrior shown interest in his lady's maid. It was other women of the household upon whom he bestowed attentions he could not cast at the wed Isa.

Wrenching her thoughts back from a place they did not belong in this moment, Aelfled said, "You think the Baron of Stern will punish all, Lady Chanson?"

She shrugged. "There was a time I would have been confident he would since he learned well his lessons from my husband. But now, with that priest at his side, I am not as certain."

What priest? Aelfled wondered.

"But one never knows when the dark of a soul might venture forth again."

Merciless Cyr, Aelfled silently named him as Campagnon had done at Senlac.

"I will return ere the supper hour," the lady said and gestured for Nicola to follow.

When they were alone again, Bernia said, "Know you who killed the man-at-arms outside Lillefarne?"

Aelfled hesitated, said, "Vitalis told it was Sigward."

Bernia made a sound of disgust. "That worm rot upon an apple's backside," she muttered. "It is good it is him."

"Good?"

"As Cyr of the silver told, that miscreant was beaten well. If one must be handed up, better he who dealt the offense. Now another question. Did you speak true that you know naught of the missing D'Argent?"

"I do not know if Guarin D'Argent is alive and where he might be found, but neither am I entirely ignorant of him." Aelfled told her what Isa had said at Senlac that evidenced her encounter with a D'Argent, then of the dagger found in the passage that was in Mary Sarah's possession.

"If naught else," Aelfled said, "I believe Isa knows what became of Guarin D'Argent. And it seems likely Vitalis as well."

"Isa," Bernia said. "I do not—could not—wish her venom cured by death, but if its pall falls upon her, taking the last of the family of Wulfrith, better done now."

The last... "You ought not speak such, Grandmother."

"Be assured, I pray for her, though more for her heart than body." Bernia slid a seeking hand across the coverlet between them.

Aelfled covered the thin, aged hand with her own, said, "I also pray for her."

"But still do not believe He hears you, hmm?"

"I see no evidence of it."

"It is not required He give proof, Child, but He does. Methinks, you are neither listening well nor looking in the right place."

Aelfled muffled a disrespectful snort. "I am in England. It is conquered. I am upon Wulfenshire. It has been cut and parted to award Normans. I am at Stern. It is my prison."

Bernia turned her hand up into her granddaughter's. "I am corrected. You are looking in the right place. However, you are more blind than this old woman who sees Cyr D'Argent in England, upon Wulfenshire, and lord of Stern. A prisoner you are, aye, but of a man who has more a care for you than what he fears Vitalis feels."

Aelfled sighed. "You are fanciful, you who yet feel love for my grandsire though he is many years dead."

"Of course I still feel for my man. Though many say love resides in the heart, I say it is not of the body. It is the breath made of two souls. Though the body passes and returns to dust, that breath remains—sweet amid the stench of the world. I wish that sweet for you, Child."

Such pretty words and sentiment, Aelfled thought, then slipped her hand free. "I am tired," she said and turned away.

Was Sigward the one? Or merely the easiest to sacrifice to a Norman's wrath?

Cyr broke his stride beneath the portcullis, drew a breath to ease the roiling. After seeing the remains of the missing man-at-arms, he had ignored Fulbert's entreaty to join him in the chapel. That he could not do whilst vile images sprang at him from every corner of his mind.

The men who located the man-at-arms and had been attacked by rebels shortly after bringing him out of the wood had warned the body wrapped in a blanket was unsightly, having suffered desecration not unlike that done Saxons at Senlac by Normans who thought it would ease the ache of their own losses—that to which Cyr had nearly succumbed.

He took another breath, then looked behind at the paddock which held the rebels. When he had entered it and ordered Vitalis to come before him, he had known he presented as fearsome to men of the sword deprived of swords. But the warrior had not hesitated. Hands bound at his back, he had halted near enough to be struck without inconveniencing his captor and met the gaze level with his own.

Cyr had demanded the name of the murderer of the Norman in the wood. When Vitalis remained close-mouthed, he had warned all would be punished.

That had pleased Merle and his men in the opposite paddock who called for the blood of cowardly Saxons they believed should have been shed with their countrymen at Senlac.

It took Theriot and his men little time to quiet them.

Before Cyr could issue a final warning, Vitalis had settled into his heels and nodded at the corner where Sigward slowly succumbed to internal bleeding Chanson told could not be stemmed when the symptoms were described to one whose kin refused to allow her near the rebel.

Cyr was not surprised the murder of his man was blamed on one soon beyond the reach of justice. Though he knew it possible the warrior did not lie, he was fairly certain that if another had cast a stone at Aelfled and suffered the same as Sigward, that one would have been named. He had mocked Vitalis over the convenience of crediting the murder to one he so disliked that he and others of his men had ensured Sigward would not rise again.

Vitalis had shrugged, said, "I see you have two choices, Norman. Take my head since all these men serve under me and I am responsible for their actions, or ask Aelfled the name of the one I revealed to her killed the man set to watch the abbey."

Proof Aelfled was more deceptive—had lied in telling she did not know his man's fate? Though Cyr hoped Vitalis spoke false, there was also hope she would verify what he told the sooner to be done with the matter and satisfied as much as possible.

When he entered the chamber minutes later, he found Aelfled seated in the chair from which he had watched her sleep, her grandmother on the floor with her back against the younger woman's legs.

Aelfled looked up, and the long plaited braid with which she crowned the old woman's head slipped from her fingers.

"Ah, look what you have done, Cyr of the silver," Bernia named him though he had spoken no word to identify himself. "Distracted my granddaughter. Now she will have to begin again."

"I have naught else to occupy me," Aelfled said and raised her eyebrows. "What do you require, Baron D'Argent?"

Deciding to speak in her language to ensure Bernia fully understood and her reaction might be gauged, he said, "Only the truth," and closed the door and crossed the room to stand over the two. "As thought, the man I sent to the wood at Lillefarne is dead. I would have from you the name of the rebel who killed him, Aelfled."

When she could not hold his gaze, Cyr stepped alongside the chair and caught up her chin. "Do you have a care for Vitalis and his men?"

Her lids sprang wide. "Of course I do. They are my people."

"Then you will aid them in an entirely different manner. You will forget I am Norman, forget you are Saxon, and speak one name in truth. Can you do that?"

She swallowed loudly.

"Mayhap this will aid in loosening your tongue," he said. "It was no quick, thoughtless kill. The young man in my service, hopeful of a good life in England, was mutilated."

The warmth of her breath against his hand cooled, and he heard Bernia catch her own breath.

"Mutilated?" Aelfled whispered.

"Aye, whoever slew him took pleasure in what he did. Now a name else others shall be punished for his crime."

She shook her head. "I do not believe you would harm innocent men to ensnare the guilty."

"Neither would I have believed it, but after what I have seen, I am nearly there again."

The old woman shifted around and gripped her granddaughter's knee. "Tell him."

Emotions struggled across Aelfled's face, then she reached up and drew his hand from her chin. "When Vitalis came to me in the garden, he told your man had been slain by the rebel scout and his body hidden so it could only be known he was missing."

"The scout's name?"

She moistened her lips. "He who injured me—Sigward."

Cyr delved her face. Was this truth? It was the same Vitalis told and the man had no opportunity to alert her, but that did not mean she did not guess well. Still, leaning toward her speaking true, he strode to the door.

"Do you believe me?" she called, and the distress in her voice nearly moved him to offer assurance. "Cyr! You will not harm the others, will you?"

He stepped into the corridor and closed the door.

"I gave what you asked of me!"

Rather, what he had forced from her—again. Continuing to the stairs, he wondered if it would always be thus with them. Would she who professed to be more conqueror and Norman in the eyes of her own ever trust him enough to willingly give what he asked of her?

Halfway down the stairs, he halted at the realization he was not thinking days and weeks ahead. He was thinking months and years—of a long future with his little Saxon.

"She distracts me," he rasped and moved his thoughts back to his purpose in seeking her out—to verify what Vitalis told.

Though it seemed too easy Sigward was the murderer, he believed it, causing relief to thrust up through blood-watered ground that had begun to encourage the merciless side of him to send out roots and once more grow like a weed.

Cyr closed his eyes and thanked the Lord for this mercy, then asked for another—to find Guarin alive. And another—to be rid of Campagnon against whom he had no proof it was at his bidding Merle and the others sought to destroy the lord's hay. Thus far, the only thing he had was a missive from Campagnon expressing shock and outrage over men he had mistakenly trusted.

But Cyr would lay hands on more. And soon.

285

Castle Balduc
England

TOO MUCH WINE, though Campagnon named it inferior. Too much food, though he named it bland. Too much brooding, though he named it sorrow. All because too much he found himself watched by Cyr D'Argent's men whom he did not wish to know how great the raging of one who claimed to be betrayed by those whose lives he had saved at Senlac.

"Liar, knave, miscreant," breathed the one who now watched Campagnon as he and others became sluggish over the meal sloshing about their bellies and a day that had turned night well before they rose from supper to converse, boast, jest, and engage in games of chance. "You will suffer what is due you. I vow you will."

The little finger hooked between two gathered curtains widened the slit to better view Balduc's castellan as he wove a path from two mercenaries who had yet to fail him as the imprisoned Merle had done to the servant refilling her pitcher at the sideboard.

Leave her be, the hidden one silently commanded. *There is naught there for you, devil's spawn.*

Still he groped the woman, and when she tried to pull away, gripped her by the throat and kissed her hard on the mouth. Then he thrust her back and shoved his tankard at her.

As the woman refilled it with a hand that shook so greatly it seemed a miracle she did not slop drink on him, the one who watched whispered, "Do with me what you will, Norman, I shall see you broken long ere you break me. It is me you ought to fear. Strong of mind, body, and spirit, I am Saxon. Never shall I forget it. Ever shall I embrace it. Be it by my hand or another's, you will breathe your last." A long, slow release of breath. "Pray soon, Lord."

Now it was time to send word.

CHAPTER THIRTY

Stern Castle
England

*C*yr did not know how the confession was obtained. It was enough to know Maël persuaded Merle to set in writing that it was Campagnon who ordered the burning of his liege's hay.

And as Sigward's passing neared, yet more the day delivered. Theriot having given watch over the rebels to men familiar with their language, the Normans had drawn near when Vitalis challenged the dying man to prove he was not a coward—that it was not fear that made him flee Lillefarne but loyalty to one he esteemed above others. It had been a good tact, Sigward confirming he acted on the orders of one he called a Saxon *true to the blood, the bone, the marrow.* No name had he given, but it was clear he referred to a man rather than a woman.

What little more was spoken between the two was cryptic, but from what Cyr had surmised of that night at Lillefarne, there was dissension among the rebels. Because Lady Hawisa was Dotter and, now too ill to lead, others vied for her position? So ferociously they handed up their own to eliminate contenders?

Cyr nodded. Whomever Sigward served, it was hoped the Baron of Stern and Balduc would be in the wood that night and capture—if not kill—Vitalis and his men.

"With whom are you in agreement, my son?"

Wishing he could say it was the Lord—that he had not drifted away from Him in this holy place—Cyr looked to the priest on the kneeler beside him. "I agree with myself that I am made an instrument of the rebels. And how well I shall like making an instrument of them."

"You speak of vengeance?"

"I suppose there is that, but more there is Guarin. This day, I shall send word to the rebels and, God willing, they will agree to my terms and deliver my brother to me."

"And if they do not? Or have only a corpse to bargain with?"

Though were Guarin already dead Cyr wished his body returned, he would yield naught to the rebels for anything less than a brother who yet breathed for fear a lesser bargain could see Guarin murdered. "They give me what I want or their fellow rebels accompany Campagnon and his men to King William." Campagnon whom Cyr would remove from Balduc on the morrow.

Fulbert thought on that, said, "What of this Aelfled? Will she be part of the bargain you make?"

"Non." With any other, Cyr would have been ashamed at his lack of hesitation.

"What will you do with her?"

"As told, I think it unwise to deliver her grandmother and her to another shire. Even if the rebels do not root her out, the king could, and she would suffer his wrath for harboring rebels. Were she alone, it is possible she could lose her pursuers, but not in the company of an old blind woman who would slow her and render her more recognizable."

Fulbert sighed. "It is unfortunate you did not leave her at Lillefarne."

"I do not think so. Rather than take vows, I believe she would have left, collected her grandmother, and fled Wulfenshire. And what remained of their lives would be spent running and hiding. Non, my only regret in forcing her out—and it is great—is the injury done her."

The priest raised his eyebrows. "So I ask again, what is to be her fate?"

Cyr moved his gaze to his loosely clasped hands on the kneeler's shelf, stared at them, closed his eyes. *Lord, what do I do with she who has been made more the conquering Norman than a Saxon by association with me? How do I keep her safe in this changed world? Where do I tuck her away so she may live again?*

A hand settled on his back. "The fight is over, my son. You have but to cease struggling."

Cyr breathed deep, opened his eyes. It *was* over. He knew what must be done. But ere delivering tidings to his little Saxon, he would set in motion Guarin's release.

"YOU KNOW I am aware Sigward betrayed you and your men?"

Chest forward, shoulders back—doubtless more a show of aggression than a result of hands bound at his back—the Saxon glared.

A grunt sounded from the right, and Cyr glanced at Theriot who stood outside the paddock, arms propped on the fence's top rung, in one hand a small dagger, in the other an apple whose skin he sliced away in one long, narrow spiral.

Cyr returned his regard to Vitalis whom he had summoned to the far corner of the paddock distant from his men. "The same as you, I do not believe fear caused your scout to desert you at Lillefarne. I believe he did as planned in the event I brought forces to the abbey, and once it was verified I had, he slipped away, his absence allowing one of my own to number amongst yours. And I believe you and your men were sacrificed in what was hoped to be a river of blood with few if any survivors. Thus, it requires no imagining to conclude there is great division between you and Dotter or you and others who serve Dotter."

Vitalis continued to stare, the only movement about him glittering eyes, flaring nostrils, perspiration coursing face and neck.

Cyr stepped nearer, and breathing the odor of the man's long unwashed body, said, "I require something of you, *housecarle.*"

A flicker in his eyes.

"Aye, though you no longer wear the finery of an esteemed warrior, I know what you are. Thus, I set you a task."

Still Vitalis did not rise to words in the hope of more quickly gaining answers to the questions slamming about his head.

"I have a message that needs delivering. Do you agree to what I propose, this day I shall provide a horse and send you to your leader."

The man gave a bark of laughter. "I am to believe you would have *me* play the herald?"

Cyr smiled. "Either you think yourself too valuable to be released, else you fear whomever you answer to. Since that may be the one who sought your death, it is not entirely shameful."

"I am too valuable, as well you know, D'Argent. Hence, I question why you choose me."

"I have watched you as have my men. You are protective of your own and it is clear their loyalty is well-earned. Thus, I am assured my message will be delivered quickly the sooner to see your men freed."

"Freed?"

Cyr inclined his head. "I wish to bargain with your leader— trade nineteen men, twenty do we count the deceased Sigward —for one."

"One?" He glowered. "Never."

"I do not speak of Dotter."

The Saxon narrowed his lids.

"My brother for your men—*if* he lives."

"The same brother whom this D'Argent"—Vitalis jutted his chin at Theriot—"sought these months with no proof of his existence other than a rumored sighting?"

"I believe Guarin is alive and has been held by your rebels since the great battle." *Lord,* Cyr sent to the heavens, *let my hope be worthy of belief.*

"For what would we hold a Norman noble if not for ransom, which would have been demanded long ago?"

"That is a question I shall ask my brother."

"*If* he lives and your terms are met. What if he is long dead?"

"Though I would recover his corpse and see him buried in holy ground, if he is not delivered to me alive and well, we have no bargain...no trade." Cyr looked to the rebels beyond Vitalis, saw as much as felt their curiosity. "I shall give your men into King William's hands."

Vitalis followed his gaze, and when he looked back around, set his eyes on his captor's sword belt.

"Because of the dissension among your own," Cyr continued, "what I require could prove difficult to carry out, perhaps so much it may be best you not deliver my message but act on it yourself."

The Saxon looked up.

Cyr raised his eyebrows. "I care not how you gain my brother's release and return him to his family, only that it be done."

Vitalis kept him waiting, finally said, "I have no cause to value the word of a Norman, but I would have it given on the hilt of your sword that do I deliver your brother alive—and hear me, I am not saying it is possible—you will release all my men. And only to me."

Further proof of dissension among the rebels.

Cyr set his hand on his hilt. "In the sight of God, I give the word of Cyr D'Argent of Stern and Balduc that do you meet my terms in full, I shall release every rebel in this paddock only to you."

The man dipped his head. "You have made of this warrior a herald—for a day."

Cyr drew his dagger, stepped around Vitalis, and as he cut the rope binding his hands, said, "I know about the hay and crops, that the bulk is not burned but sold to ensure the villagers want for naught."

The warrior stiffened.

"A good thing you are not as dangerous as believed, Vitalis."

"And that you are not as merciless as told," the man retorted.

Regardless of whether that was meant as an insult, Cyr did not take it as one.

The rope fell away, and Cyr motioned forward the lad who held the reins of a saddled horse.

"You are sure of this?" Theriot asked.

Cyr saw that though his brother had looped the long apple peel over the fence's rail as a treat for the birds, he had yet to enjoy the fruit of his effort. "I am sure of naught, but I think it our best course."

Theriot nodded, took a bite of apple.

Once Vitalis was mounted, the Saxon looked all around, then to Cyr who held the horse's bridle. "You will have me followed to discover the one to whom I answer?"

Squinting against the sun past the man's head, Cyr said, "It was a consideration, but as your attempts to lose my men would delay the delivery of my message, you will not be followed. Nor do I believe it of benefit to me." He patted the horse's jowl. "A fine mount you have been given—as swift as those that carried you and Aelfled onto Wulfen a sennight past."

The man could only dampen his surprise.

"As told, of no benefit to me." Cyr released the bridle and stepped back. "Godspeed, Vitalis of Wulfen."

CHAPTER THIRTY-ONE

*I*t was not much of a garden, but one could be made of it, just as one had been made of that trampled by Norman captors and Saxon captives.

"My aunt says dirt betwixt fingers and toes will do me good," Nicola D'Argent said as she dropped onto the bench beside Aelfled. "I do not know she is right, but I am loath to test her belief. Not that I am lazy. I am happiest out of doors with a swift horse beneath me or stealing tree to tree with my pretty bow nocked and a quiver of arrows on my back."

Aelfled slid her gaze from her grandmother who moved among the tangled roses on the far side of the garden, to the young woman. "You know archery?"

Nicola's mouth bowed wider, and Aelfled thought she might have more teeth than herself were it possible. But it was not unsightly, only stunning. "I do, and I am proficient enough to take big game." She gave a quick laugh. "Well, with some small help. I must needs strengthen my drawing arm."

"Your family allowed you to be instructed in weaponry?"

"Be assured my mother protested. However, my eldest brother is of the belief a woman ought to be able to fend for herself and vows when he weds he will teach his wife the dagger and bow so she is as fearless as he in protecting and feeding their children. Unfortunately, that did not persuade our mother."

"What did?"

"His assurance it would calm my restlessness. *That* she much desired."

Aelfled smiled. "You speak of Guarin, oui?"

"Of course, he who is the greatest of..." Like something dropped from on high, her smile fell, and in a voice pushing past tears, she said, "Every night I pray him back to us, suffering aching knees to beseech the Lord not to allow the godless Saxons who took Dougray's arm and disfigured Maël's beautiful face to—" She clapped a hand over her mouth.

Feeling her nails in her palms, Aelfled forced her hands open. Though Nicola offended, she could be forgiven. She was young, and just as Aelfled had yet to master thinking before speaking, so must she of fewer years. Too, just as Saxons blamed Normans for those injured and lost to them, so this Norman blamed Saxons.

Nicola blew breath up her face. "That was not well thought nor said. I forget you are one of them, and how could I not? You and your grandmother are civilized, and you are sufficiently educated to know my language such that only if one listens closely might they hear the common of your own tongue."

Offended again, and yet...

Aelfled did not know how she was capable of laughter in such grim circumstances as those which reduced her to captivity, but she laughed, and felt fall upon her the gaze of the man-at-arms whom the lady's youngest brother, Theriot, had insisted accompany the women outside.

"What is funny?" Nicola snapped.

Aelfled drew a breath, sat back. "I would not name *funny* what you speak, but *delightful*. You are very...alive."

The young woman's eyebrows clipped. "And you are not?"

Two years ago and beyond, Aelfled silently answered. *Before you Normans came.*

She shrugged. "You must know the world has gone dark for my people."

Concern replacing annoyance, Nicola said, "I do know, and I am sorry. This day as I stood upon the inner wall with my cousin and looked down at the rebels in the paddock, I tried to imagine how I would feel were they Normans and were it your people upon our soil."

Before Aelfled could ask after the Saxon captives, the young woman continued, "Next I imagined how I would feel were I you." She shuddered. "I fear I would not know how to pull myself out of that hole. But you will find your way out—will come alive again, be happy again, will you not, Aelfled?"

Her concern was so sincere it hurt. "At present, the possibility is distant, but it is my hope." *Though not much of one,* she silently added.

Nicola set a hand over Aelfled's. "Worry not, Cyr will make it as right as possible."

"I will make what right?" asked the one who had entered the garden unseen and unheard.

As Aelfled shot her gaze to where he stood in the place no longer occupied by the man-at-arms, Nicola jumped up, hastened to his side, and kissed his cheek. "Aelfled fears never to be happy again, and I am all assurance you will aid her as best you can. I speak true, do I not?"

Past her, he met Aelfled's gaze. "You do. Now go find our aunt and tell her I require her attendance a half hour hence."

"For?"

"Go, Nicola."

Muttering something, she left Aelfled and her grandmother alone with Cyr.

He strode forward, and as she started to rise said, "Pray, do not disturb your repose." He halted before her, sent his eyes all around her face then down her figure. "You look improved."

She touched the bandage. "I am, much gratitude to your aunt."

"Certes, she is gifted with healing hands."

Aelfled inclined her head. "Will you tell me how your captives fare?"

Displeasure flickered across his face, but he said, "This day Campagnon's men departed under guard of a half dozen of my cousin's men who shall deliver them to King William for punishment."

"And the Saxons?"

"Sigward has passed, his life forfeited not by way of a Norman but his own people. As for those he leaves behind, they are well and shall soon aid in retrieving my brother."

Aelfled longed to ask how that would come to pass, but certain he would not tell, said, "I pray you recover him in good health. But if you come seeking my aid, I say again I know not if he lives nor where to find him."

"But you know something of him, oui?"

It was difficult to hold his gaze. "Very little, but what I know I have no right to tell."

Another spasm of displeasure. "As I believe I possess the means of retrieving him does he live, that is not why I am here. Thus, until I better prove worthy of your trust, keep your secrets, Aelfled."

She frowned. "You make it sound as if I will be here a very long time."

"You will. To speak on that is why I sought you out."

Telling herself providing her grandmother and she continued to be treated well she could tolerate being his captive, she looked to the far end of the garden. Though Bernia kept her back to them, from the angle and lean of her body, she listened.

Returning her regard to Cyr, Aelfled said, "As you know, my grandmother is aged and unseeing, but do you make a place for us here, I shall do the work of two in whatever capacity you decide, be it serving in the kitchen or at table, keeping chambers or—"

"I would not make servants of you."

She raised her eyebrows. "Then what? Surely we are not to dwell amongst you as guests?"

Movement at his sides drew her attention to large hands folding into fists. "What I have determined to do, I want no more than you. The Lord knows, it is far from the plans I had when I came to England."

"What speak you of?"

He breathed deep. Then he turned, took two strides opposite, came back around, and took one stride forward. "I planned that did I not find my brother alive, I would petition the king to pass these lands to one or both of my brothers, return to Normandy, and take my place as our sire's heir. And did I find Guarin alive, I would resolve myself to remaining in England and joining with a noble Saxon lady in possession of a sizable dowry, that alliance more quickly gaining me acceptance from her people now made mine."

Wishing it did not hurt to imagine his life with another, Aelfled said, "It is no different from that done by Normans come before you. For what do you tell me?"

"Because what I shall do *is* different—of no benefit to my holdings, coffers, or relations with those of these lands. Indeed, it could be of detriment."

"I do not understand."

He took a stride nearer so she had to tilt her head back to hold his gaze. "You are not noble, possess no lands or dowry," he said in a rush as if there was too little time to speak measuredly as she had only known him to do except when greatly angered. "And the more you are believed a traitor to your own, the more difficult it will be for me to gain their trust and respect."

Still she did not understand. Unless he was saying... She caught her breath. Was it possible? Did he suggest they...

His face, the garden, her grandmother who now moved toward them all began to tilt as if to topple, then waver as if sinking beneath water.

"Aelfled?"

She squeezed her eyes closed, opened them wide upon Cyr's above her, was relieved he presented right side up. "You speak of this Saxon commoner wedding you? A Norman noble?"

"I do."

She shook her head. "It makes no sense for you to join your life with mine when, as you say, it is of no benefit and may even prove harmful. Thus, either you jest—and I cannot believe you so cruel —or you are not thinking right."

"No jesting, though it is possible my thinking is not right. Unfortunately, I can resolve myself to no other way of saving you."

He wishes to save me, she thought with no small wonder that made her terribly aware of the beat of her heart. But then she recalled what he had spoken first—*unfortunately.* How could one word cause so great an ache?

Because it fit, though more clearly he had voiced how regrettable his decision when he told he wanted it no more than she and it was far from his plan of wedding one of good benefit.

Aelfled thrust to her feet and, finding herself too near him, sidestepped. Chin up, hands clenched at her sides, she said, "I thank you for being so honorable you would wed one such as me despite the many sacrifices required of you, but it is not for you to save me. I decline."

"Aelfled!" Bernia protested where she had halted to the right of Cyr.

"I decline," she said more forcefully. "Better the Baron of Stern and Balduc wed a Saxon noblewoman like Lady Hawisa." The moment she spoke her lady's name, more greatly she hurt over the possibility of him wedding another, but she pushed the blade deeper. "It is her hand you ought to seek. If for naught else but to see made whole the demesne off which your king carved great pieces, she might agree."

Cyr was a long time answering, finally said, "She would fit my plans better, but though I believe her also in need of saving, it is you I shall wed."

"This *commoner?*" Her voice rose sharply. "She who possesses no lands nor sway over her own people?"

Beyond strands of silvered black hair, his brow rumpled. "I but state facts, Aelfled. It was not my intention to offend."

Remembering Nicola's own offense, she almost laughed. "Though offense seems something at which D'Argents excel, I do not argue your facts. But this I contend—honorable though your sense of responsibility, it is misplaced. I am not your problem, will not allow myself to be made that, and the best thing you can do for all is to release my grandmother and me." She stepped nearer, set a hand on his arm. "My word I give we shall depart Wulfenshire forthwith and never again shall you set eyes on us."

His nostrils flared. "Non."

A cry of frustration parted her lips, but before she could add words to it, her grandmother said, "Aelfled, I know enough of what is said to side with Cyr of the silver. Do you accept his offer of marriage, we need not flee our home nor fear for our lives, and once he makes babes on you, the blood of Saxon and Norman shall become one."

Heat so suddenly flushed Aelfled she might have stumbled were her hand not upon Cyr. And when she snatched it back, her feet nearly did fall out from under her. Holding his gaze, she said, "I will not accept. Thus, we shall remain at Stern until you tire of us or we slip free. And so we not burden you, I shall make myself useful in whatever position you entrust to me."

"I am glad to hear it," he said, too accommodating for one who had lost the argument. "The position with which I entrust you is that of wife and mother of my children. Now come, Father Fulbert waits."

She gasped. "You think it in your power to command me to wed? It is not!"

He reached. Before she could jump away, he took hold of her shoulders and drew her to him. Lowering his head so near she felt the warmth of his brow on hers, he said, "Why do you not wish me to save you?"

She did wish it, but...

Throat tightening, eyes stinging, she lowered her gaze and noted his upper lip was thin relative to the full lower lip. But already she knew that, not only by sight but feel.

"Tell me, Aelfled."

She swallowed, looked up. "If you would wed me only to save me, ever you will suffer for so great a sacrifice. Each time you look at me, you will see and feel the mistake you made. As will I, and that will not do. Far preferable I leave Stern and you wed one who betters your lot."

He considered, and she wanted to feel relief when he said, "Very well."

Though his concession was best for both, it made her ache that he was letting her go—would not save her.

"I shall bare myself, Aelfled."

Then he did not concede?

"Though great my wish to save you, I would not wed you for that alone."

Mouth going more dry, she whispered, "What else is there?"

"Our kiss." He drew a hand from her shoulder up over her neck, cupped her jaw, and touched a thumb to her lips as if to quiet her. "I would have from you what comes after."

Distantly hearing her grandmother's chirp of satisfaction, Aelfled choked, "After?"

"More than any woman I have known, I want you in my arms when I lie down at night, want to find myself curled around you come morn."

"You...lust?"

He growled low. "That is a crude word for desire, especially when it is given answer only after vows are spoken. But call it what you will, I want you, my little Saxon. And I believe you want me."

Aelfled could not think what to say. She had believed him attracted to her, but so greatly? More than any woman before? Surely he but fashioned words to gain what she refused?

"Of course she wants you," her grandmother said, and Aelfled felt Cyr's stiffening as much as her own, but though he drew back, he did not release her.

With what seemed a smile in Bernia's clouded eyes, she stepped alongside, set fingers on Cyr's arm, and trailed them to his hand on Aelfled's jaw. It was then he loosed his hold and stepped aside.

Bernia moved in front of her granddaughter, set her palms on either side of her face. "You will be happy with him. I imagined it when you told what this Norman did for you upon Senlac, and more so when first I met him. This is as the Lord ordains, Child, even if only the blind see His hand in it." She turned her face to the man beside them. "Did I not tell babes are the way, Cyr of the silver?" When he did not answer, she said, "I did and am pleased you did not fail me." Her sightless gaze returned to Aelfled. "Go with him, and before God bind yourself to this worthy man."

Aelfled looked to Cyr. Longing to agree to what her silly heart sought to persuade her would make her happy again as Nicola wished, she said, "Cyr?"

He raised his eyebrows.

"You will not regret it terribly, will you?"

"That both of us suffer as little regret as possible, I vow to do my best—that I will make you a good husband, our children a good father."

"What of your king?"

"*Our* king. He will not like it, there being no way to hide you aided rebels, but he knows what it is to want a woman of a different class."

William's illegitimacy and his mother being of the common having nearly denied the duke the woman of royal blood he wished to wed, Aelfled reflected.

"Once he cools," Cyr continued, "I believe he will forgive me—providing the rebellion on these lands ends, which I am confident a D'Argent will effect, whether it is done by me or one of my brothers."

"One of your…"

"As told, if my eldest brother is dead, I shall return to Normandy. And as my wife, you will accompany me." He held out a hand. "Come be my lady, Aelfled."

Lady. It was one moment thrilling, the next frightening. Having not been raised nor groomed for that responsibility, she would not know what to do and could easily shame Cyr.

He caught up her hand. "Before God, a priest, and witnesses, you have but to repeat vows agreeing to become one with me, then it is done."

She moistened her lips. "And when it is done?"

"We feast, then being joined in holy matrimony, experience what comes after a kiss."

"Babes," Bernia said.

Though Aelfled's face warmed again, she summoned a smile. "Wed me, Cyr D'Argent."

A SIMPLE CEREMONY. A tense ceremony. More disapproval than approval.

The only witnesses clearly in favor of the union were Nicola who could not contain her smile and gasps of pleasure, and Bernia whose face had never appeared so tranquil.

Lady Chanson, Theriot D'Argent, and Maël D'Argent

presented as grim. And Dougray D'Argent come late to the chapel had turned on his heel and stalked away after learning the reason for his summons. Nor had he been amongst the confused and curious retainers and servants during the feast.

"Ah, Dougray." At table, Nicola had leaned near. "It is not you. It is all Saxons. But though he is broken over the loss of an arm, my brothers are putting him back together with every piece they drag out of him. And I say, he is more tolerable now than when first we arrived at Stern. Be patient, dear Aelfled. He will come around."

I think I shall love this sister made mine, Aelfled mused as she reflected on the few bright spots during a meal that had lasted too many hours. Another bit of bright had been Cyr feeding her the choicest pieces of meat from the point of his dagger as Isa's husband had done his lady. Even better, beneath the tablecloth he had covered her fist on her thigh, eased open her fingers, and raised their joined hands to the tabletop for all to see.

Now standing in the solar beneath a window set high in the wall, its open shutters letting in the light of falling night to play among the golden flicker of candles, she raised her left hand and once more considered what passed as a ring. Not until they were at the chapel door was it discovered Cyr had none to place on her finger. Lady Chanson had not offered one of hers, Nicola's fingers were bare, and Cyr's ring too large.

Bernia solved the dilemma. Her betrothed having no coin for a ring when they wed scores of years ago, the young woman had herself provided one. Now an old woman, she had instructed Nicola to cut the longest lock she could find upon her brother's head, then a lock of Aelfled's hair. The two were gathered together, divided into three, and tightly plaited. Thus, it was a silken ring fashioned of golden, black, and silver hair placed on Aelfled's hand, and she thought it more lovely and meaningful than any band of precious metal. It would not last, her grandmother said, but would suffice until the baron commissioned a ring worthy of the Lady of Stern and Balduc.

Aelfled turned her palm up, and as she confirmed the joined ends of the braid tightly bound with a stout thread from her grandmother's hem remained secure, caught the sound of the one come unto her.

Since entering the solar a quarter hour past, she had become oblivious to the din in the hall beyond, but as the curtain was thrust aside and before it fell back into place, it became louder. Now she heard his boots over the floor and the length of his stride.

It was time for what came after a kiss. And she was glad, longing for the nervous knot made of her insides to loosen and the satisfaction of curiosity.

Cyr halted at her back, and when she did not turn, said, "All is well?"

She peered over her shoulder at her husband and raised her left hand. "I think this beautiful. See how the black and silver and gold take the light over their crossings? And where they go under before coming up again on the opposite side, the dark of them is so soft and silken." She sighed. "If only it would last that ever it be upon my hand."

"Then you are pleased to be my wife?"

She hesitated, said, "I am, but—"

"Non, Aelfled. This is not a night for discussion. It is a night for knowing and feeling." His eyes moved to her temple. "If you are well enough."

She fingered the bandage. "As I have hardly thought on this since ere we spoke vows, I must be."

"Then shall we know? Feel?"

She drew a shaky breath. "Pray, let us." She started to turn to him, but of a sudden his hands were in her hair.

Running his fingers over and through it, he gathered the

tresses and draped them over one shoulder, letting them tumble down breasts and abdomen.

"Do you remember I told you were not meant to be a nun, Aelfled?"

The brush of his stubbled jaw and warm breath in the curve between shoulder and neck making her shiver, she nodded. "You said I was meant to be here with you. Like this."

"At last you are." He drew back and began loosening the laces coursing her spine. "Like this, Aelfled." He slid the shoulders of her gown down her arms to her elbows, exposing the thin, short-sleeved chemise that was all there was between her skin and his fingertips. He kissed her neck. "And like this." He pushed the gown's sleeves lower, trailed his finger over her arms to her wrists, rasped, "My wife is too soft to wear coarse material. I shall see her garbed in the finest weave and loveliest colors."

With the night air slipping through the window, she should not have been so warm she felt faint, but she was. And more so when he pushed the sleeves off her wrists and the gown dropped around her feet, leaving her clad in only her chemise.

"I do not know what to do, Cyr. And I think I am afeared."

"Think?" There was a smile in his voice.

"For what else would my heart beat so fast and breath be difficult to draw?"

"For this." More closely he fit his body to her back, slid his fingers through her splayed ones and curled them into her palms. "I will not hurt you." He kissed her neck, jaw, the corner of her mouth. "I will love you well."

Love? Though Aelfled longed to question that word, when he turned her into his arms and closed his mouth over hers, all that mattered was what he made her feel—and the hope she could make him feel half as much.

She returned his kisses and caresses, and for a wondrously long time they learned each other. But when he gentled her back on the bed, Aelfled of Senlac nearly cried when he said, "This night and every night and day hereafter, you are mine as I am yours, Aelfled of Cyr D'Argent." Burying her face against his shoulder, she held fast to him, and he stroked her hair and soothed her with sweet promises.

When finally she asked him to show her what came after, he kept every promise. And ones not made.

IN HIS ARMS. It was what he had wanted, what he had gained. No regret—terrible or slight—did he feel, only gratitude he had ceased struggling before it was too late to himself discover what came after with Aelfled.

He smiled into the dark of candles long guttered out, listened to the quiet of a hall settled into sleep, and once more slid his fingers from the crown of his wife's head resting on his shoulder to the ends of her hair splayed across his chest.

He had been confident he knew what followed a kiss such as theirs, but would wager he was nearly as surprised as his little Saxon who had shed self consciousness and given as she received —not wantonly but with sweet, reverent fervor.

Moving his fingers off the silken strands to her hand on his abdomen, he touched the ring braided of gold, black, and silver, wondered how to preserve it so she might wear it always as wished, then pressed his lips to the top of her head.

This night he had loved her as told. But as not yet told for being heretofore unaware—or was it resistant?—beyond the pleasures of the body he would love her to their end days. Though attracted to and protective of her since that morn at Senlac, he did not understand how he came to feel so much for one who had defied and frustrated him.

Was it her courage and resolve? That.

Strength and loyalty? That.

Compassion and willingness to sacrifice herself for others? That.

Spontaneity which often made her speak ahead of thought, evidencing she was not easily given to deception? That.

For this and more he loved her. God willing, one day he would love her for how well she loved him.

Unbidden, Hugh rose to mind. How he would scorn his nephew—after striking him upside the head. Or worse. A warrior was not to allow a woman to incite him to emotions only she should feel. Too much they distracted, threatening to soften the steel out of which men of the sword were forged. Though good to be protective and passing fond of those who bore worthy children to carry their sire's name into the ages, that was all. It was as Cyr believed before the bloody battle sent him in search of answers God had provided through Fulbert who would have him believe love for others gave a man greater purpose and more reason to survive the battles he must fight—especially love for a godly woman.

Godly. Though many her deceptions and lies, they had been in service to her people whose lives were dependent on her holding close their confidences and giving aid in an England ruled by men they had cause to fear. He would have to be patient with his Saxon bride. He would have to earn her trust. He would have to make allowances for secrets not her own. And of the scattered faith of she who had challenged his own at Senlac...

He lowered his lids, murmured, "I will help you gather up what has fallen away and put it back together. I shall be your Fulbert, Aelfled of Cyr of the silver."

CHAPTER THIRTY-TWO

*S*he had fallen asleep in his arms and now awakened with him curled around her, his chest to her back, arm over her waist, hand on her belly. A belly that would swell had they made a babe on the night past and nine months hence birth a son or daughter of mixed blood. It was as she hoped and as she would pray.

Though for nearly two years her faith had been terribly tested, and time and again she failed it, perhaps the Lord had not entirely turned His back on her and her people.

Was this not answered prayer—peace between conquered and conqueror, even if only here between one Saxon and one Norman? And surely across England there were others like Cyr and her. A small beginning, but the same as in centuries past when the people from whom she was descended had fought over these lands and slowly mixed to become Anglo-Saxons.

Unseeing Bernia saw that and believed it the way forward. Though other Saxons did not yet see it, many a Norman did. Self-serving, aye, but if those from across the narrow sea kept hold of this island kingdom, eventually most of those sprung from them would be of mixed blood. What then might they be called? Anglo-Saxon-Normans?

The man at her back stirred, caressed her belly.

Opening her eyes on morn whose misty light swept the wall opposite, Aelfled slid her hand atop her husband's. "I dreamed of you." Before speaking, she made no attempt to think those words front to back and top to bottom, having no care where they led since she could not imagine being more vulnerable to Cyr than she had on the night past. There were truths not her own she could not yet discuss—if ever—and blessedly he told he did not require them, but she could speak her own truth to one who had not been self-serving in taking her to wife.

She heard his breath, felt it expand his chest and the hair on that muscular plane rasp her skin. Then he rose, eased her onto her back, and lowered his face near hers. "I dreamed of *you.*"

She peered into green eyes shadowed by hair fallen forward, drew strands of silver and black through her fingers. "I speak not only of the night past," she revealed another of her truths, "but of many a night since you left me in Andredeswald."

A smile parted his lips, tempting her to touch strong white teeth that had grazed her skin as they made love. "As told you at the stream when first I kissed you, Aelfled, you have been with me since we met, visiting me at night whilst there was a sea between us. I am pleased to know I was visiting you as well."

Remembering the hopeless kiss that was hopeless no more, she said, "Oui, it is as you told me that day, but I dared not believe it. I thought…"

He grunted low. "I admit to motive beyond emotion—an attempt to soften you to gain your aid in ending the rebellion—but it was no exaggeration, no lie. That I chose as my reward these lands upon which you could be found ought to bear witness to that. And though it is true the sighting of Guarin is the foremost reason I returned to England, I had other reasons—you around whom I cannot think quite right as is very wrong for a warrior."

Aelfled could not keep her mouth from bowing. "I pray when you must take sword in hand to defend your life and the lives of others, you think only there the sooner to return to me here."

He brushed his mouth across hers, then trailed fingers down her neck to the hollow of her throat. "There are many who would think me a fool, but they are not here with you."

"Like this," she repeated his words of the night past.

"Like this," he murmured, then more slowly, gently, sweetly made love to his wife.

Afterward, with his heart beating beneath her ear, his hand once more in her hair drawing out tresses and winding them around his fingers, he said, "Should I prove my sire's heir, do you think you could be happy in Normandy?"

So earnestly was it asked, she knew that though great his hope of recovering his brother, great also was doubt.

"Aelfled?"

She looked to her hand splayed on his chest, upon it the ring fashioned of Cyr and Aelfled. "I could be happy there. Mayhap more so."

He was silent a long while, then lifted her chin to move her gaze to his. Head propped on the arm angled behind it, he frowned. "Truly?"

She had said it, and with not much thought, it being more feeling than consideration. "Oui, providing I am with you—and my grandmother."

He raised his eyebrows. "You surprise, my little Saxon. I feared you would not like to leave the country of your birth."

"I do not wish to, but…England hurts."

"It will heal."

"I pray you are right." She smiled sorrowfully. "Beyond your brother and me, what other reasons had you for returning to England?"

He released her chin, and when she resettled her cheek on his chest said, "Two, if they can be named reasons—Nicola and

Dougray. My sister was caught with a stable boy in a manner unbecoming a marriageable noblewoman. Though to save his life she submitted to an examination and proved she remained virtuous, the damage was done, the scandal far flung. Thus, it appeared all that remained for her was the convent—until I determined to return to England. It is hoped here might be found a suitable match either unaware of her past or willing to overlook it."

It was a sorry, ruinous thing to be so compromised, Aelfled reflected, whether in Normandy or England, and whether a woman was of noble or common blood. And yet one would not know the lively Nicola had been sent out of her country—in a manner, banished. "I like your sister."

Cyr gave a murmur of agreement. "She is reckless and fierce in all things in which she takes an interest, be it family or matters of men. Had she been born a male, I do not doubt the feats of *Nicholas* would have brought honor to the D'Argents—once control was learned."

Aelfled smiled. "She told she knows the bow."

"It is a weapon favored by Guarin who instructed her in its use —and the dagger."

"Not a sword?"

"That our mother would not permit."

"Nor your sire?"

After a long moment, Cyr said, "Nor him though much he indulges Nicola."

Aelfled's curiosity was piqued over the man who fathered her husband, but there was now time aplenty to learn more about one whose brother, Hugh, seemed to have been more a force in Cyr's life. "What of Dougray?" she asked.

"He requires more telling, and further back I must go to well before Duke William began assembling his great host to invade England and take the crown from Harold. As you may have guessed, the reason Dougray's hair is not black marked with silver is he was not sired by a D'Argent. I will not elaborate now, but suffice to say the circumstances of his conception outside the bounds of marriage allowed my sire to accept his wife's child and give his name to him. But for all that, it is well known Dougray is misbegotten. Though his brothers and sister count him fully kin and equally worthy of the D'Argent name, he struggles over the whispers and mockery of those outside our family. And in more recent years the limitations."

"What are those?"

Lowering to his chest the hand wrapped in her hair, he said, "He thought himself in love with a noblewoman, and she was taken with him. But her sire refused a match, citing Dougray's illegitimacy and landlessness. He became so sullen that when I determined to cure my own landlessness by joining the campaign to gain England's crown, I set to persuading him to do the same. He resisted, not out of cowardice but the belief it an ill and unjustified business destined to shed the blood of thousands and subjugate innocents. It was my suggestion lands of his own could prove sufficient to gain his heart's desire that moved him to pledge his sword to the duke's cause."

Feeling what had been relaxed beneath her tense, Aelfled looked up. "You suffer guilt that rather than lands and his heart's desire, he lost an arm."

Down the length of his nose, he met her gaze. "I do. And guilt over Guarin as well."

"Why?"

"When he tried to dissuade us from crossing the sea, I accused him of not understanding the need since he was to have lands of his own and a prosperous future. I knew he did not seek to deny his brothers the same, that he foresaw the slaughter and sought to protect us, but my need to prove my prowess that had earned me the name *Merciless* during contests of arms bade me challenge him to join the invading army and fight with us. He accepted and has been lost to us since."

She considered the dagger found inside the abbey's walls and longed to tell him of it, but so dear to him was his brother she feared in seeking answers from his captives the merciless side of him would show were he denied them. Though he might learn it was Vitalis who carried the weapon, Isa's man would own to naught.

"You may yet recover him," she said.

"That is the plan." Before she could question it, he said, "As for how Dougray became a reason for my return to England, so bitter was he over the loss of an arm that made his lack of lands and illegitimacy lesser things, it was hoped removing him from D'Argent lands would loose him from the miserable existence in which he wallowed. Though he is coming around and has resumed training to reclaim the warrior left upon Senlac, methinks that a long road, especially with such scarcity of faith."

"Unlike yours."

He smiled. "As told, I met Father Fulbert on pilgrimage, and he has been my dear companion, confessor, and conscience since. Of Saxon and Norman blood, he instructed me in your language lest my destiny prove that of an English rather than Norman lord."

"Spoken English only?"

"Written as well, mostly taught by way of..." His brow rippled. "I have something for you." He eased her onto her side, and as she snatched the sheet over her bared body, rose.

A flush heating her head to toe, she watched him move to the trunk at the foot of the bed and raise the lid that stole from sight all beneath his upper chest.

He bent, paused to looked at her, grinned. "If my lack of modesty makes you uncomfortable, Wife, you could look elsewhere, though I vow I will not look elsewhere do you come out from beneath your sheet. What too little light denied me on our wedding night, daylight will allow me to know and enjoy in full."

She warmed further, too late averted her gaze.

He chuckled, and she heard him rifle through the trunk. Shortly, he returned. "This," he said.

She chanced a look at him, was grateful he had donned a robe —and jolted by what he held. She gasped and, gripping the sheet to her chest, sat up and reached to that which he told he would return to her the first day he had come to Lillefarne.

Before she could close a hand around the binding, she faltered, then drew back. She knew to expect evidence of Wulf's blood on the cover, but though much lightened, the stain slapped her back to that chill morn when she had cradled Isa's boy in her lap and mourned the numbered heartbeats of an unfinished life.

"I am sorry," Cyr said. "In anticipation of returning this, I had the cover cleaned, but the stain could not be entirely removed."

Of course he had shown such consideration. *Lord,* she silently entreated, *how could I not love this man? I do. Truly, I do.*

She breathed deep, scooted forward, and took the psalter. "This aided in learning our written language?"

He hesitated, said, "Father Fulbert began my instruction by writing words in the dirt and progressed to these pages. But more than teaching me to read and write English, it provided prayer and guidance to aid in governing my new people as you suggested."

"I am pleased but also ashamed."

"Why?"

"Though that day I believed you more in need of prayer and guidance, whilst you found your way, I lost mine. For that, the abbess would not allow me to give my life to the Church."

He drew the backs of his fingers down her cheek. "I cannot bemoan that. Tell me that if ever you did, you do not now."

"I do not now."

He bent and kissed her mouth open. When he drew back, it was to turn an ear to the din of the risen household beyond the curtains. "Soon it shall be time to break our fast. I am thinking you prefer we do so here."

"I would like that."

He strode to the curtains, exited, and returned moments later. "It shall be done," he said and lowered beside her. "Now you, Aelfled."

"Me?"

"I have told of my guilt. I would know of that weighing upon you—Wulf."

"Oh."

"If you can," he added.

Could she? He ought to know, even if only to better understand lies told to protect her lady. "I can." She passed the psalter to him, and when he set it on the bedside table said, "You must understand that though Lady Hawisa wed for alliance, she grew fond of her husband. When he was killed at Stamford Bridge after sending Wulf and her south, unaware he sent them into the teeth of a greater battle, she grieved." She shook her head. "So tired and dispirited was she that all grew concerned. And as Wulf made it worse with his anger over the loss of his sire, I entreated my lady to give him into my keeping so she might rest. Now much to her regret, she agreed."

When Cyr closed a hand over hers on the mattress, she realized she had made it into a fist. Opening it, she turned it up and gripped his fingers.

"When we learned your duke had landed nearby with a mighty army," she continued, "I was more vigilant, though the Penderys with whom we stayed were Normans and assured us we had naught to fear from their fellow countrymen. However, the danger did not come from without. I did not know my charge's mind—that though he could not touch those who slew his father, he plotted vengeance against the new invaders. Under pretense of play, he gathered village boys to his side. Though I followed wherever they went on the demesne, given his word he would behave I kept my distance so as not to embarrass him. On the day of the battle, I fell prey to trickery. Wulf and his friends entered the stables, and for an hour I waited outside as done each day, certain they played games of dice in the loft. When still they did not come out nor answer when I called, I entered. Except for the restlessness of horses, it was quiet, and soon I verified the boys had stolen away."

Momentarily, she closed her eyes and took comfort in the hand holding hers. "Much time I wasted looking for them, certain they were near. When I could not find them, I went to Hawisa—Isa as I was yet permitted to call her—and confessed my failing. As she was aware the battle between Saxons and Normans had commenced that morn near Hastings, and it was reported three horses were missing, she guessed her son and his friends had gone seeking vengeance against the invaders. With dusk approaching and without assembling an escort, she and I followed. As we neared Senlac, we happened on fleeing Saxons who told King Harold was dead. Though we were able to question only a few, I thought I would die when one reported having seen boys on the battlefield." Eyes moist, Aelfled met Cyr's gaze. "As you know, we came too late. The innocents Wulf persuaded to join him were slain and him nearly so. Thus, it is not the death of one boy on my conscience. It is five."

He pushed a tress off her brow, tucked it behind her ear. "You were deceived."

"That does not absolve one who assured her lady she would allow no harm to befall her son."

"You could not have known the lengths to which Wulf would go."

"It is true I did not know him capable of such, but my ignorance cost my lady her son."

"And Lady Hawisa's ignorance," he said firmly. "She who ought to have known him better than you should have entrusted his care to warriors. Does she know how he deceived you?"

Aelfled shook her head. "My grandmother believes I should

tell her, but of what use? It would not bring him back and could tarnish the character of a well-loved son."

"Still she ought to know. And even if she will not forgive you, you must forgive yourself."

She smiled sorrowfully. "As you have forgiven yourself?"

He inclined his head. "And as I continue to do every day. Though I remain burdened by knowledge I could have felled those boys the same as my uncle—and may ever be burdened, which is not a bad thing for one who wields a blade—much peace I find in daily prayer for forgiveness. I want that for you, Aelfled."

Throat so tight it ached, she whispered, "Will you help me find it?"

"For better, for worse," he reminded her of their vows spoken on the day past. "Whatever you need, I will give you."

A sob escaped, and he held her close until she settled and said, "When first you came to me at Lillefarne, I told I did not pray for you."

He drew back. "A lie?"

"Not entirely. Though I resisted your attempts to intrude on my time with the Lord, at times you were so persistent I could quiet you only by keeping my word to pray for you."

He kissed her brow. "Those prayers were heard, my lady. And answered."

She smiled, and as she started to tuck herself into him, a woman's voice called from beyond the curtains, "My lord, I bring your meal."

Cyr pulled away, rose, and turned the coverlet over his wife. "Enter!"

The servant shouldered open the curtains, with eyes lowered crossed the solar and set a tray on the bedside table. She glanced at Aelfled, next her lord, then curtsied and hastened away.

Side by side, they ate mostly in silence, and though comforted by Cyr's assurance he would help her find peace and forgiveness, Aelfled was grateful they did not return to that discussion.

Cyr drained his cup and set it aside. "Would that I could remain abed with you all day, Wife."

Aelfled finished chewing a slice of crisp apple. "Why can you not?"

"There were three momentous events on the day past, one of which was our marriage."

She smiled. "The other two?"

"A means of removing Campagnon from Balduc and—"

"How?" she exclaimed.

"Dougray obtained a confession from Merle that his lord ordered the hay upon Stern put to flame."

She knew the name, recalled the face. "He was with Campagnon at Senlac." She nodded. "When I arrived at Stern, I recognized him in the paddock opposite the Saxons. Do you think he speaks true?"

"I am not certain. It is possible he acted on his own. However, I cannot pass on the opportunity to be rid of Campagnon, especially as under such circumstances the king is likely to approve and be eager to himself confirm the truth of it. Thus, this day I ride to Balduc to remove Campagnon, set him on the road to William, and install Theriot as castellan."

"I am glad he is leaving. All know him to be of wicked bent," Aelfled said. "Now what of the third momentous event?"

"It is possible I am near to retrieving my brother."

She sat straighter. "How?"

His gaze sharpened as if to ensure her reaction to his words did not escape him. "I sent word to the rebels I wish to strike a bargain, that I shall release to them all my Saxon captives if they release to me one man."

"Guarin."

He inclined his head. "Only if he lives, in which case, never will they have better cause to return him."

"I pray they do."

"And I pray Vitalis does not fail me."

She frowned. "Vitalis bears your message?"

"He does."

"But he is—"

"The most valuable and loyal of those taken at Lillefarne. For that, I believe he has the power to make good the trade, even if he must act against his own to ensure his men are freed."

"What do you mean—act against his own?"

"I think there dissension in their ranks, Aelfled."

She held her tongue a long moment, said, "I fear the same."

Cyr's smile was slight. "If not that it could make it more difficult to gain Guarin's release, I would think it a good thing since it lends itself well to disbanding them, internal fighting having destroyed many a good—and bad—cause."

"When do you expect the rebels to give answer?"

"I do not think this day, but possibly the morrow—all the more reason to finish with Campagnon so I am present to receive Vitalis."

Once more, he stood from the bed. "Now I must prepare to depart for Balduc."

Guessing he had watched her closely as much for her response to the dissension as to Vitalis, she said, "Cyr, as not told, once I had a care for Vitalis. As told, naught came of it." She felt herself flush. "And now I am glad."

He leaned down and kissed her.

"We will be happy, will we not?" she asked when he drew back.

"Will be? In this moment, I am happier than ever I expected with my choice of bride. And that happiness shall be nearly complete do I restore Guarin as my sire's heir."

He will come to love me as I love him, she assured herself as she laid back. "Be of good care, Husband, so sooner you return to me."

A quarter hour later, he told her he would hold her again come night and departed. But no rest was she allowed following her wedding night, Bernia led by Nicola entering after the closing of the great doors sounded from beyond the curtains.

Aelfled should not have been surprised the women did not come merely seeking assurance that Cyr's bride had weathered her wedding night, but their talk of hanging out the sheets to prove she had been a maiden discomfited. The evidence was present, and Nicola's pronouncement that none could dispute Aelfled's virtue was gifted her husband had the bride pleading they do what must be done and speak no more of it.

They complied, but when later Aelfled stepped from the solar wearing a pale grey gown with her psalter on its girdle, she knew from the looks castle folk and soldiers cast her way—some understanding and approving, others sly and knowing—the matter remained under discussion.

There was naught to be done, and so she turned her thoughts to other things, above all becoming the lady Cyr D'Argent had made her.

CHAPTER THIRTY-THREE

Castle Balduc
England

I am glad to have your company, Dougray."

Having slowed his mount alongside Cyr's on the final approach to Balduc, Dougray looked to his older brother, then Theriot beyond. "Woe to me should I miss the opportunity to see Campagnon bound over the back of a horse."

"That I would also like to see," Cyr said, "but unless he turns violent, he must be afforded a measure of respect since it is for William to determine his culpability."

"Then let us hope he turns exceedingly violent."

Fulbert would not approve, but neither would Cyr mind if his castellan took extreme measures to resist being unseated. But it was not only that hope which incited Dougray to join the ride to Balduc. As revealed by Maël who was left in command of Stern, it was with Dougray's aid Merle's confession was gained—and only after a beating, though well-deserved, Maël told.

Whilst being questioned over Campagnon's involvement in the plot to burn Stern's hay, Merle had begun taunting Dougray over the interest shown his lord's slave. And when Dougray rose to it, the fool went further, claiming Campagnon used Em as a reward for men who served him well, and many a night and day he had enjoyed her.

That had begun the beating that required Maël and his men to intercede. But no sooner was Dougray sufficiently calmed to be released than Merle boasted the *whore* was worth every tooth and claw, bite and scratch.

It was more difficult to pull Dougray off the second time, and then only after Merle sustained broken ribs, teeth, and wrist—and turned fearful as he should have sooner.

Maël had used the moment to good advantage, stating a signed confession would put the greatest distance between Merle and the man who would kill him first and worry second on what King William thought of the *slaughter* of a fellow Norman. Thus, by questionable—albeit satisfactory—means, a signed confession was gained.

To Cyr's surprise, when next Dougray spoke, he revealed what surely did not wish to. "What happens to…" He made a face. "I forget her name. What shall become of Campagnon's slave when he is sent to the king?"

With reluctance, Cyr confirmed what his brother had to know. "As his property, I think she must accompany him."

"Did he not face the charge of treason, oui," Dougray said. "But under such circumstances, dare he take her with him? William sets no store in slavery—indeed, looks ill upon the practice."

"In Normandy, Brother. Though I believe he will abolish it in England, at this time, the share he earns from the trade is a good source of revenue with which to stitch back together a country torn by war and rebellion."

Dougray turned thoughtful, finally said, "If William accepts Merle's confession as truth, what will become of…the slave?"

"Unfortunately, I do not believe Campagnon will suffer much. Should William accept Merle's confession, I trust I shall be rid of the knave entirely, but likely he will return to the work of a mercenary. If he remains in England, he may keep Em—that is her name, Dougray." As well he knew. "If he returns to Normandy, he will have to sell her."

"Like an animal," Dougray growled.

"I like it no more than you. Thus, should you contrive a means of rescuing her without risking recourse for theft, you can be assured of my aid."

Dougray's chin came around, and there was light in his eyes and a curve to his lips that could not be attributed to bitterness nor scorn. However, immediately he shifted his regard to the fortress and shrugged. "It would be the godly thing to do—free her and send her on her way. I shall think on it."

"A rider approaches!" Theriot announced.

As that one came off the drawbridge and headed toward them at good speed, Cyr and his entourage urged their mounts to a gallop and moments later met one of those Cyr had set to keep watch over Campagnon.

"You could not have come at a better time, my lord," the man-at-arms said.

"What has happened?"

"Not a quarter hour past, a great commotion arose in the hall."

"The cause?"

"I have yet to learn, my lord. Myself and two others were commanded to secure the outer bailey whilst the rest of your men put finish to whatever goes."

Cyr urged his horse forward and, upon entering the bailey, gave command of the garrison to Theriot and a dozen warriors.

Shortly, with Dougray striding alongside, chevaliers and men-at-arms at their backs, swords drawn, Cyr entered the hall and found Campagnon at the center of what remained of a disturbance put down by soldiers who stood with weapons drawn before the dais.

As the men acknowledged the arrival of their baron with grim mouths and curt nods, Balduc's former castellan shouted at the woman who stood before the chair in which he was seated, "Be done with it, wench! I have prey to take to ground!"

"What is this, Campagnon?" Cyr demanded.

The man jerked so hard his chair jumped back a space, snapped his head to the side to look to the one advancing on him, then knocked aside the servant to reveal a bared and bloodied shoulder crudely stitched closed. "What this is," he snarled, "is what happens when a Saxon—and a slave at that—knows not her place. But be assured, I shall teach it to her when I have her hair in one fist, her throat in the other."

Senses assaulted by Dougray's surge of anger, Cyr growled low, "Stay your hand, Brother. This is for me to give answer." He ascended the dais and considered Campagnon across the table between them. "You are saying a woman did this to a warrior who survived the great battle?"

Campagnon sneered. "The witch caught me unawares."

One of the men-at-arms snorted, and when Cyr commanded him to speak, he said, "Hardly unawares, my lord. He was shouting and beating her, causing a great clatter with all he felled in chasing her around the solar."

Yet more aware of Dougray, Cyr hoped he would not have to intercede as Maël had done with Merle. "What cause did you give her to stick you with a blade, Campagnon?"

Cyr expected the man to draw around him the mantle of ownership and refuse to answer, but he said, "Though my coin bought her, her actions are also of your concern since they threaten the demesne."

"Speak!"

"I discovered she has been passing information to the rebels which, doubtless, was used in their most recent attack on the castle."

Cyr had guessed Balduc hosted one or more rebel supporters, but if it was Em who passed along the plan to attack Stern's hay, there was good in it. That she was the cause of him losing his position seemed fitting justice for one who abused and made of her the basest of chattel.

As if suddenly aware of something he should have been sooner, Campagnon demanded, "For what have you ridden on Balduc?"

Ignoring his question, Cyr said, "Where is the slave?"

"Your men let her get away."

Cyr wondered if Dougray was also thinking here the means of getting the woman out of Campagnon's clutches. Were she not found, she could not accompany him from Balduc.

"But I shall drag her from whatever corner she huddles in," the knave boasted, "and upon threat of death she shall reveal the nest of rebels within my walls."

"*My* walls," Cyr corrected. "And now my brother's."

Campagnon's lids narrowed. "Of what do you speak?"

"This day, Theriot D'Argent takes your place as castellan of Balduc."

The man lurched out of the chair, groaned and clapped a hand to his wound, braced his other hand on the table. "The king made me your liegeman!"

"A mistake, as I believe William will agree when he learns it was under your orders my hay was to have been burned."

"A lie!" Campagnon's saliva misted the air between them. "I had naught to do with that. You know I did not."

"I do not know that. Thus, it is for the king to determine whether your man, Merle, speaks true or false. And as I am sure he will wish to do so quickly, this day his men shall escort you to him." Cyr motioned the chevaliers forward. "Take him into custody."

Campagnon stumbled back, snatched his dagger from its sheath.

It was no contest, though he was skilled enough it would have been a good fight were he not weakened by his injury.

When the warriors had him facedown on the dais, he howled, doubtless over the pressure on his wound.

"As soon as you have his dagger," Cyr said, "get him on his feet."

The one with a knee planted in the knave's back, scorned, "You sound like the one you were beating, Campagnon. A woman."

It was not he who paid for the insult but his fellow warrior trying to grasp the flailing, dagger-wielding arm. The blade sliced the man's palm, causing him to rear back.

"I would say he has turned violent, would you not?" Dougray drawled.

Cyr inclined his head. "Wish granted."

Thus, it was Dougray who relieved Campagnon of the dagger with a deft sweep of the hand. Gradually, he was reclaiming the warrior he had been.

"My slave goes with me!" Campagnon shouted as he was carried from the hall. "It is my right! Find her!"

"We must," Cyr said when the doors closed behind his protests and threats.

Once more Dougray was all glower. "You will not send her with him, will you?"

"Non, but as he was beating her, her own injuries may require tending, and there is the matter of her being an informant. I would have from her all she knows of Campagnon and what she passed to the rebels." The shift in his brother's eyes revealing he did not like it, Cyr added, "However I can, you know I must stop the insurrection, Dougray. Too, if she supports Merle's confession—"

"You think a Saxon...a slave...one who aids those opposed to William's rule would be believed?"

"If her tale is the same as Merle's—a Norman and a warrior—it is possible." Cyr stepped nearer, lowered his voice, "Are you aware of how much concern you show for one whose name you cannot recall?"

Cyr glimpsed alarm, then denial in Dougray's eyes before he pivoted away.

"I will find the wench," he said and strode toward the kitchen passage where servants had gathered to watch from a safe distance.

An hour later, despite the efforts of Dougray and a half dozen men-at-arms, the search for Em proved fruitless. Either she had become a mouse in a hole of which none knew, else amid the commotion she had escaped Balduc.

The latter, Cyr guessed—and that she made her way to the rebels she served. Regardless, she had freed herself of Campagnon.

CHAPTER THIRTY-FOUR

Stern Castle
England

*T*he dagger of Hugh D'Argent.

It made Aelfled falter and Lady Chanson look up from the scabbard-less blade. With a taut smile, the woman said, "Join me, Lady Aelfled."

Telling herself she must become accustomed to the title that she not always be wincing, Aelfled glanced at where the woman's son stood before the hearth in conversation with three chevaliers.

"Pray, Nicola, assure Cyr's wife I am capable enough of defending myself I need not call on my son should the need arise," the lady said with a light tone that made the young woman at Aelfled's side giggle.

Aelfled set her shoulders back, circled the dais, and as she lowered into the chair on one side of Cyr's aunt and Nicola on the other, said, "I hope you do not believe the need will ever arise where I am concerned, my lady."

"As oft my departed husband said, certainty in anything, be it of flesh, strategy, or emotion exposes one's neck to the blade." The lady touched a finger to the dagger's point, then raised her hand to reveal a drop of blood. "As sharp as ever. Do you think it last bled my husband?"

Aelfled wished she had not allowed Nicola to persuade her to seek her aunt's counsel over how to bring the household under her command. But though this was not a conversation she wished to have, here it was, and she supposed it must be had eventually. "It is possible, my lady."

"You gained the dagger from Lady Hawisa's son?"

"I did—as he breathed his last in my arms. I know not how it came into his possession, nor whether it was before or after he was dealt the blow that proved his own death."

"So you cannot say my husband slew him and the other boys?"

Aelfled moistened her lips. "As your husband warned, one cannot be certain of anything, but that is as it appeared."

After a long moment, the woman said, "Though he had a reputation for being vicious in battle, he would have been appalled over his end and theirs."

"Cyr believes he must have been severely injured by King Harold's men to have fallen to boys."

Lady Chanson nodded. "I suppose that is of some comfort."

"I am sorry for your loss and your son's, my lady. I know it is great."

The lady pressed a thumb to the pad of her crimson-beaded finger, sat back. "Not as great as it could have been. Hugh was not one to welcome love, and so it was gifted at one's own peril and pain. He was different from his brother who sired my nephews and niece."

Curiosity roused again over Cyr's sire, Aelfled leaned nearer. But it was Hugh the lady returned to. "Thus, bit by bit, disappointment by disappointment, one reeled in that love." She looked to her son. "As did Maël, and yet methinks he suffers the loss more than I."

Aelfled could think of no response, and was glad one was not sought over a matter beyond her knowledge and understanding.

Nicola patted the woman's arm. "My cousin will come around, Aunt."

"I pray so, but I see little evidence. When I told him he should keep his sire's dagger, thinking he would be comforted, he became angry. If only I knew what is in my son's mind—more, his heart."

Certain she trespassed on intimate discourse and now was not the time to seek Lady Chanson's advice on ordering Cyr's household, Aelfled sat back and wondered how best to approach the cook to discuss the menus. Occasionally, she had been present when Isa coordinated the meals at Wulfen. Much was required to feed so many, but there had been logic to the planning—a balance between using the best ingredients whilst in their prime and making use of foodstuffs of which there was an overabundance or approached a ripeness that would soon see them fit only for pigs.

As Nicola spoke soothingly to her aunt, the great doors swung inward, and the soldier who strode inside announced, "Sir Maël, the Saxon has returned, fully armored and accompanied by ten men similarly outfitted and with extra horses."

Vitalis. It had to be.

As Cyr's cousin made the fewest of strides between hearth and entryway, he demanded, "My cousin accompanies him?"

"I do not know, Sire. All but Vitalis are beneath hoods."

As Sir Maël and his man exited, Nicola leapt to her feet. "Guarin is sure to be without. I must see for myself."

"Non," Lady Chanson said, "remain with me. Soon enough we shall know what goes."

"I cannot sit still. Devise a punishment if you wish, but I shall sooner than later be reunited with the brother two years denied me." As she descended the dais, she called, "Accompany me, Aelfled."

Aelfled rose and followed. Other than visits to the garden, she had not been outside since her arrival at Stern when Sigward's stone dropped her over the horse's neck. Though Cyr had borne her through the inner bailey, she had been too dazed to look near upon it, but hardly was she able to do so now with Nicola nearly running to overtake her cousin.

When they entered the outer bailey, Aelfled hesitated at the realization once more she must pass the rebels. But assuring herself they knew it was Sigward who betrayed them at Lillefarne, she continued forward and followed Nicola and Sir Maël up steps to the wall walk above the great doors that were open though its gate remained lowered.

Cyr had sent Merle and his men to his king, but the eastern paddock was no more empty than the western, the rebels having been divided between the two, doubtless to exercise greater control over their numbers.

It was difficult to meet the eyes of her fellow Saxons who might think she flaunted her freedom among Normans, but she looked between them and was glad they did not yet know she had acquired the surname D'Argent.

"Non, Nicola," Sir Maël said when he noticed the two women. "Return to the donjon, both of you."

"Only do you serve as escort," Nicola said as she and Aelfled halted before him.

Annoyance lined his face, and when the young woman pushed onto her toes and tried to look past him to those outside Stern, he gripped her shoulders and set her back against the rail. "Stand there—and you as well, Aelfled. Providing you stay out of sight, you may remain. Interfere and I will have my men put you over a shoulder and carry you from here."

"Just one peek," Nicola entreated and again tried to peer past him.

"Non, Nicola!"

She rolled her eyes. "Very well, we shall remain out of sight."

He pivoted and, a moment later, showed himself to those below.

"Sir Maël!" Vitalis's voice bounded to the top of the wall as if carried by his long legs.

"You return sooner than expected," the king's man called down. "I am thinking it is not because you are unable to keep the bargain. Were that so, you would surely flee."

"You do not know me, Norman," Vitalis called, "and you are not the one with whom I bargained. I would speak with Cyr D'Argent."

"Regrettably, he is gone, and it may be night ere he and his men return."

A long silence, during which Nicola hissed, "Does he or does he not have my brother?"

Finally, Vitalis said, "Do you have the power to act on your cousin's behalf?"

"I do."

"Then soon we shall be done here. My leader agrees to the terms, but there is one thing required beyond my men's release."

"Dear Lord, he has Guarin," Nicola gasped. "He lives, at last shall be reunited with us."

"The bargain was accepted by both parties," Maël said. "It stands as is."

"Then it falls," Vitalis said.

"Maël!" Nicola squeaked. "No matter what he asks, Cyr would agree."

His head came round. "Be silent!"

"I will not! You know I speak true. Give him what he wants."

Anger coloring the face Sir Maël turned back to those beyond the walls, he called, "What else does your leader require?"

"Aelfled."

She of that name nearly choked on her tongue, and Nicola coughed hard as if to dislodge her own from her throat.

"I do not believe my cousin would agree to that," Maël called. "Hence, your nineteen rebels for—"

"Ere you give answer," Vitalis spoke over him, "look upon this."

Beside Aelfled, Nicola drew a sharp breath, on its exhale whispered, "You think it my brother?" Then she hastened forward, knocking her cousin's shoulder as she joined him at the wall. "Guarin!" She gripped Sir Maël's sleeve, cried, "Dear Lord, what has been done him?"

Feet feeling as if shod in lead, Aelfled dragged them forward. As she neared, she heard Vitalis call, "Your brother is not well, Lady. Though I assure you he is not mortally ill—at this time—of great benefit would it be were you to persuade your cousin to reconsider."

"Maël?" the young woman shrilled.

Aelfled closed a hand around the psalter on her girdle, stepped to Nicola's side, and peered down at those before the castle—a score of horses, only half of which carried riders. And of those riders, all were hooded except Vitalis who was already known to the Normans and the one between two others whose hood was around his shoulders to reveal his hunched figure.

Though the man's hair was long and tangled as it had surely not been when he wielded a sword against Saxons at the battle that passed England into the hands of the Normans, it was ink black and liberally streaked with silver. As she stared, he gave evidence of life by lifting his head and, with what seemed great effort, turned up his face. It was bruised and cut, but not gaunt as if he had been denied adequate sustenance. When his head dropped, a great sob sounded from Nicola.

"Aelfled, you are summoned," Vitalis shouted, and she was reminded of when he had said her time at Lillefarne was over—that she was to return to her lady's service. Now that she was wed to Cyr, that was no longer possible, but the trade was.

Feeling soft ridges beneath thumb and forefinger, realizing she had moved her hand from the psalter to her beautifully makeshift wedding ring, Aelfled looked to Sir Maël. He watched her, and she felt his struggle which would have been non-existent had he not witnessed vows spoken on the day past.

She stepped back from the wall and skirted Nicola. Knowing how greatly Cyr needed his brother restored to his family, and certain he would yield his new wife even were Guarin not in need of medical attention, she touched his cousin's sleeve and when he looked to her said, "I know you wish to do as he bids."

"I would were you not Cyr's wife."

She inclined her head. "Allow me to solve your dilemma. Guarin has been Cyr's beloved brother and your cousin far longer than I have borne the name D'Argent. For him, Cyr returned to England. Now that he is within your grasp and in dire need of care, you must surrender me."

"It is what you want?" he snapped. "To be with your own?"

She nearly confirmed it in the hope it would make it easier for him to trade away his cousin's wife, but the thought of Cyr being told such was painful. "I wish to be with the one who left me this morn and said he would hold me again this eve, but I fear that is not the one who shall next stand before me if his brother is lost to him."

His eyes delved her face as if searching for falsity, but he would find none. Finally, with what sounded desperation, he said, "Cyr could return soon."

"Oui, but it might also be hours—or even the morrow—which could make the difference between his brother living and dying. Pray, Sir Maël, do not let me be the cause of your family losing another member."

Still he hesitated.

"They will not harm me." Of that she was fairly certain since it was now known Sigward was the betrayer.

He nodded. "As you say, I have no choice. Hence, I will release you to them. However, I think you must agree it will be safest for you if those outside these walls remain ignorant of your marriage." His jaw shifted. "Were it thought you carried a Norman's child…"

Was the beginning of a babe within? Determinedly keeping her hand from her belly, Aelfled mulled his concern. Vitalis would be repelled by her union with Cyr, but even if she need not fear him, there were others among the rebels who could prove a danger. What the chevalier suggested was for the best. For now.

"I agree, Sir Maël." Ache in her breast, she removed from her finger the ring woven of hair, next the psalter from her girdle. "Give these to my husband." She tucked the former between the pages of the latter. "Tell him I pray they—more, he—shall soon be returned to me."

When he took the psalter, impulsively she added, "I am sorry your sire's dagger pained your mother and you. I meant no harm."

He nodded, then turned to his cousin who continued to stare at her brother outside the wall. "Go with Aelfled to the bailey, Nicola. There you shall be reunited with Guarin."

She turned moist eyes on him, then gripped the hand Aelfled offered and followed her sister-in-law down the wall walk.

"We are in agreement," she heard the chevalier call. "Prepare to trade your captive for ours."

She who was no longer Cyr's captive was met by Father Fulbert as she came off the steps.

"Nicola," he said. "I must speak with Lady Aelfled."

The young woman's face was all confusion, but she continued toward the portcullis.

"Father?" Aelfled prompted.

"Methinks you do this not only to see your people freed but that a beloved brother be recovered ere the chance of saving him is lost. Thus, I believe I speak true in saying how difficult a thing it would be for Cyr to do were he here. You care much for your Norman husband, aye?"

"I do."

"May I pray for you?"

"I beseech it. Since Senlac..." She shrugged. "'Tis as if my voice is too small to reach the Lord's ear."

"No voice is too small, Child." He raised his hands, and when she set hers in his, bowed his head. "The Lord be with you. The Lord embrace you. The Lord comfort you. The Lord return you to your family. The Lord give peace to you and yours, Aelfled D'Argent. Amen."

That was all, and yet so sincere was his beseeching that no more seemed needed.

When he released her hands, she opened her eyes and saw Sir Maël bounding down the steps. "Will you tell my grandmother what has happened and I shall return as soon as possible, Father?" *Pray, let me not be long gone from her,* she silently beseeched.

"I shall tell her, my lady."

The exchange happened quickly, the bound Saxons marched from the paddocks under guard of chevaliers and men-at-arms and assembled before the portcullis two abreast. When Cyr's cousin placed Aelfled behind the rebels, Nicola hastened to her.

"What do you?" she demanded of Sir Maël, confirmation she had been too emotional to understand the bargain was altered.

"What must be done to return your brother to you, Nicola. You want that, do you not?"

"Of course, but—"

"Neither do I like this, but it is done. Now stand aside."

Nicola turned stricken eyes upon Aelfled, started to speak, then hastened away.

As clattering chains announced the raising of the portcullis, Aelfled said, "Pray, Sir Maël, tell Cyr I shall return to him."

He raised his eyebrows. "I believe he will himself retrieve you, my lady. And should he require it, I will aid him."

Words that did not sound mocking nor falsely confident helped Aelfled to place one foot in front of the other when the rebels were ordered forward.

The armed Normans stayed close as their captives passed beneath the portcullis and over the drawbridge. Once on firm ground, the rebels were commanded to halt, and the king's men sliced the ropes binding their hands. Then the mounted Guarin D'Argent was led forward by hooded men on either side.

As the two parties passed, Cyr's brother, gripping the saddle's pommel, turned his face toward the rebels for whom he was being traded.

Did he recognize any? Likely, considering how long he was held captive.

Aelfled stumbled when eyes like Cyr's in shape and color passed over her and immediately swept back. Just as she had not known he was the rebels' captive, she had never met him, but there seemed recognition there. Though he was surely on the verge of collapse, he was alert enough to have attended to the negotiation that saw the ranks of captive rebels swell with the addition of a woman.

Had he heard of her? Did he know of the aid given the rebels during her stay at Lillefarne? When she returned to her husband —and she had to believe she would—might Guarin D'Argent be so bitter he would try to turn Cyr against his wife? And if he did...

He will return to Normandy, she assured herself as he passed. *Happily, he will leave behind a land and people he must detest and a brother who wed a Saxon commoner of no benefit to him.*

As hooves on the drawbridge sounded, Aelfled peered over her shoulder and saw the eldest D'Argent cross it alone, his rebel escort having turned back. Striding toward him was his cousin, beyond him Nicola whose eyes were all for her beloved brother.

"Mount up!" Vitalis commanded his men who immediately set themselves at the spare horses that would carry two riders each, then his eyes landed on Aelfled. "Come!"

She hitched up her skirt and hastened to him. "Why me?" she asked as he settled her on the fore of his saddle.

"Still she has a care for you," he said.

That she need no longer have, Aelfled reflected and was tempted to reveal to Vitalis she was wed to the man Isa feared would harm her, but he would deliver her as commanded.

She looked to the fortress and beyond the lowering portcullis saw the injured D'Argent being lifted down and his sister anxiously peering around the men who would convey Guarin to the donjon.

"Fear not," Vitalis said, "you are free of them."

As she did not wish to be, but better he believe it so no guard was placed on her to prevent her from returning to Cyr.

"You ought know Dotter does not hold you responsible for what happened at Lillefarne," he said as he turned his horse aside.

As thought, it was Isa to whom Vitalis had gone with tale of Sigward's betrayal, and the men who accompanied him to Stern were her housecarles. "I am glad," she said.

"Vitalis!" a shrill voice sounded, causing those departing to look around.

Nicola was on this side of the wall, and ducking beneath the portcullis were two men-at-arms who sought to drag her back inside. "If he dies, Saxon pig," she called, "I will kill you!"

"Methinks I would like to see the silvery-haired termagant try," he murmured, then chuckled softly when the young woman yelped as she was swept off her feet and carried back across the drawbridge.

Aelfled met Vitalis's gaze over her shoulder. "Will her brother die?"

His slight smile disappeared. "He was badly beaten, and not by me, but Guarin D'Argent is strong. I believe he will live."

He spoke as if he knew him well. But then, likely it was amongst the rebels Cyr's brother had been imprisoned all this time.

"Ride!" Vitalis commanded.

Aelfled turned forward and wished the back against which she settled and the arm around her waist were another's.

CHAPTER THIRTY-FIVE

a wife lost. A brother found.

The price for the latter ought not seem so high, but in his hands Cyr felt emptiness despite the dig of nails that would draw blood were his palms not so calloused by weapons—weapons to be wielded eagerly once assurance was given Guarin would not expire in the space between Cyr once more departing Stern and returning with Aelfled.

"My brother will live?" he asked of the two women who had paused in tending him.

Chanson straightened, turned to Cyr where he stood just over the threshold. "He is badly beaten, but providing there is no serious internal bleeding, I believe he shall fight at your side again."

"Is it not wondrous?" Nicola exclaimed where she sat beside her eldest brother, in her hand a damp cloth with which she had been swabbing his neck and shoulders. "He is returned to us!"

No better tidings could Maël have delivered the moment Cyr swung out of the saddle. And the only tidings worse than that Cyr would not hold his wife this night was if the sacrifice of Aelfled proved for naught—if Guarin died.

It was good Father Fulbert had been present during the telling of what had transpired. Holding Aelfled's psalter between whose pages was tucked the ring evidencing they were bound for life, Cyr had nearly forgotten the blessing of his brother's return as he stared at his cousin who claimed he had no choice but to yield Aelfled a paltry half hour earlier.

The priest had snatched hold of Cyr's arm, and with ferocity few would guess a man of God possessed, kept the fist from Maël's face. "He speaks true," Fulbert had entreated. "As you will see the same as did he and your wife, in that moment Guarin was of greatest import."

He did see, though hardly recognizable was his brother propped on pillows on the bed Aelfled had occupied during her recovery. Not because Guarin's short, cropped hair was long, unkempt, and more silvered than two years past. Not because his body had wasted to skin and bones, for it had not. Because of bruises, cuts, and swellings visible on face, neck, and chest. Doubtless, his lower body was similarly abused. The bargain made had required Guarin be alive and well. He was alive, but not well.

"I will kill Vitalis," Cyr snarled.

He did not realize how loud he spoke until Nicola said, "If you do not, I will."

As Chanson motioned them to silence, a low groan sounded from the large figure on the bed, then with eyes closed, Guarin said, "Beware Vitalis."

"I will kill him," Cyr repeated as he strode forward. "He shall pay for every—"

"It was not him." Guarin lifted his lids only enough for the light within the chamber to reflect in eyes that appeared as black as pitch though of all the D'Argents his were the brightest green. "He did not do this."

"Not Vitalis?" Nicola gasped. "Truly?"

Cyr stepped into the place yielded by Chanson and bent near. "It matters not if it was done by his hand or he ordered another."

"Not by his orders." Guarin swallowed loud and dry.

Nicola on his other side snatched up a cup, and Cyr took it from her and set its rim to his brother's lips. "Drink."

He gulped, and when he had taken the last drop, Cyr instructed Nicola to refill it.

Having reined in his anger, he returned his regard to Guarin, and finding himself watched, said, "God's sweet mercy, I am glad you are returned to us. We feared you dead."

"Far from it, though had Vitalis not..." He groaned as if sharp pain tore through him.

When the tension in his face eased and he settled more deeply into the pillows, Cyr said, "If you can, tell me what I ought know about the knave as quickly as possible, for I must pursue him whilst there is yet light."

"He is a knave," Guarin breathed, "but he is not the dangerous one. Rather, not as dangerous as...Jaxon."

"Jaxon?"

"The first in command ahead of Vitalis. I believe it was he who ordered the deaths of the Norman family passing over Wulfenshire."

"He answers to Dotter?"

A hesitation, then, "Oui, but only if he determines Gytha would approve. If he thinks not, he answers to himself."

"You speak of King Harold's mother?"

A slight nod. "She remains determined to return her family to power."

Unsurprised the wily old woman's reach extended into Wulfenshire, Cyr said, "Continue if you can."

"Long Jaxon has wished me dead, but ever Dotter and Vitalis stay his hand."

"For what if not ransom, a demand for which we never received?"

Something passed over Guarin's face that did not match his words. "I cannot say."

He could not? Or did not wish to? There being no time to pursue the matter, Cyr said, "What else can you tell?"

"Jaxon seeks to come out from under the watch of Vitalis that Dotter sets over him, even if it means turning on her and sacrificing the lives of rebels."

"Lillefarne," Cyr said. "You heard Vitalis and his men were captured there?"

"Oui, and I saw the look on Jaxon's face that told he was not displeased. I am guessing it was his man, Sigward, who set all in motion."

"You guess right."

"Thus, he turned on Dotter, and sure of his success set to ridding himself of me. But no swift death, though I nearly wished it these past days when he and his supporters beat a chained man unable to defend himself." He nodded. "As told, Vitalis did not do this. Had he—" His face spasmed and he coughed with such force it ended on a shout of pain.

"Enough, Cyr." Chanson gripped his arm, and a glance at Nicola revealed fear all about her. "Your brother must—"

"Non," Guarin said. "I covet sleep, but when I awaken it may be too late." He set his gaze fast upon Cyr. "Had Vitalis not stolen into the camp and brought me out, this eve would have been my last."

"You are not saying he is your friend?" Cyr unleashed incredulity.

"Non, but neither is he the murderer Jaxon is. Vitalis has a reason for what he does that I would act on were I in his place."

"And Dotter?"

"I believe her actions more justified than William's in gaining England's crown."

"You have met her?"

Guarin inclined his head.

"You know whose face she hides behind?"

This time no response as if... "Do you protect your captor, Guarin?" When still he did not answer, Cyr said, "You know the woman who was traded for you is Lady Hawisa's maid?"

Guarin breathed deep, groaned as if pained by pressure on bruised or broken ribs. "I know."

"On the day past, I wed her." As surprise bloomed on his brother's face, Cyr continued, "She is Lady Aelfled D'Argent."

"I did not know. And I am guessing neither did Vitalis."

"Where would he take her?"

"Not the camp from which he freed me."

"Where?"

He shook his head. "Methinks he will not harm her."

"Where, Guarin?" Cyr said sharply.

"You care for your Saxon wife?"

"I do, though I would have done the same as Maël to safely deliver you inside these walls. When there is time, I shall tell you how we came to be. Suffice to say, I want her back."

Guarin momentarily closed his eyes. "As you have guessed, Lady Hawisa is Dotter, and I believe she tasked Vitalis with retrieving her maid, but not to do her ill. As the lady does not know you, nor that Aelfled now has the protection of your name and position, she must fear for her."

"Then it is from Wulfen Castle I ought to retrieve my wife."

"I believe so, but be of great care, Brother." His lids lowered. "I would guess Jaxon and his men destined there seeking Vitalis who they likely believe stole me from them."

Cyr gripped a hand over Guarin's atop the coverlet, once more sent thanks heavenward he lived and the guilt twisting Cyr's insides since first his brother was lost might finally find some ease. "Ere I ride on Wulfen, I shall send word to Theriot and Dougray at Balduc you are returned to us. Rest well." He straightened from the bed, looked from Chanson to Nicola, and crossed to the door.

"I want your word!" his brother croaked.

Cyr turned. "Anything."

"Whatever happens, keep the Lady of Wulfen safe, whether it be her own come against her or ours."

What had transpired between them? Cyr wondered, but that tale must save as well. "I shall do all I can." Seeing no reason to clarify Aelfled's safety was of greatest import, he said, "We will speak more later." He exited and, gripping the leather pouch on his belt into which he had placed his wife's psalter and ring, went directly to the stables where his men waited with fresh mounts.

In the soft oranges and greys of a day moving toward night, he dropped his weary body into the saddle and, flanked by his men, spurred toward Wulfen Castle.

~

Wulfen Castle
England

"CERTES, WE HAVE COME TOO LATE," Vitalis rasped.

Aelfled's heart sank further as, the same as the others in the wood this side of Wulfen Castle, she watched the forces slip from the trees opposite. Were they not all the rebels upon Wulfenshire, then nearly so.

One score. Two. Three. Now four. Perhaps as many as five.

For fear of this, Vitalis had taken his men to the trees well before the final approach and watched as three riders before the raised drawbridge requested entrance. The answer was long in coming, during which torches were lit on the walls, and when the visitors withdrew, it was to the wood.

Afterward, Isa's housecarles had encouraged Vitalis to ride forth, but he had suspected the men turned away were rebels and had not come alone. Now his patience was rewarded as he would not wish it to be.

Though Vitalis's ranks were thirty strong and ten amongst them were housecarles, against more than eighty it could prove a slaughter, the rebels of Wulfenshire being no ordinary disaffected Saxons capable of little more than swinging scythes, rakes, and sticks. They had been trained in the ways of Wulfrith, and those who this eve might seek to cleave Vitalis's head owed much to the deadly skills imparted by this very man.

Once more aware of the pad of her thumb sliding across the base of her finger, finding absence that ought to be more familiar than a ring worn only one day into the next, Aelfled peered across her shoulder. "What do they intend, Vitalis?"

"As Lady Hawisa has refused them entrance, I believe they will go over the wall."

"For what?"

"This day, all comes to a head, the taking of the wolf having made—"

"The wolf?"

A slight smile stretched his mouth. "It is as Guarin D'Argent is known amongst the rebels though much it offends our lady."

Of course it did, though surely the Norman was named that in jest.

"The taking of him has made us the enemies of Jaxon and those rebels who lean more toward him than me," Vitalis continued. "As for those caught in between, many of whom I believe would side with me given the opportunity, I fear they are trapped on the side of Jaxon. Thus, with so great a force, he seeks to take our lady's place."

Aelfled gasped. "She is their leader!"

"No longer. Even did they not suspect she sent me to free Cyr D'Argent's brother, many would be rid of her."

"But this—Wulfen-trained rebels—all began with her."

"So it did, but though she remains opposed to Norman rule, too long she has been absent from her rebels."

"She is ill!"

"Aye, and feared soon for the grave."

Aelfled shifted around to more fully face Vitalis. "They are wrong, are they not?"

Distress tightened his face. "Though this morn she appeared improved over when last I was here, nearly every stride forward is snatched back by her unwillingness to be still. Thus, even if it cannot be proved she acted against Jaxon in freeing the wolf, that she is believed no longer of benefit gives him the excuse to rid himself of her."

He spoke of death. "Excuse," Aelfled breathed. "You think revenge moves him?"

"It does, but there is something of greater consequence—wresting control of Wulf Fortier from her."

Aelfled frowned. Jaxon knew as well as Vitalis and she the boy had no true claim to that name, that he was a pawn to ensure Isa did not become a possession and tool of one of the conqueror's favorites. "What does Jaxon want with him?"

"As the boy is believed half-Norman and the heir of Wulfen, he is the means of keeping this demesne in rebel hands in plain sight of the Normans—specifically, Gytha's hands."

"Gytha," Aelfled breathed the name of the departed king's mother who time and again tested the mettle of England's new ruler.

"Aye, ever she wishes more from Wulfenshire than what Lady Hawisa is willing to give. She sees the ruse of burning crops to ensure the survival of our people as petty, that it is the deaths of Normans in great numbers to which we ought to turn our efforts no matter how many of our own yield up their lives. And methinks that is what Jaxon seeks to give her—the lives of more of her enemies, whether they be warriors, women, or children—by making Wulfen a base upon which her followers can amass and lead attacks."

He looked past her to the rebels gathering before the castle. "Do we not stop them, they will breach the castle and all the more easily with so many of our lady's best men this side of it." He cursed under his breath. "I have weakened her defenses."

"But the walls are high and of stone."

"The buildings in the inner bailey are not, constructed of wood and thatch. For such an attack against the Norman castles rising across England, I have been training these men, and I do not doubt Jaxon thinks to put that training to good use against our own."

"How?"

"Among the great advantages the invaders had at Senlac was an abundance of men proficient in the use of bows—a lesson well enough learned that many of our rebels are now equally skilled. Thus, soon you will see fire rain down over Wulfen, and the need to put out the flames will draw Lady Hawisa's men off the wall. Then more arrows will be loosed, these with hooks and ropes to scale the walls."

"Dear Lord," she breathed.

"They make ready now." Vitalis looked to his men on either side of him. "We must prepare to stop them."

Aelfled followed his gaze, saw from the faces of housecarles and rebels that though they numbered far fewer than those under Jaxon's command, they awaited orders that could mean their deaths.

"We cannot abandon our lady," Vitalis continued. "Even do we fail, we must try to save the last of the family of Wulfrith." He returned his gaze to Aelfled. "Dismount."

"I can help," she said and heard the sniggers and snorts of others.

Vitalis looked ready to refuse, then frowned and lowered his gaze over her. "I believe you can."

"Tell me."

"Dismount."

"But—"

"Dismount, Aelfled!"

She grabbed the saddle's pommel, twisted around, and slid down the horse's shoulder. She thought the only aid required of her was her absence, but when she stepped back, he slid his meat dagger from its sheath and extended it.

It was a wicked little thing and would prove of better defense than her own should she find herself surrounded by Jaxon's men, but Vitalis quickly dissuaded her of that notion. "Remove your gown."

CHAPTER THIRTY-SIX

*F*ire in the night.

Proof it was here Vitalis conveyed Aelfled? Merely another distraction? Or a genuine attack against the fortress?

Though Cyr had hoped to find his wife at Wulfen Castle, so ominous was the sight he revised that hope. Even if it took him days longer to locate Aelfled, he would not have her here. And greater that hope when he and his warriors ascended the last rise and he saw the chaos before Wulfen Castle that was better lit by fire rising from the outer bailey. As the drawbridge remained raised, it had surely been set by flaming arrows sent over the walls.

It was no easy thing to resist riding into that mass of warring men among whom Aelfled might be found, but he held more than his own life in his hands. Two dozen chevaliers and men-at-arms had accompanied him. He must think first how to preserve the lives entrusted to him, second how to use their skills to defeat what appeared a host numbering more than three times his own. And that was best done from the bordering wood so the enemy did not know who came at their backs until the last possible moment.

That Hugh-worthy decision allowed Cyr to study those before Wulfen and determine they did not attack the walls as a united force. They battled amongst themselves, and it became apparent they differentiated friend from foe. Of fewer number, those around whose arms were tied strips of pale material fought those lacking such.

From what Guarin had revealed of the division between the rebels and that Maël told those who departed Stern with Vitalis numbered thirty, the rebels wearing the pale had to be led by the man with whom Cyr had struck a bargain.

Though tempted to allow the two sides to finish what was begun, leaving the Normans fewer rebels to put down, Aelfled might be in their midst. Too, there were men not of the pale scaling the walls of the Lady of Wulfen who, as yet, William believed yoked to him. But the Norman attack on the rebels would not be indiscriminate as it would have been had Guarin not assured his brother Vitalis was not to blame for the injury done him—and that he who had taken Aelfled would not harm her.

Not allowing himself to think long on where she might be lest he render those under his command vulnerable, he turned his mount and addressed them. "They are rebels all, but this eve we side with those who wear the pale on their sleeves. When you ride amongst them, put down their opponents with the cry, *God and Vitalis!* in their language." Cyr spoke it for those unfamiliar with Anglo-Saxon, then continued, "Regardless, watch your backs. They shall know us for Normans, and we cannot be certain our aid and battle cry will persuade rebels of the pale we fight with rather than against them."

As told by lined brows and mutterings, there was unrest among the men, many of whom would have answered to Maël had not Cyr once more given him charge of Stern.

Praying they would trust him, he said, "Those are your orders, as are these—to preserve your lives and the lives of your fellow

Normans, cut down whoever aggresses against you regardless of whether he wears the pale. If you can render him harmless without taking his life, do so. If not, dispatch him that he sooner answer to the Lord."

More murmurings, these of agreement.

Reining his mount around, Cyr shouted, "To arms!" and sword in hand spurred out of the trees and across the meadow.

SHE HAD INTENDED to stay the wood as Vitalis ordered, but then glimpsed movement at the base of the fortress along the side and knew Jaxon's men sought the sally port. Under cover of trees she had followed their progress, thinking to shout a warning to Wulfen's defenders in the unlikely event the hidden entrance was unsecured.

Not until Jaxon's men were near enough to make good targets had those on that section of wall shown themselves between the battlements and loosed bolts from bows.

Aelfled had tried to think clearly in order to act wisely, but there being little time, she had run from the wood, calling to the men on the wall.

It had to have been the shock of seeing a woman clad in a thin chemise that kept an arrow from her own breast, and when she was near enough to identify herself as Lady Hawisa's maid, orders had been shouted to those below.

The men above kept their arrows trained on her, surely lest she was joined by others seeking to enter uninvited, then the hidden door opened, she was yanked inside, and the sally port secured.

Though she had recognized the soldiers who had hold of her just as they recognized her, they did not trust her—a credit to their faithfulness and duty to Isa. They checked her for weapons, but all they found was her own meat dagger, Vitalis's returned to him after she cut her pale grey gown into strips that were fastened around the arms of all who stood with him. There had been extra strips, and those he also distributed, speaking the names of a dozen rebels who were likely before the castle but who he believed would turn his side given the opportunity.

The first name had been that which always made her smile, not only for how unique it was but that it belonged to one from her own village of Ravven whom she had thought the kindest and gentlest of men. He was a warrior now, and she prayed the offer to abandon Jaxon would be received before he was cut down or did unforgivable harm to Lady Hawisa's men.

Now as Aelfled entered the hall, she glanced over her shoulder at the fire delivered by arrows during her escort from the outer bailey to the inner. It was as Vitalis predicted and she had prayed he could prevent. But blessedly, here another benefit of stone. Though the wooden buildings the water did not save would collapse into smoldering piles, the walls enclosing them would stand, only their blackened surfaces testament to their own battle against flame.

As the doors closed behind her, Aelfled looked forward. The great room was filled with castle folk whom Isa had surely commanded to the donjon to protect them from the fires and blades of their attackers.

Doubtless, enough drink and food was stored here to sustain them for weeks providing those seeking to take the outer bailey did not also gain the inner. Did they, within days—at best—they would break through the donjon's defenses and put all within to the blade.

"Lord," she whispered as she searched for her lady who was not upon the dais nor before the hearth. As ill as Isa was, she must be abed, but it was not to the curtained solar Aelfled was led.

"Remain here." The housecarle named Ordric jutted his chin at a bench before the hearth. "I will ask Lady Hawisa to grant you an audience."

"Tell her it is of import, that I—"

"Sit."

She lowered beside a boy of five or six whose knees were drawn to his chest and arms wrapped around them, blue eyes wide with fear above those knobby joints. Aelfled slid an arm around him, and he did not resist when she drew him against her side.

"All will be well," she murmured as she watched the housecarle ascend the dais and disappear behind the solar's curtains. It was then she became more aware of eyes upon her—likely as much for her immodest state of dress as that she who had not numbered among those of the household for nearly two years had returned. On such a night as this, she did not need to feel their suspicion and distrust to know of it.

When Ordric reappeared and motioned her forward, Aelfled eased the boy away, stood, and smoothed the hair back off his brow. "Where is your mother?"

"I-in the kitchen. Gatherin' food. She told me to wait here."

Aelfled smiled. "I am sure she shall return soon."

He nodded, and she patted his shoulder and turned toward the dais.

An unexpected sight greeted Aelfled when she passed through the curtains the housecarle parted—as surely unexpected as was the sight of Isa's former maid wearing only a chemise. Her own surprise was not that her lady kept company with others in the torchlit solar, but that she stood before the iron-banded chest at the foot of her postered bed and the bold manner in which she did so.

She was erect, shoulders level, chest forward. Beneath a sheen of perspiration possibly of fever, color swept cheeks above gaunt hollows. Though her golden hair remained the dark of long unwashed tresses, it was braided back off her face, exposing a regal neck. And she was clothed in crisp—albeit dusty—garments far from those of a lady.

Isa's husband had forbidden her to don men's clothes that, as the daughter of Wulfrith, she had occasion to wear before her marriage. Even when he summoned his wife to the training field to confirm the techniques taught those who would become England's greatest defenders remained true to the reputation of Wulfrith, she had been required to wear a gown.

Now she was a sight to behold. Though not unusually tall nor broad for a woman, and her figure possessed more curves than Aelfled's, her bearing made her appear so formidable that were tales of shield maidens true, such women would look like Hawisa Wulfrithdotter who wore tunic, close-fitting chausses, boots, and a wide leather belt fit with both long and short scabbards from which projected the hilts beneath which would be found killing blades.

"As you know, Aelfled," she said in a voice strained enough to betray her, "Wulfen is under attack by those who are no longer our own. What you also know that I do not is how you are here without Vitalis."

"He is at Wulfen, my lady, having made the trade you required for the release of Guarin D'Argent."

Striking grey eyes widening, Isa retreated a step, felt a hand behind, and lowered to sitting atop the chest. It took her some moments to settle whatever was unsettled, then she said, "Tell me all and quickly, Aelf."

Heart bounding over being named that again, she swept her gaze over the other occupants of the chamber. There was the one who had taken Wulf's place, watchful where he stood before the hearth. Alongside him, and inappropriately near, was a young woman whose chin was down as if the white-knuckled hands clasped against a worn and torn gown were more interesting than the men and women with whom she kept company. Wondering who she was, Aelfled looked to the others—three housecarles, two of whom were also arrayed in dust.

Aelfled returned her gaze to her lady. "May I approach?"

Isa inclined her head.

She halted a reach from her and told all that was relevant, which did not include her marriage to a Norman. "And that is what goes in the outer bailey and beyond your walls, my lady," she said and once more found her thumb seeking the ring of braided hair.

Hands curled over the chest's lid, Isa leaned forward. "When Jaxon demanded entrance, I knew the release of our Norman prisoner brought him to my walls and the time had come for him to move against me. Thus, though Vitalis's numbers are far fewer, I prayed for his speedy return so he might aid in defending Wulfen."

"Your prayer is answered, my lady."

"But for what? I know he is the best of all that remains of my sire's legacy, as are those who look to him ahead of Jaxon, but is it enough? Or will it see my man dead?" She shook her head. "This night, he and his faithful do not fight astride, do they?"

"Nay, my lady. They dismounted."

She nodded. "Though I ordered Jaxon to develop methods to provide our men the advantage the Normans had upon Senlac, ever he fought me over instructing them to wield weapons astride. Thus, Vitalis sought to train himself and those closest to him, but they had too little practice." She rubbed her forehead. "So dare I risk remaining here in the hope it is Vitalis who comes to the donjon? Or do I risk shepherding the castle folk from Wulfen?"

Wondering if her lady's prolonged illness had affected her mind as well as her body, Aelfled sank to her knees and caught up Isa's cold hands. "Even if the outer bailey—and sally port—have not yet fallen, it is not possible to take the castle folk from Wulfen."

"You are wrong, though only hours past did it become possible. But as told, there is risk there as well." Isa considered Aelfled. "You are yet faithful to me?"

"I am, my lady."

She pushed upright. "Come." She crossed to the far corner of the solar where a tapestry hung that only then Aelfled realized was a source of light beyond candles and torches set around the chamber.

"My lady?" a housecarle said and started to follow.

She flicked a hand. "I do not require your accompaniment. Keep watch over Wulf."

Wulf, not *Wulfrith,* meaning that affection was no longer reserved for the one of her body and heart?

Aelfled followed her lady behind the tapestry and past the door left ajar that had allowed the glow of a single torch within the passage to cross the threshold. She knew of the hidden places here, having been present when the stone walls were erected and witness to arguments between husband and wife over their construction, the latter determined if she must give up her timber house and live in one of cold stone she would make the most of it with the addition of passages similar to the one she later added to Lillefarne's outer wall. Isa's Norman husband had yielded, though not entirely, determining it too costly and dangerous to add a passage coursing underground to the wood.

Aelfled peered left up the stairs that fell into complete darkness beyond the tenth step, then to the right where her lady moved through a short passage lit by the torch taken from the sconce. Here was the source of dust seen upon Isa's garments and those of her housecarles. As if stirred by a breeze, it danced in the warm, flickering light.

Rubbing her itching nose, Aelfled set after her lady and, as the woman turned right, called, "You think to hide the castle folk within these passages?"

"Nay, beyond."

"Beyond?"

Her lady did not speak again until they passed two more sets of stairs and turned right again.

"This is familiar to you?" Isa asked.

"Aye, my lady." Aelfled had explored the passages years past, and well enough to now notice the addition after descending toward the cellar where food and drink were stored. A short passage branched off that landing, then more steps appeared of a descending rather than ascending nature, so crudely constructed Aelfled was more grateful for torchlight and her lady going before her. When she reached the next landing, she saw the walls of an incredibly long passage ahead were fashioned of dirt and chipped away rock. Though they lacked the reinforcement of stone blocks, many were the timber posts set in the sides and overhead.

She halted, as did Isa who turned and raised an eyebrow.

"When you said *beyond,* you spoke of the wood," Aelfled said.

"I did. Construction began after Duke William crowned himself king of England. It has been work without cease with several lives lost to collapse, but ever it resumes for such a time as this. Though often these past months we have thought we were close to breaking through into the wood, it has been one disappointment after another. Then on the day past, as I was resolved to once more being abandoned by the Lord, word came of how near we were, and once more I let myself believe it possible. This day at noon, my men broke through not far from the great waterfall." Her mouth curved. "If we must flee, this is the way out, Aelfled—be it to escape Jaxon's grasp this day or the usurper's another day."

"But where would you go, my lady? And are you well enough for the journey?"

Though Isa shrugged a shoulder, Aelfled knew it was not a gesture of uncertainty. She had told all she wished to tell.

Aelfled glanced past her to where light did not reach, likely from a turn in the passage. "You said there is a risk in taking the castle folk from Wulfen."

"Aye, as there is no time to reinforce the most recently mined walls, the greatest risk is panic should we have insufficient time to flee. Thus, I must decide soon, not only that we may proceed cautiously to prevent the passage from collapsing, but to ensure it does fail once we are through should it be discovered and we are pursued." She put her head to the side. "What think you I should do?"

Vitalis's thirty against as many as one hundred... "I think you must leave Wulfen until certain of the outcome, my lady. If your man wins the night, on the morrow you can return."

Isa nodded. "The thought of retreat sours my belly, but I believe it the best course for those owed my protection. Come, we must prepare." She advanced, and Aelfled stepped against the wall to allow her past in the narrow confines. Almost immediately her lady came back around and Aelfled nearly trod on her feet. "What have you not told me?" she asked with the confidence of one who could well guess the answer if she did not already know it.

Aelfled longed to lie, but as it was now only the two of them, it was easier to speak the truth though it might earn her the back of a hand never before dealt. "I am wed, my lady."

Isa startled, evidence she had not guessed as far as that.

"I am now Aelfled D'Argent."

Another startle though slighter. "Cyr D'Argent," her lady rasped, then gave a sharp laugh. "You are not *merely* Aelfled D'Argent. You are Lady Aelfled D'Argent. In William's England, you are now more titled than I."

Wondering how Isa could appear so calm, Aelfled said, "I am, though it seems a gown too wide and long for my body, as if never will I keep it on my shoulders and ever I shall be soiling its hem."

"Norman wed," Isa said, "the children you birth Norman-bred."

Aelfled lifted her chin. "And Saxon, equal both sides."

"I ought to hate you," her lady said without venom.

"I pray you do not."

"Were you forced to speak vows?"

"Nay, my lady. I care for him as I think I have since the day..."

"My son died," Isa finished what Aelfled should not have begun, eyes and lashes suddenly bright with moisture.

Aelfled touched her arm. "As Cyr proved upon Senlac, he is a good man, not just a good Norman. Honorable."

Isa closed her eyes. "The D'Argents are different," she said, and Aelfled longed to ask how the eldest brother had become her lady's captive and how well she had come to know him. But before she chanced it, Isa muttered, "We are fools, women all."

Meaning she counted herself such? If so, was it in regard to her husband or...?

Nay, impossible.

Aelfled moved her thoughts back to Roger Fortier. From all she had witnessed, theirs had been a fairly good marriage though much Isa resented the power wielded by the Norman she grudgingly wed. Other than forbidding her a role beyond advisor in the administration of her family's holdings, he had been good to her and rarely raised his voice when she defied him or argued over what she believed the best course for Wulfen and those whose training was entrusted to them. Even her husband's dislike —and disparagement—of Saxons had lessened the longer he was gravely a minority amongst them. There may not have been love between the two, but affection enough that neither had been miserable.

A snort of disgust returned Aelfled to the underground. "Make haste," Isa said and led the way to the solar. There she received tidings of the state of Wulfen upon which she based the decision to risk the passage if the inner bailey could not be held.

After issuing orders to prepare the castle folk for departure, she sent a housecarle outside the donjon to instruct those defending it to retreat the moment it was determined it was lost. Those men would be set amongst the castle folk to ensure a cautious, orderly passage through the underground, housecarles bringing up the rear to defend their backs if necessary.

As Aelfled distributed to men, women, and children packs of

provisions sufficient for five days in the wood, someone touched her arm. She turned to the young woman who had stood alongside Wulf in the solar and gasped at the direct gaze of greater note than the bruises and abrasions across her pretty face.

Her eyes were otherworldly, so much it surprised she had reached adulthood amid the superstitious. But there was something more disturbing about them. They were harder—or might it be better said near hollow?—than Aelfled had seen a woman's, even Isa's upon losing Wulf and vowing vengeance against the Normans. If not for slivers of what seemed fear and sorrow, one might name them inhuman.

What had she lost? And was it possible to recover from something so terrible? Surely not in the absence of faith.

"I am Em," she said. "I am to aid you."

CHAPTER THIRTY-SEVEN

Though many of those engaged in hand-to-hand combat had seemed unaware of the approach of mounted warriors amid the din of steel on steel, bellowing, grunting, and cursing, some of the combatants had begun to fall apart when the Normans entered the fray. Amongst these, Cyr and his men first rode, striking at those whose arms did not bear the pale strips of material and shouting the battle cry that caused Vitalis's men to falter over aid given by one who had imprisoned all but the housecarles who had accompanied their leader to Stern to make the trade.

As upon Senlac, the use of mounted warriors proved as great an advantage as had William's numerous archers, and though some rebels boldly turned their efforts to hewing down the great beasts, others scattered. Even so, they were not easily taken to ground, further evidence of the excellence of training afforded men born to the soil. For this, King William had wished Wulfen to remain active in training warriors to defend England—*his* England.

Over and again, the battle cry of unity with rebels of the pale was loosed, and Cyr hoped Vitalis heard, understood, and embraced what they did—that even if only this night Normans and rebels united to defeat a common enemy.

So great an impact had Cyr and his men and those of Vitalis that when Jaxon's rebels who went over the wall gained control of the gatehouse and lowered the drawbridge, it was not only to their own admittance was offered. More it was the Normans warily followed by rebels of the pale.

Belatedly, Jaxon's men this side called out warnings to drop the rising portcullis before which the contest between unlikely allies and Gytha-bent rebels raged. And it was a familiar figure amid smoke on the other side who frustrated the efforts of those reversing the chains.

Beyond the lowering portcullis, Cyr glimpsed Vitalis whom he guessed had scaled the wall after Jaxon's men whilst the Normans rode on Wulfen.

Cyr returned his gaze to the opponent he had thrust backward a moment earlier, knocked aside the man's next swing, then holding to the saddle with his thighs, swung his dagger-wielding hand down and slid the short blade into the rebel's side. The man came off it with a cry, dropped to his knees then face on the drawbridge.

When Cyr returned his regard to Vitalis, he saw two rebels not of the pale on the ground behind him, and the one who had slain them was at the chains driving a dagger's blade between the links to prevent the portcullis from lowering further. The rattling ceased and the gate shuddered and stilled three feet from the ground.

Vitalis met Cyr's gaze across the distance.

Glimpsing no surprise on the rebel's face, Cyr guessed from atop the wall he had seen what transpired below.

"Aelfled?" Cyr called.

"In the wood, but the little fool did not stay."

Of course she did not, just as at Senlac.

"Where?"

"I saw her running toward the eastern wall. And that is all."

Then she remained outside the fortress? Or had she sought entrance by way of a sally port guarded by Lady Hawisa's men? Would they have let her in? Possible only if they yet held the outer bailey—before the survivors retreated to the inner bailey and donjon.

"Jaxon is mine!" Vitalis shouted and, as he pivoted, added, "God and *Wulfrith!*"

After fending off a blade aimed at his calf, Cyr did not slay his attacker whose youthful face and build told he was only recently deemed a man. He brought the hilt of his sword down on the rebel's head, rendering him bloodily unconscious. Though that one's defeat and several others cleared the way forward into the bailey, Cyr hesitated.

Was Aelfled outside or inside? If he guessed wrong and sought her where she was not, it could mean her death—were it not already dealt.

Inside where the danger was greatest, he determined. Assuring himself that even if he chose wrong, her inability to enter the fortress would force her to return to the safety of the wood, he dismounted with his men and ducked beneath the portcullis.

Trusting what remained of Jaxon's men outside the walls would be put down by the Normans and rebels of the pale coming behind, cautiously Cyr led the way forward through a haze of smoke lit by the fire's glow.

Thus, they were not taken unawares as they neared the inner bailey. The contest that followed was more ferocious than that fought outside Wulfen, proof Jaxon had taken his best men over the wall. And now those rebels sought to breach the inner wall defended by Lady Hawisa's men, many of whom had surely withdrawn to that bailey when the outer was lost. With their lives they would defend their lady in her donjon, but what they could not know unless Vitalis had made it to their side was salvation did not entirely depend on Saxons faithful to the lady but those against whose rule they had struggled these two years.

Of good benefit to those opposing Jaxon and his rebels was they had not breathed the smoke as long and were only beginning to cough and eyes to stream as they swung and parried, thrust and sliced while advancing on the lowered portcullis beyond which stood armored men a dozen strong.

Once more Cyr's sword skill was challenged, this time against a man of good width and less than average stature whose coarse voice sounding the Saxon battle cry *Out! Out* evidenced his life before the great battle was that of a laborer. Because of his bulk, he was deceptively fast, and whereas Cyr had thus far sustained minor injuries, few of which would require stitches, this man landed a blow that would have made a good start of severing Cyr's head from his neck had he not leapt backward. Instead, it sliced the flesh of his collarbone above the neck of his mail.

Feeling the warmth of blood run with perspiration, Cyr roared and lunged. The rebel returned stroke for stroke but gave ground as he was beaten back toward the portcullis.

Keep your sides in sight, Cyr silently counseled, *beware your back.* It was as Hugh had instructed, drilling into his pupils that no matter the strength of the enemy faced, one ought ever be aware of others seeking to enter through side and rear doors.

Cyr's own men were fighting all around, and among them were rebels of the pale who appeared to engage Jaxon's men with equal ferocity though they had trained, raided, and burned alongside one another since taking a stand against the conquerors.

Cyr's next swing caught the flesh of his opponent's forearm and made the warrior stumble against the gate, but he pushed off and with bared teeth moved his blade toward his enemy's abdomen. It was deflected with an upward swing that, at its end, gave Cyr's steel a taste of the man's brow. But still the rebel came.

"Nay, Zedekiah!" a voice shouted. "You are my man. Mine!"

The Saxon reacted as if dealt a fist, sharply turning his head as Cyr was tempted but dared not. He knew it was Vitalis who called and hesitated in delivering a death blow. When the rebel leader came into view, once more on the opposite side of a portcullis, beyond him Cyr saw the defenders of the inner bailey retreated toward the donjon with the reluctance of men who preferred to battle to the death but had been ordered otherwise. And they had good reason to withdraw, many of those not of the pale streaming into the inner bailey.

Lest Vitalis soon lay dead, Cyr called, "They come for you!"

"As mine come for them," the warrior snarled and thrust a hand through the bars, in it pale grey cloth. "Put this around your arm and live, Zedekiah," he demanded as Cyr once more ensured his sides and back were not vulnerable.

The man looked between Cyr and Vitalis, back again. "These are Normans!"

"Aye, and this eve they are with me—as are you do you don this."

The man hesitated, then snatched the strip and sidestepped as if for fear of being slain by Cyr as he bound his arm.

"You can trust Zedekiah," Vitalis said.

Cyr hoped it was true but did not believe it. Thus, he kept the man peripherally in sight as others of the pale on the other side of the portcullis rushed toward those who sought to end their leader's life. As the divided rebels met at swords, others of Jaxon's men ran for the donjon and flung themselves up the steps as the great doors closed behind Lady Hawisa's men.

"Jaxon's men have control of the gatehouse," Vitalis said as one of Cyr's own slew a rebel to the far left. "Use the ropes with which they scaled the walls and come over." He swung away. Sword piercing the air before him, he ran to aid his men struggling to cut a path through those loyal to Jaxon who stood between them and the ones assaulting the doors of the great hall.

"It looks I am your side now, Norman," Zedekiah said and jerked his banded arm. "This eve only."

As the wary allies turned aside, Cyr heard Vitalis shout, "I come for you, traitor!"

A glance through the portcullis brought to Cyr's regard not the largest nor broadest of the men at the doors, but the one who responded to Vitalis's threat was of good size. Though balding, the hair at the sides and back of his head was bound at the nape, and a length as thick as a horse's tail hung to his hips. Of further note was a beard gathered and tied beneath his chin that hung to the center of a belly as flat as his arms were thick with muscles. Here was Jaxon, and if Vitalis did not make good his threat, Cyr would.

"Try, poltroon!" the man called. "And fail." Then he returned to hacking at the planks that stood between him and Lady Hawisa— and possibly Aelfled.

It was a challenge to reach the ropes, the way blocked by rebel battling rebel and rebel battling Norman. Many fell before Cyr, Zedekiah, and a dozen others their side were able to climb the wall and pull the ropes up after them to protect their backs.

As they ran the wall walk, Cyr saw the donjon's doors had come down. Those fighting in the inner bailey having moved their struggles to the steps and the hall, from the gaping mouth of the great room came the sound of men fighting for their lives and the sight of torch and candlelight licking keen blades.

There was no time to take the gatehouse to raise the portcullis, and it was for the best. Of those barred from the inner bailey, Cyr's men and rebels of the pale now outnumbered their opponents and would keep them from adding to Jaxon's forces inside the donjon.

No sign of Vitalis, Cyr led the way down into the inner bailey, then up the donjon steps, swinging his sword only when necessary to make a hole through which he and his men passed.

Shortly, they entered the hall. The dead and dying were

scattered across the floor, and though here Jaxon's rebels were of greater numbers, among them were those of the pale and two housecarles. And no castle folk, blessedly.

A shout sounded from behind the dais.

Recognizing Vitalis's voice, Cyr lunged toward the solar, but before he reached it, a great tearing of cloth sounded as a curtain was ripped from its ceiling hooks. It fell, revealing Lady Hawisa's bedchamber and a snarling, sword-wielding Vitalis advancing on the heap of material from which Jaxon struggled to rise—whilst another rose from the floor behind Lady Hawisa's man. One not of the pale.

"Your back!" Cyr shouted a moment ahead of Zedekiah, then both were forced to turn their attention to two of Jaxon's men running at them.

Moments later, the enemies-turned-allies fought side by side, exchanging blows with Jaxon's men, one of whom taunted Zedekiah over betraying his people. It did not have the effect hoped for, turning the man more vicious, and it was he who put down his opponent ahead of Cyr felling his own.

Noting his men who had come over the wall had made it into the hall and set themselves against the enemy, Cyr started for the dais. And faltered at finding the solar empty—rather, what could be seen of it. Were Vitalis and his opponents behind the one remaining curtain clinging to its hooks?

Cyr sprang onto the dais, trod the heap of material, and entered the solar.

To the right at the base of the hanging curtain, Vitalis was down. Eyes squeezed closed, panting between his teeth, he pressed a bloodied hand to his side.

"Vitalis!" Zedekiah reached him ahead of Cyr, and when he dropped to a knee, the rebel leader opened his eyes. "Stop them," he rasped.

Cyr halted over Vitalis. "Where did they go?"

"Behind the tapestry." His eyes moved to the one most distant. "Hidden passage. Stop them!"

Zedekiah started to rise, but Cyr said, "Remain to ensure none finish him."

"I will not be...your prisoner again," Vitalis called to Cyr's back.

"Not this eve," Cyr said and thrust aside the tapestry and entered the passage.

It was dark, the only light provided by the solar and muted by the effort required to bend around the side of the tapestry and slip beneath its hem.

Cyr cursed the delay that required him to return to the bedchamber and retrieve a torch, but the light that would allow him to proceed without great stealth to ensure the one who had stuck Vitalis did not stick him would make up for time lost. Unfortunately, it would sooner alert the ones he chased that the predators were also prey. But at least one of them already bled, which was how Cyr knew not to explore the stairs ascending from the level of the hall.

Following the spots of blood on the floor and streaks on stone walls, Cyr was surprised they did not end on the steps he guessed led to the storeroom beneath the kitchen.

The passage did not confine itself to the castle walls. It went underground and quite distant he realized as he followed the trail. To the wood, he guessed and marveled at the undertaking that required so many timbers to keep the passage hewn more of dirt than rock from collapsing.

As Cyr approached a bend, he caught the scrape and thud of footsteps and, more distant, the murmur of voices. Guessing the former was Jaxon and his man, the latter those fleeing them, Cyr halted and peered around the corner. Though he held back the light, enough swept past to reveal this next section of passage was narrower, at best allowing two of slight build to walk shoulder to shoulder.

Ahead, moving toward the distant flickering light of a torch borne by those of Wulfen Castle were the two who felled Vitalis. Within minutes they would reach their prey—unless Cyr reached them first. And he must, especially if Aelfled was down here.

He set the torch at the center of the passage where it would burn itself out amid dirt whilst casting enough light around the corner to allow him to more quickly overtake the rebels.

"Lord be with Aelfled, Lord be with me," he rasped. And ran.

PROGRESS WAS SLOW, there being two score to move through the ever-narrowing passage whose timbers creaked and groaned, causing dirt to sprinkle down each time a shoulder or foot jarred a support.

"We are close," Isa said. "I smell the falls, feel the wet on the air. Soon we shall be above ground."

Aelfled peered past her to the housecarles who led the way with a torch borne high, then behind at those following single file. Placed at regular intervals among the castle folk were soldiers to ensure all proceeded as instructed and put down panic when it arose. Thus far, there was only one instance, that of an elderly man who feared being buried alive and demanded they turn back. Before he could rouse others, he was knocked unconscious and put over the shoulder of a man-at-arms.

Center of that long column was another torch, this one held aloft by Ordric, and a third was carried by one of two housecarles bringing up the rear.

"There," Isa said.

Aelfled followed her lady's gaze and nearly asked the purpose of the rope wrapped around the bottom of a post, but when she tracked its length tucked against the base of the wall and saw it extended thirty feet ahead and was wrapped around each successive timber, she guessed here was the means of bringing down this section of tunnel to ensure any who discovered the passage would have to turn back, giving Isa and her people more time to escape.

Doubtless, the task of toppling the timbers would fall to the housecarles behind.

"Will it work?" Wulfrith asked. Sounding more curious than concerned, the boy reminded Aelfled of his namesake and made her question how far Isa had gone to present him as her husband's heir. He would have received some training at arms alongside lessons in speech and gentility, but perhaps his facility with weaponry had progressed to the strategy of warfare, so at ease did the commoner seem in the skin he now wore—even absent being displayed before Normans.

"I have been assured it will bring down the walls." Isa looked over a shoulder at where he walked behind Aelfled. "And possibly those ahead lacking sufficient support. Thus, all must be well clear of the passage when it is sealed off."

Assuredly they would be, Aelfled told herself, and once above ground she would slip away, returning to her husband and grandmother. Hopefully, in the midst of so many, she would find the opportunity and Isa, aware her maid was now joined for life to another, would not try to stop her.

A shout from behind startled all, and the shower of dirt evidenced one or more reacted violently enough to jostle the supports.

"Calm!" Ordric shouted from behind. "Though pursued, we must consider each step. Move quickly but remain center, and do not touch the timbers. As soon as all are clear, we shall collapse the passage atop those who follow. Go!"

Heart straining against her ribs, Aelfled complied but was shoved forward by those who feared they would breathe their last underground.

"Fear not!" shouted a housecarle ahead. "The warriors at our backs will keep us from their blades."

Another shout sounded from deep in the dark behind the last torch, and it was of one who should not be here.

Aelfled spun and collided with Wulfrith who grabbed her shoulders to steady her.

Isa pulled her back around. "For what do you endanger all?" she demanded and without awaiting an answer, said, "Come!"

Aelfled strained backward. "Pray, do not collapse the passage. My—"

The slap never before dealt landed, and she dropped to her knees.

"Get up!" Her lady yanked on her arm, attempting to drag her forward as the press of those behind threatened to trample her.

Aelfled wrenched free, scrambled to the wall opposite the one whose posts were bound together. And glimpsed more alarm than anger on her lady's face before Isa had no choice but to continue forward.

Aelfled rose and pressed herself flat to the dirt wall so she would not impede the progress of others. Though several stepped on her toes, they seemed not to notice her—except Em.

The young woman's eyes, less startling in so little light, met Aelfled's. With a bitter bend to her mouth, she said, "The Normans must die. One and all." Then she was past.

Soon Ordric at the center appeared, but though Aelfled feared he would try to drag her along, he was too occupied with keeping order to more than flick his frowning gaze over her.

After he passed, there came the sound of blades at the rear and shouts amid which she heard that familiar voice again.

Though she longed to push through those who moved too slowly, she forced herself to remain still and once more found herself seeking proof of the ring gone from her hand. Pressing her fingers into her palms, she told herself that even if she could aid her husband in battling the housecarles seeking his death, any attempt to reach him before all were safely past could sooner collapse the passage and brand her a murderer of many.

"Please, Lord," she whispered. "Please be here...be now...be merciful."

Each clang of the sword and shout jolted, but more she was struck by what the torch at the rear now borne by a gangly youth revealed. It was not Cyr whom Isa's warriors fought thirty feet back but a good-sized man whose hair was bound at his back and beard at his front. Jaxon.

Might Aelfled have been wrong in believing she heard Cyr's voice? Considering how unlikely he was at Wulfen, she must be. But then he shouted again and she glimpsed well beyond the battling housecarles two other figures trading sword blows. It was him.

She struggled against shoving past the last of Isa's people, and a moment later saw a housecarle collapse, leaving Jaxon only one other to defeat—unless Cyr prevailed against his opponent who must be one of Jaxon's men.

As the youth carrying the torch brushed past her, fear contorting his face, Aelfled heard Ordric shout, "Collapse the passage!"

She snapped her head around and saw him cautiously push through the people toward the rear. Did he not see the housecarles were unable to carry out his order, one likely dead, the other struggling to remain alive beneath Jaxon's vicious blows?

"Do it, Aelfled!" Ordric bellowed.

She startled. He did see and believed she possessed the strength to topple the timbers. Did she? Regardless, she could not test her ability whilst Cyr was on that end, as was the housecarle who might prevail against Jaxon.

And if others of Jaxon's men are coming? reason countered. *Men who will slay all in their path to reach Isa?*

Aelfled looked to Cyr, knew him from the height and breadth that differentiated him from one who seemed equally matched at arms, then swept her gaze to Jaxon and the housecarle—just as the latter flew back against a timber and collapsed in a heap.

For a moment, she thought his blood sprayed her, but it was the dirt loosened from the ceiling as told by the creaking and shuddering of timbers and beams threatening to collapse. And bury her husband.

"Cyr!" Aelfled called and regretted it when he shouted again, not only with anger but what sounded pain.

"Run, Aelfled!"

In the next moment, she better understood his urgency that was not all to do with the passage's collapse. Jaxon sprang toward her, what remained of torchlight streaking his blade.

She ran, though it was surely too late to escape.

As if Cyr also realized it, he commanded her to do as Ordric had done. "Collapse the passage!"

Then he would die to keep her safe?

She peered over her shoulder, and there was hope in seeing her husband was now a lone figure running toward Jaxon and her. But lacking wings, he would not reach her ahead of the rebel. The collapse of the passage was the only hope for Aelfled and those of Isa's people bringing up the rear, and it was a thin one.

Just past the support where the last of the rope lay between wall and floor, Aelfled snatched up its end and swung around to face the men advancing on her. As feared, Jaxon was too near.

With a sob, she wrenched on the rope and the timbers creaked and gave slightly. Far more effort was required to bring them down. But then, as if slapped by the hand of God, Jaxon stumbled and dropped to a knee, and when Aelfled swept her gaze to Cyr, she saw he no longer carried a sword. Had he thrown it?

"Collapse the passage!" he roared.

Surely there was no need now Jaxon was down. However, the rebel was rising, and though he clasped his left hand over his shoulder as if pained, once more he set his sword before him and lunged at her.

"Do it, Aelfled!"

"Lord, preserve him!" she cried, then hearing her husband's name sobbed over and over, gripped the rope tighter and threw all of her weight backward.

Something slammed into her from behind, knocking the breath from her, and yet she possessed strength she should not, and as she was propelled backward, saw the timbers fall inward and beams crash down before the haze of dirt and sting of flying rubble stole all from sight.

Amid receding consciousness, Aelfled sent pleadings heavenward that Cyr survive what she could not, these lands know peace under his rule, he care for Bernia to her end days, and he find happiness that might have been for them.

CHAPTER THIRTY-EIGHT

*S*he thought it rain, but there was no wet upon her face. The sound had to be the nearby waterfall. She thought it sunshine, but too much it flickered. The light penetrating her lids had to be of torches.

Aelfled opened her eyes, flung up a hand to shield them, and from beneath its shadow saw standing around her those who had departed the passage ahead of her. It would be a miracle were Cyr among them, but she had to believe he had made it past Jaxon, and it was he who carried her from the collapsed tunnel.

Cool fingers settled on her shoulder, and she shifted her narrowed gaze to where a woman had lowered beside her. "Cyr?" Aelfled rasped and coughed against the dirty saliva cast down her throat. "H-he made it out?"

Though her eyes were too gritty to clearly focus, she saw her lady's frown deepen. "What say you, Aelf?"

"D'Argent was in the passage, my lady," Ordric said, and Aelfled knew without moving her gaze from Isa he stood alongside.

"You say it was not Jaxon down there?" Isa exclaimed as Aelfled coughed again.

"The traitor was there, my lady, but giving chase was the Norman who stole your lands, and it was the throw of his sword that slowed Jaxon enough for us to collapse the tunnel on both."

"Both," Aelfled gasped, then a wail rent the air—immediately stifled by a hand over her mouth. She did not fight it, instead let the pain trapped within pierce her insides.

And more bloody they became when her lady demanded, "Aelfled aided in collapsing the passage?"

"Though I commanded her to it, she did not until D'Argent ordered the same. When I reached her to give aid, she…"

He trailed off as if to spare Aelfled the humiliation of others knowing how over and again she had sobbed Cyr's name as she dragged on the rope.

I die inside, she thought, and remembrance of the hollowed-out Em rose to mind. *This is how one becomes like her. This is how one empties out. This is how one loses what little faith remains. This.*

Still holding a hand over her maid's mouth, Isa bent near and brushed the hair out of her eyes. "Brave Aelfled."

Body continuing to spasm with trapped cries, Aelfled was almost moved to shame that she who had lost less than Isa should grieve in this woman's presence. *Almost,* for did she not have the right to express pain over love lost no matter how recently gained? Even though it was love for a man with whom she had wished to make a child and not love for a child stolen away? Even were that love not returned?

In some measure it was returned, she corrected as her thumb probed the base of her ring finger. *And were it but a sip, still I would savor it.*

"It seems we are not all the fools of men," Isa continued. "You did what had to be done, Aelfled. I know there is pain in that, but there is joy in having saved so many—and of your own."

Aelfled's chest heaving over the next stifled sob, her lady removed her hand from her mouth. "It is much to ask, but you must be strong again. Can you?"

Again? Emotions so tossed Aelfled could not reconcile how being responsible for the death of Cyr made her strong rather than weak and self-serving, she could only stare.

Isa looked to those gathered around. "We dare not return to Wulfen. Though Jaxon is dead, some—perhaps many—of his followers live. And of greater threat is the usurper. After what was wrought this eve, he will question my allegiance and if he does not remove me from Wulfen shall take steps to better control me, forcing me to wed one of his own. And I will not..." She cleared her throat of what Aelfled knew was great emotion. "Never will I, the daughter of Wulfrith, be the prize of a Norman, valued only for bedding and making children to bear *his* name. Thus, elsewhere we shall gather our strength and prepare for the day we take back what belongs to us."

Then she yet believed it possible to rout the Normans? For Saxons to reclaim their country though among them were men like Jaxon who had sought to take from Isa the same as Normans?

Aelfled knew she was not right enough of mind to make a good guess at what the future held for her people, but one word pressed against the backs of her lips—*hopeless*. And all the more were Cyr dead.

If. That word slammed into *hopeless* with a force nearly as great as that which had slammed against her back in the underground which she now knew was Ordric, he whose strength added to hers had brought down the passage. But had it come down on Cyr? Was it not possible the ceiling above him remained intact? That even now he made his way back to the donjon? Would soon mount a horse and find his way to her?

There was the word *hopeless* again, but when Isa said, "It is time to depart, Aelf," she knew she would not leave Wulfen. Perhaps later she would join her lady, but only if Cyr were truly lost—and they had not made a child.

She did not resist when Ordric lifted her to her feet, and it would have done little good she discovered when an ankle went out from under her and she was surprised by pain she marveled she had not felt sooner.

"I feared that," Ordric said as he steadied her. "Your foot was pinned beneath a timber."

She looked up, guessed her clothes, face, and hair were as ravaged as his—torn, nicked and bruised, fouled.

"You shall have to carry her through the wood, Ordric."

"Nay," Aelfled countered Isa. "I do not go with you."

Her lady's eyes widened, then she ordered those gathered around to prepare to depart. As they dispersed, she said, "There is naught for you here, Aelfled."

"If Cyr is alive, there is much for me."

Isa made a sound of disgust. "Tell her, Ordric."

When Aelfled shot her gaze to him, he said, "You must know there is little chance he survived."

"Little, meaning not impossible," she countered.

His eyebrows pinched. "The passage is down, so filled with rubble that were there light on the other side one could not see it."

Pressing a thumb hard to the base of her ring finger, Aelfled said, "That does not mean he is buried the same as Jaxon."

"Jaxon is not buried—not entirely. He was near us when the passage came down." At her sharp breath, he continued, "Dead, but as D'Argent was not far behind, I wager the Norman is well enough buried he could remain there were it consecrated ground."

Such cruel imaginings had Aelfled of Cyr in a grave she helped make for him she feared all the bones would go out of her. "I wager against you," she retorted and needed none to tell her how petty her argument nor the odds such a wager would see her lose all.

She looked to Isa, said past teeth beginning to chatter, "Even did I wish to go with you, I would slow you. Pray, leave me."

"Here?" Isa gestured at the moonlit wood—trees, foliage, and the wide stream carrying away water spilled by the great fall whose veil sparkled in the distance. "There is no time to deliver you nearer the castle, and I will risk no life for so distant a hope it will be safe for you there. Come with us."

"Nay. Find me a sturdy stick, and I can make my own way out of here."

Her lady breathed deep. "Your path is your own. I will not stand in the middle of it nor force you onto mine. I..." Momentarily, she closed her eyes. "It is hard to forgive, Aelf, but I try. I do."

Emotion nearly choking Aelfled, she rasped, "I thank you, my lady."

Isa shifted her regard to her housecarle. "See her sheltered upstream near the falls lest any venture here in search of us. Provide her a good stick and provisions, then we leave." Once more she addressed Aelfled. "Do not risk the journey ere dawn. After all you have endured, you must rest, and regardless of the outcome of the attack on Wulfen, it will be better seen in daylight and aid in determining the way forward."

Aelfled had not thought that far ahead but accepted the advice, at the moment too pained, weak, and chilled to remain upright without Ordric's support. "I shall journey forth at dawn," she said and grasped a handful of the housecarle's tunic when he lifted her into his arms. "Godspeed, my lady."

"My lady," Isa murmured, then said, "If you are still *Lady* Aelfled, and my fate lies beyond Wulfen's walls, I am no longer that to you."

Through fresh tears, Aelfled said, *"Ever* you shall be my lady."

Isa gave what sounded a muffled sob. "Godspeed, Aelf." She swung around, stumbled as if the sudden movement made her light of head, then strode away.

Ordric carried Aelfled upstream to the waterfall she had visited with Isa and her son in his early years. They had spread a blanket beside the pond and eaten cold meats, fruit, and bread there. They had waded in the cold water, swum, and splashed each other. And once, beneath a full moon, they had ventured there before dawn to watch those who trained at Wulfen run the ridge above. Isa's husband had not been pleased to learn she was there, though he would not have known had she not advised him on a crossing atop the falls that would more greatly challenge the boys and young men—as it had challenged Ordric when he trained beneath Isa's father.

Now that boy-turned-warrior settled her on moss-covered ground in the shelter of towering rocks that formed a wall on one side of the falls, near enough the pool into which water tumbled that she could easily reach it, but not so near she suffer the spray. Here was only mist.

He left her and returned with a blanket he draped around her shoulders, a walking stick, a pack of provisions, and splints.

As he bound up her ankle, she stared at his bent head crowned with hair fairer than hers and remembered the boy he had been when Isa's father took the orphaned youth from Ravven and gave him a means of venting so great an anger it had frightened little Aelf. A warrior he had become and nearly as esteemed as Vitalis.

"I pray you find your way," he said.

"I thank you, Ordric. Keep our lady safe."

"'Tis my duty and honor." He rose and ran to overtake those venturing deeper into the wood—her people who, perhaps more than she, must find their way.

Drawing the blanket over her lower face and body, she dropped her chin to her chest and prayed for them and those fallen and injured this night. And Cyr.

Some might wonder how she could feel so much for him in so short a time, but in that moment she understood. What she felt was not only of the heart and mind, but the soul of which her grandmother had spoken—as if since Aelfled met Cyr upon Senlac, their souls had been together every hour of every day. And still hers felt joined with his, though he might no longer breathe.

She clasped her hands tighter against her chest. "Do You save him, Lord, I will praise You to my end days. Never again will I question…" She gasped, shook her head. "I think to test You as if I were the instructor, You the pupil. Forgive me." She swallowed. "No bargains. No matter how great my loss, let me not become hollow. Help me that even when I think You cannot see me because I cannot see You, I remain in Your presence. Help me that even when I believe You lost to me, I remember never am I lost to You. Amid my darkest days, reveal Yourself even if only through Bernia and others more faithful than I. And if Cyr is gone…" She nodded. "Let me remain with You who are forever."

Aelfled did not know she slept until awakened by the pound of hooves what might have been minutes later or hours. Not of one or two horses. Four or more.

Her first thought of Cyr, she nearly called to him. But more than the likelihood he would not hear her over the hooves and waterfall, what closed her mouth was the possibility it was Jaxon's men, either fleeing or come in search of their leader.

The hooves slowed, ceased, and though from where she was tucked between jagged rocks she could not see them, she knew they were near the underground passage's opening. Catching their voices, she strained to determine if they were of Normans or Saxon, but so distorted were they by distance and falling water, she would have to draw nearer.

Heart beating hard, she retrieved the stick, pushed upright, and whimpered when her ankle protested the weight given it. Ordric had assured her it was not broken, but it was damaged, and she would go nowhere without the stick's support.

She drew the russet-colored blanket up over her head, ensured it covered her down to her ankles, and started forward.

Progress was slow as she kept to the wall that transitioned from rock to foliage-ladened earth, her movements hampered by the need to keep weight off her ankle and the persistence of the blanket clasped at her throat to catch beneath foot and stick. Upon reaching the last outcropping, she peered around it and saw five horses, their riders scattered in all directions as if searching for the passage's opening.

Wishing they were near enough one another to converse that she might determine how great their right to be upon Isa's land, she looked from one to the next. Hope leapt when her eyes settled on the fourth man a moment before he hunkered down.

Was it him?

Wishing away the canopy of branches and leaves that cast shadows across moonlight, she pressed her lips to keep from calling his name.

And heard hers called.

~

FROM THE PASSAGE'S TURNS, bends, and courses, he had guessed right. Near the great waterfall was where the earth opened up to expel dozens of Saxons, including Hawisa, warriors, castle folk, and—he entreated the Lord—his wife.

Once more tortured by the possibility she was buried beneath timbers and rubble that had nearly become his own grave, he called again, "Aelfled!" and began his descent into the hole around which was scattered the dirt and debris of the collapse that had aided in its discovery.

"Cyr!"

He snapped his head around. Though he could not pick Aelfled from the shadows, she was near. He sprang out of the hole and ran to overtake his men who moved toward her voice.

Then there she was, darkness falling away to reveal hair and chemise not as pale as when he saw her in the passage, but enough to light the way to where she stood with a blanket down around her feet.

Though alarmed by the stick she leaned on, he saw no evidence of great injury and was further reassured by her gentle smile and tear-bright eyes.

"I have her!" he called. "Stand watch!"

As his men veered away, he took the last strides and caught her up against his dirt-clad body, the garments of which adhered to his skin wherever blades had rent the material and drawn blood.

With a cry, his wife dropped the stick and wound her arms around his neck, as unmindful as he they were much in need of bathing.

"Merciful Lord, you are here, Aelfled! Tell me you are not badly hurt."

She hiccoughed softly, shook her head. "The worst is my ankle, and it is not broken."

"I feared—" Reining in words loosened by imaginings of her breathless beneath timbers, he swept her up and carried her to a fallen tree.

As he lowered to it, she said in a rush, "You have seen your brother, Guarin? He is well?"

"I saw and spoke with him." He shifted her atop his thighs, easing her around to face him. "Though terribly beaten, there is much hope he will recover."

"Praise the Lord," she breathed, then her eyes widened. "You know I did not wish to leave you? That for the sake of your brother I persuaded your cousin to trade me? That I wanted—needed—you to come for me?"

He cupped her jaw. "I know. As you must know my desire and need are the same." He kissed her, and she sighed into him. But there being pressing matters to attend to and the Lord having assured them of time later to linger over each other, he drew back. "I must know what happened to the other Saxons come through the tunnel, Aelfled."

It took her a moment to return to that place she surely did not wish to go. "All of Lady Hawisa's people made it out, though had you not slowed Jaxon with your sword, I..."

"Slowed," Cyr muttered. "A dagger would have served better,

but I had no time to draw it. Thus, the hilt rather than the blade struck him in the back. Such a poor throw."

"But one that ensured he did not reach me."

Much too narrow a save, Cyr silently berated, then asked, "He is dead?"

"I lost consciousness, and the housecarle who helped me collapse the passage brought me out. But my lady told Jaxon is no more."

He would have to see the body himself before resting easy where that rebel was concerned. "Where are Lady Hawisa and the others?"

"Gone deep into the wood."

"They left you behind?" he growled. "Because of your injury?"

"Non, Cyr. They would have carried me, but I clung to the hope you lived and would come for me. As I had revealed our marriage to my lady, I told her I would remain and she did not gainsay me."

"Will she return when she learns Wulfen did not fall to Jaxon's rebels?"

Hesitation, and he guessed she weighed confidences in her keeping against loyalty to her husband. Such quandary, in this instance where there need be none. "Aelfled, already I know what you fear to tell, and I understand why you hold it close. Guarin confirmed Lady Hawisa is Dotter." The catch of her breath slight, he continued, "He beseeched me to keep her safe from ours—and those of her own who betray her."

Wide-eyed questions and discarded answers flitted across her face, and one word was all she could summon. "Then...?"

"I know not what there is between them, Aelfled, only that he is sympathetic. And may be as ensnared as I by a Saxon woman met upon what seemed a godforsaken battlefield."

More unanswered questions moved across her lovely face, then she sighed and said, "I fear your brother has little hope where my lady is concerned, but there is hope elsewhere—that as you say, Senlac only seemed godforsaken. As does England. As do —*did*—I."

He raised his eyebrows. "Did?"

"Whilst I waited for you this eve, I prayed, and though I began to bargain with God—promising all did He keep you safe—I ceased and held to Him." She drew a sharp breath. "And now you are here as well. Where you are meant to be. With me. Like this."

Moved that she fit him into words spoken to her when he told she was not meant to be a nun, he said, "A great truth, Aelfled, as are our vows that were kept this day and shall be every day into the hereafter." He reached to his purse. "I have something for you." He withdrew her psalter and opened it to the pages between which her wedding ring was pressed.

"As if I have worn it always, I have missed it," she said.

He slid it on her finger. "This eve, nothing mattered more than returning it to your hand," he said and once more clasped her close. "Did I not tell I would hold you again come night?"

A sob slipped from her. "I know you love me."

Though certain he had heard right, he drew back.

She smiled tremulously. "I know it."

He chuckled. "Is that not for me to say?"

"Not if you have shown it, and you have—far more than I."

"You are saying *you* love *me?*"

"I am. I do. Methinks since first my soul met yours." She reached up, drew through her fingers the dark and silver of his hair. "Do you believe it possible?"

With so much to feel—relief, gratitude, happiness—it was hard to think clearly. Blessedly, the answer required little effort. "I feel as you feel. Should I speak it into you?" When she moved her face nearer, he touched his lips to hers. "I love you, my little Saxon."

He felt her mouth curve against his, heard and breathed the words she spoke into him. "I love you, my honorable Norman."

EPILOGUE

Wulfen Castle, England
Autumn, 1068

*T*he rebellion was not done. Merely dormant. England was not on its knees. Neither on its feet. And in the space between the conquering and the bridling, a new day cast light across the dark. But on this autumn morn, two years beyond and scores of leagues distant from Senlac, a beautiful thing it was.

Something to behold, breathe, cherish. The same as the woman who shared his saddle.

"Breathtaking," she said in that sweetly husky voice.

Holding his gaze to the sky above Wulfen Castle as its ink-black dissolved beneath a tide of sapphire blue and brilliant gold, Cyr slid his hand from his wife's waist to her abdomen. "Aye, and more so now," he said in her language.

She peered over her shoulder, raised her eyebrows. "'Tis the dawn I speak of."

"As do I, for that is what you—and this child—are to me."

Now came the sun, her smile warmer and brighter than that

which had yet to mount the sky. Lowering his head, he kissed it open.

Aelfled turned into him, and as the blanket slipped from her chemise-covered shoulders, she slid her hands around his neck.

He groaned. "Perhaps we ought to have remained abed."

"And miss the sunrise of this our last day at Wulfen?"

As she had said dawn was most spectacular from the western knoll, he had kept his word to bring her here before they returned to Stern. With the waning of night, he had wrapped her in the coverlet and scooped her up. She had drowsily protested being carried, then curled against him as he conveyed her through the great hall where he exchanged a nod with Wulfen's long-haired, bearded castellan who opened the door for them. Only when they reached the outer bailey and Cyr ordered the yawning stable lad to saddle his horse had Aelfled roused. Or so he thought until she expressed concern over the castellan who looked to have found no rest on the night past.

"'Tis stunning, is it not?" she returned him to this moment—their moment.

He kissed her again. "I would not be anywhere but here with you, Wife."

She drew a hand from his neck and over a jaw bristling with whiskers to which he ought to have taken a razor a sennight past. He would see to it upon their return to Stern.

"Yours shall soon be a proper Saxon beard," she said. "Is that what you wish?"

He grinned. "Better the question—is that what *you* wish?"

She made much of considering his face. "I am partial to the Norman style that allows me to dwell on all your face, but I would not object did you wish to abandon the blade's uncomfortable and tedious scrape."

"Then there my answer. For my lady wife, I shall continue to suffer that keen edge. Now look. Here comes the sun."

She turned forward, caught up his hand, and resettled it on her belly that would soon become more than a handful.

Peace. It poured through Cyr, though he dare not allow it to brim lest it make him vulnerable to stirrings amongst the Saxons. The resistance across England continued, but upon Wulfenshire, that rage was reduced to restlessness—an uneasy acceptance of Norman rule, specifically that of the D'Argents.

Cyr upon Stern.

Theriot upon Balduc.

Guarin upon Wulfen.

Cyr closed his eyes, saw again his brother who had surely slept little last eve. He was changed, as were all who had done battle upon Senlac, some for the better, others the worse. And those who survived were not the only ones affected. Whether by great or little measure, no life either side of the channel would be as before that autumn crossing of the narrow sea.

Of further testament to that was Maël who refused to speak of his demons and Dougray who continued to struggle to reclaim the warrior's mantle. Then there was the Bloodlust Warrior of Hastings, recently come out of the monastery following the murder of the brother to whom he had given the demesne awarded him. Once more Maxen Pendery had donned chain mail to take possession of rebel-plagued lands near Hastings and avenge his brother's death by hunting down the Saxons hiding in Andredeswald.

Two years gone since Cyr aided Aelfled in those woods. How many more before the healing of England began in earnest?

Pulling himself back to the woman with whom he wished to be present, he opened his eyes. But despite the beauty before him, his oldest brother's foot remained in the door that should not have been opened to him here and now.

Cyr had loved the brother Guarin had been before 1066. He loved this one. But it was hard to be at ease with the latter. Ever

Guarin's siblings had deemed him fearless, but he was more thoughtful and watchful now, and it was not of one hunted. Rather, of one who hunted. And yet he was not the same as Dougray who had breathed in and breathed out vengeance when first he came to England. He was...

Different. Guarin having spoken little of what he endured during captivity, one could only guess what prowled his mind, but Cyr did not believe he hunkered low awaiting an opportunity to wreak havoc on his former captors.

Unlike Maël and Dougray, he had supported Cyr's decision to return to their villages the injured rebels who survived the attack on Wulfen—specifically, Vitalis's men and those of Jaxon for whom Guarin vouched. Thus far, there was no cause to regret the decision, though the former rebels were watched closely to ensure they were not moved to take up arms again. And all the more imperative it was now they were honed warriors rather than wielders of whatever tool or stick could be brought to hand.

Since many were of Wulfen, a fortnight past they had begun answering to Guarin. And Guarin answered directly to the king who, angered by Cyr's marriage, commanded the eldest D'Argent brother to remain in England and, once sufficiently healed, administer the demesne abandoned by Lady Hawisa. Without objection nor a brief return home to provide living proof the heir lived, Guarin had assumed the post.

Regarding William's anger toward Cyr, Maël believed it was less for wedding a commoner than *plans gone awry*. The king had thought to match the Baron of Stern and Balduc with the Lady of Wulfen. Of course it was of no matter the moment her demesne was forfeited for the traitor William named her, though no proof of that had he from a D'Argent—certainly not the one long imprisoned who had identified only Jaxon as his captor.

Once more, Cyr wondered what had transpired between the lady and his brother, next where she and her people had taken themselves, including Zedekiah and the injured Vitalis who had been gone from Wulfen when Cyr brought Aelfled out of the wood that night—just as the corpse of the one named responsible for the murder of the Norman family had disappeared.

Debris had been removed from the passage in the event further collapse had covered Jaxon after Aelfled was carried out, but his body was not found. Since there seemed no reason Hawisa would take the betrayer with her had he lived, it was concluded he had dragged himself away. Were that so, he might have been in the passage into which Cyr had begun his descent when Aelfled called to him. And in that dark with moonlight at Cyr's back, Jaxon might have slain the one who had slowed him with the throw of a sword.

More reason not to be lulled by peace.

More reason for the D'Argents to keep close watch on their backs.

More reason for Guarin to reroute Wulfen's underground passage, ensuring its exit remained secret, and install iron gates along its course.

More reason to hunt down Jaxon who tempted William to make good his threat to harry the shire.

As for Campagnon, he had evaded the charge of attempting to burn Stern's hay, allowing Merle and the others to take full responsibility—and punishment. Thus, once more the miscreant hired himself out as a mercenary and, it was said, searched for the slave who fled him. Hopefully, Em would remain hidden until her tormentor returned to France. *If* he returned. Whilst Saxons continued to spurn their Norman king, there would be work for men like Campagnon.

Blessedly, it was a good portent the son recently birthed by William's queen had entered the world by way of Yorkshire—Henry, the first of their growing brood to be born on English soil. But though England might soon flourish again and Cyr believed he could make a good life here with the woman he loved, he yearned for Normandy which, until the night past, had seemed well beyond his grasp.

Over a goblet of wine, seated before the hearth where Lady Hawisa had first received Cyr in that great hall, Guarin had mused England suited him. Then in a tone too teasing for one of so altered a disposition, he suggested Cyr remain their sire's heir.

Though Stern and Balduc were more extensive and boasted greater potential than D'Argent lands in Normandy and would nearly double in size were Wulfen stitched back to the other two baronies, it was not greed that sent those words from Guarin's mouth. Had Cyr to guess, it was a woman, though before Aelfled never would he have thought the fairer sex possessed such power over men.

Did Guarin cede his inheritance, their sire would be disappointed. Though proud of all his sons—to a lesser degree the one not of his body—he could not disguise his greatest joy was his eldest whom he, rather than Hugh, had first begun shaping into a warrior, nor that among his greatest sorrows was that which removed him from the training yard and, for a time, the marital bed. As for the former, there were things in which a warrior must be schooled beyond weaponry, and Guarin had been their sire's best pupil. As for the latter, to the surprise of many, Theriot and Nicola came after Dougray.

"There!" Aelfled jolted him back to the present.

Glad to return to her, he followed her regard to the golden-orange rim rising above the castle.

"Did I not name it spectacular?" she exclaimed.

He narrowed his gaze against the brilliance. "You did."

As she lowered her hand, a ray glanced off gold, slid across plaited blond, black, and silver strands, glanced off gold again. To ensure the ring over which their vows were spoken was ever upon her hand, Cyr had commissioned one of gold with a channel all around into which the braided ring was set. Atop where the ends met, four prongs cradled a square sapphire.

She was his, he was hers. And so well they knew each other, he did not believe any secrets remained between them. Did any, then on her side only, though not her own secrets. And he was well with that.

She looked around. "I thank you for bringing me." Her smile widened. "You know not how much I love you."

"I know it is not as much I love you."

"Should we argue?"

"We could, but I would win, Aelfled of the Saxons...of Wulfenshire...of Stern and Balduc."

She wrinkled her nose as ever she did when he embellished her name.

Cyr's teasing reminding him of Guarin's, he said, "Do you recall what I told of my conversation with my brother last eve?"

"I was half asleep when you joined me in bed, but it was too curious a thing to forget."

"The morning after our wedding night, you told it was possible you could be happier in Normandy. If Guarin wills it, would you become Aelfled of Normandy?"

"Nay." It was said firmly and without hesitation, but before he could be unsettled by her change of mind, she added, "No matter where I am, ever I am Aelfled of Cyr. And that is all. And everything."

He set his brow against hers, and feeling the new day's sun upon them, said, "As ever I shall be Cyr of Aelfled."

Dear Reader,

There being many wonderful books in one's to-be-read pile, I'm honored you chose to spend time with Sir Cyr and Aelfled. If you enjoyed the first Wulfrith origins tale, I would appreciate a review of MERCILESS at your online retailer—just a sentence or two, more if you feel chatty.

For a peek at FEARLESS, the second book in the Age of Conquest *series, an excerpt is included here and will soon be available on my website: www.TamaraLeigh.com. Now to finish that tale for its Spring 2019 release.*

Pen. Paper. Inspiration. Imagination. ~ Tamara

AUTHOR'S NOTE

Thus we have the eleventh-century beginnings of the twelfth-century Wulfriths of the Age of Faith series. I hope, dear readers, you enjoyed the journey back to the time of the Norman Conquest. I certainly did, though MERCILESS is not my first visit. If you have read LADY OF CONQUEST, you will recognize the characters of Maxen Pendery—the Bloodlust Warrior of Hastings—his sire Baron Pendery, Edwin Harwolfson, and the white-haired woman dragging a housecarle off the battlefield (yes, that was Dora and Edwin). Being mostly a seat-of-the-pants writer, I can't say how much overlap there will be between these tales, but as I write FEARLESS, the second Age of Conquest book, once more LADY OF CONQUEST is making her presence known in ink upon paper. I look forward to sharing the next tale with you. And all those that come after. Blessings!

FEARLESS EXCERPT

THE WULFRITHS. IT ALL BEGAN WITH A WOMAN

From USA Today Bestselling author Tamara Leigh, the second book in a new series set in the 11ᵗʰ century during the Norman Conquest of England, revealing the origins of the Wulfrith family of the AGE OF FAITH series. Releasing Spring 2019.

CHAPTER ONE

Sussex, England
14 October, 1066

*D*anger. With each drag of her hem over dirt, through blood and other things heretofore unimaginable, it seeped into this bodily vessel, filling eyes, nose, mouth.

Danger. It chilled, making her soul a quaking thing desperate to catch hold of the unsullied hem of the Lord.

Danger. It pressed in on all sides, sweeping over the silent dead in their heaps, the groaning dying soon to join those above and below.

"Not my boy," Isa Wulfrithdotter Fortier gasped as she veered away from a jumble of Saxons and Normans whose bodies were too great of size to include the one for whom she searched. "Lord, do I not find him, let it be he was never here, else returned to the wood...making his way back to safety...back to me."

She halted. Clasping her short mantle at the throat to prevent the hood from falling and making a beacon of her hair, she stared.

A body slight of stature and clothed in red lay face down on one of greater height and breadth. But before her breaking heart could snatch back a soul straining to reach the Lord's hem, she saw here was a Norman. Rather than long hair, his was cropped, the red he wore not of cloth but chain mail coated in crimson. So much blood, but not her boy's.

"Praise You, Lord," she breathed and swept her gaze around this portion of the battlefield she had been searching since shortly after her arrival on the meadow of Senlac where the forces of Duke William of Normandy had defeated the army of England after slaying its rightful king.

In the hours since, most of the victorious enemy had retreated from the carnage to celebrate, tend injuries, and rest. However, there were enough moving across the meadow, searching for their own or desecrating the fallen by relieving them of valuables, that she and other Saxons who had not yet received permission to retrieve their dead were in great peril—as was her maid, Aelfled, who had gone in a direction opposite Isa when the two ventured out of the wood at twilight.

Might she who had failed her lady have redeemed herself by finding Wulf alive and well? Or was he—?

"Nay, Lord," she beseeched. "If the one most precious to me is here, let him not number among the dead."

Breath catching, chest jerking, she told herself she would not be ashamed of this fear even were her sire here, then continued forward, altering her course when her path was blocked by bodies or she happened too near Norman scavengers who made her hand convulse on the dagger at her waist.

Once again, a figure more a boy than a man captured her regard partway up a gently sloping hill. Pinned beneath a heavily-armored Norman, he had hair of a familiar length and color.

She ran and dropped to her knees. "Wulf!" His name left her lips a moment ahead of her vision adjusting to the shadow cast across his face by the Norman atop him. They were not her boy's unseeing eyes upon hers, not his cheeks, nose, mouth, and chin. Just barely a man, this defeated Saxon was another woman's son.

"Well you served England in putting down this animal," she said, though she could not know it was true. It could have been a nearby Saxon who felled the Norman pinning this warrior. "One less of his kind means one less we must battle to hold what they seek to take from us. Be with God, faithful defender."

With trembling fingers, she closed his eyes, then dropped back on her heels, clasped hands over nose and mouth, and thanked the Lord there remained the possibility her son lived.

She started to rise, but the voices of those speaking in the Norman tongue stilled her. Looking around, she saw two moved in her direction, a third following at a distance.

She raised the hood that had dropped down around her shoulders and covered her hair. Knowing she would more easily come to notice if she retreated, she bent and placed her face near the dead Saxon's. Between sips of air heavily fouled by death, she swallowed convulsively to keep the contents of her stomach from climbing her throat, hoped the dark lump made of herself escaped the enemy's notice, prayed soon she would find Wulf.

"No more loss can I bear, Lord," she whispered, "especially that of my son. If I am the last of the line of Wulfrith, I will break. If only for my departed sire, preserve his grandson."

Blessedly, the Normans turned aside, as revealed by laughter in which only victors lacking heart would indulge in the midst of slaughter that included their own who whimpered, groaned, and cried out as death languorously claimed them.

She shuddered, certain such men would try to make her their reward for having survived the battle, just as they would do Aelfled who, seven years younger than her lady, of smaller frame, and having little training in defense, would stand less chance of escape and survival.

Despite how enraged Isa was with her maid for allowing Wulf and his friends to slip away from Trionne, she ached over the possibility Aelfled might become a play thing of the Normans.

"Lord, keep her safe," she rasped. "Defend her life and virtue as you defend mine. Above all, protect Wulf. Reunite us."

She opened her eyes upon the shadow her hood cast over her head, sat back and peered around. Dozens of figures moved over the battlefield, most of whom had to be Normans, all distant enough to allow her to resume her search.

She stood and began forging a winding path among the slaughtered to the base of the hill atop which a skeletal tree reached gnarled fingers to the heavens.

More suffering she heard here than other places she had passed, and the ground writhed with men whose struggles to rise or crawl would likely prove for naught.

Here a Norman. There a Saxon. Another Saxon. Yet another.

"Find your boy," she commanded and began her ascent of the hill. Halfway up, her trailing skirt so firmly snagged on something her forward motion could not free her. Dropped to her knees, she slapped hands to the ground to keep from landing face down in a glistening stream of blood, twisted around to free her skirt, and stifled a cry when she saw the material was grasped by neither root nor rock.

Falling onto her backside, she snatched at her skirt to pull it from fingers clenched upon it. But the one who had her held fast to the hem whose dark material was darker than that above, having been soaked in blood and other evidence of death on which she had tried not to think and sought not to think now with her belly threatening to purge itself.

"Aid me," the man said in her language.

She stilled in drawing her dagger, sent her gaze up the man's hand to his head propped on the shoulder of the extended arm he lay upon, his face framed by long hair and short beard.

"Be merciful," the Saxon said. "I must die...with my king. Pray, end it."

A royal housecarle. Even had he a chance of survival, he did not wish to suffer the indignity of surviving King Harold whose life he had failed to preserve.

She knew what he required of her. She knew her sire would not hesitate. And from all the blood, the pale cast of his face, and the absence of a physician, she knew he had no chance of life beyond this eve and it would be merciful to end his suffering. But her heart and mind protested, splaying her hand off her dagger.

"Lady," he choked. "Could I, I would do it myself."

She shook her head.

A guttural sob opened his mouth wide, but he snapped his teeth closed and said between them, "Show me your dagger."

"I do not—"

"You lie. Show me, Woman!"

Though she meant to refuse him, the tears pooling alongside his nose spilled onto the dirt before his extended arm. Great his pain, and greater if she left him like this, whether death circled for hours or the Normans made sport of him whilst divesting him of splendid mail tunic, gold necklace, rings, and fine leather boots.

He groaned, said more gently, "I am Edwin, Lady. Pray, your dagger."

Beneath her short mantle, Isa touched the hilt of the deadly weapon she wore opposite that for cutting meat, moved her hand to the latter and drew it from its scabbard.

"A wicked little thing," he said with what sounded approval, though if he saw the other dagger he would think this a dull thing.

He released her skirt, moved his hand to his neck. "Here. The great vein."

He will die regardless, she assured herself. *It is not murder. It is mercy.*

But horror over bleeding him was stronger than reason, and she said, "Forgive me, Edwin. I cannot do it."

"Lady—"

"I cannot!" She leaned near and, taking the hand with which he pointed the way to his demise, set the hilt in his palm and folded his fingers over it. "It *is* a wicked little thing, requiring less strength to do the deed than hold to my skirt."

Seeing anger flash in moist eyes lit by the moon, she drew back and surged upright lest he catch hold of her again. "Forgive me," she repeated. "I..."

His lids closed, and the hand holding her dagger dropped to the ground.

Praying his suffering was at an end, that he had not lost consciousness lest he regain it and suffer more, Isa left him the dagger should he yet require it and turned away.

Feeling sticky moisture and grit on her hand, she lifted it before her face. Blood and dirt, doubtless gained from the housecarle's hand when she placed the dagger there—some of which he must have gained from her hem.

"Find Wulf," she told herself but delayed further by dragging up her skirt. Aided by the deadly dagger, she cut away two hands' width that bared ankles and lower calves beneath the hem of a short chemise. It was necessary, not only to prevent her from being distracted by the horror of that bloodied span of material but to keep others from seizing her as she passed.

She cast the jagged strip aside, returned the dagger to its scabbard, and refusing to look behind at Edwin, continued up the hill.

The nearer she drew to the tree, eyes delving the sprawled figures for a boy of good size though not yet eleven years aged, the more quiet and still it became. The voices of the dying were lower and of fewer number, the movement of their pained bodies sluggish in places, absent in others. But that was surely due to more blood and carnage here where the dead lay deeper. So deep her boy might—

Feeling as if she walked the edge between everything and nothing, that slippery ridge threatening to tip her into inescapable darkness where one with the blood of Wulfrith did not belong, she gave her head a hard shake.

Returned to this moment to which observation—not imagination—was due, she looked nearer on all ahead and to the sides of her. Much had gone here as further evidenced by the royal housecarle who wished to die with his king and other soldiers whose clothes, armor, and weaponry revealed neither were they of the class of ordinary housecarles who served thanes. King Harold might have fallen here, but even had he not, this place was too central to the battle for mere boys to have reached it. Or so she prayed as she continued toward the tree past which she would begin her descent to the other side.

During her search, she had happened on many horses whose lives were sacrificed to carry their riders through battle lines. Norman only she was certain, the Anglo-Saxon army not given to fighting astride though her sire had admired mounted warfare and sought to persuade King Edward and the earl who would later succeed him—the fallen Harold—to adopt the strategy. Here were more steeds transported across the sea, and partway down the hill one that would appear peacefully at rest where it lay with forelegs tucked under and head up if not for the rider slumped over a grey-black neck across which a pale mane flowed.

Distantly aware once more she broke stride, she stared at the animal who turned its head in her direction, startled when it seemed all the light that could be found in this darkness shone from its eyes.

Yanking her thoughts back to the one who was her only

reason for being upon Senlac, she said firmly, "Wulf," and stepped forward.

"Non, destrier," spoke one whose language and accent spun her around and up against one taller and broader than she.

Finding her palm empty as it should not be, she jerked her elbow back and closed fingers around the hilt.

Before she could pull the blade from its scabbard, the Norman seized hold of her arms beneath the mantle.

Unworthy! she silently denounced as her sire had done when he instructed the girl she had been in the defense of her person until finally he pronounced her otherwise. Now a dozen years later, aged twenty and five, once more she proved unworthy. And might die for it once the plunder made of her was beyond tarnished.

Cease, Hawisa Wulfrithdotter Fortier! she silently commanded. *You will not dishonor your sire and his name. Fight!*

She wrenched backward. Glimpsing the grinning, clean-shaven face above hers as hands tightened around her lower arms, she slammed her knee up between her enemy's legs. And made contact in the absence of chain mail surely shed following the battle.

The Norman cursed and lurched forward. If not for his chin clipping the top of her head, she might have gained her release. Though the pain weakened her knees and blurred her vision, she clung to consciousness and strained to free her arms. Then of a sudden, the ground was at her back and a great weight atop her.

"Whore!" the man spat.

As she translated his slur into her own language, easily done having been wed to a Norman, her assailant turned his mouth to her ear. Bristling jaw grating against her cheek, he said, "After I have used you up, I shall give the husk of you to my men. Here you shall die, Saxon."

Strained breaths wasted on attempts to dislodge him, Isa heard her sire bellow, *Know when to be still, Daughter of Wulfrith! Know when to wait and watch!* Imagined though it was, she felt his saliva fleck her face.

"Aye, Father," she whispered.

The Norman's head came up. "What say you, *Saxon?*"

Though earlier he had understood the name he believed the word *wolf* of the four-legged variety, likely he was minimally conversant in her language. But if she proved she knew his, perhaps he would release her—or at least be rendered vulnerable by surprise.

Using the thin stream of breath allotted her, she said in his language, "I am a lady, a Saxon wed to a Norman. Great ill you do my husband in attacking me. He will—"

A hand snapped up and gripped her chin, then he raised himself slightly to peer into her face.

Inwardly bemoaning the arm he had released was not the side from which her one remaining dagger could be had, she ground her teeth and returned his scrutiny. Though his countenance was more shadowed than hers, she guessed he was two score aged.

"You are pretty and fairly young," he said. "I shall enjoy this all the more."

Then he was not moved to learn she was joined with one of his own, would *use her up* regardless? "My husband is Norman the same as you," she tried again.

He laughed. *"Not* the same as the esteemed companion of the mighty King William."

King. Already the invader named that as if all was decided here, as if Harold's death was the only thing required to crown him.

Let it not be, Isa sent heavenward. *William may have carried the papal banner into battle, but it is for You to decide, Lord! Pray, come back to Your faithful!*

"Not the same," her assailant repeated and dug his nails into her chin. "That honor was lost when your husband sullied his line by wedding one of inferior race. And did he fight against William this day, what I shall have from you this night will be more due your traitorous husband."

"He did not take up arms against your duke," she exclaimed and dared not reveal Roger had died in the north at Stamford Bridge while defeating the invading Norwegians alongside King Harold. Nor that had he survived, he would have been obligated to fight his fellow Normans, having pledged his allegiance to King Edward and his successors in exchange for the great demesne given him through marriage to the only surviving child of the formidable trainer of warriors and thane of Wulfenshire.

"I care not what he did or did not do," the Norman said. "Though paltry your contribution toward a debt that can never be paid in full for the Normans slain by your Saxon dogs, still payment shall be made." He loosed her chin, reached down, and began dragging up her skirt.

"Nay!" Resuming her struggle, Isa swept her free hand over the ground in search of something weighty to slam down upon his skull. Finding only pebbles and dirt, she closed her hand over his upon her leg and tried to pull it off, but the calloused fingers continued upward, scraping over calf and knee.

She screamed, tried to bring that knee up again, but his legs were too heavy on hers. Another scream, a failed attempt to sink her teeth into his jaw, a successful snap of the forehead against his chin that pained her nearly as much as when her crown had struck that same bony prominence.

Blessedly, that last caused him to remove his hand from her leg. But her Saxon's triumph against a Norman was fleeting. He slapped her hard, knocking her head to the side and cutting a lip that bled onto her tongue, then clamped his hand around her neck.

Denied breath, she hooked her fingers over his and pried at them. To no avail. She dragged her nails down his jaw and neck. To no avail.

I fail you, Father! she silently called to he who had lived long enough to learn he was to be a grandfather and name the unborn babe Wulfrith.

Dirt, she heard him growl as if he were with her now. *A woman's weapon but effective.*

Remembering the girl of her grumbling it was the sword and dagger she wished to learn, not the scramblings of weak women, and for it he had dashed dirt in her eyes that incapacitated as if she were stuck with a blade, she flung her arm out to the side and drove her fingers into the earth.

As the lack of air caused bursts of black to obscure her vision, blotting out the Norman's face and dulling the pain of a body vulnerable to deeds most foul, she scraped dirt into her palm until it was filled enough she could barely close her fingers over it. Then with what consciousness remained, she brought her hand near her ear and cast that weapon of women.

Her assailant released her neck, reared back onto his knees, and as he cursed and ground his palms against his eyes and her throat creaked open and she wheezed in breath, she found her right hand was freed the same as her left.

The deadly dagger within reach.

CHAPTER TWO

Curse all, he had not time for this! Certainly not whilst he had three brothers, a cousin, and an uncle to account for, all of whom he had become separated from when day yet shone across a lovely meadow that had become a bloody battlefield. Then there were his injuries that needed tending, many of which pained though none would kill—providing infection did not set in.

His barely godly uncle would not approve of him being distracted from his purpose, and though his overly godly sire would understand, neither would he approve of the risk to life and time lost seeking other sons.

Still, the heir of the family D'Argent ran to answer the cry for help, doubtless of a Saxon woman who herself risked all to discover what would likely be the remains of a loved one.

Another scream. As with the first, it drew the attention of others moving amongst the bodies. It was not fellow Normans searching for kin and friends who made Guarin stretch his legs longer beneath the weight of chain mail, but those with whom he would not associate for the opportunity they made of men far less fortunate than they—and the prey they would make of the Saxon at that place her king had fallen.

"Fool woman," he bit as he swept his gaze up over the reeking bodies he negotiated to the flat of the moonlit hill out of which grew an enormous tree that, had it boasted fruit this year, might never again were it poisoned by great quantities of blood seeking its roots.

To the right of it, one of Guarin's own sought to defile the Saxon. The big Norman having taken her to ground, even now he might be violating her as she continued to fight and voice outrage.

What had she been thinking to venture here where what was likely the greatest battle fought on English soil had raged from mid-morning until dusk? Not only had night fully fallen, but Guarin's liege, Duke William, had yet to grant permission for the Saxons to retrieve their dead.

Reaching the base of the hill, he looked ahead of his feet and had only a moment to adjust his course to avoid one of his countrymen who had died with the pole of the duke's pennon clutched to his chest, Saxons scattered left and right.

Guarin drew his sword, began his ascent of the hill, and halfway up returned his gaze to the scene near the tree. He halted abruptly, causing the links of his mail to ring more loudly. He knew himself to be a seasoned warrior and more so after putting down Saxon after Saxon who sought to rend his life and the lives of those he fought alongside, but there was something stunningly disturbing about that to which he bore witness.

Light shimmered across the silver wielded by the one with her back to the ground, and as she drove that blade into the neck of the one whose hands clawed at his eyes where he had risen atop her, in the Saxon tongue she screamed two words he understood. "Die, Norman!"

As if following this command as he had not her others, the man jerked and collapsed to the side.

Yet another of Guarin's own slain by a Saxon. Feeling the return of anger that had made him a formidable opponent as first he fought astride and then on foot when his destrier was slain beneath him, he watched the woman shove the Norman's lower body off hers. She turned and rose to her hands and knees, stumbled upright. Once she had her balance, she reached down. When she straightened, he as much felt as saw the killing dagger drawn from her victim's body.

More anger—until he reminded himself that one's death was more warranted than those of Normans who had truly believed they fought to reform England's church that could only be accomplished by placing its rightful king on the throne.

The Norman ahead had used his greater strength to seize what the woman would not give. It was questionable whether Guarin's uncle would approve of his nephew's reasoning, but again his sire would understand. And might even approve.

Regardless of whether the Norman had gained what he sought to steal from the Saxon woman, she had ensured he could not further harm her and others. Hence, with an unburdened conscience Guarin could resume his search for those who could prove in greater need of deliverance than one who would count him her enemy.

He turned aside, but too many shadowed figures moved toward the hill, evidence he was not the only one to witness the death of a warrior outside of battle.

"Almighty!" Guarin growled. Though a fatigued, battered body once more at swords could prove his undoing, he could not leave the woman to worse than already she had endured.

No matter how quickly she moved, she had far less chance of leaving the battlefield alive than had her defeated countrymen. And being a Saxon who had slain a Norman—of greater detriment, a woman—no quick death would she be afforded. Her only hope was this enemy whose sire may have had to relinquish his sons' training at arms to their uncle but had ensured Guarin and his brothers were instructed in faith to better guide the warriors made of them—and among Baron D'Argent's tenets was that defenseless women and children must be protected.

Not that this Saxon was defenseless, but she would fall to those coming for her if Guarin did not intervene. Blessedly, he would reach her ahead of the others.

Sword once more leading the way, its presence threat enough to dissuade some of those advancing on the woman to think better of laying claim to one about to be claimed by a chevalier prepared to defend his right to this spoil of war, Guarin continued his ascent.

Despite the extent of whatever had happened to the woman, she had enough wits about her to note his advance and the others', as evidenced by the single step she took opposite Guarin before whirling back around, dagger in hand.

Such gold hair she had, more visible across the distance than the face beyond unraveling braids. But in the moment before he returned his attention to negotiating the ground, he glimpsed enough of her features to guess she was between twenty and thirty years—and of slender figure, the short mantle fallen back off her shoulders revealing the only swells of her body were a generous one above a narrow waist and a gentle one below.

Reaching the crest of the hill, he slowed only enough to avoid trampling the dead scattered wider and higher here. Though the woman would surely believe he meant her harm, if he approached more cautiously, he would lose much of his lead over those who did think to act against her.

"Come no nearer!" she shouted in her language.

He glanced at where she had retreated to the other side of her assailant as if to make a barrier of his corpse, saw her sweep the bloody dagger before her. And noted—as well he should considering his training—it was no desperately careless attempt to defend her person. Her wielding of that blade and stance bespoke training of her own. Of less, albeit worthy, note was her garments. Though the gown was of simple design and its lower edge torn away, the bodice's neck and sleeves were edged in lustrous fur. Here a lady.

"I will cut your gullet," she spat and kicked the body at her feet. "The same as this vermin!"

Guarin was unable to interpret her every word, but he was familiar enough with Anglo-Saxon—and more than conversant in these circumstances—to understood her threat. And after witnessing her assailant's fate, he believed it. No ordinary lady, this.

Clearing the last great heap of bodies across which the barren tree cast knobby, grasping shadows, he lowered the point of his sword and raised his empty left hand. "I mean you no harm."

Beyond braids draping shoulders that rose and fell with great breaths to mist the air, out of a battered face shone pale blue—perhaps grey—eyes wide with hatred.

"Out! Out!" she chanted the same as her menfolk had done in answer to the Norman battle cry *Dex Aie!*

Guarin stepped around the splayed body of one of his own, causing her to lurch back a step and search left and right for a means of escape.

He followed her gaze and was relieved all but two of the roused Normans had returned to their scavenging. Injured though he was, the worst being a wound to the side bound up at battle's end, he should be able to stave off attempts to take what others would believe he wished for himself.

Returning his regard to the woman, finding she had returned her regard to him, he halted three strides distant. After a brief struggle for words in her language, he said, "Fear not. I—"

She lurched forward, jolting the body at her feet, and slashed the air between them.

Though Guarin could himself lunge and arc his sword upward, were she well enough trained, she might evade his attempt to knock the dagger from her hand. And did he succeed, it could put her to flight that would place her in the path of one or both scavengers.

"I would aid you," he said.

Once again, her dagger slashed the air and she cried, "Out! Out!"

"Others are coming, Woman! They will—"

"Heathen! Barbarian!"

Though loath to render himself blade-less, he assured himself he could quickly return his sword to hand, then with great show to ensure she attended to it, set its tip at the scabbard's throat. As he slid the blade in, he looked nearer on the dead man responsible for her belief Guarin was cut from the same cloth.

That Norman's face was turned toward her, but Guarin need not see it to know this was no common soldier. Though his clothes were begrimed, ripped, and bloodstained, better they were named finery. Here was a wealthy chevalier at worst, a lord at best who ought to have been resting or celebrating were he not searching for those lost to him.

Guarin knew depravity came in all forms, ranks, and ages, but had he not witnessed this Norman's assault, he would have believed outright murder more likely his end than defense—or retaliation—against ravishment. Yet more reason to get the woman away quickly.

Summoning Anglo-Saxon words, putting them in what he

hoped was the proper order, he looked up. "I am sorry for what he did to you. It is wrong."

"He did naught!"

"I saw him. Now we must—"

"Naught!" She shook her head, and he wondered if more she sought to convince herself than him. Regardless, she had suffered enough that, despite her aggressive stance, she might be near emotional collapse.

"Hear me," he tried again. "We must get you away."

A thrust of the dagger. "He did naught!"

He shifted his tightening jaw, glanced between the Normans who had begun their ascent of the hill—one on the right, the other far left—and was grateful they were slowed by bodies the same as he had been.

As he took another stride forward, she jerked back and one of her braids lost what remained of its crossings. Like a curtain of the finest weave, the hair swept down over that side of her face. Though in moonlight she did not present as beautiful, that softening of what had appeared stern made him stare, then rebuke himself and slam himself up against the reason he was here when he ought to be elsewhere.

Jutting his chin at the man who had taken a blade to the throat, he said harshly, "You tell he did naught? That for *naught* he is dead?"

She blinked. "I…" He heard her swallow, saw her eyes begin to lower then quickly return to his. "I slew him ere I could…ere he could dishonor my…I vow I did."

Though her words were a swiftly-moving stream rerouted time and again by thoughts thrusting up through disturbed silt like jagged rocks, it gave him time to make sense of them. Time he did not have.

"You must…" He struggled for the right word. "…permit me to see you away from here, else what this one began others will finish."

"And you will not do to me what...?" She choked on a sound of distress, then kicked the corpse again, causing its head to turn toward Guarin. And his fear for her to treble.

A wealthy chevalier and lord, indeed, but one thing more and of greater import—here was one of the duke's *companions,* so esteemed that even if Guarin bore witness the man sought to ravish the Saxon woman, William's wrath could prove deadly.

Certain the time for persuasion was past and the woman would present no better opportunity to subdue her, Guarin lunged. An instant ahead of catching the wrist of her dagger-wielding hand and yanking her forward, he felt a sting across the underside of his jaw. Then her feet caught on the body between them, toppling her toward another Norman who sought to capture her though for a far different reason.

He let her drop to her knees, certain the jolt would loosen her grip on the hilt. It did. As she screamed and pushed upright with the other hand that had taken some of the impact from her knees, he tossed aside her keen weapon.

"The word of a D'Argent I give," he said and caught hold of her other wrist. "I will not..." Another elusive word that gave him pause. "...harm you. I will see you to the wood and that is all."

No reasoning with her. He saw it in her wide-flung eyes a moment before she became all teeth, hands, knees, and feet. Using that gift of a moment, he released one wrist, drew back a fist, and said in his language, "Pardonne-moi. C'est nécessaire."

All of her jerked when his knuckles struck her jaw, then her chin dropped, and he caught her up against him.

He had never had cause—nor desire—to strike a woman, it being an abhorrent act against the weaker sex, but surely he was justified. He but tried to keep safe this Saxon whose warranted fear of assault by another of her enemy and the lack of time and occasion to prove he sought to aid her had earned him no trust. No choice had he.

Feeling a trickle down the side of his neck, he swiped a hand across it and considered palm and fingers bloodied by the dagger that had sought to do to him what had been done William's companion.

"No choice," he rasped, then wiped his hand across the back of her mantle, the material of which would better clean it than his chain mail.

It was no easy thing to put the woman over his shoulder, not because of her size and weight, though she was no tiny thing. The difficulty was his side injury that shot pain to his hip as he raised her.

A moment later, her arms flopped against his armored back, and he knew were she conscious she would grab at the weapons on his belt. This was for the best, the bruise sure to rise on her jaw dealt to aid rather than harm as had other bruises gained from her attacker.

"Eh, chevalier!" called the Norman on his left nearing the top of the hill. "A good blow to the Saxon witch. When you are done with her, let your good friend, Guillaume, teach her further respect of her Norman betters."

"And your friend Joan," shouted the second Norman who was no more a friend—nor acquaintance. "A better lesson I shall teach her ere doing to her what she did to our countryman."

No choice at all, Guarin reaffirmed, then shifting her into a more comfortable position, called, "I share with no man, friend or foe. What is mine is mine." He anchored her with his left arm around her upper thighs, drew his sword lest these common soldiers challenged him. "When I am done with her, *I* shall ensure she bleeds no more Normans."

He turned. Hoping when he came back around both would be in retreat, he flipped William's *companion* onto his belly with the thrust of a booted foot that further pained his side. And belatedly realized it was a waste of time to hide the identity of the slain man. The soldiers had only to search the area for the warmest body in the freshest pool of blood to see the man face up again.

Certes, they would discover him, not only for curiosity's sake but because this place provided some of the best pickings for those bent on desecrating the dead.

However, here was the means of ensuring these two did not challenge him. Guarin turned back and did not like how near they had drawn. "Better your efforts spent on relieving our enemies of all the gold around their necks and silver on their belts ere others sniff it out."

Both halted, looked around.

"Many a woman's favors you can buy with such spoils," Guarin said and began descending the hill toward the horse earlier noted in the midst of slaughter, seemingly untouched by death beyond the potent stench of blood and its master's collapse over its neck.

The men did not continue their pursuit, and shortly Guarin had the unfortunate chevalier off a dark grey destrier that appeared too young to be battle-hardened and likely suffered from shock.

Getting astride took more time, not only because the animal was exceedingly skittish, but the unconscious woman had to be settled atop without setting the horse to flight before Guarin could mount behind. Once done, he adjusted the woman's seat between his thighs, causing her head to tip back and unraveled hair to fall away from a face fully exposed to moonlight.

It was cut, scratched, bruised, and bloody, but not so much it disguised her looks and age. Though her face was strong boned, it was pretty with large eyes and a mouth whose lower lip was full beneath an upper lip that would present as thin if not for high arches reaching toward a fine nose dilated by breath. She would live and…

He glanced at her hands in her lap, saw she wore a wedding band, hoped this day she was not made a widow and her children fatherless. Were she, the lady ought to have little difficulty acquiring another husband, especially had she lands to her name. But as it was not his concern, the sooner he delivered her off the battlefield, the sooner she would become another man's problem and he could resume his search for Cyr, Dougray, Theriot, Maël, and Hugh.

CHAPTER THREE

DESCENT of the hill and negotiation of the meadow was slow to avoid further alarming the quivering horse, trampling the fallen, and to remain clear of scavengers, but finally the wood into which surviving Saxons had fled was before Guarin.

Having stayed far right of that section of Andredeswald that had swallowed the majority of the defeated and a great number of victors who gave chase and met their end at the bottom of a fosse known only to Saxons, he entered the trees.

There were Saxons here. Though likely too seriously wounded to flee beyond their enemy's reach, Guarin's senses confirmed they watched. Keeping one arm around the woman, he released the reins and, continuing to guide the destrier forward with the press of his thighs, drew his sword.

He would take the lady only far enough to ensure she did not become easy prey to men who would do to her as William's companion had done, then send her and the horse opposite. That would be the end of it, allowing him to return to his duty and her to praise the Lord she had escaped far worse than whatever she had suffered—and return home to a world she would soon find much changed with the duke's foot firmly on England's throat.

Reaching his senses in all directions, Guarin urged the destrier deeper into the wood. Minutes later, as they passed beneath a gap in the leaved canopy that shone moonlight over their path, he caught movement and sounds not of nature but neither from a distance. Right in front of him, in fact. The woman had regained consciousness, though she was quick to still and quiet as if gone under again.

Likely, she assessed her situation and would offer further resistance, but he did not tighten his hold lest he alert her to his own level of consciousness. Thus, she was not as cautious as she might have been in reaching for his dagger.

"Lady," he growled, "do not."

She did not, though he sensed she would once she adjusted her plan and expectations of the Norman who had struck her senseless.

Readying his hand around her waist to intercept hers, he said, "I did not like to do it. I but wished to see you off the battlefield. Ahead, I shall..." He did not know the Anglo-Saxon word for *démonter*. "I shall get off this horse, and you will ride it to your home. That is all, Lady."

As evidenced by her grab for his dagger, no more did she believe him now than before.

He gripped her hand, but she was as prepared for his defense as he was for her offense, shooting the other hand past and seizing his dagger's hilt.

He released the first hand and captured the second before she could fully unsheathe the weapon. As he thrust the blade back to the scabbard's depths, she cursed him for a Norman, twisted around to face him, and drove an elbow into his injured side.

The pain, hesitation over further harming her, and determination to hold to his sword that was his best defense against any lurking among the trees handed her the advantage—until the young destrier protested the skirmish on its back and swung to the side.

The only way to retain hold of the woman capable of finding his vulnerable places past chain mail was to release his sword. With a curse, he tossed it aside and grabbed the saddle's pommel a moment before the destrier reared. The return of its hooves to the ground was so forceful both riders lurched over its neck and the woman cried out. Now, given the chance, the beast would run.

Guarin straightened, snatched hold of the reins, and dragged on them, causing the horse to whinny, toss its head, and turn side to side before shuddering to a halt.

Seeing his sword lay ahead to the left, its blade reflecting moonlight, Guarin determined it was time to part ways with the woman. He gripped her tighter—even cruelly—pinning her arms against his chest. "We are done," he growled. "Now you go your way, I go mine."

She strained backward, raised her face. So much hatred masking fear there, but if his life depended on knowing one thing about her character, it was that her hatred was directed more at herself for her fear of him. Her eyes flicked left and right of his face, and he saw in them the question to which he was long accustomed the same as nearly all his kin—how was it possible one of relatively few years had so much silver in his hair?

She blinked, hissed, "I do not believe you, *barbarian*."

Reminding himself another had given her cause to name him that, he loosened his hold. "Turn forward, Lady." When her eyes widened ahead of argument, he snarled, "You have the word of Guarin D'Argent. It will have to be enough."

Further hesitation, then she jerked around and he felt the strain of her arms testing the strength of the one preventing her from gaining his dagger.

When she settled, he said, "Do you not move, all the sooner you shall be rid of this *barbarian*."

She gave a defiant jerk of her shoulders.

"Be still!" he growled, then released her and, retaining hold of the reins lest she try to trample him beneath the horse, swung a leg over. Grinding his teeth against discomfort, hoping his side did not bleed again, he dropped to the ground.

The woman watched as he moved to the destrier's head. Though he would have liked to immediately retrieve his sword and start back, ever he had been good with horses, and this one who had survived what its battle-hardened fellows had not, needed reassurance were he to accept a woman rider and heed her commands.

Guarin smoothed its pale mane, patted its great jaw, in his language said low, "You will see her safely home, eh?"

The great steed eyed him.

"Indeed you will. You are Norman-bred, brave, true. It is your duty and privilege to aid this lady and prove to her what she will not believe of me." Feeling the animal's quivering begin to ease, he looked to the Saxon and glimpsed what seemed uncertainty before she lifted her chin and peered down her nose through narrowed lids.

It was a show. Though she made it appear her fear was in retreat, it remained nearly as present as though there were a third person here with them.

Taking hold of the bridle, he led the horse to where his sword lay, bent, and swept up the weapon. "I leave you now, Woman. This fine destrier will carry you well." He frowned. "You will return home, will you not?"

No answer.

He stepped nearer, causing her to shift opposite. "I did not suspend my own search for family to bring you here that you return to where you are not welcome. For the family that remains to you, Lady, await the duke's..." He fumbled for the word. "... permission to seek your dead."

"My son is my only family," she rasped.

"Then for him—"

"He is upon Senlac. But ten winters aged."

Correctly he translated what confirmed her son was yet a boy as he must be for one as young as she, but Guarin failed to make sense of what sounded as if he might be found on the battlefield. He nearly asked for clarification, but he was too long in being reunited with kin.

He looped the reins over the saddle's pommel and drew his dagger, causing her lids to spring high. He paused over relinquishing something so cherished, which would not have been necessary had he not cast her weapon aside, then extended it hilt first. "Should you need it. Now go home."

She blinked and so forcefully snatched at it, she took his hand with it.

He pulled free, and she caught up the reins and put heels to the horse.

Here the end of it, Guarin assured himself. And a moment later discovered he was very wrong on two fronts—the first when she turned the horse back the way they had come, the second when a half dozen bearded and long-haired men came out of the trees.

For him.

Dear Reader,
I hope you enjoyed this excerpt of FEARLESS: Book Two in the Age of Conquest series. *Watch for its release in Spring 2019.*

For new releases and special promotions, subscribe to Tamara Leigh's mailing list: www.TamaraLeigh.com

PRONUNCIATION GUIDE

Aelfled/Aelf: AYL-flehd/AYLF
Aethelflaed: EH-thul-flehd
Alfrith: AAL-frihth
Bernia: BUHR-nee-uh
Boudica: BOO-dih-kuh
Campagnon: CAHM-paan-yah
Chanson: SHAHN-sahn
Cyr: SEE-uhr
D'Argent: DAR-zhahnt
Dougray: DOO-gray
Em: EHM
Mary Sarah: MAA-ree-SAA-ruh
Merle: MUHRL-uh
Fortier: FOHR-tee-ay
Fulbert: FOO-behr
Gerald: JEHR-uhld
Guarin: GAA-rahn
Gytha: JIY-thuh
Hawisa/Isa: HAH-wee-suh/EE-suh
Hugh: HYOO
Jaxon: JAAK-suhn
Maël: MAY-luh
Nicola: NEE-koh-luh
Ordric: OHR-drihk
Raymond: RAY-mohnd
Rixende: RIHKS-ahnd
Roger: ROH-zheh
Sigward: SEEG-wuhrd
Theriot: TEH-ree-oh
Vitalis: VEE-tah-lihs
Wulf: WUULF

Wulfrith: WUUL-frihth
Zedekiah: ZEH-duh-KIY-uh

PRONUNCIATION KEY

VOWELS
aa: arrow, castle
ay: chain, lady
ah: fought, sod
aw: flaw, paw
eh: bet, leg
ee: king, league
ih: hilt, missive
iy: knight, write
oh: coat, noble
oi: boy, coin
oo: fool, rule
ow: cow, brown
uh: sun, up
uu: book, hood
y: yearn, yield

CONSONANTS
b: bailey, club
ch: charge, trencher
d: dagger, hard
f: first, staff
g: gauntlet, stag
h: heart, hilt
j: jest, siege
k: coffer, pike
l: lance, vassal

m: moat, pommel
n: noble, postern
ng: ring, song
p: pike, lip
r: rain, far
s: spur, pass
sh: chivalry, shield
t: tame, moat
th: thistle, death
t~h: that, feather
v: vassal, missive
w: water, wife
wh: where, whisper
z: zip, haze
zh: treasure, vision

GLOSSARY

ANDREDESWALD: forest that covered areas of Sussex and Surrey in England

ANGLO-SAXON: people of the Angles (Denmark) and Saxons (northern Germany) of which the population of 11th century England was mostly comprised

BLIAUT: medieval gown

BRAIES: men's underwear

CASTELLAN: commander of a castle

CHAUSSES: men's close-fitting leg coverings

CHEMISE: loose-fitting undergarment or nightdress

CHEVALIER: a knight of France

COIF: hood-shaped cap made of cloth or chain mail

DEMESNE: home and adjoining lands held by a lord

DONJON: tower at center of a castle serving as a lord's living area

DOTTER: meaning "daughter"; attached to a woman's name to identify her by whose daughter she is

EMBRASURE: opening in a wall often used by archers

FEALTY: tenant or vassal's sworn loyalty to a lord

FORTNIGHT: two weeks

FREE MAN: person not a slave or serf

GARDEROBE: enclosed toilet

GIRDLE: belt worn upon which purses or weaponry might be attached

HILT: grip or handle of a sword or dagger

HOUSECARLE: elite warrior who was a lord's personal bodyguard

KNAVE: dishonest or unprincipled man

LEAGUE: equivalent to approximately three miles

LIEGE: superior or lord

MAIL: garments of armor made of linked metal rings

MISCREANT: badly behaving person

MISSIVE: letter

MOAT: defensive ditch, dry or filled with water

MORROW: tomorrow; the next day

MOTTE: mound of earth

NITHING: derogatory term for someone without honor

NOBLE: one of high birth

NORMAN: people whose origins lay in Normandy on the continent

NORMANDY: principality of northern France founded in the early tenth century by the viking Rollo

PARCHMENT: treated animal skin used for writing

PELL: used for combat training, a vertical post set in the ground against which a sword was beat

PIKE: long wooden shaft with a sharp steel or iron head

POLTROON: utter coward

POMMEL: counterbalance weight at the end of a sword hilt or a knob located at the fore of a saddle

PORTCULLIS: metal or wood gate lowered to block a passage

POSTERN GATE: rear door in a wall, often concealed to allow occupants to arrive and depart inconspicuously

QUINTAIN: post used for lance training to which a dummy and sandbag are attached; the latter swings around and hits the unsuccessful tilter

SALLY PORT: small hidden entrance and exit in a fortification

SAXON: Germanic people, many of whom conquered and settled in England in the 5th and 6th centuries

SENNIGHT: one week

SHIRE: division of land; England was divided into earldoms, next shires, then hundreds

THANE: in Anglo-Saxon England, a member of the nobility or landed aristocracy who owed military and administrative duty to an overlord, above all the king; owned at least five hides of land

TRENCHER: large piece of stale bread used as a bowl for food

VASSAL: one who holds land from a lord and owes fealty

ALSO BY TAMARA LEIGH

~

CLEAN READ HISTORICAL ROMANCE

THE FEUD: A Medieval Romance Series
Baron Of Godsmere: Book One
Baron Of Emberly: Book Two
Baron of Blackwood: Book Three

LADY: A Medieval Romance Series
Lady At Arms: Book One
Lady Of Eve: Book Two

BEYOND TIME: A Medieval Time Travel Romance Series
Dreamspell: Book One
Lady Ever After: Book Two

STAND-ALONE Medieval Romance Novels
Lady Of Fire
Lady Of Conquest
Lady Undaunted
Lady Betrayed

~

INSPIRATIONAL HISTORICAL ROMANCE

AGE OF FAITH: A Medieval Romance Series

The Unveiling: Book One

The Yielding: Book Two

The Redeeming: Book Three

The Kindling: Book Four

The Longing: Book Five

The Vexing: Book Six

The Awakening: Book Seven

The Raveling: Book Eight

AGE OF CONQUEST: A Medieval Romance Series

Merciless: Book One

Fearless: Book Two (Spring 2019)

INSPIRATIONAL CONTEMPORARY ROMANCE

HEAD OVER HEELS: Stand-Alone Romance Collection

Stealing Adda

Perfecting Kate

Splitting Harriet

Faking Grace

SOUTHERN DISCOMFORT: A Contemporary Romance Series

Leaving Carolina: Book One

Nowhere, Carolina: Book Two

Restless in Carolina: Book Three

~

OUT-OF-PRINT GENERAL MARKET REWRITES

Warrior Bride 1994: Bantam Books (Lady At Arms)

*Virgin Bride 1994: Bantam Books (Lady Of Eve)

Pagan Bride 1995: Bantam Books (Lady Of Fire)

Saxon Bride 1995: Bantam Books (Lady Of Conquest)

Misbegotten 1996: HarperCollins (Lady Undaunted)

Unforgotten 1997: HarperCollins (Lady Ever After)

Blackheart 2001: Dorchester Leisure (Lady Betrayed)

*Virgin Bride is the sequel to *Warrior Bride; Pagan Pride* and *Saxon Bride*
are stand-alone novels

*For new releases and special promotions, subscribe to Tamara Leigh's
mailing list: www.TamaraLeigh.com*

ABOUT THE AUTHOR

~

Tamara Leigh signed a 4-book contract with Bantam Books in 1993, her debut medieval romance was nominated for a RITA award, and successive books with Bantam, HarperCollins, and Dorchester earned awards and places on national bestseller lists.

In 2006, the first of Tamara's inspirational contemporary romances was published, followed by six more with Multnomah and RandomHouse. Perfecting Kate was optioned for a movie, Splitting Harriet won an ACFW Book of the Year award, and Faking Grace was nominated for a RITA award.

In 2012, Tamara returned to the historical romance genre with the release of Dreamspell and the bestselling Age of Faith and The Feud series. Among her #1 bestsellers are her general market romances rewritten as clean and inspirational reads, including Lady at Arms, Lady of Eve, and Lady of Conquest. In November 2018, she released MERCILESS, the first book in the new AGE OF CONQUEST series unveiling the origins of the Wulfrith family. Psst!—It all began with a woman.

Tamara lives near Nashville with her husband, a German Shepherd who has never met a squeaky toy she can't destroy, and a feisty Morkie who keeps her company during long writing stints.

Connect with Tamara at her website www.tamaraleigh.com, Facebook, Twitter and tamaraleightenn@gmail.com.

For new releases and special promotions, subscribe to Tamara Leigh's mailing list: www.tamaraleigh.com

59106609R00267